Haarun Brothers

HAARUN BROTHERS

Kleptocracy, Resistance, and the Search for Meaning

Greg Olmsted

Dirty Business Publishing

Washington, D.C.

Library of Congress Control Number: 2020902644
ISBN: 978-1-949203-23-3
ISBN: 978-1-949203-24-0 (trade paperback)
ISBN: 978-1-949203-22-6 (E-book)

FIRST EDITION

Edited by Lori Stone Handelman, PhD
Cover design by Kerry Ellis
GregOlmstedBooks.com

DirtyBusinessPublishing.com

Dedicated to Rodney and Andrew.

Thank you for saving my life.

Contents

ALSO BY GREG OLMSTED

STRONG CURRENT TRILOGY

UNDER WATER

UNDER GROUND

UNDER THREAT

OTHER NOVELS

ISTINA AND THE APOSTATE (RELIGION, GENETICS, AND THE SEARCH FOR MEANING)

MARITAUQUA ISLAND (WE SHALL COME AWAKE)

Prologue

A lilac-breasted roller chased his mate tree-to-tree across the well-kept grounds of the Home for Pregnant Women. It was a day between spring and summer, and the breeding season had already passed. Young birds were emerging from nests in the trees.

The male roller rose a hundred feet and then descended in a swoop to perch high in the branches of a tree across the street from the maternity home and adjoining orphanage. Its harsh cry blended with the happy shouts and laughter of girls and boys playing together, kicking a green soccer ball up and down the neighborhood street.

Hugo sat on his sister-in-law's stoop in the shade of the tree, drawing pictures of the boys and girls. Except for the lilac-breasted roller and the joyful sounds of children, the street was quiet. Not a car in sight. His sister-in-law, Saba, sat on the porch swing of her two-bedroom home, hemming a traditional tribal dress that rested on her lap. A finished Fazidis cloak, from the same clan, lay on the seat next to her. She did piecework for her neighbors to supplement her income.

The soccer ball rolled to within reach of Hugo. He put his drawing tablet and pencils down just long enough to roll it back to the kids. The ball was indestructible, made of the same material as croc shoes. The local school system had received special bulk pricing, and consequently had purchased soccer balls for schools across the community. The soccer balls – blue, orange, green, and pink – were now everywhere. Available to all the children.

Hugo never tired of drawing the children playing. He

never thought about their vulnerability, that their parents had passed away or that their mothers couldn't care for them due to poverty. Today they were happy. He was doing what he loved most, drawing pictures of children. One little girl in particular was exceptionally graceful, and Hugo had half-filled his tablet with drawings of her.

Saba, Hugo's brother's ex-wife, was doing what she loved, too: sewing. She taught sewing skills to the unwed mothers who boarded at the maternity home, and occasionally to the older girls at the orphanage. The maternity home and orphanage had partnered with a fair-trade fashion company and hired Saba as seamstress and trainer to give apprenticeship lessons. She enjoyed it and found it personally rewarding. Everyone needed pillow cases and simple baby blankets.

The road rumbled as it did when cars passed through, so the children stopped playing and stepped to the curb. One of the larger boys picked up the green soccer ball from the middle of the road. The stoop beneath Hugo rumbled, too. He looked up, expecting to see a large truck coming down the road. Instead, he saw a convoy of soldiers. They were approaching fast.

The first vehicle struck the boy in the middle of the road, knocking him out of his small shoes. The shoes remained in the road where he had been standing. The front tire of the Humvee rolled over the green ball, pressure kicking it sideways across the lawn of the orphanage.

Hugo rose to his feet. Only the ball was indestructible. The rest would be a massacre of innocents—women and children.

Before Hugo could react, Saba ordered him into the house and closed the door behind them. Hugo could now only imagine what was happening outside, and perhaps that was worse than seeing it.

Children were butchered in the street. The maternity home was set on fire with women and children inside. Those running out of the flames were chased down, laughed at, and slaughtered.

Hugo looked out the window as soldiers rushed forward, over the stoop and onto the porch. They had swords, knives, and machetes.

They didn't knock at the door, they just entered. Hugo stood, unmoving, next to the window.

A soldier walked across the room, raised his machete, but then balked, backed up. His gaze had focused on something behind Hugo.

Hugo slowly turned.

His sister-in-law stood behind him, wearing the traditional Fazidis cloak and dress she had hemmed for a neighbor.

She stepped forward to Hugo's side and took his hand in hers. "What have you done?" she asked the soldier.

"Cut the unborn from the womb of the mothers."

Another soldier entered and began walking around the small room. He carried the drawing tablet Hugo had left on the stoop.

The first soldier looked at Hugo from head to foot. "And why are you inside? Why are you not helping us?"

"I was drawing," he said.

The first soldier slapped Hugo and he stumbled against the window, cracking the glass. In that instant Hugo looked through the broken pane to see the young girl he had been drawing. Her graceful body lay in the street without arms or legs.

"It is true," Saba said. She pointed to the drawing tablet in the soldier's hands.

The first soldier took the tablet and opened it. He glanced at the sketches and then closed the book, handing it back to the soldier. "Burn it with the orphanage," he commanded.

The first soldier then said to Hugo's sister-in-law, "Their tribe must bear their guilt, because they are vermin. They will fall by the machete. Their little ones will be dashed to the ground. Their pregnant women ripped open."

And then they left.

A short time later another soldier walked over the stoop and onto the porch. He carried the small arm of a child. Blood still dripped from the limb. The man drew a red X on the front door using the child's blood. The marking indicated that a search had been made and completed in the house. In his other hand, he carried a can of red spray paint. Below the X he painted '2 live.'

Saba and Hugo stayed inside during the next two days and nights.

The morning of the third day, a couple knocked on their door, peering in their window. At the sound of a fist pounding wood, Hugo's heart raced.

Saba opened the door, welcomed them.

It was clear to Hugo that the wife was pregnant, but this was no place for a child! Nevertheless, the couple accepted the offer of the small room in the back.

Hugo ventured out. The orphanage was burned to the ground. The fire had burned hot and consumed the leaves in the tree in front of their house. It was a miracle that their home had not also caught fire and burned to the ground. The tree trunk stood black and leafless. Hugo wondered if even it was dead now. The birds were gone.

Hugo found no one living. He walked the immediate neighborhood gathering stray livestock, now ownerless. He secured three small goats and a sheep and a cow in his sister-in-law's small, fenced-in back yard.

Several days later the couple's baby was born.

That evening the soldiers returned, but this time they stopped and knocked on the front door. After all, it was marked that two lived inside.

Hugo saw the fear on Saba's face. She ordered him to go out the back door and run. He refused, and she ordered him again. Again Hugo refused. After he disobeyed her third order, she finally opened the door.

The soldier was not happy that he had been kept waiting. He strolled in as if it were his home, not hers.

Hugo stepped forward and stood beside his sister-in-law, taking her hand in his. He glanced at her simple, everyday clothes. She'd had no time to don the magic cloak – the Fazidis dress that had protected them the last time the soldiers had intruded.

And then the baby cried.

The soldier bolted into the next room, Saba right behind him. Hugo was unable to move. He could only observe. He could only imagine what was occurring in the next room.

And then Saba stepped out, the baby swaddled in her arms. The soldier followed her into the front room.

"Congratulations," he said to Hugo.

But it is not my child, Hugo thought, naturally.

Suddenly soldiers appeared at the front door, too excited for the circumstances. They rushed through the front door and into the back room where their leader and Saba had just been. After a moment they reemerged.

"There are goats and a sheep in the back yard!" one reported. And so the backyard feast began. Barbequed goat and bottle and bottles of beer. *Probably stolen locally,* Hugo thought.

The soldiers offered Hugo beer, and he drank with them. Not to celebrate, but to wash his mind of all he had witnessed. Soon he was so drunk he could barely sit upright, yet he kept drinking. He hoped the alcohol would kill him. He knew it was possible, alcohol poisoning. They gave him another beer and he chugged it. A soldier patted him on the back.

He felt that he would soon begin to cry. Surely that would bring all the machetes down on him? To be the one man to weep as other men celebrated?

The soldiers brought a man and women into the back yard. They had found them in the neighborhood, hiding. It was the couple who had sought refuge with Saba. Hugo understood then that his sister-in-law had sent them out the back door when the soldiers arrived.

"Kill every women of their tribe who is not a virgin," the leader said.

They sodomized her. Tortured her. And then burned her alive. All this in front of her husband. And then it was his turn.

"We will skin you alive," one soldier said.

Hugo knew the soldier's boast was true. They would skin the man alive.

And then Saba appeared at the back door. She stepped into the yard and walked to the central fire, carrying the infant in her arms.

She carefully pulled back the simple baby blanket that

covered the infant's innocent face. She held the baby so the soldiers could see his face, and then she slowly walked around the fire, showing the face of the infant—her infant—to each soldier.

And then she tilted the babe in her arms so that his real father could see his face: his eyes, nose, pursing lips. The infant had a head of black hair.

Hugo saw the father smile at his son.

Saba then turned and walked back into her home.

The smile of the father followed his son as Hugo lunged forward, grabbed a machete lying on the ground in front of him and slashed the man's throat.

His death was quick and merciful.

PART I

1

I'm Not Responsible

Where is my Uber? Zahi checked the app on his iPhone. The driver was ten minutes away, dropping off another customer. *I have less than an hour to get to the airport or I'll miss my flight back to New York.*

"You abandoned my sister, your wife."

"Abandoned?" Zahi looked up from his phone at Haleh. He gazed into his sister-in-law's black, kohl-rimmed eyes. "No. I divorced Saba. I did not abandon her."

"You abandoned your brother," she said.

Zahi stared across the small living room at his sister-in-law. She was dressed Western style in blue jeans, a cotton pullover top and open-toed sandals. Her home was a cheap one-story concrete structure built on a slab, a Western style that had become popular after the civil war. The house was nothing like the two-and-a-half story adobe home that she and Saba had grown up in.

"I am not Hugo's keeper," he said. *You have no idea what you're talking about.*

"You abandoned your country."

"The Republican Emirates?"

"Yes, what other country would I be talking about?"

Zahi read the disdain in her face: a lack of respect. *Why? What did I do?*

"Thank you for the makroudh," he said. The tone of his voice was irritated and dismissive. "And the limonana." He placed his hands on the armrests of the chair, preparing to stand up. "I need to use the bathroom."

Her thick eyebrows came together, forming a deep, vertical furrow between her dark eyebrows. The frown caused shallow, horizontal furrows to appear on her forehead. The furrows and her downturned mouth framed the disdain in her eyes and showed her age. Saba had been beautiful. This woman, her sister, not so much.

I can find it myself, he thought, pushing himself out of the blanket-covered chair and to his tired feet. He crossed the small living room and stepped into a short hallway.

Abandoned my country? He paused to think about it. He looked at the mostly blank walls. *What a stupid thing to say.*

What happened in the Republican Emirates had happened in Egypt, Yemen, Libya, Syria, and Bahrain, and it had all started after a poor young street vendor, Mohamed Bouazizi, set himself on fire in a region of Sidi Bouzid, Tunisia. His self-immolation had set off street demonstrations across the Middle East. That is when the Republican Emirates became the Republican Democracy.

What does that have to do with me? "I had nothing to do

with the riots," he mumbled. "Or the civil war. Or the genocide."

He took a few steps down the hallway. "It was the Arab Spring. I had no responsibility."

He stopped to look at a framed snapshot of Haleh. "Stupid woman," he muttered. He recognized the colorful abaya she was wearing. Saba had designed it. She had been so talented. She loved to sew and needlepoint.

Regimes fall. Is that my responsibility?

First, Egypt. After two weeks of massive protests, Egyptian President Hosni Mubarak resigned. He had been president for thirty years. Zahi had watched it on TV. Then Yemen descended into chaos. Thousands of Yemenis protested in the streets. And then Libya imploded. Zahi recalled that French aircraft had attacked a long convoy of vehicles carrying Muammar Gaddafi, killing one of his sons and the head of his army. Colonel Gaddafi fled on foot but was captured. His captives sodomized him and then murdered him. Shot him in the head. It had not interested Zahi.

The following month, the Republican Emirates descended into a civil war and then genocide. *But I was already living in Washington, DC and working across the Potomac River in Virginia. I had nothing – nothing at all – to do with the civil war or the genocide.*

Was I responsible for Mohamed Bouazizi's immolation? No! Was I responsible for the four years of devastating dust storms and droughts that blanketed Syria and the Republican Emirates? No! Was I responsible for Bashar al-Assad destroying Syria, or Lil't destroying the Republican Emirates? No! Did I kill 500,000 Syrians? No! Did I make five million Syrians flee their homes? No! No! And neither was I responsible when these things happened in the Republican Emirates!

Zahi opened the second door along the hallway, the one farthest from the living room. Seeing a hand sink and shower curtain and toilet, he flicked on the overhead light. A dingy incandescent bulb threw sparse light into the cramped space. He noted that the shower was a pre-fab fiberglass unit. A piece of bar soap sat in a wall sconce above a trail of soap scum that had run down the wall. *Not clean.* Another small piece of bar soap sat on top of the sink next to the faucet handle. *Dirty.* No guest towels, no hand towels, and only a thin roll of toilet paper. *She knew I was coming but she didn't clean.* "Bitch," he mumbled.

He sighed. Many countries had had a civil war, but only the Republican Emirates had had a genocide. The destruction had been devastating.

He closed the bathroom door. He disliked his sister-in-law, but not enough to make a mess in her bathroom, so he raised the toilet seat before pissing.

The word on the street was that the current ruler of the Republican Democracy, Lil't, would soon declare himself emir. *King. The ultimate power grab.*

"And I'm not responsible for that either," Zahi said out loud as he flushed, pulled his pants up, and tucked in his shirt.

I'm not responsible for crazy world events. He washed his hands without soap and wiped them on the sides of his pants.

2

Two Peas in a Pod

Zahi stared into the mirror. The silver backing was water damaged, causing dark spots to appear on his face. It startled him.

The civil war and genocide were terrible, but I had no part in them, and I have no responsibility – to anyone – whatsoever. He dug his iPhone out of his pants pocket. *Forty-five minutes left to make it to the airport. Where is my fucking Uber?*

As he retraced his steps down the narrow hallway, something at the far end glowed and caught his eye. He walked to the source of light and peered into the room. It was dark, except for a nightlight glowing near a baseboard. He pushed the door open and saw a large bushy tree, a Christmas tree. From floor to ceiling it was covered in ornaments.

He thought that his sister-in-law was bold to have such

an overtly Christian symbol on display in her home. After all, the Republican Democracy was a Muslim country, and most of the Christians, along with many other minorities, had fled during the genocide. The ruler of the Republican Democracy, the populist Lil't, was as anti-Christian as the US President Trump had been anti-Muslim.

Zahi flicked the bedroom light switch and a thousand small, white lights lit up the tree.

It's Saba's! They had purchased the tree together in London, the day after Christmas, many years ago, long before their divorce.

He took a moment and gazed at the tree. The small lights on the artificial tree were pre-strung. The tree glowed with a sharp white light. It was beautiful!

He glanced about. *This must have been her room.* There was a single bed and a vanity and a small bench seat. *Did she sleep here? Die here? In this room? In that bed?* It was a small bed, low to the ground, nothing more than a bare, thin mattress and a worn-out, yellow-stained pillow. No pillowcase, no sheets. No bedspread. But then he realized that a bedspread had been draped over the chair in the living room. *The chair I was sitting in?* He shivered.

He looked back at the tree. Every animal imaginable was on display, domestic and wild. Saba had loved animals. Every time she found a new animal, one she hadn't collected, she bought it and added it to her tree, as if she were filling an ark. In fact, she had Noah's Ark ornaments filled with wild animals peering over the promenade decks.

Hallmark ornaments weighed down the artificial branches. Zahi admired the tree, recalling how they had added one, two or even three ornaments each year. They had shopped together, selected the ornaments together, and hung them each Christmas Eve, together. He opened the packages, and Saba hung the ornaments. He now remembered it well.

He spotted Snoopy and Woodstock, Sylvester and Tweety, and the Tasmanian Devil Taz. And a rocking horse and a chickadee. And one of his favorites, a mouse napping inside a partially opened matchbox. The small brown mouse lay on his back, wearing a red stocking cap, his two front feet gripping the edge of a green sheet that was tucked under his chin.

Zahi knew the names of the ornaments because he had stored them in their original, small boxes. He was neat and methodical and careful because he didn't want breakage. Each year, as he and Saba decorated the tree together, he would read the name of the ornament off the box, open the box, pull out the ornament, carefully unwrap the tissue paper, replace the wire hook if needed, and then hand the ornament to Saba. She placed the ornament on the tree.

It was a happy routine. Saba enjoyed placing the ornaments and he enjoyed watching her. Her happiness had made him happy. There was "slipper spaniel" and "gentle fawn" and "yule logger beaver."

And then Zahi spotted "mistletoad," one of his all-time favorites. The toad was climbing a yellow rope attached to a green leaf of mistletoe. If the rope was gently gripped above and below the toad, and both ends given a gentle pull, the toad flashed a smile. A friend's kid had broken the mechanism and then hidden the mistletoad beneath the tree skirt. Zahi noticed that the toad's red stocking cap had been replaced with a small, pink "pussy hat." Despite the unexpected emotional pain, Zahi had to smile. Saba had a great sense of humor. She must have watched the Women's March the day after Trump's inaugural.

And then Zahi saw the "two peas in a pod," his favorite. From the center of the pod, the bottom pea gazed affectionately up at the top pea, smiling, happy in the moment. They had both loved that ornament.

Zahi stepped away from the tree and to the vanity. A hairbrush lay on a book. The word "DIARY" was printed in faux gold letters on the brown cover. He ran his hands absentmindedly down the wooden handle of the hairbrush.

He moved the hairbrush to the side, picked up the diary, started to open it, but hesitated. *Should I read it?*

Curious, he turned the diary over. The back was solid brown and nondescript. Again he started to open it, and again he stopped. It would awaken memories. *I've placed all that behind me,* he thought. *I've moved on. What good will it do now?*

Nevertheless, he wanted to see her handwriting. It was a small way to connect with her, even though she was now gone. Had she written in English or Arabic? Was her handwriting as he remembered it? Precise and graceful?

Did she write about me? Did she know about my success?

He set the diary back down on the dresser. He looked at the book and wondered why he didn't feel sad. Shouldn't he? He felt nothing. He felt empty.

He stepped back from the dresser and returned to the Christmas tree. He picked the "two peas in a pod" ornament off the tree and placed it in his pocket. It was a spontaneous, almost unconscious movement.

At that moment, Zahi glanced towards the door and saw his half-brother, Hugo, standing in the hallway, watching him. They made eye contact. He saw Hugo's flash of dislike. Zahi put his hand in his pants pocket and wrapped it around the two peas ornament.

Switching off the tree lights, Zahi stepped back into the hallway and returned to the living room. Hugo stepped into the small bedroom for a moment, but then followed him. Zahi sat down in the chair and found himself enveloped once again by the bedspread. It was her bedspread, he knew it. He shivered as if she were sitting beside him. For a moment he recalled lying in bed beside her, like he used to do early in the mornings, half awake, half asleep.

Zahi looked up and across the room. Hugo stood in the doorway between the living room and hallway, staring at him.

"I am not responsible for the civil war, the genocide or what happened here," Zahi said in a matter-of-fact voice.

Haleh rose from her seat. "I want you to leave, now." She pointed toward the front door.

"It is not my fault Saba died." Zahi looked directly at his sister-in-law as he spoke. Her kohl eyes looked smoky.

"And her child was not my child," Zahi added. "Saba and I never had a child."

"Leave this house and never return!"

"She could not have children," Zahi said. "The child is a nobody. Nobody to me."

"I said, leave this house and never return!"

She walked over to Hugo and gave him a heartfelt hug. Her short, firm arms wrapped around his weak frame. They were about the same height, both short. "Hugo, you take care of yourself."

Hugo returned her hug. "Thank you ... for your kindness."

Zahi walked to the front door with his hands buried

in his pockets and pushed open the front door with his shoulder.

Hugo followed behind carrying a small duffle bag.

What am I going to do with you, Hugo? Zahi thought.

3

New York Airport

The Boeing 767 slammed hard onto the runway, bouncing on landing gear and main struts, jarring Zahi in his seat. Overhead the luggage compartments squealed. For a moment Zahi felt weightless. *Shit!* He crouched into his seat, instinctively raising his arms to protect his head. The huge tires struck the runway again, rattling suitcases, and then the nose wheel gripped asphalt, jolting the plane, forcing it into alignment. An overhead compartment burst open. A passenger yelled.

Zahi glanced sideways at Hugo, sitting next to him in the window seat. He seemed unfazed. Unconcerned. Calm. *Must be the sedatives.* At the start of the cross-Atlantic flight from Munich to New York, after the flight from the Republican Democracy, Zahi had given Hugo a heavy dose. Perhaps they hadn't worn off.

A dark blue travel blanket covered Hugo's body, leaving only his head visible. His cropped hair stood up in every direction, except for being flattened on the side where he had slept against the window. His eyes were open, but they were not alert.

Zahi looked beyond Hugo and out the window. The wing flaps were flat, not deployed. The plane had landed fast and now the pilot was braking hard. A roar of air turbulence enveloped the plane.

"Welcome to New York City," Zahi said to Hugo, his voice high in his throat.

Hugo adjusted his emaciated body in the seat and yawned.

"You need to wake up," Zahi added.

They sat together in silence as the plane taxied to the terminal. They deplaned and followed the signs and other passengers to Customs and Border Protection screening.

Zahi directed Hugo to the line for visitors, because Hugo did not have a U.S. passport. Although Hugo was a returning United States citizen, he had no passport or other proof of his citizenship.

Everything had been rushed. When Saba died she left Hugo in the care of her sister, Haleh, but that had not worked out well. Haleh felt incapable of dealing with Hugo's nightmares, insomnia, and lethargy. Moreover, Haleh believed that Zahi, as Hugo's closest living relative, should be responsible for caring for Hugo.

Zahi had taken time off work and made the long trip from Washington, DC to his sister-in-law's home in the Republican Democracy. That was the easy part. The challenge was getting Hugo out of the country and into a safe living arrangement somewhere in the United States.

The process was difficult because during the civil war, Hugo had lost all his possessions, including his passport.

Pressed for time, Zahi decided to use his local contacts to obtain a passport from the Republican Democracy and a U.S. tourist visa for Hugo. The plan was simple: Hugo would use his Republican Democracy passport and U.S. tourist visa to enter the United States. Once he was safely in the United States, Zahi would help Hugo get a copy of his birth certificate before his tourist visa expired.

Zahi felt his jaw tense as he scanned his U.S. passport at a kiosk and, after being electronically fingerprinted and photographed, entered the line for United States citizens. He left Hugo in the line for visitors.

Zahi's line moved slowly. The family in front of him was having difficulty with their papers. An immigration officer, seated on a stool inside the small booth, was firing rapid questions, and an old man, possibly the patriarch of the family, had stumbled with his answers. Frustrated, the immigration office leaned back in his seat. He pushed a button. *Was he calling for assistance or to have the family taken away?*

Zahi turned his attention back to Hugo. Hugo's line, ironically, had moved quickly, and he had already stepped up to the booth and was speaking with the immigration officer. The officer leafed through Hugo's paperwork with disinterest. He glanced quickly at Hugo and then looked back down at his passport.

Zahi thought Hugo looked a mess. He looked like he had been living on the street, and not the streets in the United States, but the streets in the Republican Democracy. His hair was wild, his eyes dilated and red, his movements slow and unsure. He was probably still drugged.

Hugo did have one possible advantage: he was wearing an official Washington Redskins jersey Zahi had brought with him to give to Hugo. Zahi hoped the immigration officer was a Redskins fan. The burgundy jersey hung loosely over Hugo's small frame, all the way to his kneecaps. It read GRIFFIN III in white letters across the shoulders in the back. Zahi thought Hugo looked goofy, but he hoped that 'goofy' was a good thing. At least he appeared non-threatening

Is he really my half-brother? Zahi asked himself. Their father had many children, all by different Caucasian women except for Zahi's mother, who was a Bedouin. That's why Zahi had dense eyelashes, bushy arched eyebrows, and a nose like a falcon. Hugo's features were more Western and his skin less olive. They had the same curly black hair, though, and dark eyes. *What have I gotten myself into? I can't have Hugo embarrassing me in D.C. What can I do with him?*

Zahi watched the immigration officer ask Hugo one question after another. Hugo appeared calm. Zahi hoped that his answers were correct. The officer closed the passport suddenly, leaned back on his stool and stared at Hugo a moment before leaning forward, stamping Hugo's passport, and waving him along. Zahi, however, did not relax because he knew more screening lay ahead.

Zahi re-joined Hugo under a wall-mounted TV monitor where he read the carousel number for their checked luggage. They picked up their Tumi suitcase and old duffle bag and then proceeded to customs.

Once in line with their luggage, Zahi felt a small measure of relief. Everything had gone smoothly, so smoothly!

A K-9 handler slowly worked a Belgian Malinois down

their line. She was a large dog, at least two feet at the withers, and seventy pounds of energetic muscle. She had a regal head, long neck, and a statuesque body covered in an ebony, long-haired coat. She was alert and watchful. Her nails clattered noisily on the tile floor as she moved gracefully, person by person, down the line.

She was tethered to her handler by a body harness and wore a dark blue vest that read "Do Not Pet" in bright red letters. When the dog reached Hugo, he dropped to his knees and hugged her, wrapping his arms around her muscular legs and upper body. In response, she buried her nose and strong muzzle into his small chest.

Her nose poked and sniffed at his shirt pocket.

Hugo laughed, uninhibited. He grabbed her long, pointed-ears, one black ear in each hand, and pulled her gently away from his pocket. For a moment they sat opposite each other: Hugo on his knees, staring into her intelligent eyes, she on her haunches, staring back into his clouded, medicated eyes. She whined and licked her lips. Hugo smiled happily.

The handler jerked the dog back and sharply reprimanded Hugo, "Don't touch the dog!"

Hugo shrugged, "She found my makroudh, she must be hungry!"

"Come with me," the dog handler ordered. "Bring your bag."

Zahi looked the handler up and down carefully. He wore a dark blue uniform with two corporal stripes on his shoulder, and his name STRUTS in white letters above his right pocket. *Shit,* Zahi thought. He followed them, uninvited.

What drugs is he carrying? Does he have a prescription? Of course not. What else is in his bag? Zahi knew that customs officials had dogs that sniffed out fentanyl and other opioids. Dogs were trained to detect gun powder and explosives, currency, and agricultural products.

The dog handler handed Hugo off to another security officer who directed Hugo to place his old duffle bag on a steel table. "Your form?" she asked, holding out her hand.

Zahi stepped forward and handed the security officer their declaration form. "I'm his brother, we're traveling together," Zahi explained.

The officer accepted the form.

"He–"

"Step back sir," she told Zahi.

He did as she ordered.

She dumped the contents of Hugo's duffle bag onto a screening table. She sifted through the contents and removed a ball of cloth. *A wadded-up shirt? Dirty laundry?* She opened the dirty white cloth and half a dozen honey-glazed, brown triangular pastries fell out onto the steel table. Zahi knew that the pastries were filled with dates.

Playing the role of an angry, older brother, Zahi said, in a loud and disbelieving voice, "Makroudhs? Hugo, why did you bother the dog with pastries? These people have work to do!"

Among the sketch books strewn out on the table, Zahi recognized Saba's diary. He glanced at Hugo. Hugo appeared confused and nervous.

What right did you have? Zahi reached out and picked up the diary.

"Don't touch anything on the table!" the security officer admonished him severely.

Zahi gritted his teeth and set down the diary.

The security officer glanced at Zahi as she picked up the

diary, unlatched it, and flipped through the pages. A photo fell out, face down. She picked it up, looked at it, and then at Zahi. Her eyebrows raised. She placed the photo back into the pages of the diary and set it back down.

Zahi was curious. What had fallen out of the diary? Why had she glanced at him? What had she seen?

She wiped the contents of the duffle bag with a small circular pad, which she inserted into a machine. After a moment she read the results. They must have been acceptable because she told Hugo, "You can put everything back in your bag."

"Except for these cakes," she said, shaking them out of the cloth and into a large plastic bin. She handed the soiled cloth to Hugo. "And don't touch security dogs in the future."

Zahi picked up the diary and Hugo reached for it, saying, "I want—"

Zahi slapped him across his face with the back of his hand. Hugo stepped back, his eyes filled with surprise and fear. Zahi placed the diary into his own leather briefcase. He looked up to see the security guard staring at him. Astonishment filled her face.

Zahi looked back at Hugo. He read the question on Hugo's face, as if Hugo were asking, "What happened to my brother? Where did he go? Who are you?"

As they cleared customs, Zahi said in a firm, loud voice for the benefit of the security officer, "I am the older brother. You must show me respect."

The expression on Hugo's face had not changed. His face still asked the question "Who the hell are you?"

Zahi clenched his teeth and said in a low voice, "She's gone now, but I'm not. There may be stuff in her diary that's none of your business. You understand? Now forget about it." *Or I'll smack you again,* he thought. He looked around the room and decided that there were too many people, too many witnesses. One man in particular seemed to be watching them. *Great. Just great!* And everyone had cellphones with cameras.

Then, as if talking to himself, he lowered his voice further and said, "I need to make a side trip to Maritauqua Island. For business. Before returning home to Washington, DC." When Hugo didn't say anything, Zahi explained, "I must look at several properties for one of my clients."

They rechecked their luggage onto a domestic flight, went through TSA screening, and hurried to the boarding gate for a connecting flight for Alabama.

While waiting to board, Zahi took out his iPhone and quickly checked his email, phone calls and text messages. The emails included a collection of notifications from the *Wall Street Journal* and *Financial Times* reporting on the latest news impacting business and finance. He had no phone calls. He found only one text message of interest: "Morocco Vacation Packages." He clicked on the link in the message. It took him to a web page with the title "Majestic Moroccan Cities." He read: "Start planning from $1325 to $1750."

As he read the advertisement, the spyware, Unicorn, secretly downloaded onto his iPhone. Lil't's Sistema could now listen to his phone conversations, read his messages and documents, record his keystrokes, activate and use his microphone and camera, and track his internet history. Zahi's iPhone was now their iPhone.

4

Hugo
Abandoned

Maritauqua Island rests in the Gulf of Mexico, south of Mobile, Alabama, accessible only by ferry, boat and helicopter. The island was a popular vacation destination for Southern gentry, descendants of plantation owners, who were intent on preserving the culture of the Old South and respect for Confederate soldiers. Foreigners were accepted if they were professionals, such as doctors, or had money. "Colored" people were not welcome. The White Christian community had erected a monument to Robert E. Lee in the town square. They believed that Lee had been a fine and considerate gentleman.

Zahi knew better, but he put business before principle. He had no intention of butting heads with the descendants of plantation owners. If all went well, he would finish his business on the island quickly and fly back to Washington, DC, hopefully before the sun set.

But first, he had to visit the mansion and evaluate the property. If the property was acceptable then he would buy it on behalf of his client Jizan "Allegro" Oldurgan, a close friend of Lil't, the dictator of the Republican Democracy. A violent violinist, Jizan had been named the People's Artist of the Republican Democracy for his outstanding re-interpretation of Allegro Barbaro, a Bela Bartok piece, which he not only translated from piano to violin but also substituted Republican Emirates tribal music for Hungarian dances, creating a wicked piece when played with gusto.

Zahi realized that he would have to hide the identity of the purchaser in order to have any offer accepted. Zahi had formed a shell company to take title for Jizan.

If Jizan subsequently encountered problems with the locals, that would not be Zahi's problem. In fact, Zahi might earn more having to dispose of the property. Jizan, not Zahi made the decision to purchase property on the Island. If it did not work out well, that was not Zahi's responsibility. Moreover, Zahi despised Jizan's music as well as his politics. Jizan was a pal of Lil't. They had attended military school together. Jizan was the best man at Lil't's wedding, and godfather to Lil't's daughter. Jizan was reputed to be the nominal owner of properties looted from the Republican Democracy that were beneficially owned by Lil't. Zahi knew that Lil't and his family and friends and associates now owned most of the assets in the Republican Democracy: oil, refineries, polymers and ethers; supertankers, railroads and airlines, cable, TV and social media; and construction companies.

Zahi had extensive knowledge of their transactions

because he helped make the arrangements; he was a 'professional enabler.' In the early days, Zahi carried suitcases bulging with money out of the newly formed Republican Democracy. Now no one carried suitcases of money. Instead, someone pushed a button on a computer and millions of dollars were seamlessly transferred across international borders.

What amused Zahi was the world's indifference to the theft. Even though Lil't had plundered his country's assets, the Western world didn't seem to care.

Zahi also knew that Jizan had made a second fortune as a pimp and child sex trafficker. Zahi had never been involved in that side of the business. That's where he had drawn the line. A real estate transaction was one thing, underage sex was something altogether different. Any idiot knew that, he thought.

"Would you like a glass of sweet tea? A mint julep?" The realtor extended a serving platter with cold drinks to Zahi and Hugo. He was stout man in his early fifties with gray hair. His mutton chops beard was well-trimmed, with the hair on his chin shaved to accent a fine salt-and-pepper mustache. He spoke with a Southern accent.

Zahi accepted a mint julep, and Hugo shook his head no.

Zahi took a sip. The drink was heavy on bourbon. *Not a bad sales technique,* he thought. *Relax the customer. Show him the real estate. Make the deal.* He took a second sip. A sprig of mint brushed against his nose. "Refreshing," Zahi said. He repositioned the sprig, using it to swirl the crushed ice.

The realtor set the platter down on a nearby table and chose an iced tea. Drops of condensation dripped from the bottom of his glass onto the ballroom floor, beading-up on the tung-oiled oak parquet. They had no napkins to catch the drips.

Strategically, Zahi hid his contempt for the disheveled realtor whose single-breasted, gray jacket appeared bumpy and wrinkled. A red pocket square peeked from his breast pocket. His shoes were a lightweight leather and needed a polish.

"The court of Louis XV was the inspiration for this ballroom. The Regency period style."

Zahi looked at the perimeter walls of the ballroom, noting the symmetry of huge arched mirrors alternating with huge arched windows and floor-to-ceiling arched double-door openings. Everything was painted antique white and accented with gold. "Is this gold leaf?" he asked. "Real gold?"

"Gold leaf and gold paint." The realtor smiled. "Ten thousand linear feet. The wall decorations, the ceiling ornamentations, and the recessed ceiling panels, everything is gilded. Even the chair rail and door fillets."

"At a cost of twenty million dollars," he added, matter-of-fact.

"And the round painting on the ceiling. What is that about?"

"The tondo?"

"Yes, and the paintings over the doors... the half-circular paintings?"

"The lunettes?"

Zahi detected a hint of condescension. "Yes, the lunettes." *Asshole.* "Who painted them? What are they about?"

"Money, sir. They are about money." And that was all he had to say about that.

Zahi turned his back to the realtor and looked at the room. The ballroom was lit by two huge chandeliers and wall sconces. Each chandelier was suspended from a recessed panel in the ceiling, one at each end of the ballroom. He judged that the chandeliers were almost six feet tall—as tall as him—and four feet wide. *The same size as Saba's Christmas tree.* He caught himself gawking at the curled glass leaves and the multi-patterned crystals. *Impressive.* He counted eighteen sconces. Each sconce displayed three candlelight branches and was hung with crystals.

"High quality lead crystal," the realtor said. "The pendeloques in the chandeliers and the wall sconces match. The chandeliers are original, removed and protected before hurricanes made landfall."

Did they save the sterling silver, too? Zahi almost joked, but he controlled his sarcasm. He took out his iPhone and snapped several pictures for his client.

So far, acceptable, Zahi thought. *Perfect for Jizan's performances, his intimate violin concerts, and his special guests.*

Zahi liked the fact that the guest house was separate. The separation was good for security reasons. The guest house accommodated twenty, easily, and featured ten bedrooms, each with a master suite. And there was a separate small cottage for his client's mistress or other "special guest." *Not bad,* Zahi thought.

The small cottage was also a good distance from the main building and the guest house. It provided privacy and discretion. *Jizan will like it.*

"What happened to the original house and plantation?"

"The carriage house and detached kitchen and slave cabins were severely damaged in Hurricane Baker. Hurricane Michael destroyed the main house." He paused for effect. "What you see is totally rebuilt, except for the foundation and thick masonry walls. They were salvaged."

Zahi nodded.

"The exterior is authentic. The interior.... well, it has all the modern amenities, including a spacious interior kitchen and a home theater. Of course the slave quarters were not rebuilt. We have no desire to attract tourists."

"Of course," Zahi said.

The realtor lead Zahi and Hugo back down the central hallway, past a room-sized mural of plantation workers toiling in the tobacco fields. *That can be painted over*, Zahi thought. *But Jizan may like it.* He took a photo. They stepped past the foyer and the freestanding helix staircase, which Zahi liked a lot, and back onto the south-facing veranda. He set his empty glass on the porch railing and looked about him. To his right and left, the porch swept around both sides of the house. *Impressive.*

Zahi scanned the freestanding columns. The grand columns rose from the floor of the porch to the second floor roofline. The ceiling was painted robin's egg blue. Zahi smiled. From the veranda, he gazed across the circular driveway, past the fountain filled with water lilies, and across the manicured green yard. The driveway was lined on both sides with majestic oak trees. The scenic view from the veranda included the Gulf of Mexico. *Very impressive.* He took a panoramic photo.

Zahi turned and faced the huge double-entry front door. The entryway was flanked on each side by floor to ceiling Palladian windows that opened onto the spacious veranda and Southern rocking chairs.

Zahi imagined that his client would redo the double doors in gold leaf and add gold door knockers and handles. He smiled. *Kleptocrats have such poor taste.*

Zahi imagined guests arriving by limousines. Chauffeurs dropping them off at the front entrance. Or they would arrive at the private heliport. Sikorsky S-76 helicopters were among his client's favorites.

"Does the property have a helipad?"

"Of course," the realtor answered. "Behind the small cottage."

Zahi concluded that this was the perfect property for Jizan. The waterfront mansion was luxurious and was built on twenty-five acres of the most valuable land in Alabama.

He handed the realtor his business card. "Send me the necessary paperwork."

The realtor looked surprised. No, he looked shocked. He extended his hand, but Zahi did not accept it. He didn't like the man, personally, and he had no reason to shake his hand. Instead, the man's proffered hand was met with a frown. "I have a favor," Zahi said.

"Yes?" Zahi now had the realtor's full attention. He felt like he had full control of the transaction.

"The man who is with me today," he gestured toward Hugo, "needs a place to stay. Something simple, inexpensive, perhaps a studio apartment?"

The realtor withdrew his smile and rubbed his naked chin.

"Close to Maritauqua Park. I think he would like the park."

"Yes, sir," the realtor said. "I will see what I can do."

"I need it tomorrow morning," Zahi said. "I am leaving tomorrow morning, but he will be staying."

The realtor looked Hugo over from head to foot.

"Send the address to my hotel. It must be furnished, and he MUST be able to move in tomorrow."

"But..."

Zahi raised his hand and cut off the realtor. "Can you deliver? Or not?"

"Yes, sir. It will be ready tomorrow morning."

Zahi now extended his hand. As far as he was concerned, the agreements had been made. From this point on it was just a matter of paperwork.

As Zahi and Hugo drove away in their rental car, Zahi pulled over to the side of the driveway. He stepped out of the car and looked back along the long allée of oaks and at the grand plantation house.

He took out his iPhone and snapped several photos for his client. This view, the front of the house, was most important. It made the first impression: power, privilege, and money. The plantation house had a two-level porch with floor to roofline columns. Zahi liked the belvedere on top of the house. He zoomed in on the belvedere and snapped another picture.

He would send his recommendation to his client this evening: buy. And in the morning he would have a place for Hugo. Tomorrow Zahi would catch a plane back to Washington, DC and be free of him, more or less.

When he got back in the car, he turned to Hugo and said, "You're old enough to take care of yourself. Aren't you?"

Zahi drove down the long driveway to the coastline and then back to the hotel. He would soon receive a sizeable real estate commission. A very sizeable commission! That was yet another way to launder money legally.

5

Saba and Her Diary

Seated in a boarding gate area in the Mobile Regional Airport, waiting for his plane to arrive, Zahi thought about his ex-wife Saba. They were divorced before she died of cancer; she had not remarried. Zahi believed that she died still loving him. But did she?

Saba had grown up in a small village in the south-central part of the Republican Emirates, and she had never visited a large city until she attended university. She was educated in the principles of Islam at an all-girls Islamic school. There were thirteen girls in her graduating class. Her father gave her permission to continue her studies and she attended university in the capital, where she met Zahi.

She was five feet, four inches tall, and much prettier than she thought she was. She used very little makeup, if any, and she kept her hands soft with Moroccan argan oil. She cut and styled her own hair, and she never had a manicure or pedicure.

She paid a great deal of attention to her clothes. In fact, she made her own clothes. As a teenager she received a sewing machine as a birthday gift from an aunt, found a sewing handbook at the local women's library, and swapped garment patterns with like-minded girlfriends. Later, Saba began designing her own patterns. When she was at the university, friends began asking her to make garments for them. After her marriage to Zahi, Saba used her talents and Zahi's business skills to establish a clothing design business. However, the business was owned by Zahi. Men purchased her designer abayas with flared sleeves for their wives. Educated and cosmopolitan women bought her western designs, placed special orders, and became her friends.

Saba had no other work. This was not unusual; fewer than five percent of women found jobs in the Republican Democracy, even though more than fifty percent of the university graduates were women. The few women who found work became teachers or medical professionals. Women were forbidden by law to drive cars, so Saba walked everywhere she went, or rode her red bicycle, or used public transportation. She disagreed with the restrictions imposed on women; she especially disliked wearing hijabs, abayas, niqabs, and black gloves covering her hands. She was ever mindful of the religious police.

Always eager to help others, she excelled in quiet strength and kindness, even during the civil war and genocide. During the chaos of the genocide she had helped a young man and his pregnant wife who knocked on the front door of her home. She invited them in, gave them food, a drink of water, and a place to rest. The woman gave birth to a healthy boy.

The young man and his wife were caught by rebels and killed in Saba's back yard. She had shielded their newborn, and Hugo pretended to be the father of the child. Together, Hugo and Saba saved the infant's life.

Now, still seated in the boarding gate area and waiting for his plane to arrive, Zahi sighed with sadness. He felt pensive. The diary was already having the effect upon him that he had feared, and he had not yet opened it.

At least he was free from the burden of having Hugo around him. Hugo was installed in a small studio on Maritauqua Island. That had worked out well. The studio rented cheap and it was furnished with at least a bed and chair. Hugo was an adult. Zahi would send Hugo an allowance for his expenses. *Beyond that, he can take care of himself*, Zahi told himself. *I'm not a babysitter. I have my own work, my own responsibilities.*

He rolled his head side-to-side and stretched his neck muscles. Earlier, he had completed the real estate report recommending purchase of the plantation house. He encrypted the report and emailed it to his client, Jizan. When he received the go-ahead, he would complete the purchase—using a shell company in Delaware, of course. It was as easy to set up a shell company as it was to purchase a pair of shoes on Amazon.

Once seated comfortably in first class with a glass of chardonnay and complimentary chocolates, he opened his briefcase and took out Saba's diary. It was hefty. He opened it, and on the first page, hand-printed in pencil, was Saba's maiden name: Charmchi. Charmchi had been crossed out in black ink and Zahi's surname inserted,

Haarun. He surmised that she had started the diary before they were married.

He turned over a page. Her writing was graceful and easy to read. The pages were written in Arabic, but she had written from the front of the book to the back, Western style. *Typical Saba. Always her own person.* He read a few pages about the small town she had grown up in and her family life. He found it only mildly interesting. He paused for a sip of wine. He read a few more pages and paused again, this time for chocolates. He turned the page and left a chocolate fingerprint.

He came to the part where he and Saba met on their first date. Suddenly interested, he wiped the chocolate off his sticky fingers and read on. This is what Zahi read:

I met the most wonderful man today.

Maryam and I were having lunch at the coffee shop two blocks from the university. She was there because a boy had asked her out on a date. Not wanting to be by herself she asked me to join her.

We sat in the family and women's section. It was noisy but friendly, as usual. I ordered my favorite, the peach tea. Maryam ordered the Arabic coffee with a sweet.

Her date sat down across from us in our booth. I didn't like him. His hair was short and messy. His blue jeans were faded, and his shirt cuffs were frayed. His shoes were all scuffed up and looked dirty, too.

We introduced ourselves and then he ordered the shakshouka. He did not look directly at Maryam or me when he talked. He looked to our right or left, or between us, or down at his eggs in tomato sauce. It was strange. He seemed shifty.

I could tell that he wasn't happy that I was there.

And then HE walked in. He was walking towards the men's section but then he changed direction and walked over to our booth. He asked Maryam's date if he had change for a hundred riyal! The note he held in his hand was red and had the green dome of the Prophet's Mosque in Medina.

Maryam's date asked if he was kidding.

He then sat down across from Maryam and me. He said his name was Zahi.

Zahi turned the page of the diary and a wallet-size photograph fell out. It floated to the aisle and landed upside down. He snatched it up before the flight attendant stepped on it. He turned the photo over and looked at it. It was a picture of him. His eyes widened.

He remembered giving the picture to Saba shortly after they met at the café. He'd had to return home for summer break, and she had stayed in the girl's dorm to study for her finals. She was such a good student. Unlike him at that time.

He remembered being anxious and thinking that they might not see each other again unless he did something to help her remember him, so he gave her his picture.

Now, holding the photo in his hand, looking at his younger self, he shook his head. "Was I ever so young?" he said out loud. "So ivory and rose-leaves." He tried to recall where he had heard that expression 'so ivory and rose-leaves' but he could not remember.

He thumbed towards the end of the diary and randomly began to read:

I think seeing Zahi off at the airport was one of the hardest and saddest things I've ever experienced! I went out to the taxi and felt so empty and disoriented. I just sat in the back seat and cried — no, sobbed — for a few minutes.

It feels very weird at home and my sewing is just there. I know we're both strong enough and smart enough to take care of ourselves but we're so used to taking care of each other, right? Definitely two peas. In separate pods. For a while.

The words were a blow to his head, and to his heart. He set the diary face down on his lap.

He opened his briefcase and searched through it until he found the 'two peas in a pod' ornament. Holding it he felt startled. Of all the ornaments on the Christmas tree, this was the one he had chosen. It must have been her favorite, too.

He thought about the afternoon he and Saba parted, and he left the Republican Emirates for his sabbatical in Washington DC. *It was just going to be a temporary trip, until I finished my sabbatical. A year. Maybe a year and a half. I was so excited. But Saba...*He thought about the words he'd just read in her diary. *She was devastated.*

He finished the wine, wadded up the uneaten chocolates, and stuffed them into the empty wine glass.

He felt his sinuses becoming dry, starting to hurt. He glanced at his iPhone. Still two hours left in the flight. He considered placing the diary back in his briefcase, but he knew that was impossible now.

He reopened the diary to a random passage and skimmed a few pages. It appeared that Saba had made only a few entries, every day or week, throughout all the years that they had been married.

He flagged down the flight attendant and requested a bourbon, neat. He needed something stronger than chardonnay.

When did she write? At night? I guess I wasn't paying attention.

He read a longer entry that started "*I had an anxiety attack while riding the bus today.*"When he finished, he closed the diary and set it on his lap. *When did she start having panic attacks?* He suddenly realized that he had no idea what she had gone through after their divorce.

He closed the diary and turned it sideways. It was a thick book. He wondered if he had time to read it and then decided that he did. *I can finish,* he said to himself, *before the plane lands in DC.* He recalled how Saba used to tease him about being so "goal-driven." He laughed even though the memory was now painful.

Where the hell is the flight attendant with my bourbon? He pushed the overhead call button. When she arrived without his drink, he changed his order, "Make it a double."

He opened the diary near the beginning and began reading. After a few minutes he began skimming, paragraph after paragraph, looking for passages about himself, which he then selectively read. That's what interested him, passages about himself.

Saba had written:

Zahi is struggling with his coursework. He dislikes his classes, but he won't admit it. He almost cries as he studies. It's not too difficult for him. He just doesn't like it. He says that it is boring. Nonsense. I think he is just not interested. I think he is spoiled.

And:

Yesterday Zahi was lost in a book, totally engrossed with what he was reading. I thought it was a thriller or a mystery. I had to nudge his arm to get his attention. Imagine my surprise when I saw the title of the book: Mathematical Proofs for Advanced Students. He was so absorbed in the proofs that he didn't notice me when I sat down next to him. Mathematics is definitely his passion.

Zahi skimmed until he found the next mention of his name:

Why is Zahi so unhappy? Why is he stumbling in his classes? Because he doesn't want to be a religious scholar? Is that it?

And several paragraphs later:

Zahi's friends were teasing him today at the café. They saw him reading one of his math books. It upset him.

And later:

Zahi is so smart. He enjoys solving math problems. It is a game for him.

I asked him why he doesn't major in math. He laughed at me. He said that he must honor his grandfather and do as he says. He said that he couldn't make a living as a mathematician.

His laughter offended me. I wasn't teasing him like his friends. So I didn't back down. I asked him if he ever thought about being an accountant. That really got him to laughing. So I suggested a degree in business. He shook his head no and again he laughed at me.

And then this:

We were studying in the library for our upcoming exams. Zahi was so sullen. He kept trying to memorize the Quran, but I could tell his heart wasn't in it.

Then he opened up to me. He said that he enjoyed the mantiq, the study of logic, more than he liked the hafiz.

I ignored him and kept studying.

He asked me what I thought.

I didn't know what to say. I didn't know what to ask. But once he started talking about money and finance, I couldn't stop him. So I suggested that he talk to an advisor. They are available for the men in the higher classes.

Zahi slipped a piece of napkin into the diary to hold his place and rested the book in his lap.

He recalled that evening in the library with Saba. He had been in a bad mood. He recalled complaining to her about his course work. She had been right to suggest an advisor. He recalled telling her that he did not want to be a religious scholar. He did not want to spend twelve years studying to earn his certificate of alim. He did not want to be a scholar or a judge or an imam.

He remembered taking an exam and later standing outside on the sidewalk, looking up at the student mosque, knowing that he had failed. That was a first for him: failure. He had always done well in his classes.

Ironically, he had felt elated because he knew that he wasn't going to be a religious scholar. He suddenly felt free, as if a weight had been lifted from his shoulders. He had failed, yet he suddenly had his freedom. It was exhilarating. A kind of madness, he guessed.

He withdrew some money from an account set aside for his room and board, left school, and disappeared for a week. He traveled around the Republican Democracy until the money ran out. He wanted to think about what he wanted to do.

Everyone had panicked.

In hindsight he realized that he should have explained his thoughts and feelings and intentions, not only to Saba but also to his grandfather and mother. But he had not told anyone. He had started out on a bus for the coast without giving notice. Perhaps it was the euphoria of the moment. After all, he felt as if his life had just changed.

After spending all of his money, he finally returned home. His grandfather was furious.

As things began to calm down, a teacher from the school visited him at his grandfather's villa. Zahi explained to the teacher and his grandfather that he didn't want to continue religious studies. He had no interest in hadiths, the recorded sayings and deeds of Muhammad, the tafsir (interpretation of the Quran), or Muslim history. He told them that he was interested in mathematics.

His grandfather wanted to send him to an asylum. Even his mother did not support him. The grandfather wrote Zahi's father about Zahi's failure at school, his running away with his boarding money, and his refusal to resume his religious studies. He wrote that he was furious and that he wanted to send Zahi to an asylum, and he requested that Zahi's father give his concurrence.

Zahi's father replied in a long letter describing the groundbreaking work of the Islamic scholar Abu Ja'far Muhammad ibn Musa Al-Khwarizmi, a great Muslim mathematician in the ninth century. He had laid the foundation for algebra and balanced equations. With the letter, his father enclosed a copy of *A History of Algebra: From al-Khwarizmi to Emmy Noether*, by Bartel L. van der Waerden. He asked the grandfather to give the book to Zahi, and he did.

Zahi remembered receiving the book. It had a navy blue jacket and a bold orange horizontal stripe. The inside front cover was inscribed in his father's strong handwriting: "Respect your grandfather and his wishes and be obedient in all things."

Zahi devoured the book. He was particularly intrigued by how Al-Khwarizmi applied algebra to solve inheritance problems. When he reached the end of the book, he discovered an inscription in Arabic on the back inside cover in his grandfather's handwriting.

"When your father left home he told me 'I must follow the bird in my breast.' He left home against my wishes and he has never returned, except for short visits. When he left he gave up his inheritance, which one day would have been yours. When he left I lost a son, who would have been a comfort to me in my

old age. Many years have passed since he left home. He has had many wives and many children. I think that your father is happy working for the World Health Organization. I believe that each day he does the work of Allah. I give you my permission to follow the bird in your breast and to study mathematics. If the bird leads you away, then I hope that it will one day lead you back to your home and family. Al-hamdu lil-lah."

At the time, Zahi had felt elated. He had received both his father and grandfather's permission to pursue his passion for mathematics.

He now regretted, however, that he had failed to return home. His grandfather had passed away many years ago. His mother had also died, and he had no idea where his father was. Everyone believed that he had died somewhere in the Democratic Republic of the Congo, doing what he loved, helping people with their health. It was now too late for a reunion.

Zahi peered down at Saba's diary resting in his lap. She was dead, too.

So I followed the bird in my breast? He shook his head.

He recalled how he had returned to the school and sought out an academic advisor. Saba had been right. He should have gone straight away to an advisor, because the advisor told him about a scholarship program that would allow him to pursue his interest in mathematics. The program was similar to the one that King Abdullah had set up for Saudis to study abroad. The Republican Emirates' scholarship program included tuition and living expenses. The advisor helped him fill out the forms and Zahi was soon enrolled in the London School of Economics and Political Science.

He stared at the blank screen on the back of the seat in front of him. It was turned off and there was no image.

Saba had surprised him by dropping out of school and making plans to go to London with him, against her father's wishes. She had stood up to her father and other family members, demanding that they let her lead her own life, but she could not obtain a passsort without her father's consent. In addition, her father confined her to her home and would not let her outside.

Soon after that, Zahi decided to marry her. What else could he do? Saba had proven, beyond a shadow of a doubt, that she loved him. Besides, his grandfather believed that marriage would be a stabilizing factor in Zahi's life, especially since he was leaving for London. And Saba's father was agreeable.

Their wedding was simple. The nikah was in Saba's home, officiated by a friend of Zahi's grandfather, an Iman.

Zahi now vaguely recalled how he had told her, while he was studying in London, that he did not want children. There were already too many children in the world, he told her. And economically it didn't make sense.

She had become very quiet. He had thought that their relationship was over, all because he did not want the responsibility of children.

When they finally discussed it again, she had asked him, "What about adoption?"

"What?" He recalled laughing at her. "Adopt damaged kids? People don't give away good children." He now recalled how he had launched into a lecture about the expense of raising a child, and how it would be ridiculous—no, crazy—to spend money on someone else's child. "No, adoption is not an option," he had told her, firmly, decisively.

It was a memory that he wanted to forget, yet he couldn't. He recalled saying "Allah forbid!"

"Do not blaspheme!" she had scolded.

"You are no more religious than me," he had replied.

It had been difficult for Saba, though. Ironically, they soon discovered that Saba could not have children. Zahi had not comforted her, even though she was devasted by the news.

His decision not to have children was a memory that he wanted to forget. *I was young and foolish. Saba thought I was special. Sophisticated. Cosmopolitan.*

Zahi and Saba moved to London, far away from the influence of their families and free for the first time to pursue their ambition. With Saba's emotional support and the scholarship program, Zahi pursued his dream of studying math. He easily graduated with a Bachelor of Science degree in mathematics.

Saba never returned to college. She never finished her studies. Instead, she focused on her sewing. She collected Western-style sewing patterns while they lived in London and expanded her design skills. It was in London that she and Zahi incorporated the clothing business. However, Zahi insisted that the business be put in his name. Zahi also refused to allow Saba to learn to drive a car. He told Saba that driving was one of his responsibilities.

Zahi continued his studies and a year later received a Master of Science in economics, also from the University of London, with honors. This was a significant accomplishment, considering that fewer than two percent of his countrymen continued their education beyond an undergraduate program. After his masters, Zahi earned his PhD in economics from the London School of Economics. He was twenty-six years of age.

Saba became homesick. Having completed his education and having no employment prospects elsewhere, Zahi agreed to seek employment in the Republican Emirates. He applied for and accepted a position as instructor in economics at the Republican Emirates University. They moved home to the capital. Zahi taught at the Univeristy for five years. Zahi was proud of his appointment because only one in four persons under the age of twenty-five was employed in the Republican Emirates. Finding a job was more difficult for Saba, especially since she had no degree, so she continued to pursue her clothing design business. Her business prospered.

Saba sacrificed for me. She believed in me and steadied me. It had been love at first sight. That's what she had always said. They had fallen in love at first sight when he walked into the café.

After they moved back to the Republican Emirates, Zahi and Saba continued to keep a distance from his family. The capital city, where Zahi lived and worked, was far from the village where his family lived.

And then Zahi came to the passage in her diary that had upset him earlier:

I think seeing Zahi off at the airport was one of the hardest and saddest things I've ever experienced! I went out to the taxi and felt so empty and disoriented. I just sat in the back seat and cried—no, sobbed—for a few minutes.

It feels very weird at home and my sewing is just there. I know we're both strong enough and smart enough to take care of ourselves but we're so used to taking care of each other, right? Definitely two peas. In separate pods. For a while.

What was I thinking when I took the sabbatical? When I left the Republican Emirates for the United States? *That I needed a change? That I needed a challenge? That I needed time for myself?*

He had thought it was going to be temporary. One year, maybe two at the most. Yet he still lived in Washington, DC and worked across the Potomac River in Arlington, Virginia.

He put his face in his hands and slumped forward in the spacious first class seat for a few moments, then he rubbed his eyes and sat upright again.

It was an opportunity for me to learn and to stretch and to grow. When I left the Republican Emirates, I never imagined that I would divorce her.

He recalled that it hadn't been just the boredom of teaching economics. It was also a desire to expand his horizons. He remembered thinking that his students were children, not worth his time and effort.

He recalled telling Saba that he was following the bird in his breast. And that was the excuse he gave her again, later, when he requested a divorce. "I must follow the bird in my breast."

He had misused his father's words, not once, but again and again, for his own personal benefit. And now, sitting on the plane, holding Saba's diary, he admitted to himself, for the first time in his life, that he had been an asshole. A real asshole. And he wanted to tell her that he was sorry.

He returned to the diary and read on.

What changed? Zahi has become a different person.

He thought, *she was so right.* Once he had arrived in Washington, DC, he felt that he had embarked on a new journey of self-discovery. However, instead of enlightenment, happiness and peace, the bird in his breast had slowly led to his divorce.

Zahi skipped several pages and then continued reading. As he read, he learned that Saba had never stopped loving him, and she had never given up on him. She held fast to the hope that "someday he will wake up" and "he will come back to me."

With the passage of time, her sentences became shorter and then just fragments: thoughts, emotions, phrases, and no punctuation. Saba described herself:

I'm a good person.
Good
Smart
I have acted in good faith.
Loyal
Patient
I'm a good person.
I don't deserve to be treated badly.
I'm just trying to understand.

And then Zahi read about himself:

I don't know who you are.
New person
Removed yourself emotionally
Prefer company of someone else
Pushed me away
Say you love me but don't act on it

She described herself again:

I am confused
Broken up
In pieces
Trying to hold it together
Don't know who I am

And then she returned to Zahi:

Always been a good man
My rock
Partner
Mentally, emotionally
Hard for me to deal with

Every day, every day
You shut me out
Emotionally and every other way
We begin to talk
Really sharing
Say you love me
But something is wrong
Now so vain, so proud
Stubbornness about it
I'm fighting for our marriage, life, future

She continued on the next page:

I am scared
I don't want him to think that I am clinging to him
He must make a choice – what he wants to do with his life

And then, after a break in the page:

Getting really really hard
I must hang in there
I love you so much
Until the point you don't want me
I can't be what you want
Can't make you happy and myself happy, too

"Unconditional love?" Zahi said out loud. "She was ..."

How had Saba felt about the divorce? He now recalled one of their last phone conversations. She had said, "You have to get a handle on yourself. I have wanted to say that for a long time. You used to be caring, attentive. You wouldn't hurt me in a million years. You never hurt me purposefully. You were conscientious about your work. We had some fun together. You're a good person. Dig deep and find the decent person that's inside. You are the only one who can do it for yourself! You need to get a handle on things!"

After their divorce, Saba lost her sewing business

because it was in Zahi's name. Under the laws of the Republican Emirates, it was not possible to register the business in the name of a female. A business run by a wife was thought to bring shame on the husband. Neither Zahi nor any of Saba's father and brothers were willing to take responsibility for ownership of a business run by Saba. They thought her incapable of managing financial matters. Moreover, Saba's father and brothers blamed Saba for the separation and believed that Zahi should support her. Only her sister, Halah, defended her, but there was little tht Halah could do to help. So, Saba took the only job available: a job working with unwed mothers and orphans for subsistence wages. She taught the mothers sewing and embroidery. Zahi's brother, Hugo, came for a visit and stayed. He moved into her guest bedroom.

Saba wrote in her diary:

Hugo likes to cook. He always clears the kitchen table and washes the dishes. He is very clean.

And:

Children fascinate Hugo. His drawings are filled with their movements and uninhibited expressions. He loves them, dearly.

Zahi discovered a narrative break of several years in the diary. She had not written during the long years of civil war and genocide. She had left two pages in her diary blank.

On the third page she suddenly mentioned an infant and began writing again.

6

Saba's Child

Is it Hugo's child? That was Zahi's first reaction. *Did Hugo have an affair with Saba?* He paused, thought about it rationally. No, he concluded. He couldn't imagine it.

But, is Hugo the father? He could still be the father, right? Zahi wanted to ask him, and decided to call him when he landed. But then it dawned on him that Hugo did not have a landline or mobile phone. *But that's not my fault. Let him get a job if he wants a mobile phone!*

He recalled how raggedy Hugo had looked. And his yellow teeth were horrible, and several were missing. When he smiled it was gross. One had to look away. Zahi was relieved that Hugo was far away in Alabama.

Didn't they have dentists in the countries where Hugo and his father had lived? Their father had worked for the World Health Organization and had taken Hugo all around the world with him, a fact that Zahi had not forgiven either of them for. Why hadn't his father taken him along, too? At least on some of the trips!

And then Zahi recalled that his father had taken Hugo to Victoria Falls for a vacation. That had been the last straw, so to speak. A vacation to Victoria Falls! And they had stayed in the Victoria Falls Hotel. A boat trip on the Zambezi River, watching hippopotamus and crocodiles. A side trip to Bulawayo, to see Cecil Rhodes' grave at the "top of the world," as Rhodes described the park where he was buried. And their father had won a giraffe at a casino near the falls. It wasn't a real giraffe, just a hand-carved giraffe feeding on a tree, but it was a beautiful solid piece of wood. *What happened to it?* Zahi now wondered. His father had gifted it to Zahi's grandfather, and that's how Zahi had learned about the vacation to Victoria Falls, the safari in Bulawayo, the gambling at the casino. He had seen the giraffe and asked about it. Zahi had never forgiven either his father or Hugo for not including him. At least once! They could have included him on at least one trip!

He picked up the diary and read until he came to the following passages:

I must feed him formula milk, but he won't keep it down. He spits up so much.

I have started giving him bottles of watered-down apple juice. He drinks bottle after bottle, and then wets himself and drenches his bed at night. I wash his cotton diapers again and again until my hands are dry and cracked and red. My hands ache but I love him so much.

Her arthritis, Zahi thought. *It must have flared up.*

The next page, and then the next and the next, were all about the infant. Saba described her joy caring for him. Zahi, however, quickly became bored, and began skimming the passages, stopping only when he came across his own name.

The next entry with his name read: I have *decided to call him Zahi.*

No, way! Zahi thought. *No way!*

But there it was. Written in black ink in her diary. She had named the infant after him! *Little Zahi is my pride and joy!* she had written.

Zahi was astounded that she had named the infant after him, especially since he had insisted that they never have children of their own. *Why would she do something like that?* he wondered.

He paused for a moment, thinking about what it meant to have a child named after him. For so many years now he had not thought beyond his own self, his own needs and desires. He had never – not once—considered the next generation. *Poor kid*, Zahi thought. *What a world you are inheriting!*

Zahi grinned. *She named the child after me. Damn!*

He tried but he couldn't imagine having an actual relationship with the child. It wasn't that he would not consider having a relationship, if the opportunity presented itself. Instead, it was because he didn't have relationships, period.

I'm filthy rich, he thought, rubbing the back of his neck. *I could find the kid.* He smiled. *Help him out.*

The next page was filled with her concerns. Where could she buy formula? And at a price that she could afford? The cost of formula on the black market was prohibitive. She worried about Little Zahi's diet, whether the tap water was safe, whether it was safe for him to go outside. A rash developed on his butt.

She nursed Little Zahi through an ear infection, and

then a cold, and then a stomach bug. She worried about measles and diphtheria and tetanus. Vaccinations were not available.

Zahi recalled a story he had read in the *Washington Post* about disease and war and children in Yemen. A United Nations representative had told an audience that "every ten minutes a child dies of preventable causes in Yemen." Had it been that bad in the old neighborhood after the collapse of the Emirate?

For the first time, Zahi wondered what had happened to the children. What happened to them during the civil war? The genocide? He answered his own question: *I don't know.*

He knew that the high death rate of children in Yemen was caused by Saudi Arabia's bombing of the civilian population and infrastructure such as roads, bridges, hospitals, and water treatment plants. But what had happened in the Republican Democracy? *I haven't paid attention,* he thought.

Zahi skipped ahead in the diary. He read: *Maybe Zahi can help?*

Really? Zahi thought. *Me? Help with what?* He backed up a page and began reading word for word:

The soldier at the roadblock told me that I was too old for having a baby. He said that Little Zahi was not my baby.

I said that I was adopting him.

The soldier asked me if Little Zahi was a boy or a girl.

I didn't know what to say or what to do. I was alone with Little Zahi. I counted five soldiers and they had rifles. They were young, not much older than Hugo.

And then one of them said that I was a child smuggler!

I told him that I was not a child smuggler but then he ordered me to give him Little Zahi. I remember yelling 'no!' again and again.

I tried to stop him but then he ordered the other soldiers to arrest me and take Little Zahi from me. He said that it was the law.

He reached for Little Zahi. I tried to back away. I begged him to stop.

His hands were huge. He reached under my abaya and grabbed Little Zahi by the head. He grabbed his head like it was a basketball. He wouldn't let go.

Little Zahi cried in pain. I screamed.

I knew that I couldn't wrestle with the soldier. It would have hurt Little Zahi, seriously hurt him.

Another soldier said that they would take care of him. That while I was in jail he would be put up for foster care.

I could do nothing but watch as a soldier took Little Zahi away from me. He placed Little Zahi in a cage with other children, a wire cage in the bed of a camouflaged pickup truck. Three other children were in the cage. They were older than Zahi.

The children looked so scared! Their eyes were wide open and frightened. The oldest child, maybe five years of age, reached down and picked up Little Zahi off the floor of the wire cage and cradled him in his thin arms.

I pleaded but they would not listen.

That was the last time I saw Little Zahi. Later I learned that the men were separating parents from their children. The parents were arrested like me, and the children were removed. They said it was for their protection, but the children disappeared. I guess I was lucky that I didn't disappear, too. But then, I am old and the soldiers had no further use for me. They held me in a make-shift jail cell in the back room of some old building. After three days they let me go.

The hair bristled on the back of Zahi's neck. He paused his reading.

Zahi had seen the special reports on television following Trump's failed immigration policies, the cruel policies that forcibly separated children from their parents at the United States-Mexico border. Psychologists unanimously agreed that separating children and parents inflicted deep, long-lasting psychological damage. And Little Zahi was how old? Zahi guessed: between one and two years of age? Or was he three?

Lil't had emulated Trump's child-separation policy, except it was implemented inside the country and against parents attempting to flee the Republican Democracy. And mostly against Christians. *That's ironic*, Zahi thought. *Trump's policy targeted Muslims, Lil't targeted Christians.* He also targeted people who were not members of his own tribe, like Saba and Hugo and Little Zahi.

Zahi now recalled that the policy was meant to keep people from traveling outside their ethnic and tribal areas. Saba had been stopped while returning home from the northern area of the country, where she had weathered the civil war and genocide, to the central part of the Republican Democracy where she had been born, raised, and where her sister lived. *Yes, that must have been it*, Zahi thought. *She was trying to return to our ancestral home with the infant and Hugo.*

According to Saba's diary, once the soldiers separated parents and children, the parents went to temporary holding areas, while the children were held for ransom or sold to the highest bidder. Parents and children were seldom reunited, even when the ransom was paid. It was all about power, privilege and money. One ethnic group had it, another did not.

Zahi summoned the flight attendant and ordered another double bourbon. When she started to object, he gave her a piercing look that said, 'Don't fuck with me. Just give me what I want.'

He stared out the window until the bourbon arrived. He drank it quickly, felt it burn his tongue and the back of his mouth. He was upset, yet there was nothing he could do. Not now. Time had passed. Saba had passed away. And the child was lost.

Saba wrote about her panic. She had sought help from everyone, including him. He now recalled the emails and letters that he had delayed opening – multiple opportunities to help that he had ignored. *I was busy*, he told himself. And he had blocked her phone after the divorce.

It was a letter from his own family that finally had gotten his attention. The letter said that Saba had died from cancer. The letter didn't mention a child, though. Of course, by then it was too late for him to help her, or for him to help Little Zahi. They were both gone.

No wonder his sister-in-law had struck out at him in anger during his recent visit. *She hates me.*

He was coming to the end of Saba's diary. She wrote about her efforts to contact him. She described reaching out to the local police, his former colleagues at the university, their friends from his school days in London. *Why didn't she call me at my office?* Again, he answered his own question: *Because I never gave her the number.*

Instead of receiving help, Saba had learned about Zahi's collusion with Lil't and his administration. He was an enabler. He was sharing the spoils.

First she had lost Zahi to a divorce. Then she had lost her clothing business. And then her country. Little Zahi had been taken from her. And then she had lost her belief in Zahi, the man she loved and never wanted to divorce. She had always had faith in him, in his character, even through the divorce, until she reached out to him for help and he had ignored her, and she had learned what he had become: a callous criminal who helped kleptocrats hide money stolen from her impoverished fellow countrymen. She learned that he was shoveling money into his pockets. Her problems and her life had become invisible to him. The only person that he now looked after was himself.

According to her diary, his collusion with Lil't and his fellow kleptocrats had been a severe blow. His actions robbed her of sleep. She stopped eating. She lost weight. And then she wrote: *I was diagnosed with cancer today.*

The cancer, having found her immune system weakened, burned through her body like a flash fire consuming a eucalyptus tree. She died within two weeks of her diagnosis.

Zahi now sat alone, staring out the oval window of the plane, sipping yet another bourbon. There were tears in his eyes. He recalled the last time that they Skyped across the internet, watching each other on their computer screens. He said, "I want a divorce." She had fallen forward in her chair, catching herself at the last minute. She had almost fallen headfirst onto the floor.

He also recalled, on the day she signed the divorce documents, that she had told him two things. First: she did not want the divorce. Second: she warned him that he would one day end up alone, lonely, all by himself.

"She was right," he murmured. "I am alone." He took another hard swallow of bourbon. "I have no one."

He was already drunk as he turned to the next to last page of the diary. He came face to face with a black and white printed picture taped onto the page. He recognized it as his profile picture from his Facebook page. It was a more recent picture of him, and he had a bit of gray hair.

He stared at the black and white picture as if he were gazing into a mirror.

He compared it to the photo that had fallen out of the diary, the ivory and rose-leaves photo.

Saba, you would be proud of me now. I am the chief economist on several major projects. Everyone wants my recommendation, even the International Monetary Fund and the World Bank. They ask me – me! – for my recommendation for big projects involving highways, seaports, and industrial parks.

And then he slowly started crying. He knew that she would not be proud of him.

After he dried his tears, he summoned the flight attendant and asked for another bourbon. She refused. His slurred reply was, "I'm not responsible." But now he knew that he was.

He turned to the final entry in the diary. He was surprised that it was not in Saba's handwriting. It was in Hugo's. The handwriting was graceful and near perfect, the handwriting of an artist.

Zahi,

I asked Hugo to write this for me. I am too weak or I would write these words to you myself. I also made Hugo promise to see that you get this diary.

Zahi, you are a fucking self-centered asshole. You have never thought of anyone but yourself your whole life. Now that I have said that, I can tell you what I really want to tell you.

I love you with all my heart. I have from the very first day I saw you. My love has never wavered. My understanding of who you are has changed, though. You are an asshole and I feel sorry for you. Still I love you.

We often feel alone in the world. But we are not alone. We have each other. Not just family and tribe and country, but something more binding. Our relationships with each other are the most important thing we have. In my relationships I have found love, joy and true peace. And that is where you can find it too. I found joy when I was serving the expectant mothers. I found love when I was serving the children in the orphanage. I found peace when I was helping Hugo and my sister.

I have a warning for you: tribalism is as bad or worse than your individualism. I have witnessed this myself. I have no doubt that the people you have surrounded yourself with are self-centered narcissists, just like you. Part ways with them. Yes, part ways with them. Serve others.

I do not know how to tell you these things or how to explain them to you. I just hope that reading my diary will help you see that there is another way to live your life. Serve your neighbor. Embrace him. Serve him. Be good and do good. That is what your father said: be good and do good.

I love you with all my heart,

Saba

Zahi blinked back the tears as long as he could, but then he started to cry, wonderful sobs that shook his whole body.

After the plane landed and taxied to the gate, Zahi stumbled his way to baggage claim. He wanted to crawl onto the baggage carousel for a quick nap, but he resisted. Instead, he sat down on a nearby bench and waited patiently for his luggage to appear. He fell asleep, sitting upright, with his chin nodding into his chest as he quietly snored.

When he awoke, a security guard was tapping him on his leg. Zahi collected his luggage, which someone had set to the side of the carousel. His briefcase was on the floor next to the chair that he had been sleeping in, but Saba's diary was gone. Lost? Stolen? Or had he left it on the plane?

At first he panicked, but then he had already read Saba's diary. He had already received her message, her last gift to him. He understood it fully, too.

He wandered out to the taxi stand. It was a fast fifteen-minute ride from the airport to his condo in the West End neighborhood of Washington, DC. *What the hell am I going to do?*

He had a headache and he was tired. *Now what?*

7

Tweed Coat

The doorman opened the front door for him, and the lady at the reception desk stood up as he entered the spacious lobby. It was good to be home. The doorman carried his bag to the elevator, placed it inside and pressed the button for the sixth floor. "Welcome back, sir."

"Thank you."

"My pleasure," the doorman said as he stepped out of the elevator. The door shut automatically and Zahi once again found himself alone.

The hallway on the sixth floor was wide enough for a car. Zahi unlocked the front door to his condo and rolled his suitcase inside. The little black wheels rolled smoothly from the gray carpeted hallway to the waxed wood flooring in the foyer.

He walked to the center of the room and lay down on the light green designer rug, fully dressed – *just for a minute*, he told himself. He fell asleep.

He awoke to the realization that he and many other 'professionals' had enabled it all to happen. All of it: the counter-revolution, the civil war, the genocide, the theft of national wealth, and even the policy that separated parents and children—the policy that had separated Saba and Little Zahi.

Zahi pulled himself up off the floor and walked to the kitchen. The clock on the microwave gave the time as 3:30am. Every bone in his body ached. His throat was dry. His head felt like cotton. He gulped down two glasses of water.

He walked to the coat closet and stepped in. He thought of something, but as quickly as it came to him, he forgot it. *I drank too much. Way too much!* He stood in the middle of the walk-in coat closet trying to remember. *What was it? It was something in the closet. Oh, yes!* In the back of the closet, hanging on a wooden rod...

He rummaged through the hanging coats and jackets until he came to an old sport coat, still wrapped in plastic from the dry cleaners. It had been hanging in the closet for years, unworn. He had forgotten about it until just now.

It was the sport coat that Saba had given him. He reached under the clear plastic film and felt the tweed material, a rough-surfaced wool. Even in the closet light, he saw the mixed flecked colors.

He carried the coat to the living room, almost tripping over his unpacked suitcase. He stood still for a moment, just staring through the plastic at the coat, afraid to unwrap it. To free it. To try it on.

His hands trembled. He turned the brown coat front to back, then back to front again. He tore off the cheap plastic wrap and removed the coat from the thin wire hanger. How could he have disrespected the gift for so long, left it hanging on a flimsy wire for so long? Did the thin wire damage it, from lack of support? He checked the inside of the coat, at the shoulders, but they seemed to be okay.

The sport coat was a brown Harris Tweed, a coat once made fashionable by Harrison Ford in the movie *Indiana Jones and the Crystal Skull*. Zahi recalled the movie fondly. He and Saba had watched it together in a London theater. Such movies were never allowed, much less shown, in the Republican Emirates. But that was so many years ago!

He donned the coat. It still fit, perfectly. His eyes brimmed with tears.

The coat was too warm to wear indoors or during most of the year in Washington, DC. It was lined and heavy. He considered altering it, removing the lining.

But then he heard her voice. *It will keep you warm.* That's what Saba had told him when she gave him the coat: "It will keep you warm." And she had said something else that had made him laugh, back then, when she said it. *And it will keep you safe.*

Instead of listening to her, he had piped up and asked: "Does it look good on me?"

She had replied, "You look handsome!"

I was such a self-centered asshole!

Ironically, he needed the sport coat now. Not to keep warm, but to calm his exploding mind. "I have been such a fool," he said to no one.

He walked into the master bathroom, flicked on the light, and stood before the mirror. "Saba, it's beautiful. Thank you! I will wear it whenever I go outside. Just like you said, it will keep me safe. In the winter it will keep me warm. In the summer I will remove the lining."

He took off the coat and placed it tenderly on a wooden hanger, then hung it in his wardrobe closet with his dress trousers, designer shirts, suits and ties. He hung it in the very front of the wardrobe closet.

He took off his clothes in the bedroom and slipped under the bed sheets. The 500 thread count Egyptian cotton felt like silk. Tears fell again, not the sobs that shook him earlier, but quieter tears.

He awoke the next day just before lunch time, having forgotten to set his alarm for his usual 6 am wake up. He dragged himself to the kitchen and pulled back the curtains to let the harsh afternoon light fill his condominium. He made two eggs, toast smothered with triple brie, and two cups of coffee, which he sipped slowly at his small kitchen table.

It dawned on him that no one had ever sat at the table with him. No one had ever shared breakfast with him. *For how many years?* He couldn't answer his own question.

He brushed his teeth and took a long, hot shower. That felt great. Then he put on his wool coat, hid the two peas in a pod ornament in the inside breast pocket and left his condominium.

As he walked from his condo towards the Foggy Bottom metro, he thought about his character as Saba had described it. *Yes, I'm a hyper-individualistic, narcissistic asshole. She's right about that.*

He put on a pair of sunglasses to defend against the overhead sun. The azure sky was tight and cloudless. *I'm not a good man.* He shuffled down the sidewalk and walked around the green-weathered statue of George Washington mounted on his horse in Washington Circle. *A rich man, yes, but not a good man.* Zahi laughed bitterly, the laughter ending in quiet tears. *I'm a really bad person.* He wiped the tears from his eyes. *That's a fact, plain and simple.*

He now recalled the advice Saba had written for him in her diary: *Dig deep and find the decent person that's inside.* As he approached the metro station, he also remembered her telling him to be good and do good.

She was such an incredibly good and kind person. He smiled. He couldn't imagine anyone else giving him such simple, yet difficult advice, especially since she knew his professional circumstances.

He rode the escalator into the metro station. *So what do I do?* When he reached the platform, he still had no idea. He rode the train to the Virginia Square – George Mason University metro stop. A few minutes later he was seated in his office. The wall clock said 2 pm. *Why did I even bother to come into work today?*

He was tired and considered taking a nap, which was a ridiculous thing, and something he had never done before. He closed his eyes to clear his thoughts, and when he awoke the clock on the wall indicated that an hour and a half had passed. No one had come by his office, but that didn't surprise him. No one ever came by his office unless they made an appointment first. He didn't have an open door policy with his graduate students.

Should I take on Lil't's Sistema? The Sistema included billionaires, businessmen and professional enablers like himself. Most were from the former Republican Emirates, but some were from the former Soviet Union. All were ruthless. The Sistema had led Lil't to the 'king's throne' in exchange for guarantees of personal safety and prosperity.

All kleptocracies like the Republican Democracy are the same. A couple dozen men steal their country's assets and become wealthy, almost overnight. These men are the untouchables. Some rewrote their own personal histories, erasing all the murders, extortion, and crimes. And some of the worst were living comfortably on Maritauqua Island, like Jizan planned to do.

The Republican Democracy kleptocrats were loyal to Lil't. They were the source of his power, having enabled him in the early days of the counter-revolution. They had been intelligence officers, law enforcement officials, and ruthless business men. They were more ruthless than smart. Ruthless meant doing whatever was necessary to protect one's power, privilege, and money. Especially one's money.

Zahi suspected that one of the kleptocrats was responsible for the death of his friend, who was a professor at the University of The Republican Democracy. His friend had been a whistleblower: he had outed Lil't's crooked public works program. Officially his friend had committed suicide. Zahi had no doubt, though, that his friend had been murdered.

His friend had never done anything illegal. He was a good man who believed in the Golden Rule: Do unto others as you would have them do unto you. Zahi now wondered, *Where had his friend's moral center come from?*

Zahi was sure that he could not rely on receiving help from anyone in the United States government for help. In fact, the United States had recently sold a Patriot missile system to the Republican Democracy at a cost of $3 million per missile. American citizens had a thirst for oil, and Lil't had a thirst for weapons.

Lil't's bottom line: if the strongest nations in the world sold him weapons, then they had implicitly given him the green light to use them, no matter how barbaric his policies. U.S. polititians looked the other way, ignoring Lil't's well-known and well-documented human rights violations and embezzlement of public funds, on the theory that, if the United States had not sold Lil't the Patriot missiles, he would have been just as happy to buy an S-400 air defense system from the Russians. Hence, they felt no qualms about making deals with the dishonest despot.

Professional enablers in the West, like Zahi, had helped kleptocrats move their stolen wealth into the United States and Europe. Professional enablers, like him, could take them down, too. In a calm, clear voice, he said, "Yes, that is exactly what I'm going to do. I'm going to take down Lil't and his government." He laughed at the audaciousness of it.

"I'm going to shine a spotlight on Lil't." He laughed again, even louder.

"Everyone will see who he is and what he's done." He laughed deep and hard until his sides hurt.

He recalled that there was a name for this kind of laughter: gallows humor. He had already had a life-changing epiphany, a melt-down and a big cry. *And now gallows humor?* He laughed and laughed and laughed: an explosion of laughter.

There was a knock on his office door.

"Come in," he said.

A middle-aged woman, the department's administrative assistant, stood in the doorway, a textbook in her hand. "Is everything okay?"

"Yes," Zahi answered. "Everything is okay."

"Do you need anything, sir?"

"No." As an afterthought he added, "Thank you."

Her face filled with surprise. He suddenly realized that he had never thanked her for her work before. She smiled and closed the door. He heard her footsteps going down the hallway.

Crying or laughing, he knew that it made no difference. Both foreshadowed the same outcome: two bullets to the back of the head.

He took out his iPhone and stared at the apps floating on the screen. He had no plan of action. He checked his calendar. This evening he had a meeting with two very powerful men, fellow members of the kleptocracy.

It's as good a place to start as any. He ran his fingers through his curly black hair and rubbed the back of his neck. *Besides, it's a meeting I have to attend.*

8

Little Neom

The driver pulled the black SUV to the corner of 9th and G Streets, pausing in front of Zaytinya, across from the Smithsonian Portrait Gallery. Two men in black suits stepped out, wearing earbuds like the Secret Service. The chauffeur drove around the corner a short distance and idled. One black suit went into Zaytinya and the other stood alert on the sidewalk, scanning.

A second black SUV pulled up. The front passenger door flew open and a third black suit stepped out. He glanced around, 360 degrees, holding his finger on an earbud. He spotted the other black suit on the sidewalk and they exchanged nods. The third black suit opened the backseat door. Zahi and two businessmen stepped out.

Still pressing the earbud, the third black suit escorted Zahi and the two businessmen past the smartly set outdoor tables, alongside the well-dressed crowd standing in line, and through the front door of the popular restaurant.

Their waiter had been alerted and greeted them at the entrance. She immediately escorted them to their reserved table in the back corner of the restaurant.

They took their seats. Zahi adjusted the white tablecloth that draped slightly onto his thighs, tucking it further under the table. He placed the white napkin on his lap and requested sparkling water for the table.

He set his iPhone to the right of his knife and spoon so he could see any important calls or urgent texts. He wanted the two men to know that he was busy and efficient and always available.

When the two businessmen picked up their menus, he did the same. He opened the menu and ran his index finger down the list of tapas, looking up briefly to note the location of the bodyguards. One was positioned in the front of the restaurant, the other in the back. The third was not visible, yet somewhere nearby.

The bodyguards were not there to protect Zahi. Yes, he had three Swiss accounts, a luxury condominium in the West End neighborhood of Washington, DC, and a vacation home on Rehoboth Beach, Delaware. In total he had amassed a comfortable fortune worth $28 million. Not bad for an associate professor of economics at George Mason University.

The bodyguards were there for the two men seated with him. Both had also done well financially: the Russian kleptocrat, Mikhail Derichenko, and the Republican Democracy expatriate, Abdullah al-Mnuchin. In public, both men presented themselves as gentlemen, and tonight they were impeccably dressed. Both were rich and powerful. In private, both men were ruthless. Both had betrayed their countrymen by stealing hundreds of millions of dollars of public funds, money that should have been spent on health care, education, and maintenance of public infrastructure such as bridges, roads and utilities. Instead, these men spent it as they pleased, on yachts, luxurious homes, casinos, race tracks, jewels, art and other personal investments as well as some seedy entertainment.

Mikhail had steadily climbed from poverty onto the Forbes list of the world's wealthiest billionaires until his personal fortune surpassed that of the brothers, Charles and David Koch. Mikhail had built his fortune looting corporations funded with privatized assets acquired from the former Soviet Union.

Mikhail pursued similar strategies in the United States as a corporate raider. For sport he had purchased American companies that were struggling, especially in the alternative energy sector such as wind and solar power just to show that they would fail. He loaded the companies with debt and sold off company assets to make a quick short-term profit. He called his business strategy "asset stripping on steriods." Occasionally he suffered a strategic self-inflicted loss by selling valuable company assets to business friends and powerful politicians at a huge discount. He had little interest in the company's future, and none in the welfare of its employees. His serious long term investments were in coal and other fossil fuels, telling the press that "Climate change is a hoax perpetrated by Americans to keep the rest of the world from developing and being competitive."

He was also infamous for having bought control of a publicly traded health care company. He fired the company executives and hospital managers, replacing them with family and friends. He then had the company issue new shares and gave stock options to the new executives. In a conversation with Zahi he had once quipped: "Dilution is the solution to health care."

Zahi knew some of Mikhail's other tricks, including making sweetheart deals with affiliated companies, inflating costs in cost-plus government contracts, and outright embezzlement. Mikhail was the true master of the deal. Everything in his life was about making money and keeping it. No one took money from Mikhail, not even Vladimir Putin. Consequently, members of the Sistema looked up to him.

Zahi, though, had never liked Mikhail. After all, only an idiot nowadays disbelieved in climate change. Zahi now disliked him for yet another reason. Now, when he looked at Mikhail, he saw his own self-centered self.

Abdullah al-Mnuchin was cut from a similar cloth. Al-Mnuchin was a power broker. Zahi admired him first and foremost because he was a successful economist, but also because he was an accomplished businessman and politician. For many years he held a lucrative position as the head of the Republican Democracy's largest commercial bank.

Al-Mnuchin was politically savvy. When Lil't came to power al-Mnuchin courted him, fawned over him, stroked his narcissism. He gave Lil't and his associates shares in his bank. As the bank's fortunes rose, they all did well, and that is why so many in the Sistema thought highly of him.

That was when Zahi became one of his enablers. He had helped al-Mnuchin move a fortune into real estate holdings in New York City. Al-Mnuchin now had homes in New York City, London and Paris.

After Lil't solidified his control of the Republican Democracy, he and al-Mnuchin created the position of Minister of International Economic Relations. No one was surprised when Lil't appointed al-Mnuchin. His first task as minister was to find a solution to the Republican Democracy's ballooning foreign debt. His seminal idea was to attract foreign investment by sponsoring a development similar to Saudi Arabia's NEOM. Al-Mnuchin proposed building a pioneering new, semi-autonomous border city, powered using the latest technology, that was intended to attract high tech industries and diversify the economy out of dependence on oil. The Republican Democracy would have their own NEOM that some jokingly called 'Little NEOM' or 'Little Mnuchin.'

After presenting this vision, al-Mnuchin stepped down as minister and, with Lil't's blessing, became the first Chief Executive Officer of the Little NEOM Private Investment Fund. As CEO of the investment fund, he traveled around the world, promoting business opportunities in Little NEOM.

This week al-Mnuchin was in Washington, DC to promote Little NEOM and his fund. At first, Zahi had believed in the man. Al-Mnuchin could be charismatic. He had described Little NEOM as a two thousand-square mile city that would be designed and constructed from scratch in the desert, along the Republican Democracy's coastline.

According to al-Mnuchin, as soon as he raised sufficient funds Lil't would break ground for a villa—actually, a palace. The Mediterranean-style villa would sport five swimming pools, each lined with ceramic tiles in traditional Islamic designs. The grounds would include stables for Arabian stallions, a golf course, and twin helipads.

When Lil't's villa was completed, then the new city

itself, Little NEOM, would begin construction and bloom. Praise be to Allah! Another oasis in the desert.

Because the city would be semi-autonomous, Sharia law would not apply. There would be no morality police to spoil the fun of the wealthy inhabitants. As a result, it was expected that the lifestyle in Little NEOM would be more hedonistic than Las Vegas.

It was rumored that once Little NEOM was completed, Lil't would crown himself king, and then convert al-Mnuchin's fund into his own personal sovereign wealth fund. Zahi knew it was not a baseless rumor. Lil't was ruthless, power-hungry and greedy.

Although Zahi admired al-Mnuchin's personal success, he doubted that Little NEOM would be successful. He thought it would become another failed enterprise, like King Abdullah's Economic City, or Abu Dhabi's city of the future, Masdar, or even Saudi Arabia's NEOM.

Even if al-Mnuchin succeeded, Little NEOM would become nothing more than a place of refuge for kleptocrats. It would be their oasis in the desert, not Zahi's, not his family's, and not his fellow countrymen's. Nevertheless, Zahi was complicit. He had amassed his wealth enabling the kleptocrats to invest in the West.

But tonight Zahi looked at Little NEOM from a new, fresh perspective: Saba's. If the wealthy relocated to Little NEOM, what would happen to the rest of the people? Especially the vulnerable populations in the Middle East? Would Lil't build a wall around his Little NEOM, just as the Israelis had in Jerusalem, or Trump on the U.S. border with Mexico, to keep out the 'undesirables'?

However, protecting Little NEOM in the future could get nasty if it became a refuge only for the very wealthy, and the resources were stripped from the rest of the country by its construction. If constructed, Zahi expected Little Neom to become a luxurious earth habitat analogous to the space habitat in the science fiction movie *Elysium*.

"I heard that our violinist friend is pleased with his new home on Maritauqua Island." Although al-Mnuchin said this matter-of-factly, it was actually a question for Zahi.

"Yes," Zahi answered. "He is." Zahi knew not to provide additional detail about the transaction itself unless specifically asked. It was acceptable, however, to talk about the property. "The ballroom has exceptional acoustics for his violin and performances."

The waiter returned with a bottle of '16 Chateau Musar. "From the Bekaa Valley of Lebanon," he said. Mikhail ordered baba ghanoush and tzatziki to share.

Zahi settled in for a power conversation, his stomach already churning with anxiety.

"And our current project?" Al-Mnuchin did not mention Little NEOM by name. It was just understood that it was the topic of their meeting and conversation.

"I'm working the numbers," Zahi answered. Working the numbers meant tweaking the data in an economic model that one of his students had developed for her PhD thesis.

Al-Mnuchin raised his glass and took a slow sip. He was focusing on both Zahi and his first taste of the wine. He frowned. Zahi wondered: *Is he disappointed with the wine, or me?*

Zahi knew that his model had serious flaws. Nevertheless, he told al-Mnuchin, "I am confident that the Old World Fund will find our model acceptable."

His statement was not flippant. Zahi had already 'negotiated' with the contractor who would review the model. Zahi had verified, ahead of submittal, that the model would be acceptable. The data used in the model, however, was questionable. But then how could the Old World Fund expect a country emerging from civil war and genocide to have accurate economic and social data?

The data that Zahi used were completely fabricated. He knew it, the two men seated at the table knew it, and the contractor knew it. Yet no one raised the issue. They didn't want to go there, they didn't want to have that discussion, and they most certainly didn't want to try to work out an alternative solution.

He had successfully used other economic models that relied on fabricated data in the past to promote other projects for his clients, although not on the same scale as Little NEOM. For example, he had used a flawed economic model and outdated data to justify the purchase of coal plants, to continue investment in oil and fossil fuels, and to overprice alternative energy options like wind and solar. His results always shot down clean technology in favor of yet more oil exploration and the production of yet more fossil fuels. After all, the Republican Democracy was a major oil exporter.

Everyone tweaks their software, he thought. It was all part of the game. Economic models, like all models, were only as good as the parameters measured and the quality of the data used. And no one took the time to review the software in his models, except in a cursory way.

Besides, didn't everyone tweak their software nowadays, too? He remembered how surprised the public was when they learned about the Volkswagen emissions scandal. It had rocked the auto industry. However, Volkswagen was just the tip of the iceberg: other automakers were using deceptive software, too. *Why would the public expect my model to be any better than the competition?*

Zahi felt his hands sweating. He started to wipe his palms on his dress trousers but caught himself. Instead, he placed his hands on top of the table, palms down, in an effort to appear relaxed. "The Old World Fund always endorses my work," he said.

The two men smiled. That was the answer they wanted to hear. That was what this meeting was all about: to hear that answer face-to-face, so there would be no misunderstanding.

They trust me, Zahi thought. But instead of feeling the tension release from his shoulders, he felt it increase. His neck muscles tightened.

He recalled how al-Mnuchin had called him last minute and asked him to escort his wife to Trump's inauguration and celebration. Al-Mnuchin had a last-minute conflict and had been unable to attend the Victory Ball. Not only had it been an honor to be asked to escort his wife, but it had been a clear sign that al-Mnuchin trusted him.

Zahi had 48 hours to learn ballroom dancing. It was impossible, yet he had tried. The waltz had not gone well and neither had his attempts at a foxtrot. He had no rhythm whatsoever. Nevertheless, al-Mnuchin's wife had enjoyed the evening. She had been gracious, kind, and forgiving. Beautiful, too. He now thought about her gown: satin, soft and blue.

She will be surprised and disappointed.

Zahi had worked hard to win their trust and respect. His reputation was impeccable. *I could still change my mind,* he thought. *I haven't done anything yet.*

He looked across the table. He saw a ruthless oligarch and a feral economist. He should feel good about shining a light on their illegal activities. He should feel proud that he had decided to do the right thing. They had stolen hundreds of millions of dollars, hurt many people, and killed some folks. *I should feel good*, he thought. *So why don't I?*

His father would not have hesitated to stop them, to take them down. His mantra had always been "be good and do good." Saba was a force for good, too. *What's wrong with me?*

He looked at al-Mnuchin. Yes, he was dishonest in business and exceedingly greedy and ruthless. He had crushed people financially. Nevertheless, there was another side to the man. Zahi had seen it. Al-Mnuchin was honest and faithful with his wife. He loved his three kids, too, and he could be generous. His two sons, Richard and Max, were around thirty. Richard, a dancer, was choreographing ballets in New York. He was married to a man and by all accounts was very happy. Max was married, had a three-year-old daughter, and worked for a hedge fund. Al-Mnuchin never talked about his daughter.

Yes, al-Mnuchin's personal life was in order and was something to be admired. *That's more than I can say for myself*, Zahi thought.

"We can arrange contracts?" Mikhail asked.

"I'm sorry," Zahi said. "I didn't hear you. It's a little noisy tonight."

"Can we arrange contracts?"

"Yes," Zahi answered, "contracts can be arranged."

The three men huddled around the table. Each understood what 'arranging contracts' meant. Contracts would be distributed, equitably, by a 'business partner' of theirs, whose nickname was Johnny Pockets. He would ensure that the Republican Democracy 'oligarchs' would benefit, along with other 'family members,' including several Russian businessmen.

Making money no longer impressed Zahi. He knew that it wasn't hard to make money, especially if you stole it from your countrymen like the two men seated at the table with him.

Zahi took a sip of the wine. He thought it was excellent, herbal and truffly. *When I first moved here, I couldn't afford this restaurant.* He sipped the wine again. *I definitely couldn't afford a fine bottle of wine.*

He looked at the two men seated across the table from him. *It's still not too late to change my mind.*

Zahi found himself unconsciously staring at one of his emerald cuff links. Perhaps because it was shiny. More likely because it was beautiful. How many professors owned a precious stone like that? His gaze slid from the cuff of his white dress shirt to his tweed coat. *It wouldn't impress Saba, though.* He nodded his head, thoughtfully. *What was her advice?* In her diary? *You have surrounded yourself with self-centered assholes, just like you. Part ways with them. Yes, part ways with them. Serve others.*

The number one rule: Never defy the leader. Zahi knew that he would have to be careful, very careful.

Lil't was becoming as anxious and aggressive as the Saudi Crown Prince, and everyone knew that the Crown Prince kidnapped dissidents, both abroad and at home. The Crown Prince arrested and interrogated those he considered enemies. More and more Lil't was using the same playbook. Similarly, the two men seated at the table with Zahi had become increasingly anxious and unpredictable, too.

They were monitoring him, and he was monitoring them. They had a lot of destructive information about him. He had a lot of destructive information about them. They had been involved in many transactions together. Consequently, all three of them felt nervous yet comfortable sharing tapas at a fine restaurant in the capital of the 'free world.'

"I'll try the fried calamari," al-Mnuchin said to the waiter.

"And the grilled octopus," Zahi added. "I suggest we share?"

"Mikhail," al-Mnuchin said, "why don't you order a lamb or beef dish or something vegetarian?"

"I'll have the pork belly," Mikhail quipped, ordering the only pork dish on the menu. "The fasolakia."

Al-Mnuchin smiled, yet with a twinge of annoyance.

Mikhail looked up from the menu just in time to catch his disappointment. "My mistake," he said, recognizing his misstep. "Waiter, in addition to the fasolakia, please bring an order of vlahotiri." He nodded in the direction of al-Mnuchin. "For my friend."

"Dates are always a good choice," al-Mnuchin responded.

"Make it two orders," Mikhail said to the waiter. His command was cold and impersonal.

Zahi looked at the two men. They were now smiling across the table at each other like two heartless sharks. *If either of them knew what I was thinking, they would kill me with their tableware.* He made a mental note that the tableware *was* sufficiently sharp.

He thought of his friend, the economist and professor, who was found hanged in his bathroom. Zahi still wondered who murdered him, but he had resigned himself to never knowing. It was possible that one or both of the two men sitting at the table knew the answer. And, possibly, one of them had ordered the murder. Probably as dispassionately as they ordered tapas.

How will my end come? A steak knife in the neck? Two bullets to the back of my head? Or suicide by hanging in my bathroom?

He took a long, deep draft of wine, half-emptying his glass. The alcohol hit his empty stomach and he immediately felt lightheaded and dangerously loquacious. *Be careful,* he reminded himself. *Don't say anything stupid.*

He continued his train of thought. *How WILL my end come? Poisoning with the rare radioactive Polonium 210? Or pushed in front of a city bus or the metro? Or suicide by multiple stab wounds. That was a good one, suicide by multiple stab wounds. Really? Or will they find traces of a poison from the gelsemium plant in my stomach?*

He noticed a slight trembling in his hand as he sipped from his glass of red wine.

"Nice sport coat," Mikhail said.

"Thank you," Zahi replied.

"Isn't it hot, though?"

Zahi shook his head no, hoping that would be the end of Mikhail's interest. Zahi didn't want to discuss Saba's gift to him.

"It's a Sherlock Holmes kind of coat," Mikhail continued, "isn't it?"

"It's similar," Zahi answered. Actually he had no idea about that. He considered it an Indiana Jones kind of coat.

"You need the pipe and the hat, though," Mikhail added.

"I don't think you can buy those anymore," al-Mnuchin said. "I never see anyone smoking a pipe. And never in public. Do you?"

Zahi shrugged his shoulders. He felt the coat readjust to his body. He dipped a piece of bread into the hummus and took a bite, being careful not to drag his coat sleeve into the sauce. The edge of the hard bread soaked up the hummus.

Zaytinya was Zahi's favorite restaurant and he knew the dinner menu by heart, having sampled almost everything at one time or another. His mind started to wander, and soon he was thinking about the impossible task ahead: whistleblowing without a protector.

He had never met Lil't. The people who had met Lil't, or knew him well, like the two men sitting with him at the table, often compared him to Trump. Lil't was the same as Trump, except his hair was black and not combed over his crown. In all other matters, he proudly imitated Trump. Even his fat ass. Lil't's administration was crazy town, too. And like Trump, people in his administration were afraid to oppose him. If the rumor was true, Lil't would one day declare himself king. Zahi believed that it would happen right after he completed the first phase of Little NEOM, if not sooner.

Sadly, the Republican Democracy didn't have the same options to remove Lil't as the United States had to remove Trump. America had impeachment and removal by Congress, the 25thAmendment, and elections every four years. To remove Lil't there would have to be an uprising, a coup, or an assassination.

Zahi finished his glass of wine. His mind whirled. He ate more bread and hummus and tried to keep his mouth shut, not speaking unless asked a question.

He knew that the two men seated with him at the table were as much indentured as he was, even though they were billionaires. They kowtowed to the leader. They were degraded just as he was. They trusted no one.

He knew there was an occasional murder. Or an arrest

and imprisonment for a long period of time, or life. The Crown Prince of Saudi Arabia had arrested dozens of billionaires and imprisoned them in a five-star Ritz Carlton in Riyadh, stripping them of their assets. Vladimir Putin had arrested Mikhail Khodorkovsky, at the time the wealthiest man in Russia, charged him with fraud, and kept him in prison for ten years while stripping him of his money. Why would Lil't be any different? Kleptocrats followed the same playbook, learning from each other's successes and failures.

Enemies of the regime died gruesome deaths: drunken falls, impalement on the spikes of wrought iron fence. Writers and outspoken critics had fingers cut off, one by one, followed by systematic dismemberment of limbs with a bone saw, their head cut off last. *Were they still alive at that point?* Zahi wondered. Sudden heart attacks. Helicopters dropped from the sky. Beaten to death. Blunt trauma injuries to the head. Poisoned by the sharp sting of a ricin-tipped umbrella to the back of the leg.

At the end of the dinner Zahi was given the check. It was one of many small humiliations.

As he paid the bill with cash, he thought: *What is moral to them is now immoral to me. They will hunt me down and kill me.*

He excused himself from the table and went to the men's room. In the toilet stall he removed the emerald cuff links. He held them over the toilet and considered flushing them. He remembered the ridiculous scene in the movie *Titantic* when the old lady dropped her emerald necklace into the ocean. *What horseshit!* So he returned to the table and discretely placed the emerald cufflinks under the cash. "The food here is excellent," he said, suddenly proud of himself. He turned the check over and wrote: 'For the waitress. Thank you for your excellent service.' She was a young, Latin-American woman and had been friendly, attentive, and quick. And now she would be surprised!

"A comment for the waitress," he said, placing the bill on top of the cash and the hidden emerald cufflinks. "Her service was excellent, yes?" And indeed it had been.

Zahi smiled, having just made another decision. When he returned home, he would make a significant donation to the World Central Kitchen. He had read that the owner of the restaurant actively fed people who needed a good, nutritious meal. *I'll make a contribution. A significant contribution.* He smiled. *Saba would like that!*

He stared across the table at the two men. He burst out laughing. He couldn't help himself. He just felt so good! This time it wasn't gallows laughter. It was pure joy.

Mikhail and al-Mnuchin were both taken aback. They scooted to the edge of their chairs. Zahi saw the closest bodyguard tense and stand a bit straighter, more alert. He took a step towards the table but then stopped, sweeping the room with his eyes instead, anxiously.

"Let's go," Zahi told Mikhail and al-Mnuchin. "I've got a lot to do."

He enjoyed the surprised expression on their faces.

9

Hugo's Court Appearance

Zahi watched from his seat in the public gallery as Hugo entered the courtroom. He was dressed in a T-shirt and unlaced sports shoes. His hair had been cut and brushed, and he was clean-shaven. He had gained a few pounds yet still looked underweight. *Why is he wearing street clothes?* Zahi wondered. *Am I supposed to buy him a suit? Plus pay his rent?* He answered his own question: *Yes, as long as he needs my help!*

Hugo was accompanied by his defense attorney, an obese white man wearing a wrinkled and ill-fitting blue and white, wide-striped seersucker suit. He wore a yellow tie, matching yellow socks, and a pair of white buck shoes. *He's lumpish*, Zahi thought. *Disheveled.*

Hugo and his lawyer were followed by a young woman leading a large, long-haired dog on a leash. Zahi looked closely at her. She wasn't blind, and she didn't appear to have a handicap, so why did she have a dog? He noticed that her hair was tinged blue. *Interesting*, he thought. He had never seen a woman with blue hair before, or a dog in a courtroom.

The elderly man in the seersucker suit, the woman with the blue hair, and Hugo all sat down together at the wooden table in the front of the courtroom facing the magistrate's bench. The Labrador mix lay under the table between the woman and Hugo. From his chair, Hugo reached down and patted the dog gently on the head. The dog looked up, they made eye contact, and Hugo smiled. The dog then quietly sat up and leaned his body against Hugo's thigh and chair. Hugo gently stroked the large dog for a while and then rested his hand on its shiny black coat. *He loves animals*, Zahi thought. *Even goats and camels.*

And then a middle-aged man and the prosecuting attorney entered and took their seats at the table on the opposite side of the courtroom. The prosecutor wore a dark blue, modern suit. The other man wore a white shirt and khaki pants.

The man sitting next to Zahi chuckled. Zahi glanced at him. He was muscular, and Zahi guessed that he was six feet, six inches tall, maybe taller. His brown shirt and pants appeared to be a work uniform. Even though the man was large, the uniform was baggy, oversized. The sleeves of his shirt were rolled up, revealing muscular forearms. He was young, in his early twenties, about the same age as the young woman with blue hair.

"Is something funny?" Zahi asked.

The man turned to face him. "Oh, nothing," he answered. "It's just... the man up there sitting at the prosecutor's table…" he tilted his head in that direction, "he's a painter, but he looks like an accountant."

Zahi studied the painter a moment. He had a thatch of chin whiskers, a goatee. He was dressed in casual office clothes. "Do you know him?"

"Heavens no. Well, that's not exactly correct. I met him in the park – Maritauqua Park – about a month ago. But I don't really know him."

"A month ago?"

"Yes. But the homeless man, the one in the T- shirt," he pointed towards the defendant's table, "he vandalized the accountant's—I mean, the painter's—watercolor."

Homeless? The comment surprised Zahi. He looked across the room at his half-brother. Hugo was clean-shaven and his clothes were clean. Zahi had set him up in a studio apartment, so he technically was not homeless. *He's scraggly,* Zahi thought, *but he's not homeless.* "Are you here for that case or another one?"

"For that case."

"On behalf of the painter or the homeless man?"

"Neither," the man answered. "I am here as a witness. To tell the truth, nothing more, nothing less. I'm not here on behalf of the painter or the homeless guy."

"I see," Zahi said. "Well, I should introduce myself. I'm Zahi. I'm the 'homeless guy's' half-brother."

"Ohhhh!" The man slowly nodded his head up and down. "I'm sorry to hear that."

"Sorry? Why sorry?"

"Well, your brother *did* vandalize the painting."

Zahi smiled weakly. "So I've been told," he said. He didn't believe it. His brother was law-abiding and had never done anything illegal, as far as he knew.

"Your name is Zahi? Correct?"

"Yes."

"Zahi, I'm Liko. I work as a security guard at a building in the park. I just happened to pass by when the incident happened."

"I'm pleased to meet you, Liko." Zahi extended his hand.

Zahi thought that Liko's hand was the size of a baseball glove. His handshake, though, was surprisingly gentle.

"Are you from here?" Zahi asked.

"No," Liko answered. "Hawaii. And before that Nevada."

"Hawaii?" Zahi looked closely at Liko. He did look different from everyone else in the courtroom. His skin color was a beautiful brown and his hair was dark black and curly. His nose was flat and large. Zahi almost asked his ethnicity, but he caught himself – *it might be impolite.* "What brings you to the Gulf?"

Liko smiled. "I'm here because—"

The clerk interrupted. "All rise."

All eyes turned to the front of the courtroom as the magistrate entered. She was petite, gray-haired, and dressed in a plain black robe. As she took her place at the raised desk in the front center of the room, she counter-ordered, "Good afternoon everyone. Please be seated."

Zahi was surprised to see a woman presiding over the court. Such things were unheard of in the Republican Democracy. Women did not practice law. And this woman had a commanding and confident voice, especially for a small woman. Women in the Republican Democracy were expected to be submissive. Even though Zahi had lived in Washington, D.C. for many years, Western culture still surprised him.

The magistrate peered over her reading glasses, first at

the plaintiff, then at Hugo, and finally at the Newfoundland-Labrador mix. A look of distaste mixed with resignation crossed her face. She pulled a Kleenex from a box on her desk and blew her nose—a preemptive strike against a sneeze.

After everyone settled in, the painter was called to the witness stand.

"Do you swear to tell the truth, the whole truth, and nothing but the truth, so help you God?" the bailiff asked.

"Yes, I do," the painter said, placing his hand on a bible held by the clerk. The edges of the black book were worn and appeared dirty white.

"Good afternoon. Would you please introduce yourself to the court? Please state your name for the record."

"My name is Kurt Kurdirtgeon."

Curmudgeon? Zahi laughed quietly.

"Mr. Kurdirtgeon, how old are you?"

"Fifty-three."

"Now Mr. Kurdirtgeon, please state your occupation."

"I am an animation system programmer."

A cartoon maker? Zahi wondered.

"Where do you work?"

"I have been employed by Cothrom Enterprises for the last thirteen years. I live and work at the Museum Hotel in Maritauqua Park." Zahi glanced again at Liko seated next to him in his loose-fitting security uniform. He found Liko listening intently to the proceedings. "Cothrom Enterprises produces popular computer game worlds, and my job is to make the interaction between game characters and their game world smooth."

"Mr. Kurdirtgeon, would you tell us why you are here today?"

"I'm here because my painting was vandalized and destroyed."

Zahi looked across the courtroom at his brother. Hugo was petting the Newfoundland-Labrador again. *He's not a vandal and he's not destructive.*

"Before we get into the details of the vandalism, I would like to ask you a few questions about your painting. Can you describe it for us?"

"It was a large canvas, 24 inches by 36 inches."

"It was a watercolor?"

"Yes."

"What were you painting?"

"I was painting the scenery in Maritauqua Park. The landscape."

"Mr. Kurdirtgeon, I know this is going to be difficult for you, but I want you to tell us about the day your painting was vandalized. Please tell us how you came to be painting in the park that day."

"It was a beautiful day outside and I wanted to paint in the park. Early in the morning I went down to the lake and set up my easel and canvas. I painted until noon, and then I needed a break, so I put my paints away and I went across the street for a sandwich."

You left your painting unattended in a public park? Zahi shook his head. *That's unwise.*

"After you had a sandwich, what happened next?"

"I returned to the park. That's when I saw that man destroying my watercolor!"

"What did you see first?"

"I saw a man," he turned in the direction of the defendant's table and pointed his finger at Hugo. "That man there. He was sitting in front of my painting with his hands on it!"

Hugo? Zahi looked at his half-brother. *That's ridiculous.*

"You saw his hands on your painting?" the prosecutor asked.

"Yes. He was smearing my painting with a wad of dirty toilet paper. It was disgusting!"

No way! Zahi thought.

"What happened after that?" The counselor raised his voice to match Kurt's excited pitch.

"I yelled at him."

"And then?"

"He jumped on the painting and knocked it to the ground. He smashed it into the ground."

Zahi shook his head. *He'd never do that. He's quiet and gentle and calm.* Zahi glanced at Hugo. He was still petting the large dog.

"And then what happened?"

"He stood up again. He still had the painting, and he was twisting and tearing it, destroying it."

"I know this is difficult for you," the prosecutor paused and looked at the magistrate, "but I want you to tell us what happened next."

The painter turned to face the magistrate, too. "He tried to run away, but instead he ran right into a security guard. He literally ran into him."

Zahi looked at Liko. Their eyes met and Zahi asked, without speaking, *What do you say?*

Liko nodded his head, yes.

Zahi scowled and shook his head, curtly, no.

Liko shrugged his shoulders, as if saying, *What can I say, that's what happened.*

"And then I called the police," the painter said, continuing. "The security guard held him until the police arrived."

Zahi looked again at his brother, but this time carefully. He recalled a medical bill he received after Hugo visited a local emergency room. Zahi rubbed the middle of his forehead. Had he stopped taking his medicines? *I should have paid more attention. I should have talked to the emergency room doctor.*

"Mr. Kurdirtgeon, do you sell your paintings?"

"Yes."

"Are any of your paintings for sale now?"

"Yes. I have several paintings for sale locally. Several are in an art gallery. A few are on display in a restaurant."

"How much do your paintings sell for?"

"My paintings sell for anywhere between $3,000 and $18,000."

"You said as much as $18,000 each. Is that correct?"

"Yes. Eighteen thousand dollars."

"Mr. Kurdirtgeon, after this man jumped on the painting, smashed it into the ground, twisted and tore it with his hands," the prosecutor paused, "can you describe for us the condition of your painting?"

"Yes, the frame was broken, the canvas ripped, the watercolor was scratched and covered with ash and charcoal—real charcoal from someone's grill—the painting was smeared with gray and black ash. The watercolor was ruined."

"Where is the painting now?"

"I threw it away. It was totally destroyed so I threw it into one of the outdoor trashcans in the park. I couldn't bear the sight of it."

"Mr. Kurdirtgeon, thank you. I have no further questions." The prosecutor sat down.

Zahi turned to Liko and asked him, "Do you think it was worth $18,000?"

The security guard smiled. "It is now."

Zahi didn't understand. If the painting was destroyed and thrown into a trashcan, how could it now be worth $18,000? Before he could ask Liko to explain, the defense lawyer stood up and cleared his throat. It was his opportunity to cross-examine.

Unlike the prosecutor, who was friendly, courteous, and well-prepared, the seersucker lawyer stumbled from one question to the next and kept glancing at his notes and a file that he carried. He appeared overworked and burned out. *Definitely past his prime,* Zahi thought.

His cross-examination was brief and ended when he asked Kurt, "Do all your paintings sell for so much money? I mean, really? $18,000?"

"No," Kurt replied. "I sometimes donate my paintings to charities and they auction them—sometimes for more than $18,000."

"Ohhh!" The defense lawyer nodded.

Hugo's lawyer began shambling back and forth in front of the magistrate, looking at her, and then the floor, and then his file, and then quickly glancing back at her again.

He then called Hugo to the witness stand.

As Hugo took the chair, an infant in the gallery began to cry. Hugo's eyes tracked the distressed cry back to the rear of the gallery. He watched a young mother cover the infant with her loose shirt, reposition the small body, and begin breastfeeding. For several moments Hugo stared intently at the crowd of people surrounding the mother and infant. All the while, his fingers picked at the hair on his forearm.

Zahi stared at his brother. Growing up, Hugo had been calm and self-assured and gregarious. The man sitting in the witness chair was nervous and fidgety and uncomfortable with the crowd. *What happened to you?* Zahi wondered. He answered his own question: *I abandoned you when you needed me. I was not there for you.*

"Please stand," the bailiff said to Hugo, "and raise your right hand."

Hugo stood up. His hands trembled slightly. The trembling was subdued, yet Zahi noticed it.

"Do you promise that the testimony you give before this court shall be the truth, the whole truth, and nothing but the truth, so help you God?"

Hugo looked up at the bailiff and smiled. A front tooth was missing, and his remaining teeth were discolored and brown; some were broken and jagged. He laughed, a gallows laugh that cut to the bone, before saying loudly, "Yes!" with a genuine, though frightening smile.

Zahi almost rose from his seat. He forced himself to remain seated, consciously. He looked at Hugo's court appointed lawyer. Visibly shaken, the defense attorney adjusted his rumpled suit.

The court reporter asked, "Will you please spell your first and last name for the record?"

Hugo looked directly at his lawyer and said, "Haarun. H-A-A-R-U-N."

"And your last name, please?" the court reporter repeated.

No answer.

"Sir, can you please state your full name for the court?"

Again, no answer.

"Hugo ibn Haarun," Zahi said softly to himself. Zahi could feel Liko turning and looking at him. Zahi repeated, "Hugo ibn Haarun ibn Ajam Ab al-Naqad."

Liko smiled. Zahi turned and looked into the eyes of the man seated next to him, this big Hawaiian man. He appeared amused. Zahi tried to return his smile, but he could not. He was too upset.

In the meantime, Hugo's lawyer had shuffled from the witness stand back to the defendant's table and had picked up a narrow file. He now turned the folder so he could read the label: Hugo Haarun. "May it please the court," he said, "my client's full name is H-U-G-O, H-A-A-R-U-N."

"You may be seated," the bailiff told Hugo. Hugo sat down in the witness chair and glanced back at the defense table. Zahi followed his eyes to the dog, sitting up and watching Hugo. Zahi had the impression that if Hugo made the gesture, the dog would come running to him.

The lawyer cleared his throat. "Mr. Haarun, according to the police report you were in Maritauqua Park the day of the incident. Please tell the court your version of what happened that day."

"I damaged the painting, didn't I? That's why I'm here?" Haarun turned his attention from the dog to his lawyer. "That's what you said, right?"

His lawyer's mouth dropped open as he looked to the magistrate for reaction or feedback.

She glanced back at him with disdain and weary resignation.

The lawyer again consulted his file as if there was an explanation buried within for Haarun's guileless behavior. A long pause followed as he shuffled through the documents.

"Mr. Haarun?" the magistrate interjected. She took a tissue from the box in front of her and wiped her nose.

"Yes?" Hugo said.

"You said that you damaged the painting?" She crushed the tissue and set it aside.

"I sketched it up?"

"You 'sketched it up.'" The magistrate looked intently at him. "Why, Mr. Haarun? Please explain for the court, why did you sketch it up?"

Hugo fell silent.

The magistrate asked another question. Again Hugo failed to answer.

The magistrate asked another question, and again Hugo didn't respond. The magistrate pulled the last tissue from the box and blew her nose, loud and dramatically. Everyone in the courtroom, even the dog, looked her way. She then stuffed the used tissues into the empty box and threw it into a trash can.

"Mr. Haarun, you may return to your seat," the magistrate said.

After Hugo took his seat at the defendant's table, Zahi was called to the witness stand.

As Zahi stood he donned his tweed sports coat, adjusting it in the shoulders, and pulling the coat sleeves down to reveal just a quarter-inch to half-inch of his pale-yellow shirt. He squeezed past Liko and the rest of the folks seated along his row, and walked confidently to the witness stand.

He insisted on being sworn in on a Koran, which the magistrate approved. After being sworn in he began his testimony. "My name is Zahi ibn Haarun ibn Ajam Ab al-Naqad. I have a Ph.D. in economics from the London School of Economics. I teach economics at George Mason University in Arlington, Virginia. Hugo is my younger half-brother. I learned yesterday that he was appearing in court this morning. I arrived on the overnight flight from Reagan International Airport earlier this morning."

Hugo's attorney asked Zahi one inept question after another, providing him only a marginal opportunity to help his brother. Nevertheless, Zahi tried to elicit the magistrate's sympathy.

He began by describing his own situation. "It was very difficult for me to get away from my research to testify today. I have research and graduate students who depend on me. As you might imagine, it is expensive to fly cross-country on such short notice, especially on a professor's salary, and there is the cost of the hotel and rental car. But I am here. For my brother, Hugo."

Zahi then tried to describe Hugo's situation. "My brother, Hugo, was born in Hawaii. His mother is Middle Eastern-American. She met my father and they moved together to Hawaii, where Hugo was born. Yes, like President Obama, Hugo was born in Hawaii. And just like President Obama's father, our father was not American. He was born in the Republican Democracy of the Middle East and never became a U.S. citizen. He moved back to the Republican Democracy many years ago and took Hugo with him. Our father moved a lot, so Hugo grew up in many different countries, mostly in what Americans call the developing world.

"I brought Hugo to the United States after the civil war in my country ended. I set him up in a studio apartment here on Maritauqua Island. The weather here is semi-tropical, so Hugo can be outdoors most of the year. He does not like to be inside or even to sleep inside. My brother, you see, suffers from PTSD—post-traumatic stress disorder. During the civil war Hugo witnessed horrific violence, including the frequent murder and abuse of women and children. Later, he survived the genocide of our tribe. He has never talked about it. The trauma is like a poison in his mind.

"Your Honor, I have not had an opportunity to sit down

with my brother. I arrived this morning on the earliest flight to Mobile and took the first ferry to Maritauqua Island. But I think my brother has stopped taking his medications. He is medicated with antidepressants such as Paxil and Zoloft, and an antipsychotic to help him sleep."

"Is your brother a U.S. citizen?" the magistrate asked Zahi.

"Yes, Your Honor, Hugo is a U.S. citizen."

"Is he employed?" the magistrate asked.

"No, Your Honor. Hugo is unemployed. Before his PTSD, he was an artist. He drew cartoons and caricatures. He sold his work on the street. To my knowledge, my brother has never hurt anyone. Hugo is a gentle person."

"Thank you, Mr. Haarun." The magistrate fired a look at the prosecuting attorney that said 'Let's wrap this up.' "Does the prosecuting attorney have any questions for the witness?"

The prosecuting attorney hesitated but then said, "No questions at this time, Your Honor."

"Seeing that there are no further questions, Mr. Haarun, you may step down."

Liko made way for Zahi as he returned to the bench and sat down. They made brief eye contact.

The magistrate was tapping her right hand impatiently on her desk. She motioned for the bailiff. He walked over and she said something to him. He then walked over to the defendant's table, picked up the tissue box that was sitting in front of the seersucker lawyer, and carried it back to the magistrate. She pulled a tissue and blew her nose, forcefully.

The magistrate continued, "I believe that sufficient evidence has been provided by a family member, Mr. Zahi Haarun, to support the request for examination of the defendant, Mr. Hugo Haarun, with respect to physical or mental disease, disorder, or defect. Therefore, the court orders that Mr. Hugo Haarun be referred to our Medical Services Division for a medical evaluation.

"Also, the court orders that a copy of Mr. Hugo Haarun's birth certificate be obtained and provided to the court."

"I don't see why a birth certificate is necessary, Your Honor," Hugo's lawyer said.

The magistrate stared at Hugo's lawyer for a moment. "In addition to the birth certificate, the court shall obtain all existing medical, mental health, social, police, and juvenile records, including those expunged, and all other pertinent records in the custody of public agencies, and shall make them available—"

"I object, Your Honor. It is not—"

Hugo's lawyer was cut off mid-sentence by the glare of the magistrate, who continued, "All such records shall be made available to both the prosecuting attorney and counsel for the defendant."

"Yes, Your Honor." Hugo's lawyer looked at his client and shook his head.

The magistrate followed the seersucker lawyer's gaze and looked at Hugo, too. He had left his chair to kneel and hug the courtroom dog. The dog had nuzzled his large head into Hugo's armpit.

As if reconsidering her court order, the magistrate added, "The right to bail, however, is not suspended."

The court recessed. As Zahi left the courtroom he walked alongside Liko.

"You did not testify today," Zahi said.

"No. I wasn't called."

"Perhaps next time."

Liko shrugged.

"My brother is a good kid."

"Sounds like he has some issues."

Zahi smiled. "And none of them of his own making."

They exited into a long hallway and walked together to the courthouse entrance. Zahi tried to start a conversation but Liko seemed defensive, even combative. When they reached the courthouse entrance they stopped and waited for Hugo, his lawyer, and the girl handling the dog.

Liko acknowledged Hugo with a nod. After introducing himself to the woman with the blue-tinged hair, Liko bent down and rubbed the hair on the Labrador's head. Liko showed no interest in being introduced to the lawyer.

"What is the dog's name?" Liko asked the woman.

"Ho'omaha," the woman answered. "It is Hawaiian. It means 'rest.'"

"I'm surprised to see a dog in court."

"Ho'omaha is a courthouse dog. He calms and comforts child victims, nervous witnesses and, today, Hugo."

"It's good to see you again, brother." Zahi reached out to embrace Hugo, but Hugo pulled away.

"How are you?" Zahi asked.

No answer. Hugo looked to the side and stared at the floor.

"Hugo, I came as soon as I got word. I arrived this morning."

Still no answer. The awkward silence between the brothers was palpable. Embarrassed, Zahi looked back down the long hallway. He sighed heavily, yet unconsciously. *This isn't going to be easy,* he thought. *Nothing is going to be easy anymore.*

Kurt emerged from the courtroom. He stood outside the huge wooden doors in front of the Maritauqua Island's crest, staring down the long hallway at Hugo and Liko, and then at Zahi. Kurt made eye contact with Zahi.

I'll talk to him, Zahi thought. *I'll pay him for his damaged painting. Maybe buy several other paintings, too, if necessary.*

Zahi adjusted his tweed coat, gathered his courage, and looked again at Hugo. His brother and Liko were petting the large Newfoundland-Labrador mix, Ho'omaha, and appeared lost in the moment.

Why hug a dog? Zahi shook his head. *It's so unhygienic.* He smiled. *Hugging people is bad enough.* He still felt embarrassed that Hugo had pulled away from him. But he knew that it was his own fault, a result of his lack of affection and total coldness. *There must be a better way to show affection, though,* he thought.

10

Jizan's Party

Zahi failed to recognize the entrance to Jizan's property. The rows of oaks had disappeared.

"What the fuck!" he blurted out. "Where are the trees?"

"Owner has allergies," said the taxi driver. "That's what we hear. He doesn't like leaves."

"You're joking?"

The driver shook his head, no.

Jizan might be an exceptional musician, Zahi thought, *but he's a fucking idiot.* Zahi stared out the passenger window. *The trees... the beautiful, stately oaks... gone!*

He gave the taxi driver a more than generous tip. As he stepped out of the back seat, he tried to pull himself together, and tried to bury his emotions deep in his bowels, but he couldn't help himself. He turned around and said to the driver through the open passenger door, "Between you and me, he's an asshole."

The driver smiled indifferently, counted his tip, and said, "Thank you."

Disappointed in the driver's muted response, Zahi shook his head. He closed the taxi door and turned to face the mansion and Jizan's party. His stomach rumbled.

He now recognized Jizan for what he truly was, one of those people who walked upon the earth with no regard for their neighbors or for future generations. He was probably among those who cast doubt on climate change and ridiculed scientists. As an economist Zahi had a deep respect for the sciences.

He climbed the steps of the portico and walked between the grand columns to the center of the veranda. He turned around and gazed down the driveway, past the huge stumps lining both sides of the entryway. Some people destroyed the environment wherever they went.

On the horizon he saw the Gulf of Mexico. *You asshole,* he thought. *Try destroying that.* But then he realized it was already happening. He recalled the explosion and sinking of the Deepwater Horizon. And Trump's executive orders had rolled back the protections that President Obama had put in place to help prevent a future disaster. No place was safe, no place was untouched, and no place was still pristine.

He turned to face the double front doors. At least they were unchanged. After the assault on the trees, he would not have been surprised to see the doors redone in high Trump style: gold-leaf trim with solid gold door knockers and gold door knobs.

Still, as he stepped into the foyer, Zahi was aware that Jizan had spent a staggering amount of money to remodel: new drapes on the floor-to-ceiling windows, all new paintings on the hand-painted ceiling, and lots of pink marble on the floors and walls.

Zahi walked to the entrance of the grand ballroom and looked in. The original chandeliers had not been touched. They had survived a hurricane, and now they had survived Jizan, at least so far. The curtains, however, had been replaced with a Versace-style fabric in bright tones of green. Chairs in the corners of the ballroom were now Napoleonic reproductions and gilded.

Couples in tuxedos and fine gowns and expensive jewelry mingled. *Jizan is performing tonight*, Zahi thought. *The viceroy is holding court in the absence of the king.*

He surveyed the guests, curious to see what 'nobility' were present. It was hard to place the men into their true social class because they were all wearing black tuxedoes. Tonight they were all oligarchs. Ah, but here was a man sporting a red bowtie. *How bold*, Zahi thought, sarcastically. *He must have influence. Perhaps he's a Russian?*

Zahi had worn the tweed sport coat. At the present moment, he felt warm and safe. He was also wearing black dress pants, a white shirt with pleats, and a well-tied black bowtie. *But I'm just a nobody*, he thought. *Just part of the retinue.*

And then Zahi recognized Abdullah al-Mnuchin's money handler. His appearance was rather comical: short, black hair combed off his forehead; black, heavy plastic glasses; an oval face; and a funny, almost clownish mouth. But he was no comedian. Zahi knew that the money handler had personally enabled—no, orchestrated—the theft of millions of dollars from a humanitarian fund designated for medicine, food, and water purification.

The money handler used to be a Republican Democracy senator, but he was now awaiting trial in France for money laundering. His work, obviously, had been a bit sloppy. *I don't make those mistakes*, Zahi thought.

Ah, he sees me. Damn!

Zahi walked over. They shook hands. "Nice real estate," the money handler said. He had perfectly coifed black hair.

"It was nicer before he cut down the oaks," Zahi said. The words just blurted out.

"He did it for security," the money handler said, defending his client.

"I see," Zahi said.

"I recommended that he add a bomb shelter." He pursed his mouth in a well-pleased smile. "And a safe room."

Zahi had no doubt that both had been added. And probably a walk-in safe, too. Everything with these people was about money. Making it, keeping it, and making sure that no one took it, or killed you for it. In fact, Zahi now recalled that the money handler had helped al-Mnuchin purchase a private Boeing 767 with a missile avoidance system like Air Force One. Of course, Mikhail Derichenko had purchased a Gulfstream G650, a luxurious business jet. Lesser oligarchs were satisfied to fly NetJets, which required a buy-in and monthly fees for a share of a private plane. *Always a pecking order*, Zahi thought.

"Beware," the money handler said.

Zahi shivered. "Of what?"

"A local reporter. From the *Maritauqua News*. He's uninvited, but nevertheless, he's here. Security is working on it."

"I'll be mindful," Zahi said. "I hope we have an enjoyable evening, nonetheless."

"I'm looking forward to the performance," the money handler said. "It's billed as an original work. And it premieres tonight."

Zahi nodded his approval. However, he was not looking forward to another disharmonious noisepiece.

The reporter was easy to spot. Besides Zahi, he was the only other man not wearing a tasteful tuxedo. He wore an old-fashioned longtail tuxedo. And it was white. That in itself was bold. It was so bold that Zahi wondered if the reporter was deliberately drawing attention to himself. Especially with the longtail tuxedo.

At the moment, the reporter was talking to a lawyer whom Zahi recognized. Zahi had worked with him on past projects, including the recent purchase of Jizan's mansion. The lawyer had established numerous shell companies in Delaware through a company that served as a registered agent. The fees were modest. The Service was excellent. And nobody could discover the beneficial ownership of the real owner.

If only the lawyer were a good guy, Zahi thought. *He has access to so many financial documents!* However, Zahi knew the man's character and he was no whistleblower. If he were questioned, or if one of his clients got in trouble, he would claim attorney-client privilege. The law did not require lawyers to screen their clients or to file suspicious activity reports. Ironically, his job was to keep everything anonymous. And he did, for a hefty fee.

If questioned by the authorities, Zahi's defense would be similar, yet different. He was 'legally blind.' As a realtor, he wasn't responsible for who his clients were. Why should he spend money and do customer due diligence when the law and regulations didn't require it?

Besides, Zahi knew that Maritauqua Island was not under the umbrella of the Treasury Department's Geographic Targeting Order (GTO). Miami was under the umbrella, and so was New York. But not Maritauqua

Island. That's why property values on the island were going up and up.

And then Zahi heard a Russian accent. He followed the voice to a tall and muscular man in his sixties, with blond hair. *A Russian in exile?* Was he seeking refuge at the viceroy's court?

If he was a powerful Russian oligarch, then one or more bodyguards would be nearby. Zahi surveyed the area around the handsome man. He spotted a strongman with an earbud plugged in, standing with his back to the wall a short distance from the oligarch.

Zahi knew that Russian oligarchs like Mikhail Derichenko were filthy rich. Disgustingly so. This oligarch's fingers, wrists, and neck sparkled with gold, diamonds and jewels. *What would his countrymen do if they saw a video of all his bling? How would they react if they saw him strolling like a peacock among his houses and cars and mistresses? Would they stone him?* But here, in the United States, on Maritauqua Island, he was untouchable.

Zahi turned and found himself face to face with the reporter. "I'm Dan," the reporter said. "I'm a reporter for the *Maritauqua Times.*"

No shit, Zahi thought. "Are you a friend of the host?"

"No, no. I'm here to cover the event for the lifestyle section of our paper."

Dan, Zahi thought, *the guests would rather you didn't.* Jizan had a public relations specialist handling his publicity. He had spent a lot of money to whitewash his criminal past. He did not want a local reporter poking around.

Zahi studied the reporter for a brief moment. Not only was he wearing a ridiculous white tuxedo with tails, but his graying black hair was disheveled.

Zahi tried to imagine what it would be like being an

anonymous source, providing information to the *Washington Post* or the *New York Times*, or to this shaggy reporter. *I have so much information, so much dirt, so many stories to share.*

A server approached and offered them wine, a choice of red or white in glasses on a platter. Zahi declined. The reporter, however, exchanged his empty whiskey glass for two red wines. Zahi watched him pour one glass into the other.

"Saves me a trip to the bar." The reporter smiled. He placed the empty wine glass on the platter.

It saved me, too, Zahi thought as he watched the man take a sip of wine. The overfull glass spilled red wine onto the parquet. *There's no way I'm risking my life talking to a lush like you.*

"Sorry, I didn't catch your name?" the reporter said.

"Zahi."

"Zahi." The reporter took another sip, and then wiped his lower lip. "Can you spell that for me?"

The reporter was already inebriated. Zahi didn't reply.

"I've been trying to get background on the new owner. Do you know him? Personally?"

"No," Zahi said.

"How do you spell your name?" the reporter asked again. He took out a pen and small notebook. In one hand he held a full glass of wine and the notebook. In the other the pen. It looked like an accident waiting to happen.

Zahi took out one of his business cards. It was almost a reflex reaction. He hesitated, but then gave the card to the reporter.

"Thanks," the man said.

A flash of bright light. Zahi turned to see a woman standing with a camera. She was short and plump, with a heart-shaped face and rosy cheekbones. Her eyes were soft brown and she had long lashes. A loose-fitting dress covered her large frame. She was a sloppy dresser.

"Sorry to blind you," she said. "I'm a photographer for the *Maritauqua News*. You'll be able to see again soon."

Zahi was aware that the flash had gotten the attention of everyone in the ballroom. "If you will excuse me," he said. He turned his back on the reporter and the photographer and walked away, through the nearest door into an adjoining room.

He saw a group of women in front of an unlit fireplace. It was constructed of beautiful dark green marble. A life-size painting of Jizan hung over the fireplace, looking down on everyone. Zahi decided to join them.

He took the measure of the women as he approached. Two were seated in a plush light green couch at a right angle to the fireplace: one fat and one elderly. One was standing in front of the fireplace, a belle in a dark green gown. Scarlett O' Hara had not been more beautiful.

"The difference between us and them is getting worse," the heavyset woman said. "I've lived on this island all my life. I've never seen it worse." She was bulging out of her tight-fitting dress in several places. "All these Blacks protesting about the police and talking about how terrible slavery use to be." She shook her head. "They have no idea."

"It was never that bad," the matronly woman sitting next to her on the couch said. "Never as bad as they say it was."

"Heavens no," the belle said. She was standing across from the couch and the two women. "They got housed. They got fed. They was looked after."

"Because they were valued property," the heavyset woman said. "You don't damage valuable property."

Zahi stepped forward and spoke up. "Ladies," he said, "I'm an economist. It may interest you to know that a slave was worth about $350 in 1800."

"That's not much." The belle flipped her curly hair back with the back of her hand.

"Their value doubled by the time of the American Civil War," Zahi said.

"Let me introduce myself." He stepped around the couch and joined the belle in front of the fireplace. "My name is Zahi. I'm a university lecturer in economics. I live in Washington, DC."

She extended her hand, palm down. Zahi took the belle's white hand gently into his. He would have squeezed it, perhaps kissed it, but Zahi was not a Southern gentleman. He had grown up in the Republican Democracy, where a man would never hold, much less kiss a woman's hand in public. He held her hand gently and smiled. He then bowed, slightly, to all of the women. They returned his smile, which pleased him. He then released the belle's hand.

"Are they trying to take down monuments there, too?" the belle asked, brushing curls away from her forehead.

"Monuments?" he asked.

"To our heroes," the belle answered, "Robert E. Lee and Jefferson Davis."

"Oh no," he said. "There are still statues in the capital honoring Confederates."

"Really?" the belle said.

"Oh, yes." Zahi replied. "Each state has chosen two statues to put inside the capitol."

"Do we have a statue?" The belle pulled thoughtfully on one of her curls. "Alabama?"

"Joseph Wheeler," the elderly woman said.

The heavyset woman turned in her seat and asked, "Who's he?"

"Fighting Joe," the elderly woman answered. "He was a general in the Confederate army."

"That's wonderful," the belle said. "I'll have to look for him next time the family visits."

"You should contact your representative or senator before you go," Zahi suggested. "He can give you a guided tour. Show you the statue."

"Yes, I will. I will do that."

The women all pursed their lips and nodded their heads in agreement.

Zahi smiled, politely.

A flash. Zahi turned to see who had taken the picture. The photographer and the reporter had caught up with him.

He now saw bright lights everywhere he looked. *Why didn't you bounce the flash off the ceiling?* He looked above and answered his own question. *Because the ceilings are way up there, 18 feet or higher.*

The reporter pulled a piece of paper out of his white jacket pocket. He unfolded the yellowed paper, looked at it for a moment, and then laughed. "According to this article from a New York tabloid, the president of the Republican Democracy intends to declare himself emir." The reporter smiled, clearly amused. "An emir is a king, right?"

His comment killed the conversation. No one wanted to discuss Lil't, especially in public.

"But there's a problem," the reporter said, continuing. "A big problem."

"What is that?" Zahi asked.

"If he is king, then his children are royalty, too. Yes?"

"And your point?" Zahi asked.

"The future king's daughter has applied for United States citizenship." The reporter smiled. "What do you think of that?" When Zahi didn't say anything, he continued. "Will the US recognize her as a princess?" He laughed out loud and spilled red wine onto the carpet.

Zahi had never met Lil't's children. Nevertheless, he knew that Lil't's daughter had plagiarized her doctorate just like Putin had plagiarized his. He also knew that she had donated millions to establish a school and scholarship in her father's name. Kleptocrats were always imitating each other. Lil't's daughter was following the example set by Ukrainian oligarch Dmytro Firtash, who had made a sizeable donation to the University of Cambridge. The university had accepted his generous donation and created a Ukrainian studies center and lectureship in his honor. It seemed like money and power in the West could buy anything. Even Trump had been given honorary degrees. Zahi laughed. It was ridiculously ironic to give Trump an honorary degree, when he had so vociferously withheld his actual grades from the public. And besides, you couldn't believe anything Trump said.

Zahi glanced at the women. *What about your children!* he wondered. They would not be princes and princesses, but they would be rich and privileged, nonetheless, and through no merit of their own. They would one day purchase sports teams and yachts and luxury homes; they would make large donations to the arts and charities. Yet most of them would never work a day in their lives.

Royalty was not Zahi's concern. The Jared-Ivanka Effect was.

Children of oligarchs, in his opinion, suffered from a tragic socialization defect: the Javanka Effect. They overestimated their skills and were quick to criticize people less fortunate. A conversation with them was like wading through mud. They were poor listeners who loved to talk about themselves. Most of them, like their parents, disliked logic and science, which only made the Javanka Effect worse; they simply didn't know what they didn't know!

Zahi suddenly wanted to leave the party. He didn't want to mingle and make small conversation. He didn't want to hear about anyone's latest experience, whether it was an around-the-world cruise, a marvelous six-course dinner, or attendance at a special concert like Jizan's, tonight. He had yet to meet someone who had paid to be blasted into outer space, although that was just a matter of time, but that didn't really interest him either. These folks collected experiences like poorer people used to collect postage stamps. *Really boring and meaningless,* he thought. *Self-centered and amounting to nothing.* And he definitely was uninterested in their latest material acquisition: yacht, super plane, or sports team. These folks, like their kids, bounced from one happy experience to another yet never experienced joy.

The only thing that everyone at this party has in common, he thought, *is a mutual distrust of each other.* Everyone was pretending to be family, pretending to be community.

What was it Saba had told him? *Part ways with them. Yes, part ways with them. Serve others.*

Zahi discreetly left the party.

11

Prodigal Student

Zahi approached the man in the dark navy blue sport coat and blue jeans. He was wearing a light blue dress shirt, and a dark blue bowtie with small red dots and flying a hobby drone in the wide open green spaces of Hyde Park, in London.

Zahi recognized the square-shaped face, the strong jaw and nose, the shiny crown, the few tufts of gray-black hair above the ears. He fondly remembered the eyebrows in need of trimming, and the large, dark eyes, warm and kind.

The elderly man was David Ludi, professor emeritus at the University of London School of Economics. He had been Zahi's doctoral advisor, economic mentor, and second father.

Lightning flashed to their right, followed by rolling thunder. The professor guided his drone to land at his feet. He picked it up, folded its wings and deposited it in a black bag, along with the controller.

When the professor saw Zahi, he quickly stepped forward and threw his arms around him in an affectionate embrace that lasted a full three seconds and ended with heartfelt pats on Zahi's back and shoulders. There was no scorn, no reprimand, no holding back.

Zahi was speechless. He had not expected a warm embrace because he had squandered his education, his PhD. He had walked away from a promising teaching career in the Republican Democracy and moved to the United States, where he had become a professional enabler for Lil't and his associates.

And the hug itself disturbed him. It was genuinely warm and affectionate. Zahi had not received such a hug in years. And he could not remember ever giving one. He no longer liked to be touched, physically.

"The London fire brigade has issued warnings about grass fires," Professor Ludi said as he released Zahi from his embrace. He immediately extended his hand in welcome.

"I heard that it's a heat wave," Zahi said, accepting the proffered hand.

"Excess heat produces the lightning."

"And it was hot today," Zahi added.

"The temperature has been soaring!" The tone of Professor Ludi's voice was one of concern.

"A heat wave?" Zahi asked. "In the heart of London?"

"We're sweltering."

"And the lightning?" Zahi asked.

"London's climate is changing," Professor Ludi said. "The Atlantic Gulf Stream is shifting. England may become the new Alaska. Imagine that!"

"But that's a worst-case scenario," Zahi said, challenging his mentor. Nevertheless, Zahi pondered the possibility. "England, the future home of polar bears and English Eskimos? The next frontier?"

"We'll be living in igloos," Professor Ludi suggested.

They both laughed. The professor picked up the black bag containing the drone and slung one of the bag's straps over his shoulder.

Walking beside his mentor, Zahi said, "Professor, I need your advice."

"Not about investments, I hope," Professor Ludi quipped, smiling. He had co-founded and was now CEO of a climate neutral investment fund.

"No," Zahi answered. "I congratulate you, though, on the success of your fund."

"So you are seeking my advice on other matters?"

"Yes," Zahi smiled. "You will always be my advisor."

The professor fondly patted his former student on the shoulder. "Then let's talk. But first, how is Saba?"

"We divorced years ago. She died this spring of cancer."

"I'm sorry to hear that. She was a wonderful, kindhearted person."

"I returned home after the funeral." He had actually returned months after the funeral, but he saw no reason to say that. "I brought my half-brother Hugo back to the States with me."

"He's a citizen. I think you told me that, right?"

"Yes, but the authorities can't find his birth certificate."

"Probably misspelled his name." The professor smiled. "Arabic names are challenging for Americans."

"Perhaps." Zahi took his business card out of his wallet and handed it to the professor. It was his personal business card, not his business card from George Mason

University. The university job was little more than a front for his other activities.

The professor reached into his sport coat pocket and took out his reading glasses. The heavy black plastic frames went well with his square face and strong jaw. As the professor adjusted the glasses, they captured the overhead sunlight.

He read the card out loud: "Zahi Haarun, Economics and International Trade, Consulting." He skimmed the contact information. The back of the card contained Zahi's picture. Of course Zahi had not used his full name on the card, Zahi ibn Haarun ibn Ajan Ab al-Naqad.

"Nice," the professor quipped.

"Thank you." Zahi smiled. His mentor was being kind and polite. He had always treated his students with respect, except for fools and idiots and twits. It was significant, though, that he did not ask about Zahi's "consulting."

Zahi swallowed, unsure how much to explain. Unsure how the professor would react. Finally he ventured, "I've been working on the infrastructure of Little NEOM." He paused to see Professor Ludi's reaction.

"And let me guess, you are doing an economic analysis?"

"Yes," Zahi answered.

They looked at each other. There was reticence in the professor's expression.

"It will impact the lives of every person in the Republican Democracy," Zahi said. "Perhaps every person in the Middle East."

"Starbucks?" David asked.

Zahi nodded approval. They walked across the green lawn and crossed the street to a Starbucks. David pulled the door open and gestured for Zahi to enter.

Zahi ordered a venti pumpkin spice latte, with an extra shot of espresso. Professor Ludi chose a tall dark coffee with room for cream. Zahi paid for both orders plus two slices of pumpkin bread. They sat at a small table in the back corner of the café.

Once they were comfortable, Zahi pulled a copy of a document out of his briefcase and placed it on the table between them. "My unexpunged analysis."

"Unexpunged?" The professor smiled.

"Heavily annotated."

The professor again took out his glasses from his inside sport coat pocket. He pulled the hefty document to his side of the table, opened to the table of contents and began reading. His finger slowly moved down the pages, line by line.

Zahi sat patiently, slowly sipping his latte, occasionally checking his iPhone. He thought, *I will add a dedication, 'Dedicated to Saba Charmchi-Haarun.'*

Forty-five minutes later, the professor closed the document, looked up at Zahi, and pushed the economic analysis back across the table to him.

"Let me see if I understand." The professor sipped a second coffee. "Your paper is an economic analysis of Little NEOM?"

"Yes," Zahi said. "Warts and all."

"The first half is a cost/benefit and a cost/effectiveness analysis?"

"That is correct."

"Based on those analyses I would NOT invest a nickel in Little NEOM." The professor looked at Zahi. "Would you?"

"No," Zahi said. "It would be foolish."

"The second half of your report is a demand analysis?"

"That is correct."

"It shows that Little NEOM will not generate benefits for anyone, except for a few well-placed elites?" The professor's voice sounded pained.

"Correct."

"A few well-placed companies and individuals will make a lot of money?"

"That is correct."

"Huge international loans will be funneled?" the professor asked, following up on his question.

Zahi nodded absolute agreement. "Money will be funneled to Lil't and his friends and associates."

"Your report appears very thorough. It includes an in-depth appraisal of Little NEOM's strengths and weaknesses."

"I drew circles around the warts. For example, I discussed the need for an environmental impact assessment."

"The kleptocrats will NOT be happy." The professor's voice now sounded concerned.

"They will be livid!"

"Present it to a large audience," the professor suggested. "The larger the better." He looked into his coffee, and after a thoughtful pause, he made eye contact with Zahi. "An international forum: the International Monetary Fund, World Bank, big money—they should all be there."

"And Lil't," Zahi added. "I wouldn't want Lil't to miss my presentation. After all, he's paying for it."

The professor tried but failed to smile. "Do you know who killed Professor Kartouzian?"

His question surprised Zahi. "I have my suspicions, but no proof."

The professor leaned over and squeezed Zahi's forearm. "Did Professor Kartouzian share his work with you?"

Zahi felt a pain in his chest. When they were students, Kartouzian had been Zahi's best friend. In fact, his only friend. They were both drawn to Professor Ludi's lectures. They had met in one of his classes and competed for his attention.

On occasion, the three of them had retreated to local pubs in London and spent evenings discussing globalization and international trade and economic theories. Zahi had fond memories of their serious, yet heartfelt discussions. He recalled sipping Strongbow Cider at the Churchill Arms pub on Kensington Church Street, watching the workers and students come and go, while he discussed the global movement of money and resources and people with his friend and the professor. The Churchill Arms held good memories for him.

"No," Zahi said. "He did not share his work with me. As you know, we took different paths." He looked at Professor Ludi. "You must be proud of him."

The professor nodded. Professor Kartouzian had been tenured, respected, and had a high moral standing in the community. Zahi never received tenure because he expatriated to the United States. He looked down at the document resting on the table. *I made a pact with the devil and I made a lot of money.*

"Did anyone continue his work?" Zahi asked.

"Yes."

"Good data? Good, solid facts?"

"Yes."

Kartouzian had been investigating the Lil't Works Program when he was murdered. Did he have evidence that government contracts had been given to Lil't's family and friends? Zahi wanted to see his documentation, his evidence.

"I'll have his protégés contact you," the professor said, smiling at Zahi.

"Thank you."

"What the Sistema did to him was horrendous."

Zahi nodded. He knew that trolls had attacked his friend's Twitter and Facebook accounts. They had made his life miserable. They had splashed disparaging information about him all over the internet. And then Lil't had personally vilified him.

Zahi's stomach growled and he felt a pain, probably gas, just below his rib cage. "How can you salvage your reputation when the leader of your country attacks your integrity?"

"You can't," the professor said. "The National Revenue Service audited him, too."

"I didn't know that." The National Revenue Service had become especially partisan, ordering audits of businesses and individuals who did not support Lil't and his political party. They were ruthless.

Zahi picked up the heavy document and returned it to his briefcase. "I need to verify some of the data in my analysis. Do you know someone who can help?"

"Yes," the professor answered. "Someone at the university who knows someone who works in the Commerce Department."

Zahi knew that the professor was referring to the University of the Republican Democracy and the National Commerce Department. "It will be dangerous for them?"

"Yes," the professor answered. "We all know the risk."

Lil't had a stranglehold on the Republican Democracy's bureaucracy because he had filled most government positions with employees loyal to his party. Apolitical employees were now a rarity, even in the Commerce Department.

In addition, the Republican Democracy's parliament had passed a law that made it a crime to protest against Lil't and his administration. Russia had used a similar law to arrest members of Open Russia, a Russian pro-democracy movement. Once again, Vladimir Putin had led the way and other kleptocrats, like Lil't, followed his success.

Professor Ludi cleared his throat. "We should be entering a post-oil era." He couldn't keep the bitterness out of his voice. "We should be shifting from oil to high tech like wind, sun and thermal energy. We should be putting ourselves in the forefront of technological advances."

Zahi knew that the professor had begun to lecture, and that it was his way of indicating that their meeting was drawing to a close. He called an Uber.

After their farewell, which included another disconcerting hug, Zahi found himself seated in an Uber waiting for the light to change. He watched his old mentor walking down the sidewalk carrying his drone. The light seemed to take forever.

Zahi watched the professor step around a homeless man who had seated himself on the sidewalk with his back to the exterior wall of the Starbucks. Between the man's crossed legs was a plastic cup for donations. Zahi felt a special disdain for such worthless human beings. The man had no shirt and his pants appeared soiled. *Disgusting*, Zahi thought.

The professor turned around. He set down his case containing his drone, took off his navy blue sport jacket and draped it over the shoulders of the shirtless man. Zahi watched them exchange words, and then they both smiled. The professor adjusted his light blue dress shirt, picked up his case, and walked on.

You're right Saba, Zahi thought. *Relationships are everything.*

He cleared his throat and said to the taxi driver, "Do you know what the most valuable thing is?"

"Money?"

"No."

"Respect?"

"No."

"Love?"

Zahi smiled a sad smile. "Maybe. But I was thinking time."

A few blocks later they were stuck in traffic.

"I'm an economist," Zahi offered.

"I've never understood what that is," the driver said. The man wore a white turban and his skin was dark brown. He seemed comfortable in the driver's seat, yet he looked bowlegged. Zahi wondered if he had problems using the pedals, accelerating and braking.

As the man drove him to the airport, Zahi allowed himself a friendly conversation, something he never did with strangers. The driver learned about several famous British economists, and Zahi learned about recent changes in London.

Traffic was heavy and he missed his flight, but it wasn't the driver's fault. He rated the driver five stars and gave him a generous tip.

He rescheduled for the next available flight to DC, which gave him hours to kill. He read the *London Times.*

He had a hamburger and fries and a Strongbow Cider. Eventually the waiting area filled with new passengers.

He made an effort to strike up a conversation with a young couple and learned that they were going to DC for vacation. He answered question after question about the city and recommended places for them to visit. He highly recommended the tapas at Jaleo, which was one of Zaytinya's sister restaurants. Jaleo's had outside seating that he thought the couple would enjoy and allow them to people-watch.

As they boarded the plane together, the couple thanked him, and he encouraged them to give him a call. He doubted they would and that filled him with sadness, which surprised him.

All these people used to be a nuisance, he thought. Now they all seemed worthwhile.

12

Arrested at SWTP

Early morning, before daybreak, the police caught Hugo with aerosol spray paints and broad tipped indelible markers at the Maritauqua Sewage Wastewater Treatment Plant. They arrested him for graffiti vandalism.

After Hugo was arrested, they took his mug shot and fingerprinted him. The routine body search revealed a key around his neck. An investigator soon verified that the key matched the lock on the SWTP's gate fence. Consequently, the key became evidence of the crime and was placed in the evidence locker room.

Hugo was charged with a Class A misdemeanor, punishable by jail and community service and a fine. The fine was substantial for a street person, up to $2500. He was also charged with second degree criminal mischief, a Class D felony, for damaging the Sewage Treatment Plant.

The police called Zahi, awakening him. He was fully clothed, sprawled out on his bed, and he was a bit hungover. The police told him about Hugo's arrest.

What was wrong with Hugo? Why would he do something so stupid? It didn't sound like him at all. Furious at Hugo, Zahi called Liko.

He hoped that the tone of his voice conveyed his disappointment. "I am busy with my research," he vented. "I can't fly to Maritauqua every time Hugo gets into trouble! I'm completing a paper for publication." *I need to finish my analysis of Little NEOM and prepare my presentation.* "Liko, can you help?"

Zahi immediately felt ashamed of himself. He regretted putting his work above his relationship with his brother, even though it was work to dethrone Lil't. And he regretted taking advantage of the kindness of the security guard, Liko. But he had so little time. He felt the tension in his neck and his ears throbbed.

"Yes," Liko said. "I can help." He agreed to go immediately to the police station and bail out Hugo. Zahi was astounded at his behavior.

Zahi poured himself a tall glass of eggnog. He poured in some brandy, almost unconsciously. The eggnog went down quick and smooth. Delicious. He followed that up with a neat double bourbon.

He decided to take a day off work and try to relax. Just one day. The pressure was becoming unbearable.

He poured another double bourbon. He gulped it down and banged the glass on the kitchen counter. He would soon be inebriated, and once again the center of his own world. *Do I drink to dream about myself?*

He walked to the bathroom and pissed, standing up, into the toilet. He looked at himself in the mirror. His eyes were bloodshot, flecked with small veins of red. He splashed hot water on his face and again looked at himself in the mirror.

I'm going to shave, take a hot shower, and dress. Then I'm going to put on my tweed coat and go out, have brunch, salvage the day, work on my analysis!

The next day, seated in his home office in Washington, DC, Zahi answered his iPhone.

"Mr. Haarun?"

"Yes?"

"My name is Janet Rehm, we met at Jizan's party."

Zahi didn't know a Janet and he didn't recognize the woman's voice. "Can I help you?"

"I'm a photographer for the *Maritauqua Times*," she said. "I took your picture at the party."

The cherubic photographer? Zahi felt the adrenalin dump. His heartbeat quickened and his body grew warm. "How did you get my name?"

"Your business card," she answered. "You gave it to Dan, and he gave it to me."

The drunk in the white tuxedo?

"We are doing a story on Jizan," she said.

"A story?"

"Yes, for the *Times*."

"Can we talk later? I am very busy right now."

"I have just one or two questions," she said.

"Sorry," Zahi repeated, his finger hovering over the button.

"Is the Republican Democracy a kleptocracy?"

Now that was an interesting question. His finger paused.

The pause prompted the photographer to continue.

"While I was checking the names of several guests, I discovered a website called The Kleptocracy Forum."

"I am busy," Zahi said, as politely as he could. "Can I call you back?"

"Is the Republican Democracy a kleptocracy?" she repeated. "Is Lil't a kleptocrat?"

"Goodbye." He disconnected.

Zahi immediately googled The Kleptocracy Forum. It was a legitimate website sponsored by the River of Freedom Institute, a highly respected think tank in Washington, DC. The focus of the website was to provide a forum to collect and distribute information about kleptocracies. According to the website, eight percent of the world's wealth was hidden away.

Zahi imagined that most Americans, including most reporters and photographers, had never heard the word kleptocracy, much less knew what a kleptocrat was. But this woman, this photographer, Janet, she knew. And that, coupled with the fact that she had been to Jizan's party, and that she had taken pictures of his guests – that was NOT a good thing. It made her dangerous. *And she has my picture, too.*

He stood up and paced back and forth. He felt his neck muscles tighten and his ears begin to pulse again. I don't need this stress, he thought. He walked from the desk in his home office to the refrigerator in his kitchen. He looked in the refrigerator but didn't see anything that he wanted. He felt suddenly tired and weak, so he walked back to his office chair and sat down.

Zahi intended to give his analysis of Little NEOM to all the major newspapers, simultaneously. It would be helpful, though, to have a reporter assist him. And a photographer? *I could use the help. But the reporter? He's a heavy drinker.* The fact that she had called him instead of Dan did not reflect well on their work relationship. Or did it?

Relationships, he thought. *What a mystery.*

He imagined the *Maritauqua Times* carrying a front page story about the economic and social impact of Little NEOM upon the Middle East. *Can she make that happen? Timing is everything.*

Zahi considered whether or not to call her back. He knew nothing about the politics of their paper, the *Maritauqua Times.* Not every paper was as responsible as the *Washington Post* or the *New York Times.* "Democracy dies in darkness," he said to himself, recalling the *Post*'s current motto. Did the Maritauqua Times have a motto, too?

He looked at the documents on his home desk in front of him. Kartouzian's protégé had sent him a treasure trove of damning information about the Lil't Works Program. The program provided public money to private contractors to upgrade the Republican Democracy's crumbling infrastructure: not only the sewers and water lines, but also the roads, bridges, tunnels, airports, and seaports.

Zahi understood, and was determined to prove, that the Lil't Works Program was a precursor to what would happen if Little NEOM went forward—bribes, kickbacks and corruption on a massive scale. It was all here. *It will make a nice appendix to my analysis of Little NEOM.*

Zahi wished that his friend was still alive so he could tell him: "Excellent work!" He decided that he would laud Professor Kartouzian in the executive summary of the Little NEOM analysis.

13

Artwork in the Park

A month or so later, Zahi was surprised to receive an email from Liko. Curious, he opened it and discovered several newspaper articles attached.

One article showed a picture of Hugo and a small dog. The dog's white coat had patches of blue and an explosion of other colors. Hugo held the dog in his lap, a puppy. Hugo sat on a bar stool in front of a paint canvas on an easel. There was a bright patch of blue on the canvas. Zahi looked at the blue on the puppy's coat. *Probably paint.* He smiled. *Acrylic or oil? What is Hugo up to?*

Zahi looked up from his laptop, across his desk, and out his office door. He saw no one. It had been a quiet day at George Mason University. None of his graduate students had stopped by to see him. Nevertheless, he got up from his desk and closed the door. He then returned to his desk and studied the photo.

Hugo's hair covered his ears. *Has it grown that much since I last saw him?* Zahi wondered.

Hugo seemed comfortable holding the puppy. And the puppy seemed comfortable cradled in Hugo's arms. *I hope he washed his hands*, Zahi thought.

He had a strange look in his eyes. Zahi enlarged the photo. He seemed to be in the moment, happy holding the puppy, content.

Zahi read the caption: "Artist Hugo Haarun and his dog Banksy."

Great, just great! Zahi thought sarcastically. *Someone will notice his last name and connect us as family. Embarrassing for me, dangerous for Hugo.*

Zahi's bowels suddenly felt loose, pressing on him.

He'd never had a problem at work with his bowels. Usually the discomfort started at home, after he got off work and poured his first bourbon. On those occasions he needed to relieve his bowels almost immediately, as if his body knew that it had to brace itself for what always followed: several quick drinks in a row and then too much alcohol.

His bowels felt that way now. He thought about dashing to the restroom. It was just outside his office and down the hall. But he decided to tough it out, hoping that he could.

The next newspaper photo looked like a painting of Maritauqua Park, perhaps a watercolor. He recognized the park, the oak trees, picnic tables and coastline. It was an area where locals relaxed, brought families, had a cookout, had a picnic.

He looked closer at the photo. The watercolor was damaged. A dark smudged figure, perhaps a woman, stood next to a picnic table. Smaller figures nearby were possibly children. Yes, several women in dresses – no, thawbs, the traditional dress of his people? The women were surrounded by children. One child was kicking a ball. A soccer ball? The other children were running, chasing each other, jumping. All the figures looked smudged, gray and black. Scratched into the watercolor.

Along the outer perimeter of trees and along the coastline were taller, larger figures. *Men?* They carried a variety of objects in their hands. Some pointed. Some long. The objects looked sharp and dangerous.

Are they soldiers? Rebels?

The caption beneath the photo read: *"The Kurdirtgeon* by Hugo Haarun."

Ahhh! So this was the picture that Hugo had damaged.

In the bottom right corner of the photo, in small font and small caps, Zahi read: photos by Janet Rehm. Another deep groan rose from Zahi's bowels.

He read the article's title: "It Can't Happen Here: Retold Through One Man's Paintings." It was written by Daniel Johnson II, a Maritauqua Times staff writer.

Zahi skimmed the article. The reporter had commented on Hugo's painting style, calling it "fearless." Hugo was quoted: "In my country, street photography is illegal." Another quote: "My neighbors killed each other. They hunted each other. They killed the children first. That was easy because the children did not know to run. Then they killed the pregnant women. And women with infants and young children. They also could not run fast. People hunted during the day. At night they drank and ate and danced. Every night they partied."

When asked if it could happen on Maritauqua Island,

Hugo's answer was quoted: "It is already happening. When it happens anywhere, it happens everywhere."

Zahi reread the quote. "When it happens anywhere, it happens everywhere." He frowned. *This is not good!*

The article stated that both paintings, *Banksy and Hugo*, and *It Can't Happen Here, Redux*– which Zahi assumed was *The Kurdirtgeon*– would be on display Sunday. Admission was free because the display would be on public property fronting a public sidewalk, The Economists Walkway, in Maritauqua Park. Zahi went immediately to the restroom.

When he returned, he looked at the letter attached to the email. It was handwritten and then scanned, which he thought was unusual, and it was two pages long. The letter was signed Liko, and included a return address: Liko Koholua, 1212 Gulf Coast Road NW, Unit 10, Maritauqua Island, Alabama. *A Hawaiian living on an island in the Gulf of Mexico.* He smiled despite the continued growling in his intestines.

The handwriting was neat. The lettering was large and confident. Occasional words or phrases were scratched out, but it was easy to read.

The letter read:

Dear Zahi,

As you know, the police caught your brother and me trespassing at the sewage treatment plant. I have already had my trial. The magistrate gave me one year in jail. She waived my jail time, but I had to remove Hugo's murals from the concrete walls with a high-pressure water spray gun. I also had to pay $2,000. I have to report back to her in 90 days.

Don't worry. I cleaned off the murals but I first took pictures. The prosecutor's office did too. They hired a professional photographer who took color photographs.

The murals are very disturbing. They must be what Hugo saw during the civil war and genocide.

When Hugo painted the murals, he was living outdoors in the park. He was not taking his medications.

I am not an art critic but Hugo's murals were incredible. They may have been masterpieces. I think your brother is a great artist.

I have a friend Arti who says that his murals are as good as Picasso's Guernica. Have you seen the Alien movies? Hugo's work is better than that.

I believe that painting is good for him. It is his way to tell us what happened to him and to his country. It is a way to show us his feelings.

I have been trying to help your brother. He and I are now living together. I rented a two-bedroom apartment and set it up for painting. I bought him paints.

Your brother needs a better attorney so I hired one.

Hugo is facing a maximum of seven years. I don't know if the magistrate will waive Hugo's jail time like she did for me. Jail time would kill Hugo.

They have postponed Hugo's court date twice. As you know, the first time was so he could be evaluated to determine if he was mentally fit for court. The second time was because I was injured in an explosion and I couldn't make it to court to testify because I was in the hospital.

If you have any friends on Maritauqua Island who can help Hugo, I suggest that you contact them.

I think you should know a few things about the murals. Hugo has different names for them like migration, protest, and genocide. Whatever you call them, they take your breath away.

I tried to think of some way to help Hugo make a living from his paintings. Every Sunday local artists hang their art on the fence at the entrance to The Economists Walkway. I helped Hugo set up his art there. You can tell by the enclosed newspaper articles that it did not work out very well. I guess that is putting it mildly.

I think Hugo's medicines have stabilized him. He is now following his doctor's directions and taking his medicines. In addition to his antidepressants, Hugo is also taking Seroquel. It is supposed to help him sleep and make him less psychotic. He is a different person now. I think that will help when he goes back to court, but I thought it was a good idea to hire him a better lawyer anyway.

I hope this letter did not upset you too much. I am trying to help your brother.

Hugo looks a lot better now and he has a lot more energy for painting. My goal is to give him a safe place to sleep and paint. He eats like a horse.

Liko

Zahi reread the sentence "He and I are now living together." He wanted to stand up and shout 'YES!' and dance around his office in joy.

He flipped to the third and last newspaper article. He stared at the large picture of Liko standing above the painter Kurt, who was crumpled on the ground at his feet. Kurt's eyes were closed and his forearm, wrist and hand looked bloody.

What the hell happened, Zahi wondered. He read the caption: "Liko Koholua and Kurt Kurdirtgeon wrestled over a can of spray paint at The Economists Walkway."

Zahi studied the picture. Liko towered over Kurt. The painting of Banksy and Hugo hung from the fence behind Liko. It was speckled with neon green paint. Kurt lay on his side, crumpled, the spray can on the ground next to him, silver with a neon green band. The sharp edge of a bone protruded from Kurt's arm, and he had had wet the front of his khaki pants.

Zahi read the newspaper story.

Liko had displayed reproductions of Hugo's 'sewage murals' on the fence along The Economists Walkway. He had hung full color three-by-twelve-foot banners during the night at strategic locations. Each banner was a reproduction of a mural. He had placed one at the Marshall and Keynes statues, another at the Friedman and Greenspan statues, and three at the end of the walkway, mixed in with the Confederate statues.

Hugo's mural artwork had also been printed onto coffee mugs, T-shirts, and mobile phone cases, and then displayed on tables. All the merchandise was for sale. Liko had hung new, original artwork along the fence, too. *Banksy and Hugo* hung at one end and *The Kurdirtgeon* at the other.

According to the newspaper, passersby and protestors had seen the murals and paintings. Some were outraged by the juxtaposition of their paradise and Hugo's reality.

The Kurdirtgeon was especially incendiary. According to the article, the common reaction of most passersby was first shock, and then visceral anger. Hostile protestors had blocked the wide walkway and a bottleneck formed directly in front of Hugo's display.

The photo of Liko towering over Kurt was explained in the newspaper article. Kurt had attacked the painting of Banksy and Hugo using a can of neon green spray paint. Liko had intervened to stop Kurt, snapping his arm when he wrestled the spray can from his grip.

An Island Commissioner of Maritauqua had read a prepared statement to the crowd of protestors, regaling them with a bizarre, racist, and xenophobic message. His message sounded like a repackaged Trump monologue. It even included anti-immigrant language. He called Hugo a "predator" and "a criminal alien poisoning Maritauqua with satanic art." The commissioner said that Hugo's art would "burn and scar" the minds of the young people of Maritauqua.

Hugo is a citizen, not an immigrant, Zahi thought. The commissioner's statements especially upset Zahi, not because they were racist and inflammatory, but because Zahi knew the commissioner. He had seen him at Jizan's party.

Dammit! he thought. *Now everyone will connect me to my brother. And kleptocrats do not like negative press.*

14

Magistrate's Decisions

The magistrate banged her gavel. "In the matter of the People versus Koholua, I find that Mr. Liko Koholua paid his fine and satisfactorily completed his court-ordered community service requirements. His completed hours are approved by this court and his probation ends at noon today."

"Thank you, Your Honor," Liko told the magistrate.

Later that afternoon, in the separate case of the People of the Island of Maritauqua versus Mr. Hugo Haarun, the magistrate agreed that Hugo had done the right thing by paying for all damages to the buildings that he had spray-painted. He had also shown that he was consistently taking his medications, no longer living in the park, and had steady employment as an artist.

Hugo was found guilty of damaging public property.

Regarding his graffiti murals, she said, "I personally find your art to be culturally transgressive." She suspected that Hugo had been the victim of racism, and that his civil rights had been violated—in particular, his freedom of speech. She referred the evidence presented in the case back to the police department, and she ordered "the Maritauqua Police Department to review the facts to determine if a hate crime has been committed against the defendants, Liko Koholua and Hugo Haarun."

Liko blurted out: "Damn right!"

In response, the magistrate furrowed her eyebrows, stared across the room at him, and said: "For the record, let it be noted that the court has still not received a copy of Mr. Haarun's birth certificate."

Sitting in the courtroom, Zahi felt heart palpitations. He said to no one in particular, "How did I forget about his birth certificate?" Everything had been going so well.

When he stepped out of the courtroom, Zahi immediately called his personal lawyer. He spelled out Hugo's full name and tasked the attorney with locating the birth certificate, and to spare no expense. The lawyer agreed to the assignment.

Zahi breathed a sigh of relief. He still felt a slight tightness in his chest, but as he pushed the disconnect button, he felt a bit better. The lawyer was a good man. Zahi felt confident that he would find the birth certificate.

In the meantime, he had a long list of action items to finish.

He had updated his Little NEOM model using accurate economic data from the National Commerce Department. He had obtained accurate data from a student at the Republican Democracy University. The graduate student, who Zahi did not personally know, had obtained the data from a source in the Commerce Department. According to his mentor in London, the student was trustworthy. His contacts had access to public data that Lil't's administration no longer made available to the public.

In fact, Lil't and his administration tightly controlled the Republican Democracy's fiscal data. They had removed all economic data from every department's website, making the information unavailable to the general public and economists. Lil't had learned this subterfuge from Trump's administration, which had censored climate change data, removing it from the US Environmental Protection Agency and other websites. Kleptocrats around the world, including Russia and the Republican Democracy, followed Trump's example.

Just before he gave his presentation, Zahi would send his analysis of the Little NEOM project, along with a copy of his paper and PowerPoint deck, to his contact at the Old World Bank. She would be blown away, appalled.

His analysis debunked the many myths surrounding Little NEOM and showed that it would be harmful to the country's middle class and workers. Only a small group of persons who were already wealthy would benefit. And the massive use of fossil fuels to build, operate, and maintain the coastal city in an age of climate change was irresponsible.

Zahi knew that after he gave his analysis to the Old World Bank and presented his paper at the conference, and posted everything to the internet, he would be targeted. A team would be sent to deal with him.

Zahi's iPhone rang. Not recognizing the incoming number, he almost ignored the call.

"Hello," he answered diffidently, his phone in one hand, his MacBook Pro in the other.

"Zahi Haarun?"

"Yes?"

"My name is Daniel Johnson. I am a reporter for the *Maritauqua Times*."

Zahi sat down heavily on the edge of the Court of Neptune Fountain near the entrance to the Library of Congress. He rested his laptop on his thigh and looked up into the bearded face of Neptune. He had come to use the research library.

"We met at Jizan's party," the reporter said.

"What do you want?" Zahi's voice was gruff.

"I am trying to understand the difference between the Republican Democracy's Little NEOM and Saudi Arabia's NEOM?" the reporter asked. "Can you help me?"

Zahi answered, indirectly, "Kleptocrats learn from each other's successes and failures. Same with NEOM and Little NEOM."

"I don't understand," the reporter answered.

"That doesn't surprise me," Zahi said. *You're as dumb as a rock*, he thought. "Do you think your stories or your coworker's photographs make a difference?"

"Probably not," the reporter answered without even pausing. "But it's my job."

Zahi shook his head in dismay. Zahi wanted to say: *If the media did not make a difference, then why did Egypt's Abdel Fattah al-Sisi, Bahrain's ruling al-Khalifa family, the United Arab Emirate's Mohammed bin Zayed, the Crown Prince of Saudi Arabia, and the Republican Democracy's Lil't – why did all these dictators eliminate all forms of dissent, including newspapers and free media?*

"You do not understand the power that you wield," Zahi said. "I need to go. Goodbye." He ended the call.

Less than a minute later, as he walked up the white steps to the entrance of the Library of Congress, his phone rang again. It was a different phone number.

"Mr. Haarun, this is Janet Rehm."

Zahi recognized her voice. She had photographed his brother and advertised his art show in the park.

"Are you Hugo Haarun's brother?"

They've put two and two together. Zahi stepped to the side, away from the entrance. He walked a short distance and took a seat on an outside bench.

"Your photographs are very good."

"Thank you."

"Do you think your photographs make any difference?" Zahi asked.

"I document what I see, what I witness."

"Similar to my brother," Zahi mumbled.

"Excuse me," she said, "I didn't hear you."

"I said that my brother paints what he witnesses, too."

"Yes," she said. "My pictures, like Hugo's paintings, are never neutral, never objective. But both of us are committed to showing the truth."

"What is your coworker's problem?"

"Alcohol," she answered, bluntly.

"Well," Zahi said, surprised. She was being candid. But could she be trusted? "I have a presentation that I will soon be giving, and a professional paper that will soon be published." He took a deep breath, and then asked, "Are you interested?"

"Yes," she said, without hesitation. "But I hope you understand. Hugo's paintings are anonymous. My photographs show faces."

"I understand," he said. "I have seen your work."

"So you know that my work is not objective?" she stated. "I don't even try to be objective. I reveal the truth as I see it. As my camera captures it."

"I do understand," Zahi said. "I just completed an analysis of the Little NEOM project. My analysis will upset many people. Some of them are very powerful."

"You can send information to me confidentially using the app Signal," she told Zahi. "It has end-to-end encryption and it does not store your contact information."

"I'll try it," Zahi responded. "I'll download the app and give it a try."

"Very good," she said. "I'll start by sending you some pictures."

"Pictures?"

"Yes, pictures I took at Jizan's party. I need help to identify several guests."

"Okay." Zahi felt a sudden throbbing in his ears. This time the pressure made him feel a bit off-balance, a little nauseous. *They're going to be pissed*

15

Heart Attack

Back in his condominium, Zahi found the pressure unbearable. Four weeks until his presentation. He wasn't having second thoughts, but he definitely wasn't feeling ready.

He decided to take a hot shower. That usually helped to relax him. He hung his trousers on the towel rack and his dress shirt on the knob on the back of the bathroom door. He neatly folded his T-shirt and undershorts and placed them on the counter.

He stepped into the shower, turned on the water and adjusted it to a very comfortable warmth. He lathered shampoo into his hair and then conditioner. Massaging his scalp with his fingers felt fantastic and seemed to be working.

Zahi suddenly felt so weak that he couldn't stand. He sat down in the shower, on the dark tiles. He felt the warm water flowing over his head and shoulders and knees. A pain in his chest and neck were suddenly crushing, and he could barely catch his breath.

I need help...now.

He stood up and pushed the glass shower door open and stepped out onto a large white cotton bathmat. He started to reach for his brown terry towel, but he knew that he did not have the strength to dry off. So he stepped to the bathroom door and pulled his trousers off the towel rack. He pulled them on without drying off. He picked up his iPhone which was resting on the sink counter next to his underwear. He walked deliberately into his living room, and then sat down on the light green designer rug. He called the front desk. "This is Zahi Haarun on the sixth floor. I need an ambulance."

Almost instantly, as quick as the elevator could travel from the lobby to the sixth floor, two men walked into his condominium. He recognized them both. One worked at the front desk as a concierge. He knew him by his first name, King. He was a humble and quiet man. The other man was the building maintenance engineer, Joseph. His hair was cut close with a small man bun in the back, highlighting a strong, youthful face. He was tall and strong and had tattoos on both arms. He had helped Zahi with different maintenance projects in the condo and Zahi respected his skill.

To reassure Zahi, King said that he worked part-time at the local hospital, in addition to his regular job at the front desk. Sitting on the floor, Zahi looked up at him and calmly said, "My life is in your hands." He found the presence of the humble man reassuring. They made eye contact and exchanged concerned smiles.

"Where are they?" Joseph asked. "They should be here by now." The residential building was uniquely situated on the street and the block itself was triangular, and the intersection of streets surrounding the building was confusing. Zahi saw the concern in Joseph's face. A missed turn could result in extra trips around the block and unnecessary delay.

Joseph left to lock down the freight elevator for the EMS crew. He made sure that there was more than one entry point to the elevator.

Zahi went into cardiac arrest and passed out.

King performed cardiopulmonary resuscitation for more than two minutes.

Both men later told Zahi what had happened. The arrival of the emergency medical service staff seemed to take forever, and even after they arrived, they seemed to take their time. A policeman at first questioned whether Zahi had taken heroin or a synthetic opioid such as fentanyl. Joseph assured the policeman that Zahi did not take drugs. The EMS still gave Zahi a shot of naloxone.

The EMS team shocked Zahi four times with a defibrillator before his heart restarted. Even then he turned purple and was gasping for breath, his left arm pumping up and down and his limbs shaking outward in tremors. The EMS forced a breathing tube down his airway. He tried to fight off the insertion. His lower left lip and trachea were badly bruised.

The EMS ambulanced Zahi the third of a mile to George Washington University Hospital. Although he had no idea what it all meant, he was told that he had been admitted for "lateral STE and emergent catheterization, found to have an acute anterior myocardial infarction with proximal left anterior descending lesion s/p 1 DES."

Later he was told that he had survived a 'widow maker' heart attack. He had suffered a total blockage of his left anterior descending artery, and King and Joseph had saved his life.

The heart attack occurred at 6pm. He woke up at 10 the following morning in a hospital bed in George Washington University Hospital. The breathing and gastrointestinal tubes had already been removed, his lip and face were bloody, and his chest felt like someone had been pushing on his sternum and ribcage, which they had. A cardiologist had inserted a drug-eluting stent in his left anterior descending artery to open his widow maker artery.

When he woke up, he found himself in much less pain than when he passed out, and he was happy. In fact, he felt downright joyful. His first thought was how grateful he was to King and Joseph. After that, he wanted to give all the staff in the cardiac care unit a heartfelt hug.

16

Television
Guest

That evening, from the comfort of his hospital bed in the cardiac care unit, Zahi watched Hugo appear on *The Tome Show*.

"My next guest is an American who has lived overseas most of his life." The television host, an actor and comedian known by his moniker Tome, gestured to his studio audience and the bank of cameras as he segued from his opening monologue to his first guest, Hugo. Zahi saw Liko seated on the front row, watching Tome work the enthusiastic audience.

Although Tome looked physically fit, wearing the typical apparel of a late-night talk show host—dark designer suit, white shirt, tasteful tie—he had begun to show his sixty-six years of age. Tonight, a red tie highlighted his thinning copper-brown hair, pallid cheeks and forehead. Cataracts had begun to cloud his gray eyes.

"Tonight, our guest is an artist who witnessed the rise of kleptocracy in the Republican Democracy. A survivor of a civil war and a genocide. A person who understands that we are children of one planet, that we share the same time together on earth – past, present and future. An artist whose work went viral on the internet. Everyone, please welcome Hugo Haarun."

On cue, Hugo stepped out from the behind the theater curtains. His baby blue suit stood out against the blood-red curtains. Medium blue slip-on loafers, a matching medium blue cotton belt, and a white T-shirt completed his outfit. He paused a moment to get his bearings.

Tome stepped out from behind his massive wooden desk and greeted Hugo with a warm, manly handshake. The audience applauded. As Hugo crossed the set, he waved joyfully.

Hugo sat on a vintage American chair. His thin body didn't even make an impression in the hard, unyielding leather. His baby blue suit, however, stood out against the spotless white leather.

Well known as a privileged, wealthy, white Republican, Tome had voted for Trump. He was one of the 'deplorables.' However, like Saul of Tarsus, while traveling from his rural home in Kansas to his talk show studio in Miami, Florida, Tome had a life-changing epiphany. The blindness of partisan Republican politics fell from his eyes. He rose from his knees to embrace the core American values expressed in the Declaration of Independence and the United States Constitution. His new mindset went so deep that he called himself a 'born again' American, and he enthusiastically spread the good news on his evening talk show.

Like Tome, his conservative audience had undergone a transformation, too. They no longer got their news from Breitbart or Fox News. Instead, they listened to Tome.

Since his epiphany, he liked to expound on the first ten amendments to the US Constitution, the Bill of Rights. Lately his show had focused on freedom of speech. Consequently, Liko was thrilled when Tome invited Hugo to appear on his show. The topic would be freedom of expression in the arts and entertainment, and the censorship of Hugo's art by the Maritauqua Island community.

Banksy burst through the red curtains and onto the set, a white cloud of dog fur with one of his ears and all four feet dyed bright yellow. He bounded across the set to Hugo and jumped into his lap. Hugo smiled and laughed. Banksy licked his face.

In the comfort of his hospital bed, Zahi shifted his weight. He couldn't help but smile and laugh, too.

Hugo scooted over and gave Banksy a little more than half the guest chair. Even though Banksy was full grown, he was not a large poodle, and together they did not fill the chair. Hugo hugged Banksy.

Banksy's alert black eyes, pink tongue, wet black nose, and floppy yellow ear all stood out against his white face and the white leather chair.

"Dogs," Tome said. "They always steal the show."

"Imagine if I'd brought an elephant!" Hugo joked.

"An elephant with pink feet?" Tome parried.

"And a little pink tail," Hugo added.

The audience burst out laughing.

"Is that why Elephant Rock is so popular?" Tome asked.

"Tell us, what is so interesting about a boulder sculpted to look like an elephant?"

Hugo smiled. "Let me tell you the story behind Elephant Rock." He paused, recalling the story, and his smile broadened. "During my travels with my father, before we settled in the Middle East, we visited the Altamira Cave Paintings in Spain. Try to imagine, if you can, a young boy, deep inside a cave, gawking at charcoal drawings and ochre-colored paintings on the ceiling, and then learning that the artists had lived more than ten thousand years ago! That young boy, of course, was me.

"Years later, I tried to reproduce that blending of nature and man at Elephant Rock, as it has come to be known. At that time I was living in the park and my friend Liko was helping me. I had hurt my hands sculpting with improvised carving chisels and claw tools, and he gave me antibiotics and bandages for my hands. He also gifted me paints and canvases.

"My medications had not fully stabilized me, and I would go a day or two without sleep. The one constant in my life was my need to express myself and to share what I had witnessed and what I was feeling. And so I created Elephant Rock."

Hugo paused and then added, "It has nothing to do with elephants except for its size."

"Great story," Tome said. "So you aren't sculpting zoo pieces?"

"No, no!" Hugo answered, smiling.

"Your art went viral," Tome said, "and you now have an international following. What is it about your art that people find so fascinating?"

"People are hungry for the truth?" Hugo offered.

"Well, tonight you'll have an opportunity to tell us your truth," Tome said. "The world as you understand it."

"Thank you for the opportunity," Hugo replied.

"Your first art show created something of a furor, didn't it?" Tome asked.

"Yeah," Hugo answered, modestly. "Fortunately, by then I was stable on my medication, and living with my friend Liko Koholua in an apartment on Maritauqua Island. Liko set up my art along The Economists Walkway. At first only a few people showed up to demonstrate. But then—I think everyone who saw my art got a bit excited—there was a crowd of protesters."

"The demonstration turned into a violent protest," Tome added. "You shut down the park for the day."

"Yeah, I did," Hugo said, shyly. "They did."

"Were you surprised by the reaction that your art received?"

"Oh yes!" Hugo bobbed up and down in his seat, ever so slightly. "My goal was to express the truth that I had witnessed. That truth connected with people. It made them feel and think and act."

"I guess some overreacted?" the host said, making a joke. The audience laughed.

"Is it true that the police confiscated your art work?"

"Yes, they seized everything."

"Did they tell you why?"

"They hid behind expressions like 'anti-terrorism,' 'secret messages and codes,' 'Homeland Security.'"

"It must be disheartening to have your art confiscated."

"Censored," Hugo said. "Not confiscated. Did you hear what our government did to the Guantanamo prisoners and their artwork? It's sad. Very sad."

"We did a piece on that," Tome said, proud of himself.

"The Guantanamo jailers promoted art classes for the prisoners, gave them art supplies. Then when the public wanted to see and buy their art, our government seized and destroyed it.

"If you're joining us from home and would like to learn more," Tome said to the cameras, "I suggest you Google 'art censorship at Guantanamo Bay.'"

"I have another example," Hugo said. "Not long ago, Berlin police seized a coconut cannon."

"A coconut cannon? Really? How did I miss that!"

"They raided Julian Charrière's art studio. He got a coconut from the Bikini Atoll in the Marshall Islands—you know, the island where Americans tested their atomic bombs? He was going to fire the coconut from an air cannon in Antarctica, to raise awareness of military proliferation into Antarctica. But they confiscated his cannon. I think the barrel of his cannon was a coconut tree, too."

"Something else to Google," the host said.

"Maybe you could invite Julian to your show," Hugo suggested.

"And he could bring a coconut cannon," Tome joked.

"Painted in red and white stripes," Hugo joked. "Like a candy cane."

"And coconut cannon balls."

"And you could test fire it, right here on your stage."

"But the Miami police would raid my set and confiscate yet another one of Julian's cannons!"

"Would it be better than a pink-footed elephant?" Hugo asked.

"Maybe..." Tome said. "So, tell us, Hugo, what secret messages are in your paintings?"

The audience laughed.

"You should look at my art and tell *me*," Hugo quipped. "Then we will both know."

The host and audience laughed.

"I am glad to hear laughter," Hugo said. He scanned the faces of the large, mostly friendly audience. "In the face of censorship, racism, and bullying, silence is deadly. Laughter is healthy."

"Hugo, tell us," the host said. "Is your art a warning?"

"People say that my art is a warning. My art helps people look inward at their dangerous complacency, their racial and sexual stereotyping, and their fear of diversity."

"Is that your message for us?" the host asked Hugo.

"We must stand up to kleptocrats and stand firm against liars and bullies. At the same time, we must find tolerance for each other. People must not be attacked simply for being who they are.

"Apathy empowers kleptocrats and bigots and bullies. They interpret lack of humor and silence and apathy as acceptance. If we do not challenge them, then we lose our freedom of speech, security, and diversity.

"It can happen all at once, like it did in the Republican Democracy, where I lived through a civil war and genocide. Or it can happen gradually, as it is happening on Maritauqua Island. Apathy, in all its forms, empowers bad people."

"Thank you," the host said. "I hope your art will soon be returned to you."

"So do I!" Hugo said.

"In the meantime," the host said, "Hugo's paintings, sculptures and drawings—those that were not seized—can be viewed at Cothrom Art Gallery, in the Museum Hotel, on Maritauqua Island."

"Yes," Hugo said. "I am one of several artists whose

work will be on display. I want to thank Cothrom, of Cothrom Enterprises, for this opportunity."

Hugo engaged the studio audience and then turned to face the camera. "I hope to see all of you there for the grand opening of Cothrom Gallery."

Zahi turned off the television and set down the remote beside him on his hospital bed. *Impressive,*he thought. *I'm proud of you, little brother.*

Hugo had friends. Zahi saw them support Hugo during his court appearance. His friends were with him when he displayed his art along The Economists Walkway, too. And Liko had provided him a place to live and paint. And he now had an art patron. *You should be okay,* Zahi thought. He was happy for Hugo.

And then Zahi thought of his own situation. *In less than four weeks I need to be at the conference in the Republican Democracy.*

He wondered if he should tell anyone about his heart attack. He mulled it over for a few minutes, sipping ice water through a bent straw, slowly.

He made his decision: He would not tell Hugo, or Liko, or anyone else about his heart attack, especially the Sistema. Why reveal his weakness to members of the Sistema? He also decided not to even say goodbye before he left DC for the Republican Democracy.

He treated himself to a package of graham crackers and switched his beverage to a small cup of orange juice, again using a straw.

He slipped into a maudlin mood. *I should contact my lawyer and update my will.* "First thing after I'm discharged," he said to himself. "I must do it before I leave for the Republican Democracy."

He had checked into the hospital Tuesday evening, and

he checked out late Friday afternoon. That left him about three and a half weeks to prepare for his flight to the Republican Democracy. Because of the length of the trip he decided to break up his flight. He would make a stop in London to see his mentor, and then he would fly to the Republican Democracy and deliver his presentation. The doctor said it was okay for him to fly—better if it was just a two-hour flight, but a longer flight was doable. In the meantime, the doctor told him to start short walks. Zahi was given five medications, and an appointment was scheduled with his primary care physician, who would help him get an appointment with a cardiologist.

The doctor warned him that he absolutely, positively, had to take the blood thinner and a baby aspirin every day as prescribed. Otherwise his body would detect the new stent as a foreign body and platelets would quickly form against it, and he would have a fatal blockage of the stent. There would be no coming back from that, he suspected.

"You must take the baby aspirin and Effient every day," the doctor said. "EVERY DAY FOR A YEAR."

It saddened Zahi when he received a six-month prescription. He knew that he would probably only need a month's worth of tablets.

PART II

155

17

An Assassination

Word spread fast among the Maritauqua Family. The journalist who had disrespected Lil't's daughter had died while jogging—the drunk in the white tux was dead. Some joked that it was an assassination. They joked that the Republican Democracy now followed the Russian and Saudi playbooks – state-sponsored murder using hit men, even against Americans who were not part of their Sistema.

An assassination? Really? Zahi doubted it. It was too convenient, too coincidental to what had occurred at the party. And Zahi saw nothing funny about an assassination or the death of a journalist. Yes, the journalist Daniel had died suddenly of a heart attack. But an assassination? Not likely.

Curious to learn more, though, Zahi checked the

internet on his iPhone. Daniel Johnson's most recent article appeared. In the first paragraph, he had disclosed information about Jizan that was publicly and personally embarrassing: pedophilia and a six million dollar trust to be held for a young girl, a victim of rape. The second paragraph described how Jizan's lawyers had coerced and silenced the parents of other young girls and boys.

Really, Zahi thought. *Where was the #MeToo movement?*

Zahi shook his head in dismay. *I misjudged Daniel.*

Zahi scrolled through Daniel's other articles, skimming the headlines, looking for anything else relevant to the Maritauqua Family. Attached to another of Daniel's articles, Zahi discovered a photo of himself. The photographer, Janet Rehm, had snapped the photo just as he had handed Daniel his business card. Zahi remembered the moment clearly.

Zahi looked at himself in the photo. He stood beside Daniel as if they were shaking hands in a friendly greeting. Zahi lost his breath as if he had been hit in the stomach. *The Sistema may already suspect me. Do they?*

The only thing Zahi liked about the picture was the tweed sport coat that Saba had so affectionately given him. "The coat photographs well," he said, softly, as if speaking to her. He tried to smile.

As his mind drifted back to Daniel's death, he felt a tightness in his chest. A bit of heartburn, he thought.

Every year well-known journalists were killed. The worst case in recent memory had been Saudi Crown Prince Mohammed bin Salman's murder of the affable Jamal Khashoggi, a journalist who wrote opinion pieces about Saudi Arabia for the *Washington Post.* Jamal had been lured into a Saudi embassy in Istanbul, Turkey, then murdered, dismembered, and disposed of. The heinous crime had put fear in all exiles, especially expatriates from the Middle East, who were living abroad in Europe and the United States, including Maritauqua Island.

Thinking about Janet Rehm, Zahi looked her up on the internet. He found two recent pictures, side by side, with her name in small caps: photos by Janet Rehm. The first picture was the rows of grand oaks at the entrance to Jizan's mansion. *What beautiful trees they were*, he thought. The second picture was two rows of grand stumps. *Well done!* he thought.

Zahi thought about Trump's claim that his inauguration had the largest crowd ever to witness an inauguration, even larger than the crowd attending President Barack Obama's inauguration. What a joke! Photos had proved that Trump and his White House staff were lying. When confronted with the truth, the White House had defended Trump's lie as an "alternative fact." Unless pictures are edited, they don't lie. Trump had requested a revised set of pictures the day after the inauguration.

Zahi continued searching for other photographs by Janet. He discovered a full-page spread of her photographs supporting an article on Jizan's party. *Small papers are like that*, he thought. *Anxious to cover local social events.* Sadly, such coverage was disappearing.

The people in the photos were identified in the captions. He had provided her their names and she had tagged them in her photographs. *When their countrymen back home see this, they will be angry! Hopefully pissed!*

And then Zahi wondered: *Is her life now in danger, too?*

He felt a bit short of breath and it felt like there was a pressure in his ears.

Double assassinations were not common, but they did occur. Zahi recalled the story about a journalist and his fiancée who had been shot and killed in Slovakia, not too long ago. The killing had so enraged the people in Slovakia that they stood up to their corrupt Prime Minister and kicked him out of government, although his administration remained in power. *Sometimes the unexpected happens,* Zahi thought.

When a member of the Sistema was assassinated, nothing usually changed. The man and his life were forgotten, as if he had never lived. The only thing anyone remembered was how he died, which was always gruesome. *How did I get myself mixed up with these assholes!*

Zahi sent Janet Rehm a quick text message: *Heard the sad news about Daniel. I hope you are okay. I saw your photos in the* Times. *They were excellent.*

His angina grew worse.

Each day for the next three weeks, Zahi walked up and down the hall just outside his condominium. He found most of the neighbors supportive of his new effort. He told his heart attack story to one neighbor and she teared up and gave him an encouraging hug. During the next three weeks, when they met in the hallway, they smiled and commented on how wonderful life was. Zahi liked that. He once again realized the importance of relationships, and how little time he had.

More than once he lost his breath and slid down the walls, sitting on the floor until he caught his breath. Each time it was frightening. Each time it reminded him of collapsing in the shower, just before his heart attack.

Gradually, though, he built up his stamina until he could walk twenty minutes without stopping. Near the end of the third week, he could walk twenty minutes three times a day – breakfast, lunch, and dinner – for a total of an hour. That felt like an accomplishment.

At the end of the third week he told himself that he was ready to fly to the Republican Democracy and give his presentation. Tomorrow he would board the plane.

18

Passing Through London

Zahi spotted his old professor, David Ludi, walking across Hyde Park towards him. Zahi had made the stopover in London specifically to see his old mentor. He felt a bit melancholy, fully aware that this was probably the last time they would see each other.

Zahi extended his hand. The professor accepted it with a smile and gave him a warm hug, patting him generously on the back. When the embrace ended, the professor continued to hold Zahi by the arm. He looked him up and down. "You look tired," he said.

"Never enjoyed flying. Always messes up my sinuses." He smiled, warmly.

"Everything's prepared?"

"The evidence is in the Apple cloud," Zahi told the old professor, proudly.

"It's ready for release?" he asked.

"Yes. In phases. Systematically." Zahi thought his hands were shaking, but when he glanced at them they were steady, except for a little tremor in the fingertips. He shoved his hands into his pockets. "Everything is set to be released systematically, according to the schedule."

The professor let loose Zahi's arm and they began walking side by side down a pathway that led along the perimeter of the park. Zahi hesitated, wondering if he was up to the walk. How long was the path? Where did it lead? *Can I finish if I start?*

He deliberately took smaller steps, effectively slowing their pace. He had not told his mentor about his heart attack. He was afraid he would intercede and stop him from presenting. Zahi smiled and felt the tears welling up in his eyes.

"In phases?" his mentor asked.

"Yes," Zahi answered. "First the shameful information about Lil't's daughter. Then revelations about Lil't's son-in-law. And then his son. All released the day before the conference begins." Zahi had gotten the idea of exposing Lil't's daughter and son from the questions Daniel had asked at Jizan's party. "After that, the morning of the conference a copy of my paper and presentation will be released. Later that afternoon, an in-depth analysis of Little NEOM."

Zahi paused in front of a bed of bright yellow flowers just past their bloom. He glanced at the yellow-brown petals lying on top of the dry, brown mulch. Rose leaves had begun to fall into the bed, too. *Were we ever so young?*

He looked at his mentor. The old man had to be in his late seventies. He had bought himself a new navy blue sports coat.

"A new coat?" Zahi asked. He knew full well that it was new. After all, he had seen the professor drape his other coat around the shoulders of a homeless man.

A flash of joy filled David's face. "Yes," he answered.

"I see you are still wearing that old tweed?"

"I am." It was now Zahi's turn to grin ear to ear.

They continued walking slowly. "Professor Kartouzian's data?" Professor Ludi asked. "Is that ready to be downloaded, too?"

My good friend's data, Zahi thought, refocusing on the task at hand. "Yes, and the illegal profits that the Sistema made – all that will be released, too."

"A phased release should heighten public interest," David stated matter-of-factly, understating the impact it would have.

"Let's hope so." Zahi nodded. He also knew it would cause panic for some members of the Sistema. Releasing the data was like poking a stick into a hornet's nest.

A feeling of great affection for his former professor overwhelmed him and he wanted to embrace him in another heartfelt hug, but he managed to hold himself back. He always held himself back. "Thanks again for your help verifying the accuracy of the information I used." Zahi smiled broadly. "Your contacts at the university and the Commerce Department were invaluable."

"I am glad they could help," the professor said. His voice was soft-spoken. "They are looking forward to seeing your work. I only wish I could be there in person when you present."

You? Visit the Republican Democracy? Zahi smiled. *I don't think so.* "We don't want them to panic," Zahi joked.

They both laughed.

"There will be drama," the professor said.

"Powerful people will be LIVID."

Zahi thought about Daniel's article exposing Jizan as a pedophile and a rapist of young girls. And now Daniel was dead. He thought about the murder of Jamal Khashoggi and Karim Fakhrawi.

"My presentation spotlights who stole the money, what they stole, and how they laundered it." He looked steadily at his mentor. "And where the money is hidden."

"Kleptocracy exposed," David said. He put his arm on Zahi's shoulder. They walked side by side for a while.

"The United States will provide no protection?"

"None." Zahi shrugged his shoulders.

They both knew that the CIA had despots like Lil't on their payroll. They influenced judges, police, and politicians, too. And enablers like Zahi. And the CIA didn't like people messing with their assets or their programs. No, the CIA would *not* be happy.

"People will die," David said.

"Yes," Zahi said. "And many will be hurt."

"They will make an example of you."

And with my heart condition, the sting of one hornet will kill me.

"I have something that needs to be kept safe," Zahi said. "Can I leave it with you?"

They stopped walking. David turned to face him. They embraced each other with their eyes. "Drama!" he exclaimed, but his voice was tinged with sadness.

"Yes," Zahi said as he handed the professor the two peas

in a pod ornament. "I had this ornament refashioned into a thumb drive."

"I *like* drama," the professor said. He placed the thumb drive in his coat pocket. He then clasped Zahi by the arm, firmly, with both of his hands, and gave a sharp shake.

"Five items are stored on it: my PowerPoint presentation, a copy of my soon-to-be-published paper, a copy of my analysis of Little NEOM, Professor Kartouzian's documentation, and a photograph of my brother Hugo and me in our father's villa. If something happens to me..."

The professor patted Zahi on the back to encourage him.

"The photo is for Hugo."

"Zahi, do you remember missing your final exam?"

"Yes." Zahi nodded his head. He remembered it well. "I thought I had failed your class."

"Do you remember why you missed it?"

"Of course. Saba had the flu. She had a temperature of 104 degrees. I had to put her in a bathtub of ice cold water. She was sick for days." *And I was unable to study for my finals.* "I missed the final exam."

"But you did well on the make-up exam," the professor said.

"Yes, I aced it." Zahi beamed with pride. "But then, you gave me an extra week to prepare for it. Which you didn't have to do."

"You were an excellent student," Professor Ludi said. His eyes began to cloud with tears. "I wanted you to learn the material."

"I know that I have disappointed you," Zahi said. *And Saba! And Hugo!*

"What you are doing is a very good thing," the professor said. "I am proud of you."

Zahi reached out and embraced his mentor with a heartfelt hug of farewell. They shook hands.

On his drive back to the airport for his flight to the Republican Democracy, Zahi felt less nervous, more confident. He knew that he had the professor to thank for that. And the tweed coat still felt comfortable.

His plan was simple: he would arrive in the Republican Democracy the day before the conference and discreetly check into a hotel across the street. He would not make an appearance until the day of the conference, and then he would be surrounded by fellow economists, most of them well known and respected internationally. No one, including the Sistema, would attack him in such a public venue.

Surviving after the conference was the challenge. He would leave directly from the conference to the airport. Again, he had coordinated his flight so he would be with fellow economists who would also be returning home. He had arranged to be on a reserved group shuttle from the hotel to the airport, too. There was a chance that everything would work out well. If not, at least it would play out in public. That, Zahi thought, was the best he could hope for.

He suddenly recalled the author of the mystery quote: *Was I ever so young? So ivory and rose-leaves?* Oscar Wilde!

19

Arrival in the Home Country

The student's mosque was rubble. Zahi stood on the edge of a deep crater that separated him from the crumbled remains of the prayer room and dome. The entire structure had been flattened, completely obliterated by a warplane or rockets. Tons of stone lay where it had fallen. The crater was the height of several men.

As a student, Zahi had passed this mosque every day on his way to classes at the university, admiring the emerald dome and the glint of sunlight reflecting off the blue and yellow mosaics on the walls and minarets.

Now, looking at the scattered stone he felt a deep sadness, a sense of being off-balance. Not because he cared about the loss of the mosque, and not because men had died inside when the roof had collapsed upon them as they prayed, and not because he was religious – he was not – but because an earthly point of reference, something akin to a surveyor's stone, something that should have been permanent and unalterable, had been destroyed, reduced to ruins.

This is where the students had risen up and demanded change, just like they had at other universities throughout the Middle East. The response had been vicious, so Syrian, so Saudi Arabian!

This was also where he had fond memories of Saba. They had met here at the university. He gazed up the slope, his eyes searching through the rubble scattered on the hillside for a sidewalk, a footpath that he knew wandered between the mosque and the Alchemist's Pond, which was known locally as Buhayrat Butr. No pathway remained.

He half-closed his eyes for a moment to refresh his memory. He recalled the path and clearly remembered the pond, which rested below the buildings on Shura Street on the slopes leading down to the mosque. The small body of water was a quiet, serene, and comfortable place to stop and think, to write or draw, to meditate.

He opened his eyes. Still standing on the edge of the crater, he failed to find any signs of the well-worn path that led up the slope. It filled him with sadness.

He walked up the slope anyway, slowly making his way over and through the rubble, careful not to overextend himself. Pieces of colorful mosaic cracked beneath his feet. Halfway up the slope he stopped, turned around and gazed back towards the obliterated mosque.

The pond used to rest here, he thought to himself. *Calm and undisturbed. And now it's gone.* Everything had been obliterated: an old stone bridge where he had proposed marriage to Saba; an open grassy area where he and Hugo and Saba had picnicked; date trees that shaded the shoreline, where he had solved mathematical puzzles while relaxed and comfortable and enjoying the companionship of small birds, watching lazy turtles glide into the water when disturbed, and huge frogs, imported from Africa, hiding among the lily pads. Pink blossoms. Everything had smelled green and earthy. And now it was gone.

The pond had been his personal time capsule. A reservoir of youthful, cherished memories. Important events in his life had happened around this pond. And now it was all gone.

He wiped the sleeve of his white shirt across his nose, smearing a line of mucous into the cotton fabric. It dried in the near zero humidity air, instantly.

The loss of the old stone bridge upset him the most. It had been a small, one-arch bridge made of imported limestone and mortar. Most stone in the Republican Democracy, including marble, was imported. The footpath had crossed the bridge atop the spillway.

He recalled how Saba had sat on the parapet capstones while he had stood next to her on the footpath, at her side. *Where did I sit?* He tried to remember, exactly. *Did I sit directly above the keystone in the center of the bridge? Is that where I sat when I proposed marriage? Yes, it must have been there.*

He recalled her surprise. Of course she had accepted. Thinking about that moment, he smiled. *I made her happy. Very happy. It's one of the best things I did in my life. And when she said yes it made me happy, too.* He now remembered it: *It filled me with joy!*

Nothing was left of the bridge where he had proposed to her. Nothing. The bridge was gone, she was gone, and only his memories remained.

He knew without going to the top of the hill for a look

that the rest of the university campus had been destroyed, too. It didn't surprise him.

The student's protests had evolved into a grassroots revolution, and that, sadly, had been usurped by Lil't. The civil war to remove him had not succeeded, and once he solidified his control of the military, he used the national forces to destroy rival clans and tribes. Revolution, civil war, and then genocide.

The driver had dropped him off in front of the café where he and Saba first met, a short walk back down the hillside and past the destroyed mosque. Hopefully the taxi driver was still waiting.

The cab driver stopped in front of Zahi's grandfather's villa. It was largely intact, while most of the surrounding homes had been destroyed. It reminded Zahi of pictures he had seen of tornado damage in Kansas: one or two houses left standing while the surrounding neighborhood was destroyed. But instead of high winds and damage from flying debris, this destruction had been caused by artillery and mortar fire.

"The weather is changing bad," the taxi driver warned.

Zahi looked to the horizon. The distant, eastern skyline, which was usually bare of clouds, had become a wall of green-gray clouds moving in their direction. A major rainstorm was approaching. He understood the taxi driver's concern. He nodded agreement. "I'll be just a minute."

He pulled his tired body out of the back seat and stood in the road, with one hand resting on top of the taxicab, steadying himself. He wanted to take a deep breath, to breathe deeply, but his ribs were still sore from the CPR of three weeks earlier. A deep breath moved his sternum, and was painful.

His grandfather and father and uncles had all moved away, or had died. His family no longer lived here. Some had not survived the civil war. Those relatives who had survived lived in suburban compounds with workers and travelers. Someone else now occupied his grandfather's great villa, the family's homestead. The smaller, detached family villas that had belonged to Zahi's father and uncles had all been destroyed.

He wanted to see his grandfather's house, the flower garden, and the two courtyards, one for men and one for women. He considered walking bravely through the open driveway gate and ten-foot-high walls that surrounded the villa. He fought to keep his impulse in check. It would be reckless to enter uninvited. If anyone was living here now, under these conditions—no water, no electricity, no services—they were unlawful squatters, and perhaps dangerous.

He recalled the layout of the once-opulent villa. Past the gate there were actually four entrances: one for men, one for women, one for guests, and one for the driver, who had his own room across from the carport. Even parked in the shade, their family car still got unbearably hot during the summer.

Zahi tried but could not remember the details of his grandfather's large business room on the ground floor, where he entertained male guests, but he did recall the raised benches on both sides of the entrance hallway, and his grandfather's communal waterpipe. He had choked a few times, smoking.

Zahi's father, on the other hand, had no waterpipe. He worked for the World Health Organization and believed that smoking was dangerous to one's health, so waterpipes had been banished from his home.

It suddenly dawned on Zahi that he had been the recipient of both his grandfather's and father's unconditional love. *How could I have been so blind? So stupid? Why didn't I see it until now?*

He recalled how his mother was often alone because his father spent weeks, months, and eventually whole years traveling for his work. How had she done so well on her own? He had never thought about it before. What happened to her collection of travel souvenirs, the eclectic gifts his father had brought home for her?

Zahi now remembered his father's marvelous collection of stamps from his travels around the world. Zahi had always thought Hugo would inherit the collection, but now Zahi suspected that the stamps had been destroyed or lost during the fighting. He remembered being envious of the Zimbabwe stamps, in particular. They had always reminded him of his father's trip with Hugo to Victoria Falls.

His father had fathered Hugo by a woman who lived in the United States. In fact, Zahi's father had several other children, each by different women, all Caucasian. He had traveled, worked, and fathered babies. Hugo was just one of many half-siblings.

Zahi also had brothers and sisters born in the Republican Emirates, but he had felt no responsibility nor desire to contact them after the civil war. *Why should I?* he had thought. *They would just want me to feed and clothe and house them.* But now he knew that he had failed them, and he had lost yet another opportunity to be good and to do good. *I'm such an asshole.* What would they say to him now, he wondered, if they suddenly met face-to-face? *It wouldn't be nice.*

It was only because his sister-in-law had written him, shaming him, that Zahi had reached out to help Hugo, to bring him to the States, to set him up in a studio apartment on Maritauqua Island. *And I had complained of the expense!* He now recalled grumbling about the cost of air fare.

Everyone fled. He looked at the rubble. No one stayed behind. His eyes skimmed for something green. He saw only rubble.

He wondered if his brothers and sisters were alive, and how old they were. The months and days and years of their births and deaths eluded him. *And I don't remember the names of their children, either. Or the names of their children's children.*

He tried to remember playing with his siblings. *We didn't. I was older, and a loner. I wasn't there for them as they were growing up.* He sighed, recalling how everything had been about him, nothing about them.

"I wasn't part of their lives," he said softly to himself, suddenly abashed at the insight. Until this moment, he had never thought or considered it. *I don't know who they are – or were. And they don't know me. I never shared my experiences with them. Or my wealth. But how could I? I was across the ocean, in another country, a world away. I had my own life, my own job, my own interests. I couldn't come back during the civil war, and after that, I just never did. Any connection we had as children, I severed. Now they're too old. Or they're dead. And now it's too late for me.*

"I'm still following the bird in my breast," he mumbled to himself. "Just as I always have." That thought, which usually gave him some comfort, now failed him. He now understood it had been a poor excuse to be hyper-individualistic, when he should have been a part of his family and community. He was all alone now, and he knew it.

The rainstorm arrived with a roar, and his shirt, pants and shoes were instantly soaked. He dropped into the back seat of the cab, moving his chest muscles as little as possible. The taxi driver began the long drive to the hotel, negotiating potholes, the daily reminders of past artillery fire.

The backseat windows of the cab fogged up, yet Zahi could still make out the ruins of the National Hospital as they drove past. He knew that the United States had sold bombs and an assortment of weapons to Lil't, and they had helped the military select targets. The hospital had been "collateral damage."

US policy towards Lil't had been a tragic repetition of the US assistance to Saudi Arabia during the undeclared US war in Yemen. During that war, the US had helped Saudi Arabia refuel planes in the air. Both the war in Yemen and the Republican Democracy's civil war had caused the death of countless women and children, reducing their lives to statistics. Like Saudi Arabia, the Republican Democracy had also targeted water treatment plants and wells and health clinics. An American-made bomb dropped on a school bus filled with children. Tens of thousands of civilians died of cholera.

Sitting in the back seat of the cab, Zahi thought, *Why had the United States supported Lil't? A narcissistic, egotistical, bully?* He scratched his head. He recalled how Jared Kushner, Trump's son-in-law, had pushed the United States into supporting Crown Prince Mohamed bin Salman of Saudi Arabia. Everyone knew how badly that had turned out. But who had pushed the US to support Lil't? Who in the administration had been that naïve?

What could I have done? he wondered. *What options did I have?*

Zahi stared out the window and into the torrential downpour. The world outside the cab had become surreal, temporarily unrecognizable. From his vantage point, the real world—consisting of his family's villas, the National Hospital, and a water treatment plant—and this other, surreal world—consisting of a war-ravaged countryside, green-gray sky, and torrential rain—seemed to coexist in the present moment: the real and the surreal. It baffled him. The fog on the inside of the windows formed rivulets of water. He felt a loss of personal equilibrium. He felt confused. And then nauseated.

"A flood is coming," the taxi driver told him.

He caught the eye of the driver in the rearview mirror. "How long before we reach the hotel?"

"Thirty minutes, sir," the driver answered.

Mile after mile, Zahi gazed out the window at the massive destruction along the roadway. He could recall the names of his peers in the Sistema, and the names, sexes, ages, and birthdates of their children. Such things were important for business. And he could recall everyone's illicit activities, the properties they purchased and the cost, the shell companies. *But I can't remember my brothers' and sisters' birthdays and I have never met their children.* "It's all so baffling," he mumbled.

"Baffling?" the driver asked. "I don't understand, sir."

"I no longer recognize anything."

"I see," the driver said.

Do taxicab drivers ever lose their equilibrium, their sense of direction? Zahi wondered. He stared into the bloodshot eyes of the taxi driver in the rearview mirror. "Can't you drive faster?"

"Dangerous, sir," the driver answered. He diverted his eyes back to the road. "It would be dangerous in this rain."

"Very well," Zahi said, hoping the tone of his voice conveyed his dissatisfaction. "I suppose you were here during the civil war?" As soon as he said this, Zahi felt ashamed. Nevertheless, he continued: "And the genocide?"

The driver made no answer. He did look in the rearview mirror and they once again made eye contact. Zahi looked away. *So much rubble*, he thought.

"You...." Zahi began, but he didn't know how to finish his thought.

"During the war," the taxi driver said, "I was in Saudi Arabia. I was an Uber driver."

"An Uber driver in Saudi Arabia?"

"Yes."

"What was that like?" Zahi asked.

"A very good job." The taxi driver smiled. "I liked driving their women around. Their women are beautiful."

Zahi smiled. He couldn't help it.

"But everything changed. Saudi Arabia began bombing our country, bombing our people, bombing the homes of my relatives." The driver frowned and one of his cheeks began to twitch as if pulsed by a current of electricity. "Just like they did in Yemen!" The taxi driver nodded his head towards the destroyed homes just outside the window.

"I was driving their women so they would be safe, while they were bombing our homes and killing our mothers and wives!"

"And our children," Zahi added.

"I quit my job and I returned home. I borrowed our

family's car and used it as an ambulance. A four-wheel drive Land Cruiser. I drove people from their homes to the hospital. Many were wounded. Many died during the ride."

"But we passed the hospital," Zahi said. "Wasn't it bombed, too?"

"Yes," the taxi driver said. "And then the soldiers stole my car."

"You did a good thing," Zahi said. "For our people."

The driver's cheek stopped twitching. He refocused on the road.

After a few minutes Zahi said, "Did you know that the Saudis paid $3.5 billion dollars to Uber?"

"No!" The driver raised an eyebrow and looked at Zahi. "This is true?"

"Yes, the Saudi Public Investment Fund wired $3.5 billion dollars to the San Francisco-based Uber. It was the largest wire transfer ever made."

"True?"

"Sadly, yes," Zahi said. "Saudi Arabia now owns a chunk, more than 10 percent, of Uber."

"No!"

"Yes," Zahi said. "And a Saudi used to sit on the Uber board."

The taxi driver shook his head. "Then I am glad I quit Uber."

"You want to know something else? Something kind of funny? Kind of ironic?"

The driver nodded yes.

"At the time, the CEO of Uber was an Iranian immigrant."

"No!"

"Yes," Zahi laughed. "The world is crazy, no?"

"How do you know these things?" the driver asked.

"I'm an economist," Zahi answered. "I watch the market. I make investments." In fact, Zahi had invested early in Uber, and he had made a small fortune when Uber went public. But he didn't tell the taxi driver that.

20

Pre-Conference Jitters

Tired from the long flight, depressed from the drive through the old neighborhood, and still soaked from the torrential rain, Zahi checked into his hotel. It was a small hotel across the street from the grand hotel where the economic conference would be held.

It's a cheaper room, Zahi thought. *I'll save a few dollars and avoid bumping into other attendees. Besides, it will be safer.*

He kicked off his shoes and left them just inside the front door. He walked in his wet stockinged feet to the closet and hung up his tweed sports coat. In the bathroom he stripped off his wet clothes, dried himself with the rough bath towel, and donned a white hotel robe that hung on a hook by the bathroom door. He washed his hands with hot water and a small bar of sample soap.

He emptied his dry clothes from his suitcase onto the

double bed. While hanging them in the clothes closet he spotted a pair of posh hotel slippers. He slipped into them.

Now unpacked and warm, he sat down at the desk provided in the corner of the room. He switched on the desk lamp and plugged in his laptop, entered the hotel password, and connected to the internet. He knew that the line was not secure, but everything he did was encrypted.

He signed in online to the economic conference in the hotel across the street. Because it was important to get the information out to people who would understand it, use it, and disseminate it, and to do it quickly, he had arranged automatic downloads of files to the economic conference members' shared drive, and to the *Washington Post's* SecureDrop – all anonymously. The downloads would be done in phases to maximize the drama. He browsed to their shared link. It was there! The file on Lil't's daughter had posted. The released documents showed that she had plagiarized her doctorate, just like Vladimir Putin. It also showed that she had donated millions to establish a school and scholarships in her father's name, using the same playbook as the Ukrainian oligarch, Dmytro Firtach. He scrolled through the other files until he found the files on Lil't's son, too. And then his son-in-law.

By all accounts, Lil't was proud of his daughter and bragged, "My daughter is beautiful and smart. Like me, she has a doctorate!" He would not be happy that confidential information, including her grades, had been posted, along with documentation showing how she sought to purchase her citizenship using a US EB-5 visa.

The data dump implicated Lil't's son and son-in-law in criminal activity—activities that would interest not only the United States Justice Department, but also the United States Central Intelligence Agency.

Zahi leaned back in the uncomfortable chair. *So it begins,* he mumbled.

He heard a knock on the hotel door. He adjusted the bathrobe and tightened the cotton belt as he walked across the room.

"Compliments of the hotel," a middle-aged man in a hotel uniform said. His pants and shoes were black, his shirt a deep red. Zahi allowed him to push a cart into the middle of the room, the only open space. Atop the cart was a fruit basket of apples, oranges and banana; hot bint al sahn on a plate; and a steaming pot of tea with milk, a small jar of honey, and cardamom.

Zahi thanked him. He stepped to the dresser and pulled a United States five-dollar bill from his wallet and gave the damp bill to the man, who then left.

Zahi sat on the edge of the bed. He tried the buttery, hot bint al sahn. *Moist!* The bint al sahn carried him back to thoughts of early childhood, his mother serving him cakes. Decades peeled away and his memories became visceral and vivid. Perhaps it was the smell of the cardamom in the tea?

He recalled Saba working on a new dress pattern. Her passion was sewing, and her joy was helping other people. She was so kind, and had such a big heart. *How could I have been so stupid? It must have been so difficult for her. Why didn't I think about her feelings and her needs?*

In her diary she told me to "be good and do good," just as my father always did. I definitely didn't follow their advice.

He lay down on the bed, still wrapped in the hotel bathrobe and wearing the warm, comfortable slippers. He was dry and warm, and tired. He was glad to give his heart a chance to rest. He fell fast asleep.

Zahi woke up. He sat up in the full size bed and didn't recognize the modest hotel room. *Saba?*He waited a moment for her to answer, and then he remembered. *I returned home today.* He remembered that he was in a modest hotel near the extravagant Four Seasons Hotel, where the economics conference was being held. He would present tomorrow.

He thought of Saba again. *I should have taken you with me when I went to conferences. We should have taken more vacations together. We should have.*

You were always so supporting... loving... attentive. You were right. You said I would one day be alone, lonely, and all by myself.

Sitting on the side of the bed, he put his head between his knees and took in several shallow breaths. That was the best he could do with his aching ribs and lungs. He had sat up too quickly and felt a little lightheaded. He shuffled to the restroom and took two Tylenol PMs. *As soon as I'm sleepy, I'm going back to bed.*

He heard a soft knock on the door. He adjusted the guest robe and slipped into the comfortable slippers. He picked up the empty plate and pinched the crumbs together, placing them in his mouth as he shuffled across the room to the door. *Still moist.* The knock grew louder. He passed a wall clock that said 7:15pm.

She would have loved this cake. He smiled and opened the bedroom door, plate in hand.

A man in black pants and a red shirt stepped forward, across the threshold, and tasered him. His legs crumpled. The plate hit the floor and bounced. The recipe card slid off the plate and glided across the wooden floor, coming to rest on the edge of the rug.

21

Torture

Zahi was led into the brightly lit room, one jailer in front of him, one behind.

The room was empty except for a large reclining chair and a stool. The navy blue recliner had a headrest, backrest, lower body section, and two arm rests. Zahi noted a foot paddle beneath the chair, probably to adjust the height and incline. He also noticed a large, grated floor drain. To the side of the chair was a porcelain rinse-and-spit bowl, the kind often used by dentists. The chair looked new and state of the art.

A tray table stood against the far wall, the kind of adjustable table often used with hospital beds. The stainless steel base reflected the fluorescent ceiling lights, and the top of the table boasted a light-colored faux wood. A white bath towel and several hand towels lay on the table next to an open box of fabric softener sheets. He smelled the scent of lavender.

Zahi was led to the large chair and forced into the seat. The two men leading him restrained his arms and legs. Working together they strapped his legs, arms, and waist against the hard plastic chair, cinching the cotton straps and buckles tight. Then they left the room.

A third man entered wearing a white lab coat, white pants, and brown rubber galoshes. His black hair was pulled back in a large man bun, and he wore large black eyeglasses with lenses as thick as the bottom of Coke bottles that distorted his eyes.

The man rolled the tray table across the room until it rested against Zahi's chair. He then walked to the head of the chair, stood behind Zahi, and looked down at him.

"Those who make my acquaintance call me Flowers, Mr. Flowers. And what is your name?"

"Zahi. Zahi Haarun."

"You know what I do here, don't you, Zahi?"

"No," Zahi tried to say, but his mouth was dry.

The man pulled a sheet of fabric softener from the cardboard box and held it near Zahi's nose. "What do you smell, Zahi?"

"Lavender."

"Very good." He gazed at Zahi. "You are here because you publicly insulted the family of the president of the Republican Democracy. You were arrested under Article 70 of the Criminal Code. Have you seen the movie *A Clockwork Orange*?"

"No," Zahi said.

"It's one of my favorites. I considered using Beethoven's *Ninth Symphony* too, but I am a man of the nose, not of the ear."

Man of the nose? Zahi thought. *What are you talking about?*

The man stretched his foot underneath the chair and pressed the foot pedal. Zahi heard the hum of a motor as the chair lowered and then adjusted to a 15-degree decline, with Zahi's head lower than his feet. Zahi found himself staring into the ceiling lights.

The man flipped a switch and Zahi heard water flowing into the porcelain rinse-and-spit bowl. The man held his finger under the stream of water for a moment and then said, "Ah, nice and warm."

He flipped another switch and Zahi heard the roar of a mechanical motor and something grinding. The loud noise seemed to come from the bottom of the porcelain bowl. Zahi thought it sounded like a garbage disposal. The man flipped the switch again and the grinding stopped.

He unfolded the hand towel and placed it over Zahi's forehead and eyes and smoothed out the wrinkles in the cloth. "Soft, isn't it," he said. "Egyptian cotton. Very good quality."

What the hell are you doing?

"Zahi," he said in a calm and comforting voice. "You have not seen them, but there are sharks in this room. I have pet sharks." He laughed. "Answer honestly and you will only have to drown once. If you lie to me then you will drown many times. And each time you drown, I will cut off a part of your body. A finger, a toe, an ear, a nose. And I will feed my babies, my baby sharks. Do you understand, Zahi?"

"Yes," Zahi said. "I understand."

"Open your mouth."

Zahi opened his mouth.

Zahi felt something enter his mouth. It was smooth and smelled of lavender. Zahi guessed it was a fabric softener sheet.

Water began to drip onto the towel, which soon saturated. Zahi closed his eyes. The towel felt warm and comfortable. Water filled his eyes, and then spilled down his forehead and into his ears. Warm water filled his ears.

The man dragged the hand towel downward, over Zahi's nose, and then over his mouth. Water flowed into his hair and down his neck and wicked into the sheet of fabric softener in his mouth.

The gag reflex was involuntary. The restraints prevented him from sitting up and coughing.

The man water-tortured Zahi for exactly twenty minutes. Every minute, for twenty minutes, Zahi thought he was dying. When he wasn't drowning, he believed he was dying from another heart attack. *My heart*, he begged. *My heart is weak.*

He gave up the names of his coworkers at George Mason University, the names of graduate students and fellow professors. *They're in the United States*, he said to himself. *They will be safe. Besides, they had nothing to do with my analysis.*

The man removed the towel, raised the inclined chair, and wiped Zahi's face dry with one of the hand towels. "Egyptian cotton," the man had said. "Very soft."

Zahi spit out the fabric softener. *Fuck you*, he thought.

He was taken to a communal bathroom where he was allowed to use the toilet. He showered, combed his hair, and brushed his teeth with a mint-flavored toothpaste. Looking in the mirror before he dressed, he noted that there were no marks on his body. *He can kill me, asphyxiate me, and not leave a mark!* The thought trembled through his body. *This monster can murder me and no one will know!* He returned to the toilet and relieved himself again. His stool was watery, as if he had the flu.

After he dressed, pulling on the light gray prison pants and an untucked shirt, he was escorted back to his cell, one guard in front and the other behind. Zahi noted that they carried stun guns in their belts. *If they stun me again, it may stop my heart.*

As he lay on the cot in his prison cell that evening, evidence about Lil't's daughter, son and son-in-law spread across internet. It had been disseminated, undoubtedly, by attendees at the economic conference who had discovered it earlier on the conference share drive, or possibly by staff at the *Washington Post.*

The next morning, before daybreak, Zahi was roughly awakened by prison guards. They escorted him back to the torture room.

"You embarrassed me," the interrogator told Zahi. "You embarrassed Lil't and his family."

Fuck! Zahi thought, as he stared at the interrogator's hands, not his face, not his eyes.

He water-tortured Zahi all morning and all afternoon.

Zahi confessed to everything and nothing. He lied and lied and lied. While the water poured over him, he could not think clearly and he could not remember coherently. The water torture continued until his feet and hands shook uncontrollably and words babbled meaninglessly from his mouth. Survival was the only thing his body understood, and animal instinct, the lizard and amphibian brain, was all that responded to his torturer. One plus one equaled anything the torturer wanted it to equal.

This time in the chair he betrayed former colleagues at the University of the Republican Democracy, where he used to teach. They had done nothing. Their names were among the dozens of names that Zahi babbled as he was tortured. The interrogator recorded all the names, which included several of Zahi's former students. Zahi gave up the name of Professor Kartouzian, but then he was already dead. Zahi did not know the identity of Kartouzian's protégé, fortunately. He gave up the woman's code name, however, a name Zahi had chosen: mistletoad. The interrogator emailed the names to the Republican Democracy's Homeland Security.

The second night, Zahi lay on the hard floor in his prison cell because he had rolled out of his cot during the night, delirious. The lights stayed on all night long. Loud music played. He woke up several times. *I have made such a mess of everything,* he thought. However, he had told the torturer nothing but lies.

In his delirium he thought: *I can give up everyone but Professor Ludi.*

22

Swigert Prison

Zahi awoke nervous, expecting either torture or execution. He did not know if it was morning, afternoon, evening or night. Two prison guards led him back to the interrogation room.

He lay on the hard plastic chair, restrained. Next to him was a second reclining chair. Zahi now noticed that both chairs were on wheels. He had not noticed that before. They had been positioned so the floor drain lay between them.

Two guards appeared with Hugo.

"Zahi!" Hugo exclaimed. "You are here? Why are you tied down? What is happening?"

With the guards in the room Zahi remained silent. He watched as the guards strapped Hugo into the reclining chair and then they left.

"Little brother!" Zahi exclaimed. "Why are YOU here?"

"I was deported."

"Deported?" Zahi's stomach twisted tightly like a wet towel in the hands of the interrogator. "But you are a citizen of the United States."

"I have no proof. All I had was my visitor's visa and my Republican Democracy passport."

"I'm so sorry."

"I went to see the Republican Democracy ambassador to extend my visa. They jumped me and stabbed a long needle through my jeans and into my thigh. It hurt like hell. When I woke I was in the back seat of a car, and then on a plane, and after hours and hours, here I am."

"Are you okay?"

"I'm okay. And you?"

"Not so well." Zahi remembered that Hugo did not know about his heart attack.

The interrogator entered carrying a small black case that reminded Zahi of a flute case he had once seen. He set the black case on the rolling table that rested between the reclining chairs and took a seat on the stool.

"I heard your brother is a painter," the interrogator said to Zahi.

Zahi did not reply. He stared at the black case, unable to look into the face of the interrogator.

The interrogator asked, "You have nothing to tell me?"

Zahi dropped his eyes. He gazed at his legs strapped to the chair. Once again they had been raised higher than his head. He felt the straps restraining his arms and chest. He said nothing. His ears were ringing so loud – pulsing – that he thought his ear drums would burst. *It's my heart*, he thought.

The interrogator opened the black case and removed a surgical saw. It was almost a foot long, stainless steel, and had a ring handle. He closed the case and set the saw on top of it so it was visible to Zahi and Hugo.

Zahi glanced at the saw and then into his brother's face.

"Nothing to tell me?" the interrogator asked Zahi.

Zahi remained silent.

"Then watch what I will do to your brother." He pinched the ends of orange ear plugs and inserted them into his ears. He picked up the bone saw. "Should I start with his right hand or his left?"

"Cut me instead," Zahi pleaded. *He's an artist. I am not.*

The interrogator stood up and moved towards Hugo, dragging the stool with one hand and holding the bone saw in the other. He reached the side of Hugo's chair and remained standing.

"He knows nothing," Zahi cried. "Nothing at all."

The interrogator grasped Hugo's right hand and pinned it palm down against the metal arm rest. He maneuvered the hand until the baby finger was suspended in air, off the edge of the stainless steel arm rest. He stepped to the side, closer to Hugo's feet, and turned his body slightly, so Zahi could see both the hand and the bone saw.

Zahi exchanged a quick glance with Hugo. Terror mixed with an unspoken pleading in Hugo's eyes. Zahi turned his head to look again at the blade hovering above the baby finger. "Please! Cut me instead, please!"

The interrogator rested the teeth against the finger where it connected to the hand. The blade gripped the loose skin as he began to saw back and forth, slowly. Instead of tearing or ripping, or even stretching the skin, the blade sliced through the skin, and then through tendons, as easily as a pocket knife slicing through kite string. The blade cut through muscles and other tissues and then slid into the joint between the baby finger and hand. That's when Hugo screamed. The interrogator pushed downward and sliced forward simultaneously. The finger fell to the floor.

He set the saw down and picked up a brown glass bottle. He unscrewed the lid and poured a yellow liquid over the small stump on the edge of Hugo's palm. Hugo yelled again.

"Topical iodine," the interrogator said. "It burns and stings, but it will prevent infection." He smiled at Hugo. "You will thank me later."

The interrogator swept his foot forward and kicked the red, severed finger onto the floor drain. The bloody finger slid between the bars of the grate and disappeared.

The wound bled profusely.

The interrogator sat down on the stool and swiveled to face Zahi. "There are sharks in the sewer, too." He laughed.

He took off his purple nitrile gloves and focused on his mobile phone, reading messages and texting, mindlessly passing the time. After a few minutes, he set the phone aside and stood up.

"Ring finger is next." He pulled on a new pair of purple gloves and grasped the finger next to the stump, which was still bleeding. "Zahi, do you have anything to tell me?"

Zahi remained quiet.

"Hugo, doesn't your brother love you?"

"He does," Hugo answered. "I know he does."

The ring finger soon fell to the floor and was kicked onto the floor drain. It straddled an opening in the grate. The interrogator poured the iodine disinfectant over the second bleeding stump. Hugo yelled again and then passed out.

"It's funny how the iodine hurts more than the saw." He looked at the bone saw. "Little teeth." He laughed again.

"Middle finger is next." He grasped the middle finger and pressed the edge of the bone saw to the skin. He didn't wait for Hugo to wake up. He cut through the finger effortlessly. It too dropped to the floor.

"Still nothing to tell me?

"Next is the index finger." He smiled. "I enjoy cutting off index fingers. Why? Because they are a *nastyfinger*." He laughed again.

"This is getting boring, don't you think? If we have to work on the left hand, then I'll use the garden shears. I must warn you, though, they are dirty and rusty. They are not like my saw. They leave a jagged, unhealable mess of a stump."

"Fuck Lil't!" Zahi said.

"Really?" the interrogator said. He banged his hand against the top of the table and the bottle of iodine fell to the floor, shattering. Yellow liquid flowed to the floor drain. "Do you want me to cut out his tongue? Is that what you want?"

"No! No!" Zahi said. "Fuck Lil't is my password!"

Zahi gave up the passwords to his Facebook, Twitter and Google social media accounts. They all followed the same pattern: FukLil't1, FukLil't2, FukLil't3.

The interrogator clapped his hands and the two guards entered the room and stepped forward. He took a pen and small notepad from his shirt pocket and scribbled. When finished, he ripped out the page and handed it to one of the guards. "Take this to the security office. Have them verify that it works, and then return immediately here. Understand?"

"Yes, sir," the guard answered. As he left the room, he

closed the metal door behind him. It made a hollow empty sound that bounced from wall to wall and floor to ceiling.

"What should we do in the meantime?" he asked Hugo. "Should I work on the left hand now?" he asked Zahi.

Zahi did not answer.

He turned to Hugo, who had regained consciousness. The interrogator asked, "Are you right-handed or left-handed?"

Zahi saw Hugo's eye widen, but he did not answer.

Zahi could not remember. Was he left-handed or right-handed? Which hand did he need to draw?

The interrogator turned back to Zahi and asked, "Should I do the left index finger? Or just saw off the whole hand?"

Hugo's face turned pale. Zahi saw panic in his eyes. They both fought against their restraints.

The interrogator donned another pair of purple nitrile gloves and walked to the other side of Hugo's inclined chair. He pinned Hugo's left hand palm up against the stainless steel armrest and pressed the metal teeth of the bone saw against the skin on Hugo's wrist. He moved the blade back and forth, slowly.

Hugo screamed.

"No! Stop!" Zahi yelled. "I'll give you the password to my Apple account. Everything is there. In the cloud. All of it."

The interrogator released Hugo's hand. Hugo had passed out.

Zahi told him the password: DermorphisDT.

"What does it mean, DermorphisDT?" the interrogator asked.

"Dermorphis is a blind amphibian." The full scientific name was *Dermophis donaldtrumpi*.

"Don't play with me or—" he began sawing again, pausing only after he had cut an incision in Hugo's wrist.

"I'm not playing with you!" Zahi yelled. "The password will work. It is D-e-r-m-o-r-p-h-i-s-D-T."

The interrogator ordered the other guard to immediately inform the security office and verify the password.

It worked. Technicians with the Republican Democracy Communications and Information Technology Commission took down Zahi's Facebook, Twitter, and Google email accounts. Everything in Zahi's cloud was erased; Kartouzian's documents, Zahi's analysis of Little NEOM, and his paper and presentation disappeared into the ether.

Zahi was returned to his cell. An hour later, the cell door opened and Hugo was led in. His wounds had been bandaged.

Zahi wanted to say something to console his brother, but no words came, even when Hugo collapsed next to him on the cold concrete floor. Hugo's face was pale, his lips chapped, and his eyes were frightened. Zahi wanted to give him a drink of water, but no water was available.

Zahi repositioned himself on the floor and wrapped his arms around Hugo and pulled him close. Blood from Hugo's bandaged right hand bled through Zahi's white shirt and onto his chest. It felt warm. Zahi softly stroked Hugo's messy, black hair. He whispered, softly and affectionately, into his brother's ear, "Why is your hair always such a mess?"

Hugo raised his eyes to his brother. His body was trembling uncontrollably.

"Your hair reminds me of the secretary bird. Do you

remember seeing it? At the zoo in the capital? You were five, maybe six years old?"

Hugo gazed up in amazement. "Was it a skinny bird? With crane-like legs and crazy feathers on top of its head?"

"Just like you," Zahi said, crying.

Hugo leaned into his brother.

Zahi looked down into his traumatized eyes. He recalled holding Hugo in his arms, against his chest, when he was a newborn swaddled in a soft cloth. "I was ten years old when I first held you."

Hugo again stared up at his brother, but this time his eyes showed his amazement. A smile spread across his face, but quickly faded.

Zahi recalled the trusting smile of the baby. The eyes moist, big and dark. Zahi had no idea how his heart kept beating.

"Did you read Saba's diary?" Hugo asked his older brother.

"Yes," Zahi said. "I did."

"I have a confession."

"What?"

"Did you read the last entry?"

"I did." Zahi gazed down into his brother's eyes. "It changed my life."

"I wrote it," Hugo said.

"Yes, I know you did."

"No," Hugo said. "I *wrote* it."

They looked into each other's eyes. Zahi smiled. "I suspected that you did, but I wasn't sure." He held his brother tightly. "Saba was too kind to write something like that." He chided, in a gentle, loving tone, "Or use that language."

"She never stopped loving you," Hugo said.

And I never stopped loving her.

23

Data Dump

Hugo was taken away early the next morning. A short time later, Zahi was taken back to the interrogation room.

He suspected that Professor Kartouzian's data had been destroyed. His research into the illegal activities of Lil't's public works program would not be shared with the economists at the conference or the *Washington Post*. He suspected that his presentation and analysis of Little NEOM had also been wiped from the cloud and could no longer be downloaded. Surely the torturer was satisfied. *Wasn't he?*

Hugo was already in the room, strapped to his chair, unconscious. His left hand had been severed. The stump was bright yellow-orange, stained with iodine disinfectant, and resting in a pool of bloody ice in a bed pan. Hugo's arm was clamped to the stainless steel arm rest.

The torturer told Zahi that he was lying. He had not given up all the data.

"I am going to kill your brother." He threw the bone saw across the room. It struck the concrete wall and the small toothed blade snapped.

"He is going to die. But you . . . you get to decide *how*. I will dismember him, piece by piece, here in front of you, or you will tell me everything you know, and I will kill him quickly. The choice is yours."

Zahi had nothing left to give up except the name of his mentor. He gave up the names of everyone he disliked in the Sistema, even though he had no reason to believe that any of them had ratted him out to Lil't. *They would have done the same thing to me*, he thought.

He also gave up the names of every student and professor he could think of who had been enrolled or who had worked in the economic department at the Republican Democracy University. Zahi had not stayed in touch with the department after he left on his sabbatical, so he didn't know who might still be at the school and who had moved on. He had severed his relationships with his students and peers, like he always did—a pattern that had followed him throughout his life.

He gave up everyone except his mentor, the old professor, David Ludi.

"You have done well," the interrogator said.

Two guards appeared and unstrapped Hugo. They pulled him from the chair and carried him from the room, balancing his upright body between them. Hugo did not raise his head and the brothers did not make eye contact.

The torturer smiled at Zahi, and then he followed Hugo and the guards out of the room.

Zahi heard a gunshot.

When the interrogator returned, Zahi saw that he was carrying a syringe.

"Your brother is dead," he said. "A bullet to the back of the head. That is as merciful as I can be."

Any illusion that Zahi had about redeeming himself vanished. Hugo had suffered through the amputation of his left hand and three fingers on his right hand, and then he had been murdered. Shot in the back of the head. *Saba was right. I will die alone and lonely. There is no forgiveness here.*

"You are a fool," the interrogator said.

Zahi saw a bead of fluid fall from the tip of the syringe. *Like a tear drop*, he thought. But then his rational mind shut down and his body convulsed, uncontrollable, as if he were filled with lightning. He could no longer control his legs, arms, or any other body part. His mind panicked and pushed against the restraints.

The needle entered his shoulder and Zahi felt the fluid displace muscle, as if he were receiving nothing more than a vaccination. The sedative almost immediately took effect and his body relaxed and his mind cleared.

Little Zahi, he thought in his last moments, *I am so sorry that I failed you, too.*

The interrogator asphyxiated him, leaving no physical marks on Zahi's body except for the small red mark where the needle had entered his right shoulder.

Zahi's corpse was placed in the morgue because he was a United States citizen, and someone might inquire about him.

That evening and during the following day, many of the students and professors that Zahi had named were arrested. Some were teaching, some were working in government jobs, and several were unemployed. They all disappeared. Several of their coworkers and family members disappeared, too.

Also that evening, Hugo was beaten by the guards and then dumped on the street. He had no left hand and he was missing three fingers on his right hand. What remained had been dosed in iodine and wrapped in sterile gauze bandages.

Hugo had a fever and was delirious. He was in worse shape mentally and emotionally than when Zahi had picked him up to fly him from the Republican Democracy to Maritauqua Island.

PART III

24

Deported

The coach handed Liko a white hand towel. "Blow your nose."

Liko blew into the frayed towel, first his right nostril then his left. He opened the towel and looked inside: a string of red had flowed with the clear mucous from his right nostril, like the unexpected red in the albumin of a fertilized chicken egg. He closed the ragged towel and ran its rough surface under the tip of his nose, cleaning away the last remnant of blood.

"Into the corner," the coach ordered.

Liko obeyed, positioning himself in the corner of the ring. His sparring partner stepped forward and boxed him in. "Listen to me carefully," the coach said. "When you're boxed into a corner or find yourself against a wall, V-step to the side of your opponent and deliver three fast upper cuts to his chin." The coach demonstrated the upper cuts, pumping upwards with his fist three times into an imaginary chin. "Then continue around your opponent with one more step while throwing alternating hooks – right, left, right."

The coach again demonstrated, taking a small step and then pumping left, right, left. "Your opponent will then find *himself* boxed into the corner or pinned against the wall. Keep him pinned with a small V-step to the right and a series of fast punches, followed by a quick V-step to the left with fast punches." He let fly a barrage of uppercuts, saying, "Attack down the center for checkmate." He took a step backwards, looked up at Liko. "Understand?"

"Yes," Liko answered, trying to pattern the movement in his mind.

"Let's see you do it."

Liko's sparring partner wailed at him and pinned him against the ropes. Liko covered the sides of his face with his red Title gloves and protected his ribs with his elbows, absorbing the blows as much as he could. The punches alternated, left, right.

"V-step, Liko!" the coach ordered.

Liko stepped to his left but still found himself pinned against the rope.

"V-step!"

Liko stepped again to his left. A surprise upper cut tapped his chin.

"No, no, no!" The coach separated the boxers. "You must move fast. Like this." The coach demonstrated. "Again," he ordered. "V-step, three uppercuts, and then step, hook-hook-hook!"

Liko stepped to his opponent's left side but his opponent countered, stepping into the space at the same time, denying Liko the position. Liko fell onto the floor mat with a hard thud.

"Get up!" the coach yelled. "Lay on the ground and they'll kick you, stomp on you, and then spit and piss on you! Get up!"

Liko groaned as he picked his large body off the black mat. He stepped to the side of the ring, steadying himself with his back against the rope. His sparring partner came straight at him, working inside with a jab and cross. Again, he threw hooks to Liko's body – left and right – and upper cuts to his chin.

"No, no, no." Liko could hear the exasperation in his coach's voice. "Don't hop! V-step!" Liko saw his coach shaking his head in disappointment, standing with his hands on his hips.

Pop! Liko felt his teeth rattle as his head snapped up and then back down. He felt momentarily dizzy. He tried to step backwards, away from the punches, but his back was already against the ropes.

"Keep your eyes on your opponent!" The coach's voice betrayed his dismay at Liko's poor performance.

Liko spotted Charla before she saw him. She was standing to the side of the restaurant entrance with her back to him, gazing down the long stretch of sidewalk, expecting him to arrive from the opposite direction. She was dressed fashionably, as always, in a casual swing halter dress in navy blue with a floral print. Her shoulders were bare and her knees revealed.

Today was their first get-together since Liko's return from the Marshall Islands. He had spent several months exploring shipwrecks and reefs and underwater wildlife as a diving partner and personal bodyguard to his employer, Cothrom.

When he had arrived home two days earlier, he was

surprised that Hugo was not there. He had been looking forward to seeing Hugo and his latest art work. His clothes were there, but he was gone. The food in the refrigerator was spoiled, which was not a good sign.

Liko had fallen asleep without any problem, probably because of the jetlag. When he awoke, he discovered that Hugo had not returned during the night. Liko searched for him in the park and along the lake shore. He visited Hugo's elephant rock sculpture-painting, hoping to find him camping nearby, perhaps among the rocks.

Hugo did not return that evening and Liko did not sleep well. It was a long fitful night.

Early the next morning Liko called Zahi, but there was no answer. He busied himself cleaning out the refrigerator. The goat cheese had spots of green mold, the string beans were mushy and slimy, and the milk had curdled. He threw everything into a trash bag and took it out to the curb before leaving for his boxing lesson. And now he was meeting Charla.

They met at the Maritauqua Tea Room for a late brunch. It was an old-fashioned restaurant inside a historic, weathered brick house. Southern cuisine. Southern comfort food. Breads and desserts baked on the premises.

"Charla!" he said affectionately, setting his gym bag on the brick sidewalk and opening his arms wide to greet her.

She spun around energetically, her arms opening to greet him. When she saw him, her smile collapsed. "Yikes!" she said, pulling away from his hug and the air kiss that he tried to plant on her cheek.

"What?" he asked, perplexed, his arms outstretched.

Her back straightened. "What is that in your nose?"

He looked cross-eyed at his nose and saw the ends of

white tissue paper. He wiggled his nose and the paper wiggled. He felt his face flush.

He pulled the tissue paper out of his nostril. The twisted end of tissue appeared rusty—dried blood. He crumpled the tissue and stuffed it into the mesh pocket at the end of his gym bag.

Charla looked at him sideways, waiting for an answer.

"Sorry," he said. "I was boxing." He pulled a clean tissue out of his pocket and dabbed at his nose. The bleeding had stopped. He stuffed the second tissue into the mesh pocket on top of the bloody one.

"Boxing?" Charla echoed. "I could have guessed it wasn't Zumba."

"No," Liko said, "not Zumba." He smiled and gave her a respectful nod, deciding to forgo a hug and air kisses. "I suppose my nose is red, too?"

"And your ears," Charla added. "Perhaps boxing is not your sport."

"I need to practice my slips and parries."

Liko opened the restaurant door for her. They were seated right away, and a waitress quickly returned with two glasses of tap water and a basket of corn bread, bright yellow.

Charla and Liko studied the menu. "Southern cuisine?" Charla said. "I don't like overcooked vegetables."

"We can go elsewhere if you like," Liko suggested.

"No," Charla said. "It's okay."

"Each dish comes with two sides," the waitress explained. "Sweet potato soufflé, collard greens, baked sweet potato, creamed corn, fried okra, fried green tomatoes, and mac and cheese."

"I'll have the four-piece fried chicken," Liko said, "and the sweet potato soufflé and mac and cheese for my two sides." He closed his menu and set it down on the plate in front of him.

The waitress turned to Charla.

"What is your soup of the day?" she asked.

"Pot likker."

"What in the world is that?" Liko asked.

Charla smiled and explained: "Turnip green broth with a bite of corn bread, seasoned with salt and pepper."

Liko grimaced.

"I'll try the grits and shrimp," she said. "For my sides I'll have fried green tomatoes and fried okra."

Liko added, "And we'll share the tomato pie."

"One tomato pie," the waitress repeated, scribbling the request into her green-lined notepad. She flipped the pad closed and quickly walked back to the kitchen.

"The last time I saw Hugo he was at the Museum Hotel," Charla said. "More than a week ago."

"What was he doing there?" Liko asked.

"The county returned some of his art work, and Cothrom was hanging it in her gallery. Hugo went down to see how it was coming along."

Liko nodded.

"He was upset," she added.

"Was he on his meds?"

"Yes, as far as I know," she said. "He was upset, but he wasn't hyper or paranoid."

"That's good."

"He told me, though, that they couldn't find his birth certificate. He said he had to find it or go back to court again. He was nervous. He also said that his brother had left for a conference, someplace overseas."

"That sounds right," Liko said. "Zahi told me that he

was going to the Republican Democracy. I tried to call him but he didn't answer. Maybe he hasn't returned yet."

"Hugo didn't know where to get help," Charla explained. "He went to City Hall and they told him to turn himself in. Can you believe that? To turn himself in? While he was sitting in the waiting area the receptionist called the police. He left before they arrived. Can you believe that? They called the police on him!"

Yes, Liko nodded. He had no problem believing it.

"He said that he had a tourist visa, but it had expired. He believed he would be deported. He said he'd called the Republican Democracy embassy in Washington DC. He said that someone in the ambassador's office called him back a few days later. They said he was in luck, because the ambassador was visiting Maritauqua Island, and that he would be staying at Jizan's Plantation. The caller told Hugo to go to there and ask the ambassador for help."

Liko looked at Charla trying to understand what in the world she had just said. He tried to paraphrase. "He couldn't find his *American* birth certificate, so he met with the ambassador from the Republican Democracy? Here locally?"

"Yes," Charla said. "A mansion owned by some famous violinist named Jizan."

Liko shook his head. "You're kidding me!"

Charla as if Liko had just hurt her feelings. "No."

Charla's shrimp and grits arrived in a shallow white bowl: three large shrimp, tails up, in a bed of pale yellow grits, surrounded by a moat of brown sauce. *What a slaughter!* Liko thought.

His dish arrived next. The skin on the chicken was crisp but not greasy. The breast meat was moist and tender, but it lacked seasoning. In fact, it was flavorless.

"I think Hugo was abducted," Charla said, lowering her voice and speaking quietly.

The waitress returned and asked Liko, "How is the sweet potato soufflé?"

"Creamy," Liko answered. "Sweeter than the cornbread."

"It's full of lard," Charla said.

"Charla!"

"The cornbread, Liko, not the soufflé." Liko frowned at her. "Southern cuisine may taste good," she paused and looked up at the waitress, "or not. Nevertheless, Southern cooking is seldom good for you." The waitress frowned slightly and walked away.

"I just wished that he had called me."

"But you were with Cothrom in the Marshall Islands," Charla said. "How could you have helped?"

"I don't know. But I should have checked in on him every once in a while."

The waitress failed to bring the tomato pie, and Liko and Charla decided not to remind her.

25

Repentant Procrastinator

Liko tried calling Zahi again. He did not answer his cell phone and his voicemail was full. A call to his office at George Mason University went unanswered, and he did not reply to his emails.

Liko thought about Hugo trying to obtain proof of his United States citizenship and failing. *I should have asked Kwon for help a long time ago.* Kwon was a friend of Liko's Uncle Keahi, who had been murdered on Oahu. Uncle Keahi had often raved about Kwon's research skills and his ability to interpret data. According to his uncle, Kwon was not only resourceful, but also a statistical genius. Kwon had the ability to find patterns and anomalies in a set of data.

As he phoned Kwon, Liko felt heavy with guilt.

"Liko?" Kwon said, answering his phone.

How did you know... of course, you have my name in your contacts folder. "Hi Kwon," Liko answered. "Is this a good time to talk?"

"Not the best," Kwon answered. "I'm at the Keck Observatory, but I'm taking a break."

Liko thought he heard Kwon sipping a beverage and munching something.

"Are you having lunch?" Liko looked at his watch; it was at least five or maybe six hours earlier in Hawaii. "Sorry if I interrupted your lunch."

"No," Kwon said. "I'm just sipping water and eating M&Ms. It helps the oxygen uptake. The observatory is at 13,599 feet elevation, you know."

"I didn't know that," Liko said.

"The summit of Mauna Kea is 13,803 feet, or 4,207 meters above sea level. The air at my current elevation contains only 59.8 percent of the oxygen, by volume, of ocean-level air."

Liko smiled. Uncle Keahi's stories about Kwon's love for astronomy and statistics were true. "I hope you are okay."

"The M&Ms help," Kwon said, crunching them as he talked. "I sometimes get a headache after my descent, though."

"Payback for the temporary euphoria." Liko laughed, slightly. "I used to get narked scuba diving."

"Similar, yet different," Kwon said. "Nitrogen narcosis does impart a similar effect, ranging from mild impairment to death. The cause is different, of course. Diving narcosis is caused by increased solubility of gases, mainly nitrogen, as a result of the elevated pressures at *depth*."

Liko heard Kwon take another sip of water and crunch more M&Ms. "I have a favor to ask," Liko said. He explained about the missing birth certificate.

Without any hesitation Kwon agreed to help. He said he knew someone who worked in the Hawaii Department of Health's Vital Statistics Office, someone who had access to birth certificates.

26

Jizan's Heliport

"I'm going to visit the mansion," Liko said. "You interested?"

"Sure!" Charla said. "I love drama!"

I know you do, Liko thought with a smile.

He pulled a newspaper article out of his pocket, unfolded it, and handed it to Charla. "This Jizan is a sexual predator and a pedophile."

"Liko!" Charla exclaimed, staring at the article, "I didn't know."

"Neither did I," Liko said, "until yesterday. I 'borrowed' this page from the library newspaper. I was curious to see what I could find out about this Jizan character."

The article was written by Daniel Johnson with photographs by Janet Mayer. The headline read "VICTIMS DENIED JUSTICE?"

"Liko!" she said, staring at him. "Do you think they did something to Hugo?"

"Maybe."

He told her that Daniel had died while jogging a few days after his story was published. A sudden, unexpected heart attack.

Liko had read his obituary. Daniel had a remarkable career as an investigative journalist and foreign correspondent before moving to Maritauqua Island five years ago. He had spent years as a military reporter covering stories in Kuwait, Iraq, and Afghanistan. In recent years he had been a foreign correspondent in the Middle East. He had won several journalism awards, and then he had suddenly 'dropped out' and moved to Maritauqua Island, where he was assigned to the lifestyle section of the *Maritauqua Times* newspaper to report on local events, including the party at Jizan's mansion.

The article Daniel wrote about Jizan was one hell of an article.

Charla and Liko's visit was a complete bust, a waste of their time. They were unable to speak with anyone other than the butler, and he was taciturn and unyielding. When they asked to see Jizan, the butler smirked, literally, and summarily dismissed them.

Standing on the sidewalk just off the veranda, Liko gazed down the long driveway. Long rows of stumps lined both sides of the driveway, and several had sprouted new growth.

"I wonder if he needed a permit to cut down all these oaks?" he asked Charla.

"It is so sad," she said, "We should report him to the county."

Liko checked the location of their Uber. He was unhappy. They had come all the way out to the mansion to be turned away before they could ask any questions about Hugo. And now the nearest Uber was ten minutes away.

"I'm going to take a walk around the outside," he said. "Want to join me?"

"What if someone sees us and calls the police?" Charla asked.

"I hope they do," Liko said. "I'll tell them that Hugo entered the house and then mysteriously disappeared. I'll demand that they search the house."

He started towards the corner of the mansion. "We don't have much time," he added. Charla followed close behind.

As they walked around the corner of the mansion, Liko spotted the guest house in the distance, and then he saw the heliport.

"That's how they did it," he suggested.

"Did what?"

"Abducted Hugo." He gestured towards the heliport. "They probably drugged him and then flew him off in a helicopter."

Charla looked at Liko sideways with a 'you've got to be kidding?' expression on her face. When he remained serious, she added, "Really?"

He canceled their Uber—a late cancel, so he had to pay a penalty. He shoved the iPhone back into his front pocket, in a bad mood.

When they reached the heliport, they stepped onto the black surface. He glanced around the perimeter and over the surface of the pad as if he expected to find something, perhaps something dropped by Hugo, but he saw nothing except for a purple ribbon. "I know this is how they did it!" He reached down and picked up the ribbon. "I just know it. I feel it."

"It's for a little girl," Charla said, taking the delicate ribbon from him. She turned it over in her hand. "A girl's hair ribbon."

Liko took out his phone and snapped a picture of the ribbon. Opening the Uber app, he said, "I want you to leave. I'll call you an Uber."

"And you?"

"I'm going to walk back towards the house with you, but then I'm going to disappear into those bushes." He pointed towards the bushes next to the guest house.

"Me too," Charla said. "You're not sending me away just as things get exciting."

"Of course I am," he said, as he continued to set up the Uber request.

She slugged him on his shoulder with enough force that he dropped his iPhone.

"Ouch!" He reached down and picked it up.

"You should know me better than that," she said.

Liko heard the determination in her voice. "Okay," he said, "but stay close."

They walked quickly to the guest house and checked the windows. They were one-piece and double-paned. They worked their way to the back of the guest house. "Would you like me to ring the doorbell?" Charla asked.

Liko gave her a condescending look and answered, "No thank you. I can ring it myself." No answer. He rang again. Still no answer. After the third ring and no answer, he tried the door. It was locked.

In one swift motion, Liko reached down, took off his shoe and broke the sidelight to the door. He slipped his shoe back on and said, "Let's check it out?"

Charla stared, open-mouthed, at the broken window.

"He's a pedophile," Liko said. "A predator. We're here and I'm searching the place."

She nodded agreement.

Liko reached in through the broken glass and unlocked the back door. They stepped inside and he closed the door behind them.

They found some unusually decorated rooms. One room was bright pink. "For young girls?" Charla suggested.

They heard a clanging. Charla jumped and their eyes locked. "Damn!" Liko said, "We must have tripped an alarm."

Liko's eyes darted around the bedroom, looking for something to use as a weapon, but he saw nothing. The one chair in the room was plush, upholstered, not wood. No lampstands or coat racks. No glass fixtures, either. The lights were recessed into the ceiling. The headboard for the bed was bolted to the wall and made of soft fabric.

He reached up to the overhead fan and snapped off a blade. He swung it back and forth like a machete, feeling its weight.

Charla said, "I could use one too!"

The fan was now wobbling, off-balance. He reached up and snapped off one of the last two blades and handed it to her. She walked over to the light switch and punched off the fan.

He threw her a look that said, *What now?*

She said, "I'll follow your lead."

Liko nodded and smiled tightly.

They heard a helicopter and looked out the bedroom window, one on each side, peeking around the edge of the curtains. The helicopter approached from the eastern side of the property, and so did a large man and two beefy guards.

"Maybe the alarm was to announce the helicopter?" Charla suggested. "Maybe they don't know we're here?"

"Maybe."

"I see three men," Charla said.

"Two guards and Jizan?"

"An ogre," Charla said, disgust in her voice.

They watched the helicopter land. The guards opened the helicopter door and took a small girl out of the passenger area. They each took one of her small hands and walked her up to the large man. He looked her up and down and said something to her and the guards.

Liko felt his stomach convulse.

The ogre answered his phone. He dismissed the guards and the young girl with a wave of his hand and headed back to the main house, walking quickly. The guards began walking the girl to the guest quarters, one on each side of her, each holding one of her hands.

"They're coming," Charla said, her voice rising.

"Let's wait down the hall," Liko suggested. "In the room that needs cleaning, the one with the messed-up bed sheets and towels on the floor."

Charla nodded agreement.

"I don't think they'd show her into a dirty room, do you?"

She nodded agreement, again.

He took Charla's hand and led her quickly out of the pink bedroom, down the hallway, and into the soiled bedroom. He closed the door and placed his finger on his lips.

They listened to the men bring the child into one of the other bedrooms. "The pink room," Liko whispered.

Liko heard an exchange of words. One of the men gave the child instructions, or perhaps a warning, his voice low and stern. Liko heard them close the bedroom door. He heard a key in a lock and then he heard their footsteps trail off as the two men walked down the hall to the front door. He cracked his door open and peeked out. Neither man was in the hallway. He heard the lock turn in the front door.

Liko walked silently down the hallway. He tried the girl's bedroom door but it was locked. He called out in a calm and kind voice, "Are you okay?"

He heard no reply.

"Don't worry," he said. "I'm a friend. We are here to help you."

He considered breaking the door down, but he knew that was movie stuff. He had no tools, and the door appeared to be solid wood, not a hollow core door. The wood framing the doorway was heavy. Ramming the door would be foolish; he had tried that once before, at his mother's trailer. The front door to her trailer had been metal in a metal frame. He remembered bouncing off the door and landing on his ass, humiliated.

He took a deep breath, turned around and raced down the hallway. He unlocked the front door, swung it open, and ran through.

The two men were surprised when he caught them from behind. The first one dropped, unconscious, after two angry blows to his liver. Liko's boxing trainer had taught him that was a very painful place to be punched. The second man swung at Liko. Liko slipped and hit him with a jab, cross, left hook, right hook, and then kicked him twice as he lay on the ground.

He searched their pockets and found a set of keys. Liko raced back to the bedroom and unlocked the door.

A small girl cowered in a corner of the room beside the full size bed. She was ten, maybe eleven years of age. Her hair was red, straight and thin, her eyes a pale blue and her cheeks white like sugar.

Charla gathered her up in her arms, hugging her gently.

They ran out the back door and traversed the property until they came to a ravine. They passed through a thick growth of scrub oaks that grew along the edges of the ravine, and they climbed down the banks to a dry creek bed. They followed the ravine, walking along the dry creek until it crossed a road. They climbed up the banks and met an Uber that Liko had requested. Even though he was picking them up in the middle of nowhere, the driver made no comment. Twenty minutes later he dropped them off at Charla's apartment.

Once they were inside her apartment, they lay the girl on the couch and covered her with a blanket. Charla tilted her head and Liko followed her into the bedroom. She hit Liko so hard that he thought he would lose a tooth, maybe two. His gums bled. "Don't you ever do something that stupid again!"

He couldn't help but grin. He had knocked out two professional guards, and they were big men. His grin broadened as he thought of them lying on the path between the mansion and the guest house. *They deserved hospital time,* he thought. *Anyone who hurts children. Or the elderly. Or the disabled. Or anyone who enables others to hurt them. All those despicables deserve time in the hospital.*

He decided that he liked Charla, a lot—not in *that* way. Then he thought about Jizan. Was he the large man who had met the girl at the helicopter? He had to be extremely dangerous to be that cock-sure and brazen. No one messed with someone who was gulo gulo: vicious.

He and Charla had been lucky. He deserved the punch to his jaw.

When the young girl awoke, Charla questioned her. Her name was Samantha. Her mother's boyfriend had sexually abused her, so she fled her rural home. Her goal was to hitchhike to her grandmother's home in the big city of Huntsville, Alabama. That's how Samantha described Huntsville: "The Big City." She was abducted at a quiet intersection just outside Gurley, Alabama.

Charla prepared a hot bath for her, washed and dried her clothes, and fed her a cheese pizza. She then drove her to her grandmother's home. Charla waited in the car as Samantha climbed the porch steps and rang the doorbell. When the grandmother and Samantha hugged, affectionately, Charla wiped a tear from her cheek, and then she drove back to Maritauqua Island.

27

An Unexpected Death

The next day Liko received a call from a law firm in Washington, DC. The caller identified himself as Zahi's lawyer, who said he was the appointed executor of Zahi's estate.

"Zahi is dead?" Liko asked. "What happened? How did he die?"

The lawyer explained that he really knew nothing except that Zahi was dead, and that he had died in the Republican Democracy. The lawyer said that Zahi had named Liko in his will.

Liko was totally surprised.

"How about his brother, Hugo?"

"He established a trust for him."

"I'll let him know when I see him." Liko told the lawyer.

"See him? Are you visiting the Republican Democracy?"

"No," Liko answered. "Why?"

"He's in the Republican Democracy."

"No," Liko said, "he lives here on Maritauqua Island, with me. Zahi brought him here several years ago."

"That's strange," the executor said. "I just got off the phone with Zahi's relatives and they said that Hugo was with them, in the Republican Democracy."

"No way!"

"Yes. Seems he was injured. Something about his hands being mangled. I asked the relatives to have him call me, but I haven't heard from him."

"What happened to his hands?"

"I don't know."

"Where is he now?"

"I don't know."

"How in the world did he get to the Republican Democracy?"

"I have no idea."

'Well," Liko said, raising his voice, his tone now irritated, "are you sure that Zahi is dead?"

After an awkward silence, the executor said, "Yes, although his relatives have refused to identify the body so it can be returned to the States."

"What do you mean?"

"They refused to take custody of his remains."

"Why?"

"I don't know."

"What's so hard about—"

The lawyer cut Liko off. "Muslim customs follow specific rites, but for some reason the family has refused to take custody of his body. Sharia law calls for burial of the body as soon as possible. First there is a simple ritual involving bathing and shrouding and then there is prayer. Burial is usually within 24 hours of death."

"So," Liko asked, "what is the problem?"

There was another awkward silence. "Zahi's will specifically specifies cremation. That is the problem. Cremation is forbidden in the Republican Democracy. I assume this is why the family won't get involved."

"What's wrong with cremation?"

"It's simply forbidden by law. Italy doesn't allow cremation, either."

"I see," Liko said. *Muslims and Catholics don't allow cremation. Stupid laws.*

"But that is my problem, not yours," the lawyer said. "I'll find a way to work it out. I apologize for venting, but I just find it all so... frustrating."

"That's all right," Liko said. "Thank you for letting me know about Zahi."

"It's my job," the lawyer said. "And as I said, you are in his will."

They exchanged contact information and hung up.

Liko immediately called Charla and told her the terrible news. She was horrified at what had happened to Hugo. Liko wished he had told her in person, instead of giving her the news over the phone. He could hear the anxiety in her voice and he knew she was extremely upset.

"Do you want me to come by?" Liko asked.

"No," Charla answered. "But someone needs to go to the Republican Democracy and bring back Hugo."

"I could go," Liko said. "I could also identify Zahi and bring back his body."

There was a long silence on the phone. After further discussion, they agreed that he should leave immediately.

Liko called the executor and proposed flying to the Republican Democracy and returning with Zahi's body and Hugo.

"That would be helpful," the executor said. Liko heard the surprise in his voice. "Identifying Zahi's body and returning it to the States *would* help settle the estate quickly. Besides," he added, "bringing Hugo home would fit in with your duties as trustee."

"I don't understand," Liko said.

"In his will, Zahi requested that I set up a trust for Hugo, and that you and I be joint trustees."

Liko shook his head. "No."

"Please reconsider," the lawyer said. "If you refuse then I must appoint someone else. According to Zahi's instructions, he believes that you know his brother well, and that you are in a unique position to ensure that his needs are taken care of."

"I consider myself his friend, and we are roommates. If I become trustee then our relationship will change. I don't think that I want that."

"Think about it," the executor said. "You do not need to make a decision right now."

Liko nodded, then said into the phone, "Okay."

"And one more thing," the executor said. "You are a co-beneficiary."

Liko wasn't sure what that meant.

"Zahi had me change his will recently," the executor said. "You will inherit half of his estate, and it is a considerable fortune."

Liko was shocked.

28

Travel and Funding Logistics

With Charla's help that night, Liko booked a flight to the Republican Democracy. He soon learned, though, that such a visit involved more than keeping track of a few details. In fact, it was more difficult than visiting Saudi Arabia.

Tourist visas had ended shortly after the Republican Emirates collapsed. Today, no one but archaeologists, expatriates, and perhaps religious zealots, had any interest in visiting. A business visa wouldn't work; Liko had no business connections who would sponsor him and no one to pay the outrageous application fees. Plus, there would be 'facilitation payments.'

Liko considered booking a flight with a layover. According to the flight schedules, if he booked a long layover he could spend the night in the airport just outside the capital. That might allow him to slip into the country and to look for Hugo. There was a downside, however; if he were caught, the penalty would be severe. He could spend years in jail.

He finally decided to enter the country legally. He would obtain a cross-country visa that would allow him to drive across the country. That would allow him the freedom to accomplish what he needed to do, he hoped.

"How are you going to pay for it?" Charla asked.

"Pay for it?"

"It's going to be very expensive."

Charla suggested that Liko ask Cothrom, the video game entrepreneur and owner of Cothrom Industries for the money. He seriously considered it.

Liko had entered into a contract with her company giving Cothrom unrestricted rights to use his image in her games, nude or clothed. That was a joke between Cothrom and Liko because he had posed for her and she had sculpted him in the nude. Fans of her video games had wanted a reproduction of one of the small, nude sculptures showing him throwing a spear. He had posed holding a broom.

He was paid well for the use of his image. Not only was his avatar used in her latest video game, which was almost as popular as Fortnite, but his likeness was also sold as an action figure at Walmart, Target, and video game stores.

Ironically, he had set up the bulk of his income to support Hugo in their apartment. Liko spent the money as quickly as he received royalties. In addition to turning their apartment into an art studio and buying art supplies,

Liko paid for Hugo's lawyer, clothing, and his health insurance and medical bills. And there was the cost of Hugo's weekly therapy sessions.

Cothrom could easily afford it. Besides, she had already established a patronage arrangement with Hugo and she proudly displayed his artwork in her gallery. She would be motivated by a sincere desire to help.

Another possibility was Liko's great-aunt. She had been *his* benefactor, just as Cothrom was becoming Hugo's. His great-aunt had paid for his travels throughout Europe, his short-lived stint studying marine biology at the University of Hawaii, and she had even bought his first pair of boxing gloves. When Liko signed the contract with Cothrom Enterprises, she had expressed her pride in him. He sent her a monthly check to repay her generous support, but so far she had not cashed any of them.

No, he decided. *I can't ask my great-aunt for money again. I'm old enough and responsible enough to support myself. I will never forget her support, kindness and love.*

"I think the best thing to do," Liko said to Charla, "is to get Zahi's lawyer to pay for it."

"It's worth a try," Charla said.

Liko called the executor and put him on speaker phone. After the customary greetings, Liko asked, "What is Hugo's official name? How is it spelled?"

"Hugo ibn Haarun ibn Ajam Ab al-Naqad."

"It was the seersucker lawyer," Liko mumbled to Charla.

"What?" the executor asked.

"The lawyer who represented Hugo at his first trial." Liko raised his voice. "He shortened Hugo's name and misspelled it. That's why they couldn't find his birth certificate."

"Damn!" Charla said. "Could it be that simple?"

"I don't understand," the executor said.

"I'm sorry," Liko replied. "The local court here on Maritauqua Island ordered Hugo to produce his birth certificate. Unfortunately, Hugo's lawyer shortened his name so they were unable to find the original certificate."

"I see," the executor said.

"I'm calling to ask you a question," Liko said. "I'm to inherit money?"

"Yes."

"A significant amount?"

"Yes. Considerable."

"A million dollars?"

"More."

Liko and Charla looked at each other. Charla raised a perfectly groomed eyebrow and Liko whistled.

"I would like you to advance me funds as beneficiary," Liko said.

Silence.

"I need funds for the trip. I will identify Zahi and I will return with his body for cremation. I will find Hugo and return with him, too."

Still silence on the executor's end of the phone.

"Not only will that help you settle the estate, but it's also the right thing to do."

Further silence.

"I expect the estate to pay all my expenses."

The lawyer broke his silence. "The estate will pay reasonable expenses to facilitate the repatriation of Mr. Haarun's mortal remains."

"To bring his body back?" Liko asked.

"Yes. That is correct. To prepare and transport his mortal remains from the Republican Democracy back to the United States."

"While I am there," Liko said, "I would like the funds to search for Hugo."

"And how will that benefit the estate?"

"When I find him, I will ask if he is okay with me accepting the position as executor of his estate, as Zahi requested. If Hugo agrees, then I will accept."

"That is acceptable," the lawyer said. "The estate will provide you the funds, on one condition."

"Shit," Liko mumbled in a low voice so Charla could hear, but hopefully not the executor. "What is the condition?"

"You must not do anything that will compromise the integrity of my law firm."

Liko took a deep breath. "Agreed."

They worked out the financial arrangement. By the time Liko got off the phone he felt the beginning of a powerful headache.

"I hate details," Liko mumbled to Charla. "I *hate* details!"

"I'll book the flight to a neighboring country," Charla said, kneading the muscles in Liko's neck, shoulders and upper back. She applied extra force to Liko's shoulder muscles.

"Ow!" he said.

"We need to decide your legal entry and exit points," Charla said. "Where you will drive into the Republican Democracy, and where you will drive out. And then I can arrange flights to and from the neighboring countries."

"Friendly countries," Liko suggested.

"That could be another problem."

Charla ran her hands through Liko's hair, working her fingers back from his hairline. *I'll leave the details to Charla*, he thought.

Liko called Kwon and gave him Hugo's full name.

29

Lost in the Countryside

Two months passed. It had been exceedingly difficult to obtain all the necessary visas, immunizations, and other paperwork, along with permission from the three countries involved. 'Details, details, details,' was Liko's new mantra.

"American?" the immigration officer asked in English.

"Yes," Liko replied.

The officer compared Liko's passport photo to his current appearance. The photo was taken the year after Liko graduated from high school. At that time, his face looked naïve and his smile soft. He had been looking forward to spending a year in Europe. Today his face carried a weary smile, and the corner of his mouth was slightly askew, hinting at unspoken sarcasm. He was not looking forward to his time in the Republican Democracy.

The officer leafed through page after page filled with country stamps that included England, France, and Italy before stamping a blank page. Next he examined Liko's transit visa slowly, carefully, taking his time, even though a long line had formed.

"You have seventy-two hours to drive cross-country?" the officer asked, his English betraying a strong Arabic accent.

"That's correct."

"There is a $1,500 penalty for each day longer," the officer said. His voice reflected his annoyance at Liko's attitude.

"I understand," Liko said.

"And time in jail," the officer added.

"Yes." Liko nodded his head. He understood.

The officer closed the transmit visa and handed it back to Liko, along with his passport. With a dismissive wave of his hand, the officer waved him through.

Liko followed the red arrows painted on the floor to the next check point: a row of tables where suitcases had been placed. Liko walked over to the table that held his suitcase and backpack and waited for someone to step forward to inspect his bags.

Hurry up, he thought. *I don't have all day.* His documents allowed him only three days to travel across the country. He would have to drive over challenging terrain and poor road conditions, and he wasn't impressed with his rental car, an old Renault.

An inspector stepped up. "Your suitcase?"

"Yes." It was an inexpensive brown suitcase Liko had bought at a Goodwill store. He had an expensive Tumi back home that he had used on his European travels, but he had decided against using it this time. Why risk having it lost, stolen, or confiscated?

"Open it," the inspector ordered.

Liko obeyed.

As the inspector poked through his suitcase with a baton, Liko recalled losing his mother's suitcase at the Honolulu Airport during his first visit to spend a summer with his Uncle Keahi. Liko had hidden money and other valuables in the liner of the bag, so the loss had devastated and angered him.

"Just a bunch of clothes," Liko explained as the guard prodded his clean but unfolded clothes. "Should be no problem."

The inspector seemed satisfied and told Liko to close the suitcase. The inspector then asked Liko to remove the contents of his small backpack and spread them on the table.

Liko obeyed, emptying out his shave kit, three coconut cashew bars, two high protein dark chocolate bars, and a lightweight Conair jacket. The yellow shave kit was a gift from his Uncle Keahi and had Liko's initials embroidered on it: LUK. The inspector directed Liko to open the shave kit, so Liko emptied the contents onto the table. The inspector removed a wine bottle opener that had a cork screw, ratchet lever and a foil-cutter blade attached.

"A weapon?" the inspector asked.

"Not hardly," Liko said. "You can have it."

The inspector placed it in his back pants pocket.

Next he removed a large nail clipper. *Give me a break,* Liko thought, looking at the shiny stainless steel.

"It's a toenail clipper," Liko said. "Go ahead, take it, too."

The inspector slid it into his back pocket.

A second inspector, noticing, walked over. He picked up Liko's designer Conair jacket and put it on. It was too large for his frame, even though he was barrel-chested.

"I'd rather you didn't try on my clothes," Liko said.

The second inspector turned and walked away, wearing the jacket.

Liko stepped after him. Just as he reached to tap the man on the shoulder, he felt something jab his lower back and he instantly stopped. He raised his hands, slowly. A baton? Or maybe a gun?

The inspector stealing the Conair jacket continued walking, never pausing or glancing back at him. Liko was furious. The humiliation reminded him of the punks in Hawaii who had stolen his sunglasses at San Souci Beach when he was visiting his uncle. He had not seen which of the youths took them, but this inspector was brazen and fearless in his theft.

The other inspector gestured for Liko to return to his suitcase and backpack. Liko complied, although he bit his tongue hard until he tasted blood. He picked up his belongings and repacked everything quickly.

Slinging the backpack over his shoulder and picking up the battered suitcase, Liko went outside to his rental car. He placed his suitcase in the back seat, threw his backpack onto the passenger seat, and hopped in. He had serious doubts whether the car would make the cross-country transit, but he adjusted the mirrors, started the car and began his adventure.

Less than seventy-five miles down the road, the temperature gauge crept into the red. Liko suspected the cooling system, a bad water pump, or a radiator problem. He knew he should pull over right away, but what good would that do? He was miles from the nearest town.

He rolled down his window and, reaching across the front seat, rolled down the passenger window, too. He turned off the air conditioning and turned on the heater, blasting warm air from the engine into the front seat. It felt brutal.

He noticed that the gas gauge read empty. *How could that be?* He realized that the rental company had not filled the tank, and shook his head. *Three days?* Liko's chest tightened.

A half-hour later he saw a service station in the distance. Colorful signs in Arabic greeted him. He parked near the entrance and went inside. He washed his hands in the restroom, which he discovered was clean and well supplied with toilet paper and hand towels. He then took a seat at the food service counter. The waiter seemed busy yet aloof. Liko pointed to a picture on the menu – everything was in Arabic – and ordered a mystery dish.

While waiting for his food, he looked around the dining area, trying to be discrete yet satisfying his curiosity. It was a small restaurant attached to the gas station. *Like a small American truck stop.* Two tables in the back were occupied. The U-shaped booths near the front door were empty. One was cluttered with dishes and Liko guessed that the customers had recently left. He did not see a tip on the table, but he recalled reading that you don't tip in the Republican Democracy. A busboy was working the table.

A saucer slipped from the busboy's grip and rattled on top of the empty table. A man sitting nearby in one of the booths said something, probably an obscenity, rose to his feet angrily, and grabbed the busboy by his hair. Liko had witnessed similar interactions many times: a bully and his victim.

The boy grasped at the hand gripping his hair and tried

to pull himself free. The man backhanded the boy across the face and he wailed in pain. The man responded by tightening his grip on the boy's hair and shaking him hard. The boy stopped struggling and went silent and limp. The man laughed and flung the small, lean body against the side of the table where his two companions sat, smiling. The boy's ribs struck the table and he fell to the floor. His two small hands went to his side and he began moaning.

The man laughed again and the two men sitting in the booth laughed with him. *Bullies*, Liko thought. Then the man grabbed the boy by the back of the neck, forcing him to his feet, and dragged him towards the back of the restaurant.

No way! Liko thought. He rose from his bar stool and followed.

Just then a woman stepped through the kitchen pass-through door and found herself between the bully and boy, and the restroom. She had a mop in her hand and was pushing a mop bucket. Glaring at the man gripping the boy, she yelled something in Arabic that Liko could not understand.

A condescending smile crept across the large man's face. The woman swung the mop at him and he pulled the boy in front of himself, grabbing his shoulders in a vice-like grip, using him as a shield.

The woman advanced again, wielding her mop high over her shoulder. Again she yelled at the man. He took a step backward, away from her, taking the boy with him. A moment later he thrust the boy into the woman and they continued shouting at each other.

The waiter appeared through the swinging kitchen door. For a moment he stood motionless, taking in the scene with his hands on his hips. Then he ushered the woman and boy into the kitchen. The woman left her mop and bucket and fled with the boy into the kitchen. The waiter stood facing the bully.

Liko calmly stepped up behind the bully. The bully glanced over his shoulder at him.

Liko fought the urge to jab him in the face, to strike him squarely on the nose. But the small boy was safe and Liko knew that he couldn't afford to attract attention. He said, "Excuse me," and bumped his shoulder into the bully, pushing him out of his way. He braced himself for the man to react angrily, to push back, but he didn't. Liko continued on to the restroom. *No battle wounds today*, he thought.

When Liko returned to his table the men were gone. He finished his meal, paid and left a generous tip. *They earned it*, he thought to himself. *And the food wasn't too bad, either.*

He returned to his old Renault and drove two hours without stopping. Liko had read that most of the country's population was in the towns and small villages in the countryside. On this stretch of highway, though, he saw no people, no communities.

As the sun streamed down on the Renault, Liko hoped the old car would make it. The dry air ruffled his black curls.

He passed a field cultivated in rows as far as the eye could see, row after row after row. It was the first fertile field he saw. He had no idea what the crop was. He knew, though, from his pre-trip research, that the country imported food for survival. During the civil war, Saudi Arabia had helped Lil't take control of the seaports, airports and border crossings, like the crossing he had entered by rental car. This had enabled Lil't to use food as a tool of war, starving his own population. Of course it had been the children who suffered the most from severe malnutrition. Some had died. The Saudis had used the same playbook in Yemen.

Liko's mind wandered back to the boy at the restaurant. What kind of life did he have? How much had he already suffered? What had he witnessed? He was younger than Hugo, yet old enough to have experienced ... what?

And then Liko saw a camel crossing sign. He scanned the horizon on both sides of the road but saw no camels and no herders. It was a goofy-looking sign, so he made a quick U-turn and drove back to the sign. He parked on the side of the road and took a picture.

Back in the car he texted the picture to Charla with the message: *Saw this sign but no camels.* He accelerated back onto the highway. *A most inhospitable country.*

Liko found himself daydreaming at the wheel. He wondered how United States policies had played out in the Republican Democracy. He didn't know what to believe when it came to news about foreign countries.

President Bush and his administration had lied about the weapons of mass destruction in Iraq. Bush had presented the weapons as an imminent threat to the United States, the Middle East, and even the rest of the world. What a horrible lie that had been! And Bush had lied about Iraqi links to al-Qaeda and the 9/11 attacks, too.

Had the United States also based their policy towards the Republican Democracy on lies? With time, everyone would know. *There should be laws to hold politicians accountable for their lies,* he thought, *especially when innocent people die.*

The Renault hit a pothole. The sudden jolt rapped Liko's head against the roof. "Shit!" he yelled. His luggage and backpack bounced, too. Liko had been racing down the road, so he slowed down and pulled the old car over to the side of the road. He got out and walked around to inspect the front driver's side wheel. The tire itself showed no bulging or loss of air.

The road, obviously, was in poor condition. "I shouldn't have been driving so fast," Liko said in a low voice, talking to himself. He kicked the tire, but not hard. There was no spare.

He continued down the road, driving slowly at first. The tire seemed to be okay, so he gradually increased his speed to fifty miles per hour.

Just as the sun began to set directly in front of him, homes began to appear along both sides of the road. Liko soon noticed a discrepancy. The homes on the driver's side were shanties. The passenger's side had much wealthier homes. The town he was approaching had a clear division of wealth, and the road conveniently divided the population into at least two classes: the poor and the extremely wealthy. How in the world did that work? What kept people from crossing the road? Just walking across the road? *I would.*

Liko opened Google maps. He typed in 'hotel' and followed the directions. As he pulled into the nearest hotel he noted that his iPhone had only a ten percent charge. His room had a clean bed and a good shower. Liko tried to plug in his phone but discovered that he had forgotten both the electrical current adapter and a universal adapter. He was tired, so he decided to deal with the phone in the morning. He called the front desk and was relieved that the clerk spoke English. Liko asked for a six o'clock wake-up call and immediately fell asleep.

When he awoke in the dark room, he looked at his iPhone to check the time but it was now completely dead.

He called the front desk. The new front desk clerk did not speak English, so Liko was unable to learn the time of day. He opened the curtains and was surprised that the sun had not only come up, but had climbed high in the sky. It was almost midday! The jet lag and long drive had caught up with him. He had received no wake up call.

From the window he could see the Renault. The tire on the driver's side was flat. He had guessed correctly: the wheel rim had dented when he hit the pothole. He surveyed the parking lot but saw nothing that would be a problem. He ate a high-energy protein bar.

The hotel was on the wealthy side of the highway, and Liko assumed a restaurant would be on that side, too. Locking the hotel door behind him, he took off down the side street. He was hungry for breakfast, hopefully toast, eggs and coffee. He expected that a restaurant would be within a few blocks of the hotel.

He wasn't sure how it happened, but he soon found himself lost and with no restaurant in sight. The blocks, obviously, had not been perfect rectangles. He continued to walk, hoping that the hotel would suddenly reappear. He had his phone in his pocket, but it was dead so he had no access to GPS. He stopped a man and asked directions back to the hotel, but the man did not speak English and could not help him.

He had always thought it would be fun to be lost, but he realized that it wasn't. Being lost felt strange, beyond just baffling. He was on a tight schedule and did not have time to spare. He had only two days left on his transit visa, he was hungry, and he had wasted the last hour roaming an unfamiliar town.

A man approached him and for a moment, a fleeting

moment, Liko thought he would get directions. In a gruff voice the man told Liko: "Hayya alas salah."

"What?" Liko asked. "Do you speak English?"

The man repeated, growing anxious: "Hayya alas salah."

Liko shrugged his shoulders.

The man pointed down the street in the direction of a small mosque.

Liko had no interest in visiting the mosque or any other religious building. He'd had his fill of churches and cathedrals while wandering through Europe, and he had zero interest in mosques.

I'm not a believer, he thought. *It's forbidden for me to enter.* "No," he told the insistent man. He pointed a finger at his own chest and said, "I am an atheist."

The man took hold of Liko's elbow and began guiding him down the street towards the mosque. Liko pulled himself free. He turned and faced the men squarely. "I am not interested." The tone of his voice was emphatic. He deliberately walked in a direction that took him away from the mosque.

He came upon three children sitting quietly on a door stoop. They looked pale and thin. They were quiet. *Cowed,* Liko thought. *That's how they look, cowed.* There was something wrong with them. It baffled him; he couldn't quite place it, yet he found it troubling. Their faces were not childlike. He looked away to avoid eye contact. He did not want to see what he was seeing.

When he came to the next group of children, he forced himself to look, because they were children. As he looked at them, he saw something in their eyes. A loneliness. A despair. And something else he could not place.

He walked on, physically lost and confused, hoping he wasn't walking in circles.

He came upon another child. For a moment Liko thought the young boy looked familiar, but that was impossible. The young boy looked up. His eyes were the eyes of an old man filled with a quiet suffering. Liko had never seen such an expression on a child's face before.

He looked at his surroundings. The poverty on the street was disquieting. The neighborhood now felt scary. He felt exposed, vulnerable, unsafe.

Life in the trailer park was a holiday compared to this neighborhood. These kids were trapped in a hopeless situation. Their poverty and their listlessness unnerved him.

What is their day-to-day life like? Where are their parents? Are they dead? What memories will these kids have when they grow up? Where do their loyalties lie?

He continued walking. He heard music, so he headed in that direction. The music sounded grating and loud; he didn't like it, yet he followed it. He wondered how often people followed and listened to music they didn't enjoy.

He was surprised when the music led him to a café. As he walked to the entrance he could hear the music better, and he realized that it wasn't a live band. It was just a recording.

The music was similar to what he had heard in the restaurant the night before. The lyrics were in Arabic or some Middle Eastern language that he did not know. It was the music of past sufferings, he thought. Lost life, lost beauty, and lost hope. It was a music for a lost people, a people without a present or a future. Listening to such melancholy music would numb anyone's soul with hopelessness. Although Liko was unaware of it, it was composed and played by Jizan. His violin sounded both sad and violent.

To his dismay, he discovered that the café was next to his hotel, on the opposite side from where he had started his walk. Had he gone left instead of right, he would have passed the café earlier in the day when he first started his search.

Instead of the eggs and coffee he'd hoped for, he ordered a local dish and wolfed it down quickly with a bottle of cold, fizzy water.

It was now mid-afternoon. Liko heard the call to prayer and suddenly understood what the old man in the neighborhood was doing when he admonished him in Arabic, grabbed him by the elbow, and ushered him towards the mosque. Liko went directly from the café into his hotel room and shut the door. He wanted no more confrontations with overbearing believers.

After what he hoped was a reasonable period of time for prayers, Liko left his hotel room and returned to the front desk, hoping to get assistance to report his damaged Renault. Fortunately, there had been a shift change and the hotel clerk spoke English. Liko explained that he didn't have a spare tire. The clerk said he would arrange for the Renault to be towed to the nearest rental car service, wherever that was. Liko smiled, happy that he wouldn't be receiving the bill—Zahi's lawyer would.

The hotel clerk hooked Liko up with another guest who was traveling in his direction, an elderly man with a dark blue turban and long white beard. He seemed friendly, but he knew no English.

"Shukraan jazilaan," Liko said, thanking the driver when they reached the capital.

30

Police Station

"I am here to claim a body," Liko said.

The policeman behind the desk stared up at him with a mix of surprise and suspicion. Liko imagined that his own expression was one of dismay and unrelieved sunburn. Riding in the truck with the Arab, with the passenger window open and the sun blaring, had ended with a bad sunburn. His arm and hand were as red as a lobster claw, and so was half his face. *I must look rather frightening.*

The policeman pushed his chair back from his desk and stood up. He was heavyset and wearing a black uniform. As he walked around his desk, Liko had two thoughts: Black is a stupid color for a uniform in a hot, desert environment, and what will happen if I have to defend myself and I hit this guy?

The policeman stepped into Liko's personal body space. His breath was horrible, pungent with some spice Liko was unfamiliar with. "Your identification?" the policeman asked.

"I am an American," Liko responded, trying to take a step back but discovering that another man stood in his way. "I am here to identify the body of Zahi ibn Haarun ibn Ajam Ab al-Naqad."

"Passport?"

Liko pulled his shirt tail out of his jeans, reached into the money belt around his waist, and took out his passport.

The policeman held out his hand and Liko handed him the passport reluctantly.

After comparing the passport photo to Liko, he asked, "Your name?"

"Liko Koholua. I am an American citizen."

"Spell your last name?"

"K-O-H-O-L-U-A."

"Visa?"

Liko searched through the papers in his money belt, found his transit visa, and gave it to the policeman.

"I'm from Hawaii, actually," Liko said. "I'm actually Hawaiian." He hoped that being Hawaiian would break the ice. When people heard that he was from Hawaii it sometimes brought a smile to their faces. He also knew that foreigners liked Canadians. No one seemed to like Americans.

The policeman didn't smile. Instead, he opened and studied the transit visa.

As Liko waited, his ear caught the music playing in the waiting area. It sounded like the same melancholy music he had been hearing everywhere he went. He imagined that the words were heart-wrenching. He had expected to see pictures of President Lil't everywhere. Instead, he heard the distinctively raw, sad, and mournful music. No wonder all the people in the country seemed depressed.

The police closed the visa, stepped back a pace and, with a wave of his hand, ushered Liko through a door. The long hall had several turns and what seemed like one or two switchbacks. By the time they arrived at a small meeting room, Liko felt like he had passed through a maze. He listened but could no longer hear the music. There would be no easy way out, he thought.

The policeman pointed to a hard wooden chair with a straight back. Liko sat, and the policeman abruptly left the room without saying anything, closing the door behind him, and taking Liko's passport and visa with him. Liko had no doubt that the door was locked.

He looked around him. One wall was glass. The other three walls were painted beige with nothing on them. A small table separated him from another wooden chair. A yellow-green light fell from the incandescent lights overhead. *Just like the movies*, he thought.

Time passed slowly and Liko wasn't sure if he waited for one hour, or two hours, or longer. With each passing hour he missed his iPhone more and more.

A policeman returned and without introductions started asking him questions. First he verified the information in Liko's passport. Then he began a new line of interrogation that Liko considered personal, firing question after question about Liko's family, friends, girlfriends, places of employment, coworkers, and on and on. Liko answered every question without hesitation.

The policeman then began asking questions about Zahi. What was their relationship? Where had Zahi worked? What were the names of his coworkers? Why had Zahi come to the Republican Democracy?

Liko answered each question as best he could, and truthfully. When he didn't know the answer he said honestly, "I don't know."

Who sent Liko to identify the body? Why? Where would the body be sent? Why? What would happen to the body? Why?

Liko found himself answering "I don't know" again and again.

"Why not?" the policeman asked.

"Because I just don't know," Liko answered. "You need to ask Zahi's lawyer."

The policeman did not yield. The barrage of questions continued.

Liko realized that the police were building a profile on him, so he started answering: "His lawyer would know. You should ask his lawyer."

"This is not the United States," the policeman finally said.

I know that, you asshole.

The policeman left.

Eventually another policeman in a black uniform entered. He handed Liko a clipboard and pen.

"Fill out these forms and then we will take you to see the body." The policeman left, leaving Liko to fill out the forms as best he could.

Time passed slowly.

The policeman returned and Liko gave him the completed forms. He told Liko to come back tomorrow.

"That doesn't work for me," Liko said.

The policeman was surprised at his response.

"I don't have enough time on my transit visa," Liko explained.

The policeman left the room but returned quickly. He

handed Liko a piece of paper with the words 'Swigert Prison' and an address.

"I don't want to go to some prison," Liko objected. "I want to identify Mr. Haarun's body so he can be shipped back home." Shipped back home didn't sound right.

"His body is in the morgue at Swigert Prison."

"I see," Liko said.

His passport and visa were returned and then he was led back through the maze and escorted to the front door and through security. Liko exited and did not look back.

"He died from an acute coronary event," the medical examiner told Liko. "A sudden, unexpected death."

A white sheet had been pulled off Zahi's body and lay ruffled at his feet. Liko stared down at Zahi's naked body. *Where is your tweed coat?* Liko wondered. *You should be cremated wearing it.*

Zahi's exposed legs were gray as stone. His hands were closed into fists on either side of his body. His face was pale, cold and expressionless. The face did not look like Zahi. It didn't show his personality. *Where is the confidence?* Liko wondered. *The mental quickness?*

Liko saw no marks on the body. It appeared to have been a peaceful death.

He wished his iPhone still worked so he could take a picture for Zahi's lawyer, to prove that he had been here, that he had seen the body, and that he had identified Zahi.

He reached and touched the sheet. It was cotton and rough. He touched Zahi's forearm. Yes, he was dead. Definitely Zahi, and definitely dead.

31

Relatives

Zahi's lawyer had provided Liko the names and contact information of Zahi's relatives, including cell phone numbers and home addresses. The lawyer had found them, easily, so why hadn't Zahi contacted them?

Liko had charged his iPhone overnight, having found a charger adapter with USB cable in a gift shop near his hotel. He also purchased a universal electric plug adapter, so he could use the charger with the unusual Middle Eastern socket types common in the Republican Democracy. It seemed complicated and an unnecessary pain in the ass. Why couldn't nations agree on something as fundamental as how to use electricity?

He only had one day left on his transit visa, so after finalizing the arrangements for Zahi's body to be shipped back to the United States, he hired a taxi driver for the day. Using Google Maps, he guided the driver to the home of one of Zahi's uncles, a sheik. Liko suspected that the taxi driver was overcharging him, but he wasn't too worried because he intended to bill Zahi's estate.

The sheik's home was a modest two-story dwelling, yet there was more than one entrance and Liko was unsure where to knock. He stood facing the adobe building, confused.

The amused taxi driver showed Liko the male-only entrance. He then returned to his taxi, lay down in the front seat, and began a nap. It had been a long drive and he had dodged a lot of potholes. Liko was tired too, and rotated his head side to side and in a circular motion. His shoulders were still tight as he knocked.

A young boy wearing flip-flops greeted Liko with a broad and happy smile, and led him down a long corridor that separated rooms on one side of the corridor from a courtyard full of fruit trees. The doors to the rooms were open and Liko glanced in, seeing high ceilings and exterior walls filled with windows of various shapes and designs—rectangular, circular, and even triangular—all grouped in interesting architectural patterns. A breeze entered through the windows and blew across the corridor to the courtyard, rustling the fronds of the palms. The young boy ushered him into one of the rooms and then disappeared.

Liko looked around the large room. In one corner was a bronze hookah on a knee-high stand surrounded by oversized chairs filled with soft-looking cushions. The bulbous body of a silver dallah with a narrow waist, spire-shaped lid, and a long spout rested on a countertop stove next to demitasse cups. *A smoking lounge*, Liko concluded.

The young boy reappeared, followed closely by a middle-aged man perhaps Zahi's age. He was short, maybe five feet tall.

"Sheik Mansour?" Liko asked. "I am Liko Koholua. I'm here on behalf of your nephew, Zahi Haarun, and his lawyer." As an afterthought Liko said, "I hope you speak English." He then added in a very low and contrite voice, "I did not think to bring a translator."

"Yes, I speak English," the man said. "Welcome. Please have a seat and make yourself at home."

"Thank you." Liko sat in the nearest chair.

"How do you know Zahi?" the man said, dropping into a chair near Liko.

"He is an acquaintance," Liko said.

The man's expression showed his puzzlement, and Liko realized that the word acquaintance was a poor choice. "I met him several times. I am sorry for your loss."

"Why are you here?"

"To take his body back to the United States," Liko answered. "In his will he requested that his body be cremated and his ashes scattered."

"Scattered? Scattered where?"

"I don't know," Liko said. "It may specify that in his will."

The man gave Liko a look as if he thought Liko was daft.

A chair on the far side of the room swiveled around and Liko found himself staring at an older man with a long-flowing white beard that covered his broad chest. He was bald and the top of his head reflected the ceiling light.

He said, "Cremation is alien to our traditions, but in Zahi's case, it will be fine."

"I apologize," Liko said, "but I did not see you sitting there. You are?"

"Sheik Mansour," the man said.

Liko turned quickly and looked at the first man.

"I am his son," the man said, bowing his head slightly to show that he had meant no disrespect.

"I see," Liko said, turning his attention to the sheik. He placed his hand on his heart and gave a slight bow. He had read in his travel guide that this was a way to show respect.

The sheik was holding a long piece of wood, perhaps a meter long. His fat fingers covered two or more holes in the far end. Liko guessed it was a flute or a similar instrument.

"My Uncle Keahi played a flute," Liko said, sharing the first thing that came into his mind. "A traditional Hawaiian flute. It was much smaller, though."

The sheik sat quietly in his chair and stared across the room at Liko.

"He caught me playing it once. Of course I wasn't playing it correctly." Liko paused and then added, "It was a nose flute."

The sheik smiled. His son, who was still sitting beside Liko, laughed.

"My uncle was a great Hawaiian chanter and a hula dancer. He loved to perform."

"So does my father," the younger man said. "He has his camel dances."

"Dancing camels?" Liko asked. "Really?" Thinking of Charla he added, "I have a friend who would love that!"

The young man laughed again. The laugh was a little longer, a little more relaxed. The sheik continued to smile.

"I have never seen a camel dance," Liko said, smiling amiably.

Sheik Mansour stood up. He was shorter than Liko expected, perhaps five feet, if that tall. And he was stout, overweight, broad-chested. He stepped to a nearby bookcase and set the flute on a mid-level shelf. He then reached deeper into the shelf and picked up a sword.

Damn! Liko thought. *I hope I didn't insult him.*

The scimitar was three feet long, the same length as the flute. The carbon steel shone as brightly as the sheik's bald and oiled head.

"I play the flute in our camel dances," the sheik said. He brandished the sword, demonstrating his skill. "But my passion is the sword dance."

"You are good." Liko whistled a high note. "Are you good with knives, too?"

The sheik stopped his sword demonstration and squared his body with Liko. Their eyes locked and they stared at each other across ten feet of floor space for several breaths, saying nothing, neither moving. The sheik returned the sword to its place behind the flute. Turning again to face Liko he said, "Let's have some refreshments."

As soon as the sheik said this, the young boy who had greeted Liko at the front door reappeared. He set coffee to boil and then disappeared again.

"Your President Trump, he danced the Ardah in Saudi Arabia?" the son ventured.

"Yes, he *tried* to dance," Liko winced, "but it was an embarrassment, no?" Liko recalled a YouTube video showing Trump bobbing and swaying while strangers surrounded him waving real Arabian swords. *What an idiot,* Liko thought. *The Secret Service must have shit their pants.*

The son smiled. Perhaps he considered Trump's performance an international embarrassment, too.

Liko leaned back in the chair. He discovered that the cushion was nicely padded and gave support to his lower back. *Very comfortable,* he thought. He smelled something delightful, fragrant, and he guessed that the cushions had been perfumed.

Suddenly remembering the reason for his visit, Liko raised himself off the comfortable cushions and moved forward to the front edge of the chair.

"I am looking for Hugo," he said.

Liko caught the surprise in both men's faces.

"I understand that he was here recently," Liko added. "I understand that he was injured and that he required your help?"

The son shifted his feet and then glanced at his father, deferring the question to him.

"That is what Zahi's lawyer told me," Liko said. "He said that Hugo was hurt, that he was here, and that you were helping him." *Am I wrong?* Liko wondered. He waited for their answer.

The young boy returned and checked the coffee. He turned up the flame beneath the dallah and set a silver spoon in a bowl of sugar.

"I know Hugo very well. We shared an apartment together in the United States."

Liko described Hugo's need to paint. All the while, he kept his eyes on the sheik. He cupped the engraved, silver-topped head of the cane in his right hand, working his hand and cane like a mortar and pestle. Liko recognized it as a formidable weapon in the hands of a man who knew how to handle a sword.

Liko described his amazement when he saw Hugo's paintings. He explained to the sheik and his son about displaying Hugo's art along the fence in Maritauqua Park, and the islanders' anger and protests. Liko swallowed hard and locked eyes with Sheik Mansour. "Hugo is the greatest painter I have ever seen. His works, every one of them, are masterpieces.

"I am sorry that I left him alone," Liko continued. "I left the island for a while, and when I returned he had left. I don't know for sure how he got into the Republican Democracy, but I have reason to believe that he was abducted and forcibly brought here against his will.

"I am here to find him," Liko added. "And to help him."

"Rampal," Sheik Mansour called to the young boy. He gestured with his right hand, palm down, his fingers summoning toward his barrel chest.

The young boy pranced to the sheik and bowed his head.

"Bring us some bint al sahn." The sheik patted the young boy on the head. "Hurry."

The sheik then turned to Liko and said, "I love honey cakes."

"With melted butter," his son added. "And warm honey."

"Have you had our honey cakes?" the sheik asked Liko.

"No," Liko said. "I have heard they are delicious."

"They are one of the few luxuries we still have," the sheik said.

"Much of our culture and our way of life has been destroyed," the son explained for his father.

Liko bowed his head and frowned sincerely. "Your people were targeted, no?" He thought about the devastation he had seen while riding in the taxi through the countryside. "And not just the roads and bridges, but the hospitals and the schools and their homes." He waited a moment and then added, "Sir, I saw it on my ride from the capital to your home."

Once again, the sheik's visage filled with genuine

surprise. And then Liko realized that he had once again made a major faux pas. In the Middle East, talking politics while you entertain your guests is considered rude. It isn't done. Liko now recalled reading that in the travel guide. *Damn!* But he wanted to know what had happened, and he wanted to hear from someone with first-hand experience. Someone who had lived through it. A witness, like Hugo. If these men would talk to him, perhaps he would better understand what had happened to Hugo, too.

"I apologize," Liko said. "I should not have brought up politics. Back home we have a saying: Never talk drugs, religion, sex or politics. So, my bad."

"My nephew Hugo was recently here," the sheik said, breaking his silence on the topic. "One hand and three fingers were cut off. I helped him the best that I could. I was able to get him antibiotics. When his fever broke and thick scabs had formed, he left. He told no one where he was going."

"I see," Liko said. And then in a weak voice, he added, "He draws and paints with his left hand." He looked at the son.

"It was his left hand."

"What happened?"

"We are not sure," the son answered. "During his fever he mumbled about being tortured, and he asked for Zahi. When his fever broke, he shared nothing further with us."

"I have only one day left and then I must cross the border. I would like to find him before I leave."

The sheik nodded. "I am sorry, but he left as he arrived, telling no one."

Liko nodded. "Do you have any idea where I might begin to search?" He pulled himself out of the chair and stood up. He felt disoriented, unsure why he stood up or where he was going. "I only have 24 hours left," he reiterated.

Suddenly he felt a hand on his shoulder. The sheik's son guided him back into his chair. Liko collapsed into the comfortable, oversized cushions. He half-sat and half-lay there, staring at the sheik yet not seeing him. Everything in the room was suddenly blurry and Liko realized that his eyes had filled with tears. He hung his head and sobbed. The tears fell from his eyes onto his chest and into his lap. He gripped the rattan armrests of the big chair to steady himself.

"You must not leave before you try the cakes," the sheik said.

Liko looked up at him, wiped his eyes on his right sleeve, and tried to smile.

Liko didn't remember eating the cakes, although there was an aftertaste of something sweet and rich. He emptied several demitasse cups of coffee, too. He appreciated the warmth.

"Khat," the son said. "Have you ever tried khat?"

"No," Liko answered.

The sheik rose from his chair and crossed the room to where Liko sat. Liko quickly got to his feet.

"I must leave you in the company of my son," the sheik said. "I hope that the rest of your journey will be safe."

The sheik offered Liko his hand. Liko grasped his tanned hand. It felt aged and dry, yet powerful.

The sheik hugged Liko affectionately, kissing him on both cheeks. "You may stay here for the night if you choose."

"Thank you," Liko said, his voice reflected his appreciation.

The sheik left the room and the son then guided Liko to

another set of chairs in a different area of the room. They sat at right angles to each other, a few feet apart. They could look at each other and talk easily.

"Where do I start?" the son asked.

At that very moment, the young boy, Rampal, returned with a large bowl of red khat leaves and a bowl of freshly fried peanuts. He set both bowls on the small table between the chairs.

The son tasted the peanuts and Liko also tried them. They were warm and lightly salted.

Liko turned to Rampal, "A glass of water please."

Rampal nodded and disappeared.

The sheik's son took a handful of leaves into his lap. "Khat," he said. He stripped several leaves off a stem and placed them in his mouth. He began to chew. "Like this." He chewed until the leaves were mashed and soft. "Make a ball of it and tuck it into your cheek. Like this." He made a face like a stuffed hamster. "But don't swallow!"

Liko stuffed a half-dozen leaves into his mouth and chewed. "It's awful," he said. He had to fight the urge to spit out the khat.

After the ball sat in his cheek for a moment, his salivary glands overflowed and he began to drool. He swallowed, involuntarily. "Disgusting," he said, still drooling. "It tastes awful." He wiped his mouth on his sleeve.

"Khat is an acquired taste," the son said.

Liko tried again. This time he fought the urge to swallow and the ball sat there, in his cheek, slowly giving him a mild buzz, like watered-down beer. It was a good buzz and he was tired and stressed and it felt energizing. Stimulated and buzzed at the same time. "Nice," he said, smiling.

The sheik's son returned his smile. "So," he said, "back to the story of my country."

He hesitated a moment, collecting his thoughts, and said, "But first let me tell you something about myself. I have a degree from Birkbeck, University of London. I am, perhaps, worldlier than many in my country." He smiled at Liko, respectfully. "I have a more... what would you say... cosmopolitan perspective?"

Liko nodded his understanding. His own trip to Europe had been an eye-opener. And his one semester in college in Hawaii had broadened his perspective, too. He had grown up in a trailer park outside Las Vegas.

"The story of our country begins with the House of Mustabid, our ruling royal family, the descendants of Muhammad bin Mustabid, the founder of the Republican Emirates, who – back in his day – seized power and declared himself King."

"I thought we were not allowed to talk politics," Liko said, half-smiling, half-teasing.

"But have you not already broken that rule, Mr. Koholua?"

"Yes," Liko answered. "I have indeed."

The sheik's son smiled at Liko. "Imagine someone declaring themselves a king or a queen. So medieval, yes? Yet look at Oman, Qatar, United Arab Emirates, Bahrain, Kuwait, and Saudi Arabia—all have monarchies."

"And Morocco?"

"Morocco is a constitutional monarchy. So is Jordan."

"Like Britain?'"

"Similar," the son said. "Yet different."

"Where was I?" he thought for a moment. "Oh yes. The kingdom was known as the Republican Emirates because we had an Allegiance Council made up of royal family members. King Mustabid appointed the cabinet." He chuckled. "Of course, the members of the cabinet were all members of the royal family. They did well for several hundred years. Sadly, however, the royals stole everything. But what royals don't?"

"And then the revolution?" Liko asked.

"Yes," the sheik's son said. "A spontaneous uprising."

"The Arab Spring?"

"Yes," the son said. "Something the royals had feared. Historically, of course, it always happens, sooner or later. Nevertheless, the uprising was a surprise. No one saw it coming. It was like the Arab attack on Israel in '73. Who predicted that? Or the Al-Qaeda attacks on your country?

"Anyway, the House of Mustabid was under siege due to a popular uprising. And then the Unites States interceded. They established a Transitional National Committee, like the one they set up in Libya to overthrow Gaddafi. They insisted that well-connected and powerful men, those who had supported the interests of the United States, be on the committee. And generals of course—one has to control the military."

"So what went wrong?"

"Lil't." The son sneered. "He became a member of the committee."

"Was he elected?"

"No, no. No one on the committee was elected. I guess the United States just looked the other way. My cousin Zahi, he personally knew one of the committee members—the head of the Republican Emirates' Economic Development Board?"

"And what happened?"

"The United States thought they had everything under

control. They thought our king would step aside. Instead, he attacked his own people."

"Like Assad did?"

"Yes. Despots seldom leave peacefully. The US went to the United Nations Security Council. They imposed a no-fly zone, a resolution supposedly to protect the civilians from our king's wrath, but... in the end, NATO worked for the United States and the rebels who opposed the king."

"How do you know that?"

"NATO began an air strike campaign. They were brutal. The king requested a cease fire. NATO and the United States refused."

"And so what happened?"

"The king was taken prisoner and murdered."

"Like Gaddafi?"

"Yes, although our king was not sodomized."

Liko cleared his throat.

"Just beheaded, as is traditional."

"And Lil't took advantage of the confusion to set himself up as the new ruler?"

"Yes! He seized power. He slaughtered the other members of the TNC. Had them beheaded, too."

"And the US? What did the US do?"

"Lil't is a master manipulator. He pledged his support to the United States. Why? Because the US has a major Navy base on our coast. Lil't used the base as leverage, his bargaining chip, so to speak. He agreed to sign an agreement giving the US unconditional rights to the port for the next 50 years. In return, the US forgave him all his past ... and future transgressions."

"Unbelievable," Liko said.

"Then he ran for president as the only candidate, but that didn't matter because the US still supported him."

"I am feeling the khat," Liko said.

"This is shami," the son said. "Grown in Yemen. It is the best on the market."

"Nice buzz," Liko added. "So no one opposed Lil't?"

"There were protests everywhere!" the son said, waving his arms in the air. "But Lil't had given his relatives positions in the military, so the military opposed the people. Rival ethnic groups and clans and tribes were not given a voice. They were... eliminated."

"And all this time the United States continued to support Lil't?"

"Of course. During the student unrest, the US sent in special Marine forces to protect the US embassy. And then we had a three-month state of emergency. In those three months, Lil't crushed the rebellion. First the students were slaughtered. Tanks rolled into the capital. Helicopters fired into our neighborhoods. This neighborhood, too! Right here! In this neighborhood! Genocide would have happened earlier if the northern tribes had not swept down to protect us."

"And that's when the civil war started?" Liko asked.

"Yes," the son said. "The northern tribes occupied the capital." He smiled, a half-smile. "They even captured Lil't and placed him under house arrest!"

"So why wasn't that the end of it, the end of Lil't and his forces?" Liko asked.

"He did resign. He even begged and received mercy. And then, when our guard was down, he dressed up like a woman in a full black niqab and escaped out the back door of his palace. He fled to one of our coastal cities, and then he fled to Saudi Arabia."

"So the civil war failed?"

"Horribly."

"But didn't the US then help?"

The son guffawed. "Remember how the US supported Saudi Arabia and the UAE in their war in Yemen? Well, they repeated the same thing here in the Republican Democracy." He sat straight up in his chair. "And no one in the US gave a damn, then or now!"

"How so?"

"The United States supplied warplanes, your Pentagon provided military surveillance, Americans sold Lil't cluster bombs, which are banned under international law, and the United States Air Force assisted him with in-flight aerial refueling, all so Lil't could consolidate his power. And that is how the hospitals and homes and schools and water treatment plants and sewage treatment plants and ports and airport runways – all were destroyed."

They chewed quietly for a while, each lost in his own stimulated, mildly intoxicated thoughts.

"Did you see him?" Liko asked. "Hugo?"

"Yes," the son answered. "I did."

"How was he?"

"His hands are destroyed."

"So he will never paint again?"Liko asked.

"No," the son said. "I am afraid he will never paint again."

"Where can I find him?"

"I have no idea," the son said. "As my father said, he left just as he arrived, without telling anyone."

"Do you have any idea where he went?"

"No, I do not."

"He's a US citizen," Liko said. "I didn't know if you knew that."

"I know very little about Hugo. He traveled with his father and was seldom here."

"I have friends trying to locate his birth certificate."

The son chewed on the khat and then said, "Hugo told us an incredible story."

"Really?" Liko asked. "Please tell me?"

"He said that he had been abducted from a mansion on an island in your country, the United States. Of course, that was too incredible to believe. He said that he was flown to a secret prison here in the Republican Democracy."

"A secret prison," Liko asked. "A 'black site?' Like Abu Ghraib in Iraq?"

"Swigert Prison."

"No," Liko said. "That can't be!"

"Why not?"

"That is where I saw Zahi. Where I identified his body. In the morgue next to Swigert Prison."

Liko remembered seeing President George W. Bush and Vice President Dick Cheney on television boasting about secret prisons, some operated by the CIA. Prisoners were held and interrogated and tortured – waterboarded, and worse. "Our President Bush promoted torture," Liko added. "Worldwide."

"Don't be surprised," the son said. "In the Middle East, torture, death and disappearance are common." He smiled, sadly. "All kings and despots have their dungeons, no?"

"But America should not be like that," Liko said. "It saddens me."

"You are not responsible for Bush and Trump," the son said. "I am not responsible for MSB or Lil't."

"But what I don't understand is how Hugo got from the United States to here," the son said, continuing his thoughts. "Surely your government would not allow someone to be abducted from the United States and taken to a prison in a foreign country. Would they?"

I don't know, Liko thought. *I really don't know.*

"In the Middle East it is not uncommon. Someone disappears and they are never seen again." The son looked at Liko with sadness on his face. "Egypt, Qatar, Saudi Arabia, Syria, Yemen, and the Republican Democracy—all have interrogated prisoners. And sometimes on behalf of the US. The UAE has prisons in Yemen, too. Syria has tortured thousands to death, recently."

He added, "You are fortunate that they did not take you into custody, or worse."

"They held me at the police station and questioned me for hours."

"Did you see evidence of torture? Marks on Zahi's body?"

"None," Liko answered.

A long silence passed between them. And then Liko added, "I can ask that his body be examined once it is returned to the United States."

The son nodded his concurrence.

They both sat quietly for a minute.

"Nice buzz," Liko said, taking another stem clustered with leaves. He was enjoying the stimulated conversation.

"Why didn't you return my calls about Zahi?" Liko asked.

"It is too dangerous," the son answered. "All our social media—emails, Facebook, Twitter, and even our mobile phones—are monitored. No communication is safe." His eyes smiled. "Unless you are my guest and enjoying my khat."

They both laughed together.

"I know very little about Hugo. He spent most of his

childhood with his father, traveling. He was his father's favorite. Zahi, though, he stayed here. He grew up in his grandfather's villa. Ironically, he was his grandfather's favorite. I knew Zahi well."

"What was he like?"

"A self-centered jerk."

"Really?"

"He never cared about his family, only himself. He moved to London. After that he had nothing to do with us, or our children. My son had leukemia, requiring intensive treatment. I doubt that Zahi even knew about it. He was too busy in his own world. When my children graduated or started a business or got married, he sent no gift, no congratulations, not even a card. And he did not help us during the civil war or the genocide. He probably never knew how upset his mother and his brothers and his sisters and uncles and aunts were with him. His grandfather was deeply disappointed. No one has forgiven him, and now they never will."

Surprised at what he was hearing, Liko sat silently in the chair.

"The right thing can be hard and dangerous," the son continued, "but Zahi took the easy way. He turned his back on family and friends."

"That surprises me," Liko said.

"Our family is descended from devout, pious Muslims," the son volunteered. "Our grandfather was very religious, too.

"When he was young, Zahi was close to him, probably because Grandfather took an early interest in him and because his father was gone most of the time. Zahi became very attached to his grandfather. He would sit on his lap and listen to his stories, always religious stories. They were very close. But then things changed, as things often do.

"Grandfather hired a mullah to teach him. At first the lessons went well. Zahi had a remarkable memory. He surprised everyone by memorizing long surahs. That pleased Grandfather. He must have thought he could mold Zahi into the next imam. It's sad, now, when I think of it."

"What happened?" Liko asked.

"Grandfather enrolled him in a state-run Islamic elementary school. He excelled. Zahi was amazing. He learned whole parts of the Quran. But then something happened. When Zahi was eleven he returned home sullen and moody. He refused to return to school.

"Grandfather was furious. You see, Zahi's father had also been rebellious. He also had a strong spirit. He had left home and become a health worker with the World Health Organization. I believe that our grandfather was determined that Zahi would obey."

"Christian zealots," Liko said, "especially fundamentalists, are just as rigid, just as dogmatic."

"Grandfather disciplined him during his summer break. By autumn, Zahi's spirit had been broken. He returned to school, passed his classes, and graduated, but he had changed."

"How did he change?"

"I think that he waited for an opportunity to run away."

"And did he?"

"Yes, but not right away. When Zahi was older, our grandfather used his influence and connections to get him accepted into the university. Of course, everyone expected him to continue his religious studies, to become a Muslim scholar, to become a great imam. But he was still discontent, unhappy.

"He started school but then he suddenly dropped out and ran away for a week. He moved to London, enrolled in the university there, and studied mathematics and then economics. His wife Saba moved with him."

It was getting late and Liko decided it was time to leave. The son looked up Saba's sister's address and wrote it on a piece of paper for him, should he need it. The son also gifted Liko a plastic bag of khat. The leaves had been ground to make them easier to chew. "I like it that way when I travel," the son said.

"Thank you for your hospitality. And please thank your father, Sheik Mansour, for his hospitality, too."

The son hesitated. He said, "It would be much safer if my nephew drove you. Having an escort will be to your advantage in case you are stopped, or something happens along the way."

Liko considered his offer. He was inclined to continue on his journey using the taxi driver. However, being escorted by someone who lived in the area and whose family had connections in the community was something that he could not turn down.

"Spend the night," the sheik's son said. "I will make the arrangements with my nephew." He looked at Liko for his response.

"That is a very kind offer," Liko said. "I accept. If you are ever in the United States, I hope that you will contact me."

They smiled and shook hands and hugged.

Liko paid and then dismissed the taxi driver, and Rampal showed Liko to his room for the night.

Liko was feeling great.

32

Birth Certificate

In the middle of the night, Liko's iPhone beeped. The small bright screen flashed a message from Kwon. Liko sat up in the guest bed, typed in his password and opened the email.

Liko,

I obtained a copy of Hugo Ibnhaarun's birth certificate. Yes, that is the way Hugo's last name is spelled on his certificate: Hugo Ibnhaarun. Is it any surprise that it was lost?

Attached is an original certified copy issued by the Hawaii Department of Health's Vital Statistics Office.

Based on the information that you previously provided to me, Hugo has dual citizenship in the Republican Democracy and the United States.

In addition to the birth certificate, I am also attaching evidence of Hugo's mother's presence in the United States at the time of his birth. It is a hospital record of her stay at Kaiser Permanente on Oahu when she gave birth to Hugo.

It is my understanding that Hugo will need both documents to obtain a US passport: 1) his birth certificate and, 2) evidence of his mother's presence in the US at the time of his birth.

Please let me know if I can be of further assistance.

I hope you are doing well. Next time you pass through Hawaii please call. I would like to 'talk story.'

Very respectfully,

Kwon

Liko was happy for Hugo, but he also felt a lump in his throat. He felt guilty for his procrastination, and the grief that he could have prevented. Hugo would not have gone to see the ambassador if he had his birth certificate, and he would not have been abducted. He promised himself, *Next time I will be more responsible.*

He swung his feet over the edge of the comfortable bed and stood up. For a moment he felt dizzy and he felt his heart rate increase. The lightheadedness surprised him because he never felt wobbly after sitting or lying down.

He sighed and surveyed the room. The chair in the corner appeared sturdy, so he used it to do twenty triceps dips and a set of Bulgarian split squats. He shadow-boxed around the room until he broke a sweat, and then he shaved and took a long, hot shower. He combed his thick black hair, brushed his teeth without swallowing the local water, and dressed.

After breakfast, Liko called Saba's sister and told her about the birth certificate. Sheik Mansour's son had provided her contact information. He emailed her a copy of the documents, just in case Hugo showed up at her home.

"What good will this do him now?" the sheik's nephew asked. "He has no hands."

Well fuck you! Liko wanted to say, but he controlled himself. He was angry, but not at the boy driving the car. He was angry at himself. He had failed Hugo.

"I want you to drop me off at the US embassy," Liko said.

The nephew's eyes widened. "Why?"

"Two reasons," Liko said. "First, my visa expired and I need their help. Second, I want to give them Hugo's birth certificate in case he needs it." Liko hoped that if Hugo didn't show up at Saba's sister's home, then he would show up at the embassy. He knew it was not likely, but it was the only idea he had.

But then he wondered, *Should I inform the police, too?*

He set his cup of coffee in the drink holder of the passenger seat. "What if the police pick up Hugo again?" He waited but the sheik's nephew had no reply. "Wouldn't it be best if they knew he was a US citizen?"

But how can I drop off the birth certificate without tipping them off about my expired visa? They demanded to see it the last time I was there.

He placed his hand over the top of the coffee and felt its warmth. He told the nephew, "Drop me off at the police station. It's only a few blocks from the embassy. I'll drop off a copy of the birth certificate and then walk to the embassy."

The nephew didn't say it, but his expression did: *You're crazy.*

33

Police Station

"Thank you," Liko told the sheik's nephew. They shook hands and exchanged kisses on each cheek. "You have been helpful. If you are ever in the United States, please look me up. I'll give you a tour, show you the sights, and introduce you to some girls."

The young man grinned ear to ear. "It's been my pleasure," he said.

"Please, thank your uncle for me," Liko said.

"I will," he said. "I wish you a safe return to your home."

They exchanged smiles and a slight bow.

Liko turned to face the police station. It was an imposing structure.

As he walked up the flight of concrete steps to the entrance, carrying the envelope containing a copy of Hugo's birth certificate in one hand and his luggage in the other, his backpack thrown over his shoulder, he thought, *All I have to do is drop off this letter and then make it two blocks to the embassy. Or is it three blocks? Details,* he thought. *I've never been good with details.*

The guard stopped him at the security check, just inside the entrance. The last time he had no luggage or backpack and the security check had been cursory. Standing before him now was a policeman dressed in a new black uniform. The man said something to him.

"I don't speak Arabic," Liko replied, shrugging his shoulders.

A second guard stepped forward. He also said something in Arabic.

"Sure," Liko said. He set the suitcase down. "Do either of you speak English?"

Liko felt the adrenaline dump. He glanced over his right shoulder and saw a third guard, suddenly standing behind him.

"I just want to drop off this letter," Liko said. He held out the letter to the guard standing directly in front of him. "I don't even need to go inside. I can leave it with you, if that is okay?"

Liko felt a push from behind, forcing him farther into the entryway.

I guess they're worried about my bags, Liko thought. *My bad.*

He reached down to open it, to show them that it was just dirty laundry. And a half-empty bag of khat. He wondered if that was illegal. "Shit!" he said, looking up at the guard in front of him.

He felt another push from behind and guessed they were going to force him to the ground. *They're police,* he thought. *Go with it. It will be okay. Relax.*

He found himself on his stomach, on the marble, with a knee in his back. A guard grabbed him by his hair and pulled his head forcefully back. Liko heard a pop as a vertebrate made a correction in his neck. *It's okay,* he thought. *Just relax.*

The guard slammed his head forward onto the marble floor. It was unforgivingly hard. He felt his nose pop and he knew it was broken.

Liko rose from the floor like a horse regaining its feet after a stumble. The guard clung to his back, yelling something in Arabic. Liko pivoted at the waist and the guard fell to the ground at his feet. He held tight to Liko's shirt and it twisted partway around his body. Liko kicked him in the ribs. He heard several snaps and knew that the guard was disabled and would not be getting up.

The first guard threw a wide right hook. Liko squatted and the punch grazed his hair and passed over the top of his head. Keeping his eyes on the man's shoulders, Liko dipped his left shoulder and rebounded with a left upper cut to the man's jaw and then a swift left hook to his ribs and another left hook to the side of his head. The man collapsed to the floor.

Liko pivoted to his right to face the last guard standing. The man stumbled backwards away from Liko. He fell and struck the back of his head on the marble.

Liko saw a policeman running towards him with a gun in his hand. He reached down, picked up his suitcase and lobbed it underhand at the oncoming policeman and yelled, "BOMB!"

The policeman dove sideways under a table, hitting his head on the bottom edge as he slid underneath. Liko heard the wood crack or the crack of the man's head; either way, he had knocked himself out.

Liko glance at the guard who had struck the back of his head on the white marble. He lay on the floor, motionless, a pool of blood beside his head. *Poor guy!* He noted the bottom of the guard's shoes: shiny leather, slippery on marble. *Stupid!*

Liko turned and ran out the entrance, down the sidewalk to the end of the block, and around the corner. He did not look back until he reached the next corner, when he realized that he no longer had the envelope and Hugo's birth certificate. He had dropped it.

He considered, for the briefest of moments, returning for it. As he hesitated, he wiped his nose and heard it pop as it moved side to side. Broken! Blood smeared the back side of his right hand and along the lower half of his shirt sleeve.

"Shit," he mumbled. "I hope they will let me in."

He could no longer breathe through his nose. A woman and two men at the corner shuffled away from him, and one of the men yelled at him in Arabic. *A curse?*

Realizing it was stupid to stop at the light, Liko ran across the intersection to the next sidewalk. Blood dripped from his nose onto the concrete, leaving a red-stained trail for the police to follow.

34

U.S. Embassy

When Liko reached the heavy concrete barriers surrounding the US Embassy, he continued running and swerved around them, untucking his money belt and fishing out his US passport. He waved the dark blue passport overhead, hoping no one would mistake it for a gun.

He was forced to stop when he reached the inner iron gate. He gripped the black bars with both hands and tried to shake them. They didn't move. He stared at the two-and-a-half-inch space between the bars, breathing heavily through his mouth. His nose was stopped up with blood. He wiped his nose with the back of his left hand. Dried blood flaked off and then his nose began to bleed again.

He glanced back at the small parking lot he had just run through and the concrete barriers he had sprinted past. He saw no one following him—not yet anyway, but they would follow the trail of blood. They would come around the corner. And they would see him.

He looked through the iron bars at the tan stucco building and located the entry door into the embassy. He surmised the wall was reinforced to protect embassy staff from automatic rifle fire and rocket-propelled grenades. He glanced to his right and left, looking for someone to let him in. He saw no one. *There have to be guards! But where?*

Recessed into the tan stucco wall, Liko saw the round embassy seal. It was the same seal stamped onto the cover of his passport: a bald eagle holding arrows in one talon and an olive branch in the other. The eagle had a shield covering its chest as if it were protective armor. *I'm in the right place*, he thought.

Above and below the eagle, carved into the stucco, were undulating waves with sharp-pointed peaks, a motif giving the appearance of mountains, or sharks' teeth, or the teeth on a chain saw.

I should have made an appointment! He grabbed the iron fence and butted his head against it in an effort to calm down and focus.

He faced the small parking lot and took out his iPhone: "Siri, please call the US Embassy in the capital of the Republican Democracy."

After a few moments, the call was answered. "US Embassy." It was a female voice, soft and calm. "May I help you?"

"My name is Liko Koholua. I'm right outside, at the gate, across from the front door." He had to pause to catch his breath. "My nose is broken. I'm a US citizen." Again he had to pause. He found it difficult to talk and breathe through his mouth at the same time.

"Do you have an appointment?" the kind voice asked.

"No," he answered. He focused on the concrete barriers. *To keep car bombs out?* "Please let me in."

"I'm sorry sir," she said, "but you need an appointment."

"My nose is broken. I'm in danger. And I'm an American citizen."

"I'm sorry sir, but you need to make an appointment."

"Then make me a damn appointment!" Liko said, raising his voice. He took a deep breath through his mouth and said, "If you don't let me in, they'll kill me."

There was silence.

"I'm in front of the embassy," Liko pleaded. "In front of the gate. I—"

The front door opened and a man dressed in a military uniform, carrying an assault rifle and with a gun holstered to his waist, stepped out. He walked over to Liko.

"Passport, sir?"

Liko handed the Marine his passport. Liko thought he looked sharp, his uniform immaculate.

Liko glanced again in the direction of the barriers. He saw someone in the distance. A policeman? "Please hurry," he said.

The Marine turned and walked back through the front door, taking the passport with him. He closed the door behind him.

"Shit!" Liko yelled.

He glanced back to the concrete barriers. Yes, it was a policeman. Actually, two policemen, both dressed in their stupid black uniforms. One looked his way, perhaps saw him. How far away were they? Two hundred feet? *Which way should I run?* He glanced to his right and then to his left. It didn't really matter. He was surrounded by uninviting administrative buildings, and no place to hide.

He shifted the weight to the balls of his feet and pivoted

to his right, preparing to run anyway. He heard the front door open. The Marine walked to the iron gate and unlocked it, allowing Liko to enter.

Once inside the front door of the embassy, the Marine directed him to empty his pockets. He put Liko's cell phone in a small box and closed the lid. "Phones, cameras, and all electronic devices, including laptops are not allowed," he said.

Liko passed through a metal detector. Something caused the alarm to beep. He was told to spread his arms and legs and a second Marine ran a wand over his body, thoroughly. He was then allowed to enter, officially, into the lobby area of the US embassy.

An elderly woman at the reception desk pointed to a registry log. "Please sign in." Liko recognized her voice as the kind and calm-sounding woman on the phone.

"Thank you," he said as he printed and signed his name. Using the old-fashioned clock on the wall behind the woman, he recorded his entry time as 10:15am. He did a quick calculation in his head: the Republican Democracy was eight hours ahead, so it was 2:15am back home on Maritauqua Island. Everyone there would be asleep. He wished that he were, too.

The woman said, "Mr. Koholua, what is the purpose of your visit this morning?"

"My transit visa expired," he said, trying to smile.

"You said your nose was broken?"

"Yes," Liko said. "That too."

"A nurse will be here shortly. Please have a seat." She gestured towards the available chairs. No one else was present and he had the reception area to himself.

"Thank you," Liko said. He collapsed into one of the sturdy, chocolate-colored leather chairs. Three bowls decorated with Islamic motifs had been set out on the coffee table in front of him, along with three small spoons and a stack of small paper cups. The bowls contained M&M's, yogurt-covered raisins, and colorful jelly beans. Liko filled a small paper cup with a little of each candy and leaned back in the firm leather chair.

With his head tilted back so his nose would stop bleeding, he tried to read the title of a document lying on the table, gazing the best he could with his nose in the air: *Republican Democracy International Religious Freedom Report.* Another document read *Republican Democracy Report on Human Rights Practices.*

After finishing a handful of M&Ms, and having grown sufficiently bored, he picked up a glossy-covered report titled *Republican Democracy Economic Future: Little NEOM.* He found it an impressive advertisement for a futuristic, cutting-edge city in the desert along the coast of the Republican Democracy. After skimming the report, Liko wished he had the money to invest. *The rich get richer and the poor get poorer*, he thought. He tossed the report back onto the table.

Feeling a sugar rush and the sudden beginning of a headache, he felt angry at himself. He closed his eyes. He tilted his head back and imagined Hanauma Bay, one of his favorite places. He imagined diving among the magnificent marine life and seascapes, being surrounded by a tornado of colorful fish swirling around him, peacefully.

When was the last time I centered myself? A week ago? A month? What's wrong with me?!

He quietly focused and centered himself for the first time in months.

"Your transit visa has expired," the chargé d'affaires said.

Duh! Liko thought. "Expired today, yes."

The man gave Liko back his passport. "Are you enjoying your visit?"

Liko looked at him for a moment, wondering if he was being sarcastic. "I came here to identify the body of someone who died, and to find a friend who disappeared."

"Was the deceased family?"

"No."

"A friend?"

"No."

"Business associate?"

"No."

"Hmm!" the man said.

"His name was Zahi Haarun. He was a US citizen. According to his will he wants to be cremated."

"I see," the man said, nodding his head up and down. "Cremation is illegal in the Republican Democracy."

"I have been trying to find his half-brother. He is also a US citizen."

"I see."

"He is my friend," Liko said.

"So how can we help you, Mr. Koholua?"

Liko thought about the incident at the police station and decided not to mention it. Thanks to the first aid given to him by the nurse, his nose was now bandaged. He had refused to answer any specific questions about how it had happened.

"I was hoping to leave a copy of Hugo Haarun's birth certificate here at the embassy. In case he shows up and wants to return to the United States."

"And would that be a problem?" the chargé d'affaires asked, looking steadily at Liko.

"Maybe," Liko answered.

"And why is that?" the man asked.

"He was mutilated," Liko offered.

Liko watched the surprise spread across the man's face. "Mutilated?"

"His left hand was cut off." Liko looked steadily at the man as he added, "And they cut off most of the fingers on his right hand."

"Who did this?"

"Someone at the local prison." Liko paused, trying to remember the name. "Swigert Prison. Yes, I believe that is what the locals call it. Swigert Prison."

The chargé d'affaires was speechless as Liko continued. "He was tortured and then he was dumped on the street. He made his way to his family, who still live here. They cared for him for a few weeks, but now he's disappeared again. I was hoping to find him so I could bring him home. Home to the United States. But as you can see, I have run out of time. My visa has expired."

Liko reached into his money belt and removed the copy of Hugo's birth certificate. He handed it to the man. "Here is a copy of his birth certificate, and also evidence of his mother's hospital record in the United States on the day she gave birth to him. She was also a United States citizen."

Liko watched the color drain from the man's face. "Excuse me," he said, standing up. He walked around his desk and past Liko. "I'll be right back." He opened his office door, stepped out, and closed it softly behind himself.

Liko waited patiently.

After a minute, the man returned with a younger colleague dressed in a nice suit and tie and shiny dress shoes. The man introduced himself to Liko as the Minister. Liko noted that he was clean-shaven and straight-faced, and what Liko thought was executive-looking.

"Mr. Koholua, would you please repeat for the Minister's benefit what you just told me... about your friend? I believe his name was Hugo Haarun?"

"Yes," Liko said. "That's his nickname, Hugo. You will find his full name on the birth certificate that I gave you. It's misspelled, though."

The man picked up the envelope with the birth certificate and handed it across his desk to the Minister. The Minister opened and perused the document for a moment. He then returned it to the envelope and rested it on his knee. He was sitting beside Liko.

"Hugo was a gifted painter." Liko turned his gaze away from both men and stared at the office wall, where there should have been a window. Instead there was a diploma, which didn't interest Liko in the slightest. Liko felt his eyes tearing up.

"They abducted him from a mansion on Maritauqua Island. That's a small island in the Gulf of Mexico off the coast of Alabama. I don't know how, but they flew him, first by helicopter, and then, probably by private jet, here, to the Republican Democracy. They tortured him. Mutilated him. At Swigert Prison. And then dumped him on the street."

The Minister's face was ashen. He stood up. "Excuse me," he said. "I will be right back." He bolted out of the office but soon returned with three women. After introductions, the three women stood in a row against the wall, in front of the chargé d'affaires' diploma, with open notebooks and pens in their hands. Liko surmised that one of them was an administrative supervisor and the other two were clerical staff. Their attention was riveted on him.

"Hugo was a gifted painter," Liko repeated. "What happened to him is a tragedy. And horrific."

"Hugo? I have not heard of him," the man seated across the desk from Liko said. "But then I don't follow the arts."

"You should Google him," Liko said. "One of his paintings, *The Kurdirtgeon*, went viral. The last time I checked, more than five million views. He probably has one or two million followers on Facebook and Twitter."

The Minister cleared his throat loudly. "I am sorry to hear that he was injured," he said.

"Tortured," Liko corrected. "Mutilated."

"Please," the Minister asked, "tell us what happened."

Liko explained, in detail, everything relevant that he knew about Zahi and Hugo, and what had transpired during his own short visit to the Republican Democracy.

Both men were speechless. One of the women was shaken. There was a brief conversation about bringing in a chair for her, but then the older woman, probably her supervisor, dismissed her and the other young woman. The older woman remained standing with her back to the wall with a small, green, Federal-issued notebook in hand, diligently recording every word spoken.

"If Hugo shows up here," Liko added, "he will need those documents so he can get a US passport. I am entrusting them to you." Liko looked at the man across the table.

Neither man replied.

"What are your names, please?" Liko asked.

"Charles Kunianski," the man behind the desk answered. "I am the chargé d'affaires."

"Ray Strauss," the Minister said, extending his hand. Liko accepted their proffered hands. Both men gave Liko their business cards.

Liko stood up. He didn't know what to do next, he just felt it was time to stand up. To do something. "I believe Hugo was abducted from a mansion on Maritauqua Island that is owned by a man – from the Republican Democracy – who goes by the name of Jizan."

Liko was surprised that both the Minister and chargé d'affaires' faces could grow paler. Liko saw their jaws drop, too.

"Are you saying—"

"Jizan, the musician?"

"Yes," Liko said, answering both men, "Hugo, an American citizen, was abducted from an old Southern plantation house in Alabama and then flown surreptitiously from the United States to the Republican Democracy, against his will."

"Did you contact the police?"

Liko thought about that question for a moment. He wanted to lie and say, "Yes, I made a report to the local police in Maritauqua before I left the US." Instead, he told the truth, as usual. "I have been thinking about going to the newspapers. Should I?"

Liko watched the man's face turn absolutely white. Liko had just told the chargé d'affaires and the Minister about a gross violation of human rights. He suspected that the relationship between the United States and the Republican Democracy would never be the same.

"Can you help me find Hugo?" Liko asked. "He is probably in need of urgent medical care. And like I said, he survived the civil war and the genocide, and he suffers from PTSD. He probably has no meds. In fact, I'm almost certain of it."

The Minister told Liko that arrangements could be made for him to stay at the embassy, pending arrangements to update his visa, and provide him safe passage back to the US. Liko agreed to their offer of assistance.

"I have one more question," the chargé d'affaires said.

"Yes?" Liko said.

"Why was Zahi Haarun visiting the Republican Democracy? What was the purpose of his trip?"

"I don't know," Liko answered. "I've talked to his relatives and his ex-wife's sister and no one seems to know."

Several days passed and then Liko met again with the chargé d'affaires in his office. "We have looked into your concerns," the man said. "It appears that Mr. Zahi Haarun was here to attend an economics conference. He died from a heart attack in his hotel room and his body was then taken to the morgue."

"A prison morgue," Liko added.

"Yes," the chargé d'affaires agreed. "A morgue next to a prison."

"Swigert Prison," Liko emphasized. "I identified his body there."

"My condolences."

"And his brother Hugo?"

"There is no record or report of Mr. Hugo Haarun being in the country."

"But that is impossible," Liko said. "I spoke to his relatives. They took care of him for several days. I also spoke to the lawyer attending Zahi's affairs, and he said that Hugo was here."

"There is no police record, or hospital report, or other sign that he entered the country," the chargé d'affaires said.

Liko stared hard at the man. "Was there any sign that he left the United States?"

The chargé d'affaires stared back at Liko. He didn't answer.

"But if he shows up?" Liko said. "You will take care of him?"

"Of course," the chargé d'affaires answered. "Is he not a United States citizen?"

"Please notify Zahi's lawyer if he shows up." Liko gave the chargé d'affaires the attorney's contact information. "And I'd appreciate it if you would notify me, too."

"Of course." The man looked carefully at Liko. "In the meantime, we have arranged a plane out of the Republican Democracy for you."

"I would rather stay here and continue to look for Hugo."

"Sir," the man said. "There was a recent incident at the police station that was brought to our attention. I believe it is in your best interest to accept our offer and leave. Don't you?"

"Very good," Liko said. It was one thing to have an expired visa and quite another to have assaulted three policemen.

"It is the next international flight home. It departs tomorrow morning."

35

Mural

The next morning, when Liko stepped into the black SUV that had pulled into the rear of the United States Embassy, he felt discombobulated. As he settled into the back seat, he entered his password into his iPhone, which an embassy attaché had returned to him as he left the rear of the building. He skimmed his new messages and emails, quickly and quietly. He found nothing from Hugo and nothing of interest. He turned off the phone and pushed it into his front pocket.

"How far to the airport?" he asked the driver.

"A short ride," came the answer. "Twenty minutes, more or less."

Liko looked at the man in the rearview mirror. He looked different than most of the locals, and then Liko realized that he must be a US citizen. His heavy accent also placed him somewhere in the southern states.

"Are you from Alabama?"

"North Carolina," the driver answered.

"You have a strong Southern accent."

"I grew up in Charlotte."

Liko nodded.

"I hope you don't mind," the man said, "but I need to stop and get some gas. You have plenty of time to make your flight."

"No problem," Liko said.

The driver pulled off the main street and drove two blocks in the direction of the sun. He pulled into a service station, parked at an island dispenser, turned off the engine and got out to fill the gas tank.

Liko was seated facing the block across the street – and a mural. A huge mural. With white doves ascending into heaven.

"Damn!" he said, jumping out of the back seat. He walked across the street and stood facing the mural.

The face of the man in the mural was unidentifiable because the artist had painted a dirty white cloth over his face. The artist had outlined the man's mouth beneath the cloth, as if he were trying to suck air through the wet cloth, as if he were gasping for air. Water flowed from the bottom of the cloth.

Waterboarding, Liko concluded. Whoever this man was, he was being tortured.

The man wore a tweed sport coat that Liko instantly recognized.

Is this how Zahi died? Asphyxiation?

In the mural, white doves rose from his body, from his shoulders, and ascended skyward. The work was huge and spray painted. The mural was rougher, the edge of the figures less defined, and the overall painting less detailed than Hugo's other works.

Liko's joy at discovering the mural was tempered with sadness. *Is this your last painting?*

He took out his iPhone and photographed the mural and posted it to Hugo's Facebook page. Almost immediately, he received a direct message announcing that someone had posted it to another site, too. The mural, like Hugo's other works, instantly went viral.

"Sir," the driver said.

Liko turned to see the driver standing beside him, also gawking at the mural. "Yes," Liko said, returning his gaze to the painting. "It's incredible, no?"

"We need to go, sir."

"Just a moment," Liko took a panoramic picture and posted that to the Facebook page, too, and then he turned to leave, reluctantly. As they crossed back to the other side of the street, he told the driver, "I knew the artist. This is probably his last painting."

"Last?" the driver said, curious. "Why his last?"

"Because he was tortured. They cut off his hand. The hand that he draws with."

"I didn't hear anything about that," the driver said.

"It happened several months ago," Liko said. "He was tortured at Swigert Prison."

The man stopped abruptly in the middle of the street, looked at Liko, and then turned back to look at the mural. "It has to be another artist, then."

"I don't think so." Liko stopped and stood in the middle of the street with the driver. "The wool coat, the white doves, it has to be Hugo."

"Well," the driver said, "this painting wasn't there a month ago. In fact, it wasn't there a week ago. I know. I topped off the tank last week, and this painting wasn't here. It had to have been painted in the last two or three days."

"No way!" Liko exclaimed. He stepped toward the painting and was almost hit by a car. He still hadn't gotten used to drivers driving on the opposite side of the road. He had glanced in the wrong direction before stepping, and the driver had pulled him back just in time.

"Whoa!" Liko yelled. "That was close." Liko now looked in both directions and then crossed the street to the mural. He placed his hand on it. The paint wasn't tacky, yet it felt fresh.

"We need to go, sir," the man said. He gestured back towards his SUV.

"I'm not leaving," Liko said, adamantly.

"Sir? You will miss your flight."

"I'm staying until I find the man who painted this mural." Liko continued to gaze at the spectacular painting. A smile spread across his face. "His name is Hugo. He is a great artist!"

"But sir, we really need to go now."

"Leave me. I'll be okay."

The driver shook his head. He returned to the SUV and drove away.

Where are you, Hugo? Liko felt certain that he was nearby. Somewhere in the neighborhood?

Liko entered the café next to the service station and across the street from the mural. He ordered a double espresso and stood at the waist-high counter stirring sugar into the hot drink until no more would dissolve. He swallowed the syrupy mixture in one extended gulp, set the empty glass on the counter and looked around the dark room as he felt the sugar and caffeine rush through his body.

"Good afternoon everyone!" Liko said in a voice that carried easily to every corner of the small café. A few patrons glanced up from their meals or drinks to look at him, but they quickly returned to their food and personal conversations. *Perhaps they don't speak English*, he thought.

"I'll pay 500 US dollars to the first person who can take me to the man who painted that mural across the street." He looked slowly around the room.

No one paid him any attention.

"Five hundred US dollars," Liko repeated.

Again he was ignored.

"A painter without hands!" he said in a loud voice.

Again, no one paid him any attention. He paid for his coffee, slowly separating a few bills from a handful of cash that he kept in his money belt, deliberately taking his time, and then he strolled to a vending machine near the front door. Liko inserted a bill into the candy-filled machine and punched the numbers that released what he hoped was a candy bar, something chocolate, hopefully. The bar fell and Liko retrieved it.

"I can take you to another painting," said a man who had fallen into line behind Liko. "It is not far." His English was excellent, but with a British accent.

"Very good," Liko said.

The man led him to a rusted motorcycle parked next to the building—more a scooter than a motorcycle. As Liko put his arms around the man he was surprised to discover that he was a she. *Damn!* he thought.

The motorcyclist drove him farther into the neighborhood. The homes were worn out. Some had shifted on their foundations and were boarded up. All needed new paint and roof repairs. The yards were asphalt or weeds. It reminded Liko of a drive he had taken along the Gulf Coast in Mississippi and Alabama after a hurricane.

Soon the battered houses began to cause Liko some anxiety. "How much farther?" he asked.

"We are almost there," the woman said. One block later the motorcycle stopped in front of an old commercial building that had aged poorly. The concrete block facade was covered in layer upon layer of graffiti. Weeds as tall as Liko had grown from the foundation, partially covering some of the tags, which were amateurish and unattractive: poorly lettered, annoying, and self-centered.

Liko noticed men gathered in small groups, some standing together at an intersection, others seated together on a nearby stoop in front of an abandoned building. A man lay face-down, passed out, his body half on the concrete sidewalk, half on the dirt and weeds.

The amateurish graffiti was not Hugo's work, not Hugo's tags, and not of interest to Liko. He sighed, disappointed.

Nevertheless, he paid the woman $500. She pocketed the money and gestured for Liko to get back on her motorcycle.

"No," Liko said. "Unless you know where there is another painting?"

The motorcyclist motioned towards two men sitting on a nearby stoop, indicating that it was not safe for him to stay.

"I'll be fine," he said.

She hopped onto her bike and sped a hundred feet up the next block, then she did an abrupt U-turn to face Liko. She sat on her bike, motionless.

The two men stood up and walked slowly towards Liko.

As they approached he held his ground. "Shit!" he said, suddenly angry. He squared his body to the advancing men, his left foot facing them, his right foot turned 45 degrees outward. "I am looking for the artist who paints doves," he said. "Do you know him?"

The first man stepped forward. As his fist came up, Liko struck him in the face with a quick jab. Surprised, the man jerked back and lost his footing.

Liko let him regain his balance.

The man again stepped forward, this time placing all his weight on his front foot. He jabbed at Liko.

Liko slipped his head to the side and the jab passed within an inch of his ear. Still balanced, Liko kicked the inner thigh of the man's front leg. The leg gave way, the man crumpled, and his head dropped onto Liko's knee. *Whack!* His body followed to the ground.

Liko looked down at him. The man had knocked himself out on Liko's knee.

The second man advanced and punched at Liko.

Liko slipped his head to the right and at the same time jabbed underneath the man's arm, aiming at his head. Liko's fist hit the man squarely in the face. As the man pulled his arm back in surprise, Liko threw all his body weight onto his front foot and delivered a right cross to the man's face and then struck him with a jab-cross, jab-cross.

The man collapsed at Liko's feet.

The motorcyclist roared down the street, stopping just outside Liko's reach. She asked, calmly, "Who is this painter you're looking for?"

"The man who paints white doves."

The woman's eyebrow raised. "The magician?"

"Yes," Liko said. A tentative smile filled his face. "Do you know him?"

"The man who paints without hands?"

"Yes," Liko said, excitement in his voice.

"Why do you want him?"

"He is my friend."

The woman smiled. "Come with me."

Liko's hunch had been right: he thought the motorcyclist knew more than she was telling him. How did he know? First, her sex had surprised him, set him on edge. Second, she had paint on her clothes and hands. But there was one other clue. Sitting behind her on the bike, with his nose in her hair, he smelled solvents and paint thinner. He had to admit, though, that when she took off on her motorcycle without him, he'd thought, for a second – just a second – that he had made a terrible mistake.

Liko climbed back onto her bike, wrapping his arms around her waist. A motorcycle would always be his last choice for transportation. *I'd rather ride a camel*, he thought. *Surely they're safer.*

The woman pulled out into the street and stopped in front of the graffiti mural. "Do you like this one?" she asked.

"No."

She shrugged. "Neither do I." She gunned the small motorcycle and together they moved down the block at a low rate of speed, but as fast as the old machine could go. "But we are learning."

<h1 style="text-align:center">36</h1>

<h1 style="text-align:center">Leader of the Insurrection</h1>

"Hugo!" Liko exclaimed. He grabbed Hugo by the shoulders and hugged him with affection. They kissed each other on both cheeks, warmly. "How are you?" Liko pulled slightly back from Hugo, yet still held his shoulders so he could take the measure of him. He was thin and his teeth were awful as always.

Hugo raised his arms and displayed the hand and the fingers that were no longer there. "Terrible, but now better." His face settled into a welcoming smile. "It is great to see you." Then, as if perplexed, he added, "But what in the world are you doing here? Are you crazy?"

"Perhaps." In a gentle, admonishing voice, Liko said, "After all, I've spent the last few months looking for you, first on Maritauqua Island and now here. You weren't easy to find!"

They hugged each other again and Liko patted his friend on the back affectionately. They stood facing each other, grinning.

"I see you met one of my protégés," Hugo said. He gestured with his shoulder in the direction of the motorcyclist. The woman had brought Liko to the warehouse, which served as Hugo's hideaway. She sat on an overturned bucket in front of a small campfire, one of two burning in the huge room inside the warehouse. Her back was turned towards them. She had removed her hat and Liko saw her closely cropped black hair.

"Yes," Liko said. "She paints not so well, though."

A smile filled Hugo's face and wrinkled the corners of his eyes. "Considering who her teacher is, she is doing well."

Liko laughed at his friend's genuine display of modesty. He then blushed, realizing the irony of his statement: how does a man with no hands teach another person to paint?

"Ahhh!" Hugo said. "You are now thinking about my loss." He shrugged his shoulders. "It is true, I can no longer hold a paint brush. But I can still hold a spray can. Actually, I have a tool that fits on my arm so I can hold it."

"So you did paint the mural of Zahi and the white doves? After you lost your hand?"

"True, true," Hugo said. "Sadly, though, Zahi is no longer with us."

"I know," Liko said. "I identified his body in the morgue next to the prison."

"The last time I saw him was in that prison. They were torturing him, waterboarding him."

"That's awful. I'm so sorry."

"I am okay, my friend," Hugo said. "After they cut off my hand they took me from the room. They held a gun near my head and pulled the trigger. The bullet entered a bag of sand. The gun was so close to my ear that I lost my hearing in that ear for a long time." Hugo held his right index finger and thumb up to the right side of his head, pointing to his ear as if he held a gun. "Zahi must have heard the gunshot. He was still in the room, strapped to a chair. I think they did it to torment him, to make him think I had been killed."

"I didn't know he was tortured," Liko said. "The chargé d'affaires at the US Embassy said he died of natural causes in his hotel room. A heart problem."

"No," Hugo said. "He was murdered."

"What happened?" Liko asked. "Why?"

"Later," Hugo said, his eyes welling up with tears. He took a breath and said, "I will tell you everything, later."

Thinking it best to change the subject, Liko said, "We found your birth certificate!"

"That's great," Hugo said. "Thank you!"

"Your last name was misspelled. Unbelievable, yeah?"

"Yes," Hugo said. "All of it is unbelievable: my abduction, my torture, Zahi's torture, his murder... our ancestral home, destroyed."

Liko looked around the room. He noticed an occasional glance in their direction. "You have fallen in with an interesting group, yes?"

"They're friends," Hugo said, proudly.

Liko doubted it. His expression gave away his concern.

"Do not worry, my friend," Hugo said. "You are safe here with me."

The irony of Hugo's statement and his newfound confidence in himself were unexpected. Liko looked closely at his friend. He saw new wrinkles around his eyes and deeper furrows crossing his forehead. The cheeks that had once held dimples were now sunken. Liko guessed that Hugo weighed less than 120 pounds, a slight weight even for someone of his short height. "You have lost weight?"

"Some," Hugo said, again shrugging his shoulders.

They were quiet for a moment, taking the measure of each other, looking for familiarities, noticing changes.

"Now that I've found you," Liko said, "we can figure out how to escape from this shit-hole country." As soon as the words left his mouth, he realized he had made a serious mistake.

"Shit-hole country?" Hugo parroted in a voice filled with surprise and admonishment and disappointment.

"My bad!" Liko corrected himself, immediately. "I didn't mean that. At least not in the context that others have said it in the past, especially Trump. Believe me, I did not mean it like that!"

"I know what you were trying to say," Hugo said. "The Republican Democracy is only a shadow of itself because of Lil't and the kleptocrats and all their enablers."

Liko wasn't sure who 'all their enablers' were. *Were they the police? The torturers?*

"I left a copy of your birth certificate at our embassy, here in the capital. You can get a passport and escape."

"But I am not leaving," Hugo said in a matter-of-fact tone of voice. "If you came to rescue me, then you have misunderstood. I do not need to be rescued. In fact, I have no intention of leaving or returning to the US. This is where I am needed. This is where I will stay. And this is where I will paint."

"No way!" Liko shook his head in disbelief. "Why would you want to stay here, especially now? After what they did to Zahi? And to you?"

"This is who I am," Hugo said.

Liko noticed a gray and white cat nosing around a cookfire on the other side of the warehouse room.

"Here Smoke," Hugo called out to the semi-feral cat. "Here, kitty kitty." He held out a chicken kebab seasoned with local spices and rosemary.

The cat pranced across the warehouse floor, avoiding scattered debris, and rubbed her head against Hugo's black boots. Back and forth she rubbed.

"She's my boot shiner," Hugo said, laughing lightly.

The large cat approached the kebab. She rubbed her head against Hugo's remaining index finger and thumb, then she pawed at the kebab with her front paws. Hugo lowered the kebab almost to the ground and Smoke nibbled.

"Smoke?" Liko asked.

"She is the color of smoke rising from our cookfires," Hugo said. "When we cook, Smoke appears. Always just in time for dinner."

Liko looked at the two fires flickering inside the large warehouse space. The smoke rose unimpeded to the rusted ceiling three stories above. "Great name, Smoke," he said.

"I named her," Hugo said, proudly.

After eating the chicken, Smoke approached Liko and rubbed her head against the outside of his thigh. Liko noticed that one of her eyes was cloudy. Liko reached out to pet her but she scampered away.

The warehouse held an odor of smoke and sweat and greasy food.

The motorcyclist approached Hugo. "When do we paint again?"

"Sit down," Hugo suggested. "Please sit down."

She sat on the floor directly across from him and crossed her legs. Several other men and women, having just finished their meager meal, wiped their hands on the sides of their trousers, walked over, and joined them. They sat on the ground in a semi-circle facing Hugo. Liko counted five men and two women. Liko sat to the side, slightly outside the group.

"Before we decide when and where, I'd like to decide what." Hugo made eye contact with each artist in turn. "So I ask you, what shall we paint?"

"A picture of Lil't behind bars."

Everyone laughed.

"Yeah, Lil't in prison."

"And his cronies."

"Paint his hair orange!"

"And a big rump!"

"Trump! Trump!"

"Had a big rump!"

"And small hands!"

"Small grabby hands."

"So many ideas to choose from," Hugo said, looking doubtful. "Not all so good, though."

Everyone laughed, again.

Hugo turned to Liko. "What do you think?"

"Me?" Liko said, placing his hand on his chest. He had been sitting quietly outside the group, listening.

"Yes, my friend," Hugo said. "What do you think we should paint?"

"Something like *Eyes in the Heat*," Liko suggested.

Everyone stared at him blankly.

"It's a painting by Jackson Pollock," Liko explained. "Enamel and oil. But you could improvise with spray paint."

Hugo smiled. "Liko, I remember a Jackson Pollock quote that you shared with me. Do you remember it?"

Liko shook his head, no.

"When I was struggling with my nerves, and my hands were infected, and I could barely paint, you shared it with me."

"No," Liko said, embarrassed. "I don't remember."

"'Every good painter paints what he is,'" Hugo said. "That's what you told me."

"Yes," Liko smiled, humbly. "I remember it now."

"Well, my friend," Hugo said, "Pollock also said: 'It doesn't much matter how the paint is put on as long as something has been said.'"

Liko's smile broadened.

"'Technique is just a means of arriving at a statement.'" Hugo said, finishing Pollock's quote.

Liko saw puzzlement on the faces of the men and women seated at Hugo's feet.

"Who is this Jackson Pollock?" the motorcyclist asked.

"An American painter," Hugo answered.

"An abstract expressionist," Liko added.

"He stopped using a paint brush," Hugo explained. "Instead, he squeezed paints out of tubes and worked it with tools. He would pour, drip, and splash paint onto large canvases. And then he would work it."

Liko now understood what Hugo was saying to the other painters. Their next painting might be a rough sketch, a crude painting, but nevertheless their message would still shine through. *I like that*, Liko thought.

"So what shall we paint?" Hugo asked again.

"Something like *Eyes in the Heat*," the motorcyclist said.

Liko glanced over at the woman. She was still sitting on the floor with her legs crossed. She smiled at him and it caught him completely off guard.

He looked at her more closely. She was scrawny and needed to gain weight. The lack of nutritious food wasn't her fault. Her hair was dry and dull, and the skin on her forearms was streaked with dirt and ash from the campfire.

The man seated next to her spoke up and his excited voice broke Liko's daydreaming. "I can spray paint and I have a paint brush." His voice was filled with enthusiasm. "Count me in."

"Me too," the others said in unison.

Liko was amazed at Hugo's transformation. His friend still needed to express himself and to paint, but now he actively surrendered himself to this eclectic group. He served them, nourished them, and loved them. There was a fusion between Hugo and the want-to-be painters. They enabled each other. Their goals were to paint the truth, to right injustices, and to fight the kleptocracy, and his goal was to serve.

You're setting yourself up for failure, Liko thought.

The man they called Doc took out a collection of pill bottles from his large fanny pack. He reached across the space between himself and the motorcyclist and handed her a large bottle. She shook out some tablets, counted out a number and passed the bottle to the next person. Liko watched each person take or decline the tablets as the bottle went around the group. When the bottle made its way back to the motorcyclist, she rocked forward onto her feet and handed the bottle back to Doc. He took out two tablets and rocked forward again, and Hugo pinched the two tablets from the palm of Doc's hand with his right index finger and thumb. They smiled at each other. *Little victories are important here*, Liko thought.

Doc repeated the process with the next bottle of pills. Occasionally someone asked him about the need for a medication and Doc gave his advice. Liko later learned that they called him Doc because he had been studying to be a pharmacist when the war broke out. He never finished his degree, but he did administer to the health needs of the painters the best that he could.

Liko noted that Hugo dry-swallowed his tablets. Most of the others, however, took their medications with a sip of water or whatever else they happened to be drinking at the moment.

"For my psychosis," Hugo said, joking with Liko. "Doc keeps us on our meds."

"Where do you get the meds?" Liko asked Doc.

Doc said, "Friends of friends. You could help."

"How?"

"Some meds are difficult to find. The supply sometimes runs out. I'll give you a list of what we need."

Liko nodded. Inevitably he would return to the US. He had no idea how he could get the medicines for Doc, but he was confident that he would make it happen. "Sure," he told Doc, without hesitation. "Give me the list, I'll make it happen." There was a tinge of sadness in his voice because he was also acknowledging to himself that he would soon leave. He turned to Hugo and smiled sadly.

37

TrackHer

"They found us!" the sentry exclaimed, waking everyone. "Let's go!"

"Police?" Hugo groaned, rolling off his makeshift mattress and onto the concrete floor. He struggled to his feet, his body waking up. Liko and the rest of the group instantly awakened, too.

"How many?" the motorcyclist asked as she slipped into her shoes and pulled on her jacket.

"Two, maybe more," the sentry answered. "They are coming down the alley."

"Back entrance?" another person asked, standing with one shoe on while layering on his clothes.

"Yes," the sentry answered. "Everyone exit out the right side, towards the front."

The group grabbed their belongings, the items within their immediate arm's reach, and moved in unison towards the side exit of the warehouse. A man placed his hand on Hugo's back to guide him in that direction.

The sentry led everyone out the exit and along a pre-set escape route to another building, an abandoned metal shop several blocks away. Liko moved with the group, his heart beating fast thanks to an adrenaline dump.

Once the last person entered the metal shop, the sentry closed the door, completing his task for the night.

The machine shop was a much smaller building, yet it was not claustrophobic because a row of high windows provided natural light. Two members of the group raised a tall ladder up to the windows. Liko suspected that the ladder had been strategically placed ahead of time. One of the two men climbed to the top of the ladder. "All clear," he called down.

The motorcyclist directed everyone to gather around a large rectangular table. Liko joined them. The table was built from two recycled doors, laid end to end, on top of four crudely constructed sawhorses. The chairs surrounding the table were an eclectic mix of moving crates, five-gallon paint buckets, and salvaged office chairs. Moonlight streamed in through the high windows and lit up the long table, the makeshift chairs, and the would-be artists.

"Empty your pockets," the motorcyclist told everyone. "Lay everything on the table." Each person stepped up to the table and emptied their pockets, leaving them turned inside out.

The motorcyclist turned on a small penlight, shining the powerful little light on her own belongings first: a folding comb, a rusty can opener, a pocket knife, and a wallet. She then turned the flashlight on the pile next to hers. Again there was a knife. Liko followed the light as it moved around the table from pile to pile. Everyone carried a knife or other weapon, except for Hugo.

Among Hugo's items was a flattened beverage cup, or what looked like a flattened cup except that it had leather and cloth straps. "For attaching a can of spray paint to my arm," he explained when he saw that Liko was curious. He opened the flattened device and slipped it onto the end of his left arm where his hand should have been. With the thumb and index finger of his right hand, he tightened and then fastened the straps. "It works well," he told Liko. "I can hold a spray can!"

The last pile was Liko's. The motorcyclist picked up his phone. "What's this?"

"My iPhone," Liko said, reaching for it.

The motorcyclist took a step backward. "None of us carry personal phones."

"Why not?" Liko asked.

"Look around you," the motorcyclist said, joking. "We are in an Orwellian state."

"What does that have to do with me?" He again stepped forward and reached for his phone, but the motorcyclist again stepped back.

"Spyware," the motorcyclist said. "Tracking apps."

Liko looked at her with disbelief.

"Unlock your phone and let me check it," she directed him.

Liko started to object. He glanced at Hugo to complain, but when he saw Hugo's stern, uncompromising expression, he understood the seriousness of the request. He looked at the other folks around the table and they all nodded agreement.

"Okay," Liko said.

The motorcyclist stepped forward and returned Liko's

iPhone to him. He entered his passcode and then handed the phone back to her.

He watched as she swiped through his apps. Almost immediately she looked up from his phone screen, and said, "As I suspected, you're being tracked!"

"No way!"

"You have an eGovernment app on your phone."

"So?" Liko said. "It's just a digital copy of my visa."

"Really?" the motorcyclist smirked. "You are being tracked."

"Using my phone?"

"Yes! It's very simple. When they approved your visa, it was electronically stamped. A digital signature? Yes?"

Liko nodded, yes.

"The electronic stamp implants a code that uploads information from your phone to the National Information Center. When did you get your visa approved?"

Liko cleared his voice. "While I was still in the United States."

"You did it online?"

"Yes."

"Well, they have been tracking you ever since."

"No way!" Liko said.

"When your visa information was uploaded, malware was downloaded." The motorcyclist shook her head. "When you cross the border, whether you fly, drive, or walk into the country, the malware alerts the National Information Center. It uses the GPS on your phone, silently. The government tracks your location while you are in the country."

"The government can find you whenever they want," Hugo explained.

"That's terrible," Liko said. "I didn't know."

"It's not your fault, my friend," Hugo said.

"The government now has a record of everywhere you went," the motorcyclist said.

"Damn!" Liko said. "Everywhere?"

"Yes, with dates and times and other metadata."

"Shit!" Liko said, turning to Hugo. "It tracked me to your relatives, and Zahi's sister-in-law. Will they be okay?"

"Many such apps exist," the motorcyclist said. "Men use apps like TrackHer to follow the movement of their wives, their daughters and their mistresses."

"It's a way for men to control women," a man standing at the end of the table said.

"And for the government to control us," the motorcyclist added.

"How do you know all this?" Liko asked the woman.

"An ex-boyfriend stalked me with the TrackHer app," she answered. "But I got away."

Liko found it all surreal. Was this country that uncivilized? That Orwellian?

Liko handed his phone back to the motorcyclist. "I imagine you know the best way to get rid of it?"

"I already did." She grinned. "I deleted the app while we were talking."

"Fine," Liko said. "I don't need it. I carry a hardcopy of my visa in my money belt, along with my passport."

She handed the phone back to him. "You should wipe it clean and throw the shell away."

Liko erased all his personal data and wiped his iPhone clean. He'd buy a new phone and start clean when he returned home. Once again he felt naked without GPS and access to the internet.

The group settled into their new surroundings and most

were soon asleep. Liko, though, found it impossible to fall back asleep.

The shop made a great hideout, with multiple exits and the high windows for surveillance. Liko rummaged around the shop, quietly looking at everything in the moonlight. There was a treasure trove of heavy, abandoned pneumatic equipment, but without electricity and a working compressor, it was all useless. He doubted that electricity was available anyway. The workbench drawers were all open, and some drawers lay on the floor. He quietly searched the cabinets. There wasn't a useful tool in the entire abandoned metal shop. Liko concluded that everything useful had already been taken.

Eventually he grew tired and sat in one of the chairs pulled up to the makeshift table. He rested his head on his arms on the table.

He surmised that he had been tracked because there was an identification tag on the suitcase he had thrown into the police station when he had yelled "bomb!" Yeah, that was probably the motivation for the police.

He finally fell asleep just as the sun came up. The group kindly let him sleep in.

"Swigert Prison?!" the motorcyclist exclaimed. "You've got to be kidding!"

"Impossible!" a man said.

"The back side," Hugo explained, defending his choice. "The outer wall."

"But that side faces the runway."

Liko assumed the man meant the runway at the International Airport.

"It has risks," Hugo said.

"How can we get in and out?"

"How can we paint that fast?"

"It's brilliant," Liko said, sharing his thoughts. "Everyone – EVERYONE – will see it."

"But everyone will see us painting it, too!"

They grew quiet. All eyes were on Hugo.

Hugo looked around the table, making eye contact with each person, one after another. Only then did he break the silence. "First we will prepare templates."

Everyone nodded agreement.

I guess they've done this before, Liko thought.

"A template of a quadcopter drone. Something like a Phantom. The perspective will be from above and below the drones."

"Multiple drones?" the motorcyclist asked.

"Yes, each of us will have a template." Hugo cleared his voice. "The color of the drones will be silver."

Everyone was riveted to Hugo. "We each paint two or three silver drones," he explained. "Then we paint whatever we want, using black, white, yellow and red."

"We must paint fast," the motorcyclist said.

"Very fast," a man added.

"I will work the center of the mural," Hugo said. "Each of you will work out from me in all directions – up, down, to my right, to my left, all around – painting as much surface of the wall as possible, as quickly as possible."

"How will we gain entry?" Liko asked Hugo.

Hugo smiled. "A double lock."

"You're kidding me?" Liko said, dumbfounded. "On the back wall of a prison?"

"We're using the same trick you used at the Sewage Wastewater Treatment Plant," Hugo said proudly. "I've learned from the best."

"A double lock on a chain-link gate?"

"Yes," Hugo said with a beaming smile.

For the first time in a long, long time, Liko felt a twinge of pride, of satisfaction.

"And we have a van," Hugo added. "We can drive right up to the back gate."

"No one should be there," the motorcyclist said. "It's not a regularly used entrance."

"That's right," Hugo said. "It's used by the grounds crew—the landscapers and trash collectors."

The group of painters nodded, giving their approval.

It sounded to Liko like Hugo was familiar enough with the area. "You will paint quickly?" Liko asked the group, although his question was meant for Hugo. "Fast, like Vincent painting in the field before the sun set?"

"Yes," Hugo nodded. "Like Vincent. But we will paint as the sun rises."

And hopefully before they arrive: the prison guards, airport security, the local police, and nearby soldiers. Liko kept his thought to himself because he didn't want to dampen their enthusiasm.

"Why paint drones?" he asked.

"To send a message," Hugo answered. "We are sending a message."

38

The Wall

Two painters dressed in white bib overalls pulled up to the chain-link gate in the nondescript panel van. They looked like professional painters, contractors.

"Nice ride," Hugo said. He was seated in the middle of the middle seat, between Liko and the motorcyclist.

"Except for no windows," Liko quipped. "Who chooses a vehicle without windows in the desert?"

The painter in the front passenger seat opened his door and stepped out. He inserted a key into one of the padlocks on the chain that held the gate closed. The double lock system worked as smoothly as its counterpart at the Maritauqua Sewage Wastewater Treatment Plant. The man opened the lock and let the heavy metal chain drop to the dirt. He walked back the chain-link gate and the van drove through.

The motorcyclist, Hugo, and Liko rolled out of the middle seat, and the driver and front seat passengers jumped out. The motorcyclist opened the back door of the van and the other painters hopped out. Everyone unloaded the boxes of spray paint and the drone templates.

Liko set a box of supplies against the faded white concrete wall of the prison. Hugo declared that spot the center of the mural. Liko then paced off eight steps, roughly twenty feet, and set down another box. Again starting from the center, he stepped off another eight steps in the opposite direction. He roughly delineated fifty linear feet of wall space that would soon become a mural.

The artists assembled a half-story scaffolding on wheels to provide height for painting. They also had two ladders.

Hugo walked to the center of the scaffold and strapped on his painting gear. "Paint time!" he said cheerfully. The team attacked the wall, too. Some held templates, some sprayed paint, and some shouted encouragement. The two men dressed in coveralls grabbed paint brushes and joined the team.

Liko stood at the entrance alternately watching the paint team and the street. He kept a sharp lookout for the police. Liko had no doubt they were close by.

They finished in fifteen minutes. They stood back and admired their work. *Wyland is famous for his whales,* Liko thought. *Hugo will be famous for his drones.* "I think Pollock would be pleased," Liko told the team of painters.

"I'm pleased, too," Hugo said. The mural was fifty feet long and twelve feet high.

It's the size of my mother's old trailer, Liko thought.

"I wish I could take your picture," Liko told the team, "and post it on the internet."

The motorcyclist stepped forward and gave him a phone.

"Really?" Liko said in surprise. It was a Mobal World Talk and Text Phone.

"It has a five-megapixel camera," the motorcyclist said.

Liko took a series of photos. In the last photo, the paint team and Hugo stood in front of the mural. Everyone on the team turned their backs to the camera except for Hugo, who smiled for the camera, ear to ear. He was still wearing his paint gear.

Liko passed the phone to Hugo, who posted the photos on his Facebook page.

Hugo then handed the phone back to the motorcyclist and she removed the SIM card.

The photos of the drone mural and Hugo and his rebel paint team went viral.

Earlier, watching Hugo paint, Liko had felt happy. Now he experienced something larger than himself: joy. He saw joy radiating from the faces of Hugo and his team of painters, too.

"Zahi asked me to tell you something," Hugo told Liko. They were in yet another abandoned building.

"When I was in prison, we shared a room. He told me about a professor who lived in London. He said that if I survived I had to look him up."

"Why?" Liko asked.

"He gave something to the old professor. Something of value." Hugo shared the professor's contact information with Liko.

"I'll stop in London," Liko said, "talk to him. Find out what he has."

"Great," Hugo said. "Thank you, my friend."

They hugged each other one last, final time.

As the motorcyclist pulled away with Liko holding on tight, Hugo raised his arm and gestured farewell. He yelled after the noisy bike, "Wadaeaan!" The motorcyclist translated for him: share.

As they rode through the neighborhood streets to the US Embassy, Liko thought, *I hope they're not upset with me for ditching my airport driver.* And then he remembered: "Dammit! I forgot to make an appointment!"

39

London

The receptionist at the US Embassy may have been surprised when she answered the phone and Liko said, "Madam, I believe we've met once before. I'm Liko Koholua, the guy who broke his nose? Remember me?"

However, her voice didn't reflect it. "Urgent appointment?" she asked.

"Yes ma'am," Liko answered. "I'm right outside."

The guard again appeared at the front gate and ushered him inside. Minister Strauss and the chargé d'affaires were amazed when he told them about Hugo painting his mural. They asked him to tell the story twice. The second time, the administrative assistant was called in to take notes. She wrote furiously, probably in shorthand, a dying art.

Again they arranged a flight for him out of the country, and this time he actually boarded the plane. He was dismayed to learn, once he was buckled into his seat, that he was in a Boeing 737, Max 8, the plane that had crashed twice in five months and that had been pulled from use worldwide. When the flight attendant came by, he asked her, "Was this one retrofitted with the latest safety software?"

"Yes," she replied. "Oh yes, sir."

She brought him free drinks from the bar during the entire flight. That helped.

As the plane took off, he looked across the seat of the passenger next to him, a petite blonde, and out her window. He saw Hugo's mural—at least the top of it. The police had attached plastic sheets to the chain-link fence in front of the mural to censor it. Nevertheless, the top third of Hugo's mural was still visible. "Yes!" Liko said.

The blonde woman looked up from her paperwork, which she had spread out on her fold-down tray. "What?" she said, removing her earbuds. "Did you say something?"

"The mural," Liko said. "Do you see it?"

She looked out the window. "Amazing."

"Do you see the drones?"

He watched her look intently at the visible third of the mural. "Maybe?" she answered, shrugging her shoulders.

"I see them," Liko said. "They are flying skyward in all directions, like silver doves. No fence, or wall, or barrier can keep them out."

"Hmmm," she said. She put her earbuds back in and refocused her attention on the paperwork resting on her tray.

After a few drinks he fell asleep. In his dream, mother ships appeared, hovering above the earth. Near the end of his dream he stood shoulder to shoulder with Zahi and Saba, Hugo and his paint team, Saba's sister, and a large group of enlightened children – all the humans who had evolved to the next level of consciousness. In his dream he knew that the rest of the world had destroyed itself or would soon disintegrate into nothingness. The chosen ones were about to transcend their earthly existence and merge with the 'cosmic mind.' And then he awoke.

Childhood's End? he thought. *I reimagined Arthur C. Clarke's classic.*

He recalled a comment that Hugo made. After the mural was painted and Hugo unstrapped his homemade prosthesis, he stood quietly for a moment admiring the new mural. He turned to Liko and said, in a matter-of-fact tone, "This is the only gift I can give them."

That was the magical moment for Liko when everything fell into place. Suddenly he understood Hugo's talent, his vocation, his calling, his murals. They had stood together, facing Hugo's newest creation, with their arms resting on each other's shoulders, experiencing a great joy.

Hugo and his team of artists had made a speedy escape, disappearing into the neighborhood, yet their gift remained on the back wall of Swigert Prison for everyone to witness.

Liko bought a disposable mobile phone and an international SIM card with prepaid minutes from a kiosk in London's Heathrow Airport. The motorcyclist had asked Liko to send her a dozen foreign SIM cards with prepaid credit so the paint team could text each other and use Twitter without being tracked by the government. *They're too expensive in the airport,* Liko thought. *I'll buy them in a convenience store.*

He called Professor Ludi.

"Have we met?" the professor asked.

"No," Liko answered. "But I believe you have something for Hugo?"

There was silence on the phone.

"Two peas in a pod?"

Liko walked around Hyde Park until he came to a field where an old man in a light tan sweater was flying three drones. Liko had seen similar skill in Hawaii, but with three kites. Instead of rolls of twine, the man held a controller equipped with antennas and buttons and control sticks.

The weather was perfect: blue skies, temperature in the seventies, and no wind. The old man stood tall in a large field of green grass, freshly mowed. He appeared to be thoroughly enjoying himself.

The drones flew in a formation, just like three kites, swooping up and down, tight and almost touching each other. They performed a loop as if they were jets, staying in their close formation. They rolled together.

As Liko approached the professor, the drones descended and surrounded him, one in front and one on each side. *Nice touch*, he thought. He wondered if the whirling blades were sharp. The drones escorted him to the professor, then they circled the professor and landed at his side, heeling as if they were obedient, well-trained dogs.

The professor set the controller on the grass and offered his hand to Liko. "Dr. Ludi," he said.

"Liko Koholua." He accepted the professor's hand, shaking it with relief.

The professor had already heard the news that Zahi was dead and that Hugo had been brutally mutilated, yet was spray-painting murals with a team of apprentices. Liko learned that Hugo had been in touch with the professor to discuss drones. Liko was curious, but he thought it best not to ask.

"Hugo told me what Zahi did," Liko said. "He betrayed Saba, abandoned his family, and worked for Lil't and his cronies. I was surprised."

The professor nodded.

"I met him a few times. He seemed like a regular, normal person except for that tweed coat. He wore it everywhere."

"It kept him in character," Professor Ludi said.

"I see," Liko said, but he didn't really understand anything. He didn't understand Zahi's relationship with Saba. He didn't understand the significance of the tweed sport coat. He didn't understand why Zahi had returned to the Republican Democracy. He didn't understand why Zahi had been tortured and murdered. He didn't understand why Hugo had been abducted and maimed. "I don't understand anything," Liko confessed.

Professor Ludi's face broke into a broad smile. He reached out and grabbed Liko, pulling him in and hugging him warmly, and said: "Saba would have liked you! I know that Zahi did. And Hugo is fond of you, too! You have made quite an impression."

He watched the professor pack up the drones into a carrying case. "What happened to Zahi?" Liko asked. "Why did he change?"

"Zahi was a great mathematician. Not a bad economist, either. But there was something wrong with him, something wrong with his heart, his soul."

"Did you know his wife, Saba?"

"Yes, I knew her. She was a wonderful, kind person. Deeply in love with him. Love at first sight, and she never wavered."

"Why did he go to the conference?" Liko asked.

"It was personal," the professor said. "A form of repentance."

I imagine he never stopped loving Saba, Liko thought. *Perhaps she was his motivation?*

"Is there something I can do?" Liko asked. "To help?"

"Indeed there is, young man," the professor answered. "I'd like to send you to Davos."

"Davos?"

"A world economic forum in Switzerland, attended by billionaires, CEOs, and heads of state, including Lil't."

"Why Davos?"

"To present Zahi's paper, to give his presentation."

"You're kidding, right?"

"Lil't will be there to talk about his vision for Little NEOM," the professor said. "You can surprise him and his family of kleptocrats by finishing what Zahi started."

"But I'm no billionaire. Don't I need credentials or something?"

"You need an invitation," the professor said. "And you have to register."

"How do I do that?"

"You pay a $50,000 registration fee."

"Oh," Liko said. "To keep out the riff-raff." *The other 99 percent of the world's population.*

"I'll see that you are invited and registered," the professor said. "You can represent me and my hedge fund."

"I would like to take someone with me," Liko said. "She is a photographer."

"Do you know her well?"

"I trust her," Liko said.

"I'll see what I can do."

Liko hoped Janet Rehm would be able to accompany

him to Davos. Since Daniel Johnson's death they had become friends. In fact, before he left for the Republican Democracy, she worked with Charla and him to prepare a photo essay about the young girl they had rescued from Jizan's. The story was still pending, but Liko knew that if the Maritauqua Times ran her article, it would be one more nail in Jizan's coffin.

The professor extended his hand. "I wish you the best," he said. "You are doing a very good thing."

"Thank you," Liko said, shaking his proffered hand. They hugged.

After their meeting, Liko copied the files on the two peas in the pod thumb drive the professor gave him to an FTP site. He sent a link and an encrypted password to Kwon, asking him to review the information and give him his opinion.

Kwon took a week to review the documents. His text message to Liko was simple: "ONE HUNDRED PERCENT PURE CRYSTALLIZED PICRIC ACID."

40

Davos

Liko walked up to the microphone and removed it from the stand. *So far so good*, he thought.

He glanced towards the front of the hall where Lil't was seated in the center of the raised platform. He was dressed in a white thawb, the traditional tunic of the Republican Democracy. To Lil't's left sat an interviewer, an older man, gray-haired and black glasses, wearing an impeccable navy blue, three-piece business suit. Undoubtedly, the interviewer had been carefully vetted, along with his questions. Everything so far appeared rehearsed. Even Lil't's answers sounded like he was reading them.

On the wall behind both men was an architect's rendering of Little NEOM. Lil't had reiterated his vision for Little NEOM the day before at the annual Davos Economic Forum. The hot topic of tonight's dinner was investment opportunities. Attendance was by special invitation only, although no one had been turned away, especially potential investors. Attendance had swelled and additional dining tables were set up.

Liko turned around for a moment to face the participants finishing their dinners at the tables behind him. They were a spattering of billionaires, dozens of CEOs, and a medley of world leaders. Folks with power, influence, and wealth to invest.

He noted teleprompters on both sides at the back of the hall. Lil't had come prepared to read his answers. Those who cried 'fake' were among the most dishonest liars. The interviewer would ask Lil't a vetted question, and Lil't would read the answer from the teleprompters. Tonight the diners had seen a tightly scripted Teleprompter't.

In an enthusiastic voice, Liko directed his first question to Lil't, speaking slowly and clearly into the microphone. "On the back of my dinner card, next to my plate, I found the following quote: *What would it take to build cities of the future in which everyone – regardless of gender, race, income, age or ability – can live and thrive?* I believe this quote is from the youthful Global Shapers Community. Can you please explain what that quote means to you?"

Liko heard the tickling of wine glasses and small plates being moved as people searched for their own dinner cards. There was a mumbling of voices as people read the quotes they found on the back side, some reading out loud to themselves, some sharing with their neighbors, some gasping with surprise.

Lil't, surprised, rambled off a typical Trumpian-like response that was so discombobulated it was meaningless. The few people who tried to follow what he said were totally confused.

A woman at a table next to Liko began reading her

quote to her neighbor. Liko stepped over to her and asked, "Madame, do you mind sharing your quote with us?"

"Sure," she answered. Liko held the microphone for her as she read: "Let us redouble our efforts to resolve shared problems—from fixing the global trade system, to fighting corruption and tax evasion, to addressing the existential threat of climate change." The woman smiled and said, "That was by Christine Lagarde, Davos 2019."

"Thank you," Liko said, smiling at her. "Ms. Lagarde? That sounds French, right? I imagine that she is a financier or economist?" *So far, so good,* he thought. "Does anyone else have a quote that they would like to share?"

Another woman raised her hand and Liko walked to her table as quickly as he could. He held the microphone for her as she read the quote on the back of her dinner card: "D.F.F.T., the Data Free Flow with Trust, should top the agenda in our new economy, Shinzo Abe, Prime Minister of Japan, Davos 2019."

"Thank you," Liko said. "Now, everyone, please check the back of your dinner card again. See the blue link? The blue link will take you to a website that contains an analysis of Little NEOM and a PowerPoint presentation prepared by the late Zahi Haarun."

Liko read the web address twice, ensuring that it was picked up by the live internet feed on a cell phone connected to the 360-degree camera that was recording everything. The cell phone and camera had been set up by Janet Rehm in the center of her table, in the center of the group of diners. Janet had surreptitiously set up the 360-degree camera as Liko walked up to ask his question.

"I encourage you to visit this site. Why? Dr. Zahi Haarun's careful work shines a light on Lil't and his administration, specifically the corruption and state-sponsored murder that is the foundation of his kleptocracy."

He turned around to address the people behind him and saw a man rushing towards him from the side of the dining hall. Liko stepped away from the microphone stand and began moving in the opposite direction.

The billionaire Mikhail Derichenko rose from his seat as Liko passed his table. As he reached to grab the microphone, Liko shifted it from his left to his right hand, just out of reach. Derichenko stepped towards Liko and grabbed again. Liko did not know Mikhail Derichenko, but the man had such a look of conceit and entitlement on his face that Liko couldn't resist parrying his grabbing hand and simultaneously punching the billionaire in the face with three quick jabs. He dropped like a slab of pork. Professor Ludi had insisted that the protest be non-violent, but this guy was so obviously a self-centered asshole that Liko felt no regret, whatsoever, at knocking him out cold.

"As a side note," Liko said, looking down at the man lying at his feet, "some of you may be interested to know that Dr. Zahi Haarun's brother, Hugo Haarun, was abducted from the United States to the Republican Democracy. He was then tortured in Swigert Prison."

Liko walked calmly around the table and came face to face with a security guard who had come from the opposite direction of the dining hall.

"Despite being maimed, Hugo still paints. We posted a picture of his latest mural, *The Drones*, on Zahi's memorial site.

The security guards had almost reached Liko. He decided not to run.

"I hope all of you enjoyed this year's Davos summit.

I think you folks are doing a great job. However, *do not* invest in Little NEOM. Invest in the Davos Climate Change Initiatives. That will better serve your family, friends, and community. Or invest in the peaceful use of drones."

Liko now turned to face Lil't. He raised the microphone to him as if offering a toast, and said, "I hope all of you will enjoy a glass of wine following your visit to Zahi's memorial site."

The two guards jumped on Liko. He was knocked against a seated diner and he tried to fall in a way that would not hurt her. Consequently, he went down hard. He didn't fight back. He didn't resist. The microphone wailed and the diners covered their ears.

Liko had achieved his goal. The victory was Zahi's, and Hugo's, and Professor Ludi's and the hundreds of other folks who worked to expose corruption and human rights violations. Liko knew that the 360-degree camera was sending out a live feed to millions of real-time viewers. The video was also uploading to Zahi's memorial site.

Two caterers removed the lids from seven serving dishes set out on a long table at the side of the dining hall. They quickly disappeared through a door that led down a service hallway and back into the kitchen.

Seven drones powered on. They rose to a height of twelve feet and then flew in unison towards the stage.

Lil't rose from his chair and yelled what seemed like an obscenity in Arabic. One of the drones accelerated forward from the formation and went straight for him, spraying him with crimson burgundy paint. The paint was non-toxic and washable.

The six other drones flew in a pattern over the diners,

dropping confetti and multi-colored streamers while playing a joyful Ardah.

The drones then flew in formation to the front wall behind the raised platform, where they joined the drone that had sprayed Lil't with red paint. Following a software program, the seven drones sprayed red, orange, yellow, green, blue, indigo, and violet – all the colors of the rainbow – covering the design-map of Little NEOM, creating a beautiful mural.

Janet Rehm rose from her table. With her Nikon camera and lenses, she calmly framed and snapped a picture of the colorful mural and sent it to her editor at the lifestyle section of the *Maritauqua Times*, along with other photos documenting the events of the dinner. She dedicated her photos to her former journalist partner, the late investigative journalist, Mr. Daniel Johnson. She attached a caption to the drone-painted mural, Zahi's Joy.

Zahi's Joy went viral.

Notes

Chapter One: I'm Not Responsible

Mohamed Bouazizi set himself on fire—Hernando De Soto, "The real Mohamed Bouazizi," *Foreign Policy Magazine*, December 16, 2011, https://foreignpolicy.com/2011/12/16/the-real-mohamed-bouazizi.

Ali fled to Saudi Arabia—Jamal Khashoggi, "With Ali Abdullah Saleh's death, Saudi Arabia is paying the price for betraying the Arab Spring," *The Washington Post*, December 5, 2017, https://www.washingtonpost.com/news/global-opinions/wp/2017/12/05/with-ali-abdullah-salehs-death-saudi-arabia-is-paying-the-price-for-betraying-the-arab-spring.

French aircraft—Tim Gaynor and Taha Zargoun, "Gaddafi caught like "rat" in a drain, humiliated and shot," *Reuters*, October 21, 2011, https://www.reuters.com/article/us-libya-gaddafi-finalhours/gaddafi-caught-like-rat-in-a-drain-humiliated-and-shot-idUSTRE79K43S20111021.

Chapter Two: Two Peas in a Pod

US President Trump anti-Muslim—

Brain Klaas, "A short history of President Trump's anti-Muslim bigotry," *The Washington Post*, March 15, 2019, https://www.washingtonpost.com/opinions/2019/03/15/short-history-president-trumps-anti-muslim-bigotry/.

Maha Hilal, "Trump's year in Islamophobia," Institute for Policy Studies, December 21, 2017, https://ips-dc.org/trumps-year-islamophobia.

Chapter Three: New York Airport
The spyware Unicorn secretly downloaded on his iPhone—David D. Kirkpatrick, "Israeli software helped Saudis spy on Khashoggi, lawsuit says," *The New York Times*, December 2, 2018, https://www.nytimes.com/2018/12/02/world/middleeast/saudi-khashoggi-spyware-israel.html.

—Loveday Morris, "Khashoggi friend sues Israeli firm over hacking he says contributed to the journalist's murder," *The Washington Post*, December 3, 2018, https://www.washingtonpost.com/world/middle_east/khashoggi-friend-sues-israeli-firm-over-hacking-he-says-contributed-to-the-journalists-murder/2018/12/03/ddcb28ee-f708-11e8-8642-c9718a256cbd_story.html.

—David D. Kirkpatrick, "Hacking a Prince, an Emir and a journalist to impress a client," *The New York Times*, August 31, 2018, https://www.nytimes.com/2018/08/31/world/middleeast/hacking-united-arab-emirates-nso-group.html.

Chapter Four: Hugo Abandoned
Robert E. Lee—
Lee's wife inherited almost two hundred slaves—David Brooks, "The Robert E. Lee Problem," *The New York Times*, June 26, 2015, https://www.nytimes.com/2015/06/26/opinion/david-brooks-the-robert-e-lee-problem.html.

Steve Hendrix, "The day white Virginia stopped

admiring Gen. Robert E. Lee and started worshiping him," *The Washington Post*, August 22, 2017, https://www.washingtonpost.com/news/retropolis/wp/2017/08/22/the-day-white-virginia-stopped-admiring-gen-robert-e-lee-and-started-worshipping-him/.

Michael S. Rosenwald, "The truth about Confederate Gen. Robert E. Lee: He wasn't very good at his job," *The Washington Post*, October 13, 2018, https://www.washingtonpost.com/news/retropolis/wp/2017/05/19/the-truth-about-confederate-gen-robert-e-lee-he-wasnt-very-good-at-his-job/.

Lil't was a kleptocrat—kleptocrat, *noun*, a ruler who uses their power to steal their country's resources. https://en.oxforddictionaries.com/definition/kleptocrat.

Jizan was the 'secret caretaker'—Kleptocrats often use 'secret caretakers' to launder and hide stolen money and assets. For example, Sergei Roldugin is Vladimir Putin's 'secret caretaker.' His 'secret caretaker' role is explained in the following article: Roman Anin, Olesya Shmagun, and Dmitry Velikovsky, "The Secret Caretaker," *Organized Crime and Corruption Reporting Project (OCCRP)*, April 3, 2016, https://www.occrp.org/en/panamapapers/the-secret-caretaker/.

Zahi was the 'professional enabler'—Ben Judah and Nate Sibley, "The enablers: How Western professionals import corruption and strengthen authoritarianism," *Hudson Institute*, September 5, 2018, https://www.hudson.org/research/14520-the-enablers-how-western-professionals-import-corruption-and-strengthen-authoritarianism.

—Ben Judah and Belinda Li, "Money laundering for 21stcentury authoritarianism: Western enablement of kleptocracy," *Hudson Institute*, November 22, 2017, https://www.hudson.org/research/14020-money-laundering-for-21st-century-authoritarianism.

Pushed a button on a computer and millions of dollars were seamlessly transferred across international borders—In Johannesburg, in a speech to a large crowd in a cricket stadium, Obama called out 'strongman politics.' Obama said "[Globalization and technology has] made it easier for capital to avoid tax laws and the regulations of nation-states – can just move billions, trillions of dollars with a tap of a computer key." "Transcript: Obama's Speech Defending Democracy," *The New York Times*, July 17, 2018, https://www.nytimes.com/2018/07/17/world/africa/obama-speech-south-africa-transcript.html.

Serial sex abusers—The character Jizdan is fictitious. The following article, however, is about the real-life serial sex abuser, Jeffrey Epstein. Julie K. Brown, "How a future Trump cabinet member gave a serial sex abuser the deal of a lifetime," *Miami Herald*, November 28, 2018, https://www.miamiherald.com/news/local/article220097825.html.

Like Trump—Peter York, "Trump's dictator chic," *Politico Magazine*, March/April 2017, https://www.politico.com/magazine/story/2017/03/trump-style-dictator-autocrats-design-214877.

Chapter Six: Saba's Child
Every ten minutes a child dies of preventable causes in Yemen—Eric O'Brien, "Yemen: A child under the age of five dies every 10 minutes of preventable causes – UN Humanitarian Chief," United Nations Office for the Coordination of Humanitarian Affairs, 2017, https://www.unocha.org/es/story/yemen-child-under-

age-five-dies-every-10-minutes-preventable-causes-un-humanitarian-chief.

Forcibly separating children from their parents—William Wan, "What separation from parents does to children: 'The effect is catastrophic,'" *The Washington Post*, June 18, 2018, https://www.washingtonpost.com/national/health-science/what-separation-from-parents-does-to-children-the-effect-is-catastrophic/2018/06/18/c00c30ec-732c-11e8-805c-4b67019fcfe4_story.html.

Trump's child-separation policy—

Maya Rhodan, "Here are the facts about President Trump's family separation policy," *Time Magazine*, June 20, 2018, time.com/5314769/family-separation-policy-donald-trump.

Amanda Holpuch, "Thousands more migrant children separated under Trump than previously known," *The Guardian*, January 17, 2019, https://www.theguardian.com/us-news/2019/jan/17/trump-family-separations-report-latest-news-zero-tolerance-policy-immigrant-children.

Chapter Eight: Little NEOM

His role models were … President Trump—Sarah Chayes, "Trump and the path toward kleptocracy," *Bloomberg*, May 22, 2017, https://www.bloomberg.com/opinion/articles/2017-05-22/trump-and-the-path-toward-kleptocracy.

—David Smith, "Trump risks US being seen as 'kleptocracy', says ex-ethics chief Walter Shaub," *The Guardian*, July 31, 2017, https://www.theguardian.com/us-news/2017/jul/31/trump-ethics-chief-walter-shaub-kleptocracy.

—Griff Witte, "Around the globe, Trump's style is

inspiring imitations and unleashing dark impulses," *The Washington Post*, January 22, 2019, https://www.washingtonpost.com/world/europe/around-the-globe-trumps-style-is-inspiring-imitators-and-unleashing-dark-impulses/2019/01/22/ebd15952-1366-11e9-ab79-30cd4f7926f2_story.html.

—Editorial Board, "Trump embraces another dictator. Congress has to do better." *The Washington Post*, April 12, 2019,https://www.washingtonpost.com/opinions/global-opinions/trump-embraces-another-dictator-congress-has-to-do-better/2019/04/12/e94e9b1c-5bb0-11e9-842d-7d3ed7eb3957_story.html.

—Sarah Chayes, *Thieves of state: Why corruption threatens global security*, W.W. Norton & Company, New York, London, January 9, 2015.

Influence network in Washington—The Republican Democracy's influence network in DC is fictitious. However, for a snapshot of a Middle Eastern country's influence network, read the following: Philip Bump and Justin Wm. Moyer, "This is what Saudi Arabia's influence network in Washington looks like," *The Washington Post*, October 19, 2018, https://www.washingtonpost.com/politics/2018/10/19/this-is-what-saudi-arabias-influence-network-washington-looks-like.

Mimic Saudi Arabia's NEOM—"HRH the Crown Prince Mohammed bin Salman announces: NEOM – the destination of the future," October 24, 2017, https://www.neom.com/content/pdfs/NEOM-Press-Release-en.pdf.

—King Abdullah's Economic City: Ahmed Al Omran, "Saudi Arabia's sleepy city offers prince a cautionary tale," *Financial Times*, May 27, 2018, https://www.ft.com/content/ae48574c-58e6-11e8-bdb7-f6677d2e1ce8.

Science fiction movie *Elysium*—Manohla Dargis, "The worst is yet to come," *The New York Times*, August 9, 2013, https://www.nytimes.com/2013/08/09/movies/elysium-sends-matt-damon-into-a-dystopian-future.html.

The 25thamendment—Rebecca Harrington, "Some of Trump's top-most advisers have reportedly discussed invoking the 25thAmendment, which lets 14 people remove a sitting president from office. Here's how it works," *Business Insider*, February 14, 2019, https://www.businessinsider.com/25th-amendment-how-can-you-remove-president-from-office-2017-3.

Chapter Nine: Hugo's Court Appearance

Maritauqua Island's crest—Maritauqua Island's crest was described in Maritauqua Island, Book One of the Current Affairs Trilogy (CAT). The description reads: "Liko had noticed the crest earlier and had Googled it. At the top of the crest was a public pavilion, where the founders of Maritauqua had once auctioned thousands of West Africans and Native Americans. In 1950, Hurricane Baker had destroyed the pavilion, and now the site held a covered amphitheater. Symphonies, operas, ballets, theater, and even comedies were now performed where slaves had once been auctioned. The shield displayed four images: the battle flag of the Confederate States of America, a cotton boll floral spray, an offshore oil rig, and a cargo container ship. The Confederate flag had been copied from the Coat of Arms of Alabama. The cotton boll floral spray could just as well have been a tobacco plant; it represented not only the cotton plantations in Alabama, but also the wave of wealthy sons and daughters of Virginia and Carolina plantation owners who had moved to the island in the early 1800s and again after the

Civil War. The oil rig and container ship represented the island's *nouveau riche*. The island's enigmatic motto—*Expergiscimini Non veniet*, Latin for "We shall come awake"—was depicted across the bottom of the crest."

Chapter Ten: Jizan's Party

Explosion and sinking of the Deepwater Horizon—Ocean Portal Team, Smithsonian Institute, "Gulf Oil Spill," https://ocean.si.edu/conservation/pollution/gulf-oil-spill.

A slave was worth about 350 dollars in 1800: Roger L. Ransom, "Economics of the Civil War," *EH.net Encyclopedia*, edited by Robert Whaples, August 24, 2001, https://eh.net/encyclopedia/the-economics-of-the-civil-war.

Statues in the Capitol honoring Confederates—

Amanda Terkel, "The U.S. Capitol is basically a Confederate statue bazaar," *Huffpost*, August 17, 2017, https://www.huffpost.com/entry/us-capitol-confederate-statue_n_5995a370e4b06ef724d6e277.

Bill Theobald, "Controversial Confederate statues remain in U.S. Capitol despite being removed elsewhere," *USA Today*, September 25, 2018, https://www.usatoday.com/story/news/politics/2018/09/19/confederates-statues-remain-u-s-capitol-despite-opposition/1269270002.

Example set by Ukrainian oligarch, Dmytro Firtach—Nick Shaxson, "Ukraine's dirty money: The Cambridge University connection," *Tax Justice Network*, March 21, 2014, https://www.taxjustice.net/2014/03/21/cambridge-university-new-ukraine-scandal/.

Couldn't believe anything Trump said—Glenn Kessler, Salvador Rizzo and Meg Ryan, "President Trump made

8,158 false or misleading claims in his first two years," *The Washington Post*, January 21, 2019, https://www.washingtonpost.com/politics/2019/01/21/president-trump-made-false-or-misleading-claims-his-first-two-years.

Jared-Ivanka effect—Michelle Goldberg, "Who do Jared and Ivanka think they are?" *The New York Times*, March 18, 2019,https://www.nytimes.com/2019/03/18/opinion/jared-kushner-ivanka-trump-corruption.html.

Chapter Eleven: Prodigal Student
Trolls attacked his Twitter and Facebook accounts—
The Saudi Arabian "Troll Master," Saud al-Qahtani, a top advisor to Crown Prince Mohammed, used Twitter and social media to attack critics of the Prince. Katie Benner, Mark Mazzetti, Ben Hubbard and Mike Isaac, "Saudis' image makers: A troll army and a Twitter insider," *The New York Times*, October 20, 2018,https://www.nytimes.com/2018/10/20/us/politics/saudi-image-campaign-twitter.html.

Molly Roberts, "Saudi ministers are harassing critics on Twitter," *The Washington Post*, October 19, 2018, https://www.washingtonpost.com/blogs/post-partisan/wp/2018/10/19/saudi-ministers-are-harassing-critics-on-twitter.

Tamer El-Ghobashy, "Khashoggi mystery fixes spotlight on Saudi official described as crown prince's strategist, enforcer," *The Washington Post*, October 12, 2018, https://www.washingtonpost.com/world/khashoggi-mystery-fixes-spotlight-on-saudi-official-described-as-crown-princes-strategist-enforcer/2018/10/12/df5b523a-cd8f-11e8-adoa-oeo1efba3cc1_story.html.

Salvaging your reputation after the leader of your

country attacks your integrity—One couple who survived such an attack is Khizr and Ghazala Khan. Katie Reilly, "Gold Star father Khizr Khan talks about love for America and family," *Time Magazine*, November 8, 2017, time.com/collection/American-voices-2017/5016312/gold-star-father-khizr-khan-talks-about-his-love-for-america-and-family/.

Chapter Twelve: Arrested at SWTP
Eight percent of the world's wealth is hidden away—Gabriel Zucman, *The hidden wealth of nations: The scourge of tax havens*, University of Chicago Press, September 22, 2015, http://gabriel-zucman.eu/hidden-wealth.

Chapter Sixteen: Television Guest
One of the 'deplorables'—"You know, to just be grossly generalistic, you could put half of Trump's supporters into what I call the basket of deplorables. Right? They're racist, sexist, homophobic, xenophobic – Islamophobic – you name it. And unfortunately, there are people like that. And he has lifted them up." Hillary Clinton, at a campaign fundraising event in New York City, September 9, 2016.

Got their news from Breitbart or Fox News—Jane Mayer, "The Making of the Fox News White House," *The New Yorker*, March 4, 2019, https://www.newyorker.com/magazine/2019/03/11/the-making-of-the-fox-news-white-house

Chapter Seventeen: An Assassination
Well-known journalists were killed—
Amanda Erickson, "2018 has been a brutal year for journalists, and it keeps getting worse," *The Washington*

Post, October 9, 2018, https://www.washingtonpost.com/world/2018/10/09/has-been-brutal-year-journalists-it-keeps-getting-worse.

David Ignatius, "Jamal Khashoggi chose to tell the truth. It's part of the reason he's beloved," *The Washington Post*, October 7, 2018, https://www.washingtonpost.com/opinions/global-opinions/jamal-khashoggi-chose-to-tell-the-truth-its-part-of-the-reason-hes-beloved/2018/10/07/4847f1d6-ca70-11e8-a3e6-44daa3d35ede_story.html.

Kareem Fahim, "Turkey concludes Saudi journalist Jamal Khashoggi killed by 'murder' team, sources say," *The Washington Post*, October 6, 2018, https://www.washingtonpost.com/world/middle_east/turkey-concludes-saudi-journalist-khashoggi-killed-by-murder-team-sources-say/2018/10/06/31ee4f86-c8d9-11e8-9c0f-2ffaf6d422aa_story.html.

Unless pictures are edited, they don't lie—Jon Swaine, "Trump inauguration crowd photos were edited after he intervened," *The Guardian*, September 6, 2018, https://www.theguardian.com/world/2018/sep/06/donald-trump-inauguration-crowd-size-photos-edited.

Journalist and his fiancée who had been shot and killed—Griff Witte, "How Slovakia stood up to a journalist's slaying and kicked out its prime minister," *The Washington Post*, March 28, 2018, https://www.washingtonpost.com/world/how-slovakia-stood-up-to-a-journalists-murder-and-kicked-out-its-prime-minister/2018/03/28/c73bb078-2c40-11e8-8dc9-3b51e028b845_story.html.

Chapter Eighteen: Passing through London
Karim Fakhrawi—Committee to Protect Journalists,

"Al-Wasat| killed in Manama, Bahrain," April 12, 2011, https://cpj.org/data/people/karim-fakhrawi/.

Chapter Nineteen: Arrival in the Home Country
Jared Kushner, Trump's son-in-law, pushed the United States into supporting Crown Prince Mohamed bin Salman of Saudi Arabia—Philip Rucker, Carol D. Leonnig and Anne Gearan, "Two princes: Kushner now faces a reckoning for Trump's bet on the heir to the Saudi throne,"*The Washington Post*, October 14, 2018, https://www.washingtonpost.com/politics/two-princes-kushner-now-faces-a-reckoning-for-trumps-bet-on-the-saudi-heir/2018/10/14/6eaeaafc-ce46-11e8-a3e6-44daa3d35ede_story.html.

The Saudis paid $3.5 billion dollars to Uber—Eric Newcomer, "The inside story of how Uber got into business with the Saudi Arabian government," *Bloomberg*, November 3, 2018, https://www.bloomberg.com/news/articles/2018-11-03/the-inside-story-of-how-uber-got-into-business-with-the-saudi-arabian-government.

Chapter Twenty: Pre-Conference Jitters
She plagiarized her doctorate, just like Vladimir Putin—"The mystery of Vladimir Putin's dissertation," Brookings Institution, March 30, 2006, https://www.brookings.edu/events/the-mystery-of-vladimir-putins-dissertation/.

US EB-5 visa—Kelly Phillips Erb, "The EB-5 visa: United States citizenship for sale?", *Forbes*, May 10, 2017, https://www.forbes.com/sites/kellyphillipserb/2017/05/10/the-eb-5-visa-united-states-citizenship-for-sale/#150b2e592cb9.

Chapter Twenty-One: Torture

Article 70 of the Criminal Code—The torturer cites the Republican Democracy's 'undesirables' law that is based on a similar law in Russia. Vladimir Kara-Murza, "The Kremlin deploys its new law against 'undesirables', *The Washington Post*, January 25, 2019, https://www.washingtonpost.com/opinions/2019/01/25/kremlin-deploys-its-new-law-against-undesirables/.

A Clockwork Orange—This is one of my favorite Stanley Kubrick movies, but not for the reasons stated by the torturer. The film is based on the 1962 novel, *A Clockwork Orange*, by Anthony Burgess.

Chapter Twenty-Two: Swigert Prison

Swigert Prison—I named this deplorable prison in honor of "Grayson Swigert," the pseudonym for one of the two psychologists who was paid millions to create "enhanced interrogation" techniques. Kierran Petersen, "CIA interrogations: 'No place' for psychologists?", *BBC*, December 17, 2014, https://www.bbc.com/news/blogs-echochambers-30509604.

Dermophis donaldtrump—Damian Carrington, "Blind creature that buries head in sand named after Donald Trump," *The Guardian*, December 18, 2018, https://www.theguardian.com/us-news/2018/dec/18/blind-amphibian-named-after-trumps-climate-change-stance.

Chapter Thirty-One: Relatives

Trump danced the Ardah in Saudi Arabia—Daniel Brown, "From selling a Saudi billionaire his 282-foot yacht to sword-dancing on his first international trip as president, Trump's ties with Saudi Arabia run deep,"

Business Insider, December 6, 2018, https://www.businessinsider.com/trump-has-deep-ties-with-saudis-from-selling-yacht-to-sword-dancing-2018-10.

US supported Saudi Arabia and the UAE in their war in Yemen—Patricia Zengerle, "Trump objects to measure ending U.S. support for Saudis in Yemen war," *Reuters*, February 11, 2019, https://www.reuters.com/article/us-usa-saudi-yemen/trump-objects-to-measure-ending-us-support-for-saudis-in-yemen-war-idUSKCN1Q102V.

Cluster bombs—Zachary Cohen, "Rights group: Saudi Arabia used U.S. cluster bombs on civilians," *CNN*, February 29, 2016, https://www.cnn.com/2016/02/29/politics/saudi-arabia-us-cluster-bombs-on-civilians/index.html.

President George W. Bush and Vice President Dick Cheney boasting about secret prisons—Human Rights Watch, "Getting away with torture: The Bush administration and mistreatment of detainees," *Human Rights Watch*, July 12, 2011, https://www.hrw.org/report/2011/07/12/getting-away-torture/bush-administration-and-mistreatment-detainees.

Secret prisons—Jane Mayer, "The black sites: A rare look inside the C.I.A.'s secret interrogation program," *The New Yorker*, August 5, 2007, https://www.newyorker.com/magazine/2007/08/13/the-black-sites. Jane Mayer also wrote the book *The dark side: The inside story of how the war on terror turned into a war on American ideals*, published July 15, 2008, Doubleday.

The UAE has prisons in Yemen—Samy Magdy, "Amnesty urges 'war crimes' probe on UAE-run prisons in Yemen," *Fox News*, July 12, 2018, https://www.foxnews.com/world/amnesty-urges-war-crimes-probe-on-uae-run-prisons-in-yemen

Fundamentalists—Brian Bolton and Pamela Whissel, "'Fundamentalist' is the correct label," *American Atheist*, January/February 2019, Vol. 57, No. 1,www.atheists.org.

Chapter Thirty-Four: US Embassy
A gross violation of human rights—David Ignatius, "How the mysteries of Khashoggi's murder have rocked the U.S.-Saudi partnership," *The Washington Post*, March 29, 2019, https://www.washingtonpost.com/opinions/global-opinions/how-the-mysteries-of-khashoggis-murder-have-rocked-the-us-saudi-partnership/2019/03/29/cf060472-50af-11e9-a3f7-78b7525a8d5f_story.html.

Chapter Thirty-Five: Mural
Illegal tampering with absentee ballots—Amy Gardner, "N.C. election officials: Harris operative collected and falsified ballots, then tried to obstruct state investigation," *The Washington Post*, February 18, 2019, https://www.washingtonpost.com/politics/nc-election-officials-harris-operative-collected-and-falsified-ballots-then-tried-to-obstruct-state-investigation/2019/02/18/6501347a-339a-11e9-854a-7a14d7fec96a_story.html.

Chapter Thirty-Seven: TrackHer
A way for men to control women—Lucas Laursen, "Facilitating Saudi patriarchy: Apple and Google blasted for carrying app where Saudi men track vives," *Fortune*, February 13, 2019, http://fortune.com/2019/02/13/apple-google-saudi-arabia-app/.

Chapter Thirty-Nine: London

Foreign SIM card with prepaid credit—Colin Freeze, "Saudi dissident in Canada spoke to Khashoggi about fighting Riyadh's communication clampdown," *The Global Mail*, October 18, 2018, https://www.theglobeandmail.com/world/article-saudi-dissident-in-canada-spoke-to-khashoggi-about-fighting-riyadhs/.

Chapter Forty: Davos

The youthful Global Shapers Community—Global Shapers Community, https://www.globalshapers.org/story.

DO NOT invest in Little NEOM—

Jeanne Whalen and Justin Wm. Moyer, "Western walkout of Saudi 'Davos in the Desert' conference over Jamal Khashoggi undermines kingdom's modernization plans," *The Washington Post*, October 12, 2018, https://www.washingtonpost.com/business/2018/10/12/western-walkout-saudi-davos-desert-conference-over-jamal-khashoggi-undermines-kingdoms-modernization-plans.

Simeon Kerr and Anjil Raval, "Saudi prince's flagship plan beset by doubts after Khashoggi death," *Financial Times*, December 11, 2018, https://www.ft.com/content/c24ab1d4-f8a7-11e8-8b7c-6fa24bd5409c

One of the Davos climate change initiatives—David Attenborough, broadcaster and naturalist, "David Attenborough: 'The Garden of Eden is no more'. Read his Davos speech in full," *World Economic Forum*, January 21, 2019, https://www.weforum.org/agenda/2019/01/david-attenborough-transcript-from-crystal-award-speech/.

Invest in the peaceful use of drones—"Advanced drone operations toolkit: Accelerating the drone revolution,"

World Economic Forum, December 2018,www3.weforum.org/docs/ WEF_Advanced_Drone_Operations_Toolkit.pdf.

The drone-painted mural—Dyllan Furness, "Spray-painting drones may soon beautify a construction site near you," *Digital Trends,* July 10, 2017, https://www.digitaltrends.com/cool-tech/drones-paint-murals/.

—J.C. Sharman, *The despot's guide to wealth management: On the international campaign against grand corruption,* Cornell University Press, March 7, 2017.

Greg Olmsted is the author of the celebrated *Strong Current Trilogy*, as well as *Istina and the Apostate* (Religion, Genetics, and the Search for Meaning). He has Master of Science degrees in Environmental Health Science and Public Health Management, and he served more than forty years in public health programs. Greg uses the arts to increase public awareness of environmental and health issues. He enjoys skiing and ballroom dancing. Readers can contact him at GregOlmstedBooks.com.